Blacktop Harvest

CLIFTON WILCOX

WINDWARD
PUBLISHING

Fredericksburg, Virginia

Print ISBN: 978-1-969770-07-4
EBook ISBN: 978-1-969770-05-0
Hardback ISBN: 978-969770-08-1

Published by Windward Publishing LLC., Fredericksburg, Virginia.

The characters and events in this book are fictitious. Any similarity to real persons, living or dead, is coincidental and not intended by the author.

Library of Congress Cataloging in Publication Data
Wilcox, Clifton
Blacktop Harvest

Windward Publishing, LLC
2026

Dedication

For those who know that some harvests

are not meant to be celebrated.

Table of Contents

Books by Clifton Wilcox

Non-Fiction

Scape Goat: Targeted for Blame

Groupthink: An Impediment to Success

Bias: The Unconscious Deceiver

Witch-hunt: The Assignment of Blame

The Fall of the Kingdom of Northumbria

Witch-hunt: The Class of Cultures

Road to War: The Quest for a New World Order

Envy: A Deeper Shade of Green

The Rise of the Nazi SS

The Horrible Void Between the Trenches

Fiction

Cool's Last Stand

Where Despair Comes to Play

The Monuments Must Bleed

Keeper of the Fallen Ages

I, Monster

Harvest of Eyes

The Case Against Jasper

Crimson Plume: The Song of Corvus

Framed in Love

Echoes of the Forgotten

CHAPTER 1

The Arrival in Redwater Crossing

The air in Redwater Crossing hung heavy, not with the scent of pine or damp earth that should have characterized its winding roads, but with a weary fatigue. It was a town that had seen better days, a fact etched into the peeling paint of storefronts and the stoop of shoulders on its citizens. The general store, once the bustling heart of commerce, now had more dust motes dancing in the shafts of sunlight than customers. Mrs. Gable, her face a roadmap of worry lines, meticulously arranged cans of beans that hadn't seen a price increase in years, her movements slow, resigned. Across the street, the hardware store's 'Open' sign seemed to perpetually hang at a weary angle, much like its owner, Ned, who spent more time staring out the window than tending to inventory. Children, what few remained, played with a listlessness that belied their years, their games lacking the boisterous energy that should have echoed through the quiet streets. Hope, it seemed, had packed its bags and left Redwater Crossing long ago, leaving behind a hollow echo of what once was.

The town square, once a vibrant gathering place, now stood as a testament to its slow decay. The wrought-iron benches, adorned with intricate, yet rusted, scrollwork, were often empty. The fountain in the center, a proud centerpiece in its heyday, coughed out a meager trickle of water, its stone basin stained with the grime of neglect. Around its perimeter, wilted petunias struggled for life, their colors muted, mirroring the faded dreams of the town's inhabitants. Even the imposing, century-old oak tree that dominated the square seemed to droop, its branches heavy with an unspoken sorrow. Each crack in the sidewalk, each loose shutter on the municipal building, whispered tales of a community clinging precariously to existence, a town teetering on the brink, its future as uncertain as the next unpredictable gust of wind that swept through its desolate avenues.

Beneath the surface of this melancholic quietude, a deeper current of desperation ran strong. The bank's notices, tacked with increasing frequency to doors, spoke of foreclosures and mounting debts. Young families, their eyes bright with the ambition that had once defined Redwater Crossing, now found themselves trapped, their dreams of a modest home and a secure future dissolving like mist in the morning sun. The younger generation, sensing the stagnation, had largely sought greener pastures in the cities, leaving behind a town populated by those too old, too weary, or too deeply entrenched to escape. This exodus only served to deepen the sense of decay, creating a vicious cycle where the loss of its youth further diminished its prospects, leaving an ever-widening chasm of deferred hopes and unspoken regrets.

The local diner, 'Sunrise Skillet,' was a hub of quiet lament. Over lukewarm coffee and plates of greasy hash browns, conversations invariably circled back to the same themes: the rising cost of living, the dwindling opportunities, the constant worry about making ends meet. Sheriff Mason Brody, a man whose pragmatic nature was often tested by the quiet despair he witnessed daily, would sit in his usual corner booth, nursing a black coffee, his gaze distant. He heard the hushed conversations, the sighs of resignation, and felt the palpable weight of hopelessness that settled over Redwater Crossing like a shroud. He'd seen good people driven to their breaking points, their spirits chipped away by the relentless erosion of their circumstances. He understood that desperation could breed a dangerous kind of vulnerability, making them susceptible to anything that promised a reprieve, no matter how improbable.

The aging infrastructure of Redwater Crossing was a constant reminder of its decline. The roads, once smooth and well-maintained, were now pockmarked with potholes, each one a miniature hazard for the already struggling vehicles that navigated them. Streetlights flickered erratically, casting long, dancing shadows that distorted the already somber streetscape, adding an unsettling edge to the twilight hours. The town's single traffic light at the main intersection seemed to operate on a whimsy of its own, often blinking yellow for extended periods, a silent metaphor for the town's own uncertain state of being. The old cinema, its marquee darkened for years, stood as a silent, imposing sentinel, a stark reminder of a time when laughter and light filled its halls, a stark contrast to the quiet desperation that now characterized the town. Even the air itself seemed to carry a fine layer of dust, a perpetual reminder of things falling apart, of a community slowly succumbing to the relentless march of time and economic hardship. This was the fertile ground where any seed of hope, however dubious, could take root and flourish, a desperate longing for a savior, a miracle, a way out of the suffocating stagnation.

The morning after, an anomaly bloomed on the dusty fringes of Redwater Crossing, where the asphalt surrendered to gravel and weeds. It was a car lot, but not just *any* car lot. This one was an explosion of color, a defiant splash of audacious hues against the muted palette of the town's pervasive melancholy. 'Earl's Honest Rides' the sign proclaimed in bold, bubble-gum pink letters, arcing over a gleaming row of vehicles that seemed to hum with an unnatural vitality. It wasn't just the paint, though that was enough to make a person blink – canary yellow convertibles sat beside sapphire blue sedans, emerald green trucks nestled against ruby red sports cars. No, it was the sheer *impossibility* of it all.

These weren't the rust-bitten, sputtering relics that usually graced the handful of forlorn used car lots in neighboring towns, if they could even be called lots. These were pristine. Each chrome bumper gleamed as if recently polished with stardust, every tire boasted a flawless, deep black. The paint jobs weren't merely vibrant; they possessed a depth, a liquid sheen that hinted at an almost impossible level of care and attention. It was as if each automobile had been plucked from a glossy magazine advertisement and deposited, still dewy from the printing press, onto Redwater Crossing's forgotten soil.

The prices, scrawled on impossibly cheerful, oversized price tags that fluttered in the gentle breeze, were even more astonishing. A sleek, cherry-red convertible, the kind one might expect to see cruising down a sun-drenched coastal highway, was marked with a price that wouldn't even cover a month's rent for a modest apartment in a city an hour away. A sturdy, forest-green pickup truck, capable of hauling anything one could imagine, was listed for less than a high-end bicycle. There were even what appeared to be luxury sedans, their interiors glimpsed through impossibly clear windows, adorned with prices that made Sheriff Brody's eyebrows shoot up to his hairline when he first saw them. They were, frankly, absurd. For a town where a broken-down tractor was a significant investment, these were not just bargains; they were miracles.

The juxtaposition was jarring, almost offensive, against the backdrop of Redwater Crossing's everyday reality. The peeling paint of the general store, the weary slump of Ned's shoulders in the hardware store, the hesitant laughter of the few children playing listlessly in the square – all these things spoke of hardship, of a slow, grinding decline. This lot, however, was an effervescent bubble of unadulterated joy and impossibly good fortune, floating right on the edge of their carefully managed despair. It was a visual paradox; a Technicolor dream dropped into a sepia-toned world.

The townsfolk, their routines so deeply ingrained they moved through them with a certain somnambulistic grace, found themselves drawn to the edge of town like moths to a particularly flamboyant flame. Whispers, tentative at first, began to ripple through 'Sunrise Skillet' and the aisles of Mrs. Gable's store. Conversations that had been mired in the usual litany of woes – the leaky roof, the rising cost of feed, the constant worry about the next utility bill – suddenly veered into speculative, excited territory.

"Did you see it, Martha?" Agnes Walker, a woman whose usual demeanor was as grey as her namesake flowers, confided to her neighbor, her voice a hushed, breathless rush. "That car lot? Like nothing I've ever laid eyes on."

Martha Pike, who had been meticulously darning a sock with the practiced efficiency of a lifetime, paused, her needle hovering. "I saw it, Agnes. Hard to miss, wouldn't you say? Brighter than a peacock's tail feather."

"And the prices!" Agnes clasped her hands together. "A car for... for pocket change! I saw a little red convertible, looked brand new. Marked at... well, I'd hardly call it a price at all. More like a donation."

The news spread like wildfire, each retelling adding a little more embellishment, a touch more incredulity. Ned, usually content to watch the world drift by from his shop window, found himself stepping out onto the sidewalk, his gaze fixed towards the horizon where the vibrant anomaly pulsed. Even Sheriff Brody, a man who prided himself on his grounded skepticism, felt a flicker of something akin to wonder, a sensation he hadn't experienced in years. He'd driven past it on his early morning patrol, his cruiser's headlights cutting through the predawn gloom. At first, he'd assumed it was some kind of temporary pop-up sale, a traveling circus of sorts. But the sheer scale of it, the multitude of vehicles, and the undeniably solid appearance of the structures – small, cheerful sales booths and even a tiny, almost whimsical, office building – suggested something more permanent, or at least, something that had arrived with remarkable speed and purpose.

The suddenness of its appearance was as bewildering as its aesthetics. One day, there was nothing but scrub brush and neglected fencing. The next, 'Earl's Honest Rides' was a fully operational, impossibly bright enterprise. There had been no construction crews, no late-night deliveries of inventory. It was as if the entire lot, with its shimmering cars and garish signage, had simply *manifested* overnight, a surreal mirage coalescing into tangible reality. This detail, more than the absurd prices or the riot of color, was what truly fueled the growing buzz of speculation. It defied logic, and in a town where logic had long since become a luxury, the inexplicable held a potent allure.

Children, their natural curiosity unburdened by the weariness of adulthood, were particularly captivated. Their games, usually played with a subdued energy, now revolved around this new, fantastical addition to their landscape. They'd gather at the edge of the lot, pressing their small faces against the chain-link fence that bordered it, their eyes wide with a mixture of awe and a child's simple desire for something new and exciting. They'd point out the brightest colors, invent stories about the cars, and dream of the day they might be old enough to drive one of Earl's miraculous vehicles. Their parents, while still grounded in the harsh realities of their lives, couldn't help but be infected by their children's unfeigned enthusiasm. A little bit of that sparkle, that impossible cheer, had begun to seep into the cracks of their own weary hearts.

The contrast between the lot and its surroundings was so stark it felt almost intentional. The weathered, sun-bleached wood of the fence bordering the lot seemed to absorb the vibrancy of the cars within, its dullness emphasizing their impossible shine. The dry, dusty earth beneath them seemed to absorb some of the cheer, leaving the area around the lot strangely, almost unnervingly, clean. It was as if the lot existed in its own separate reality, a pocket of pure, unadulterated commerce that had landed, unbidden, in the quiet desolation of Redwater Crossing.

Sheriff Brody, despite his initial skepticism, found himself driving out to the lot more often than usual. It wasn't just the potential for traffic issues or the need to maintain order; it was a morbid curiosity, a professional obligation to understand the forces at play in his town. He'd observed the townsfolk gathering, their faces alight with a hope he hadn't seen in years, a dangerous commodity in Redwater Crossing. He'd seen what desperation could do, and he knew that when hope, however improbable, flickered to life, it could blind people to risks they would otherwise recognize.

He'd parked his cruiser a little distance away, watching the activity. There was a small, almost quaint, sales office at the back of the lot, and a few cheerful umbrella-covered tables where potential buyers were being attended to. The salespeople, dressed in crisp, brightly colored uniforms that matched the cars, moved with an easy, professional grace. They were... different. Not the usual grizzled, pushy salesmen one might expect. These individuals radiated an almost unnerving politeness, a calm, collected demeanor that seemed out of place in the rough-and-tumble world of used car sales. They smiled easily, spoke softly, and seemed utterly unperturbed by the sheer implausibility of the deals they were offering.

One particular salesman, a tall, lean man with a shock of perfectly coiffed silver hair and eyes that seemed to twinkle with an inner amusement, was the most prominent. He moved through the lot with an air of quiet authority, occasionally pausing to speak with a customer, his gestures fluid and reassuring. Sheriff Brody couldn't quite place the feeling the man evoked. It wasn't distrust, exactly, but a subtle unease, like the prickling sensation one gets when a shadow moves just out of the corner of their eye.

The sheer volume of cars was also a point of fascination. There had to be at least fifty, maybe sixty vehicles, all in various makes and models, yet all somehow fitting the same aesthetic of impossible newness and outrageous affordability. Where had they come from? How had they arrived so quickly, so silently? And who was 'Earl'? No one had seen hide nor hair of an Earl. The salespeople referred to him, if at all, with a casual respect, as if he were a benevolent but distant overseer.

Agnes Walker, emboldened by the sheer absurdity of it all, had been one of the first to approach the lot. She'd brought her neighbor, Martha, for moral support, though Martha remained skeptical, muttering about hidden fees and 'too good to be true' deals. Agnes, however, was smitten. She'd walked past a sturdy, navy-blue sedan, its paint a deep, lustrous hue that reminded her of twilight skies. The price tag, a cheerful yellow sunburst, declared it was hers for a sum that felt like a generous gift.

"It's just... it's perfect," Agnes breathed, running a hesitant hand over the cool, smooth metal. "My old 'Betsy' has been making that terrible clunking noise for months. Ned says the engine's about to give out entirely. But this..." She gestured to the sedan. "This is like a dream."

The salesman, the silver-haired one, approached them with a gentle smile. "A fine choice, madam," he said, his voice smooth as polished agate. "The 'Aurora.' A pleasure to drive, and even more of a pleasure to own, at this remarkable introductory price."

"Introductory?" Martha interjected, her voice laced with suspicion. "How long will this... introductory price... last?"

The salesman's smile didn't falter. "For a limited time, of course. 'Earl' believes in spreading good fortune. He's very... generous." He emphasized the word with a subtle, almost imperceptible nod.

Agnes, caught in the intoxicating aura of the car and the salesman's calming presence, barely heard Martha's interjections. She imagined herself, no longer shuffling along in her worn-out 'Betsy,' but gliding through the streets in this elegant, new vehicle. She envisioned the surprised looks of her neighbors, the envious glances. It was a fantasy, a vivid, intoxicating escape from the drab reality of her daily life.

Meanwhile, across town, young Tommy Miller, a scrawny teenager whose ambition had been stifled by the lack of opportunity in Redwater Crossing, was staring at a sleek, black motorcycle. It was the kind of bike he'd only seen in movies, a symbol of freedom and rebellion. And its price tag was ludicrously low. He'd been saving for years, working odd jobs, dreaming of escaping Redwater Crossing on two wheels. Now, it seemed, escape was not only possible, but within his immediate grasp.

The arrival of 'Earl's Honest Rides' was more than just a new business; it was a seismic shift in the quiet, predictable rhythm of Redwater Crossing. It was a sudden, almost violent, intrusion of hope into a town that had long since learned to live without it. And as the townsfolk, their hearts fluttering with a dangerous mixture of excitement and disbelief, began to tentatively explore the possibilities laid out before them on that impossibly cheerful lot, a silent question began to form in the mind of Sheriff Mason Brody: where had all these cars come from, and more importantly, what was the true price of Earl's honesty? The gleaming chrome and vibrant paint seemed to promise salvation, but beneath the surface, a disquieting feeling lingered, a sense that this sudden windfall might be too good to be true, and that such extraordinary offerings often came with an equally extraordinary, and perhaps even terrifying, cost. The air, usually thick with the scent of pine and decay, now carried a faint, sweet perfume, like overripe fruit, a scent that was both alluring and faintly unsettling.

The air around "Earl's Honest Rides" hummed, not just with the subtle thrum of impossibly smooth engines, but with a palpable wave of manufactured charm. At the center of this dazzling display stood Earl Maddox himself, a man who seemed to have been spun from sunlight and sweet-talk. He was a vision in a tailored, powder-blue suit, a shade that dared to compete with the cerulean sky above, and his silver hair was impeccably styled, catching the light like a polished halo. His smile, a broad, unwavering crescent, was his primary tool, capable of disarming the most hardened cynic. It wasn't just a smile; it was a performance, a carefully calibrated expression that promised warmth, understanding, and a secret shared only with the person on the receiving end.

He moved through the lot with an almost balletic grace, his presence a magnet for the curious townsfolk who had, by mid-morning, begun to trickle in, their initial apprehension slowly melting under the sheer audacity of the spectacle. He didn't merely greet people; he embraced them. His handshake was a firm, confident clasp, often accompanied by a gentle squeeze, a silent affirmation of shared humanity and mutual respect. His eyes, a startlingly clear shade of azure, seemed to hold a genuine sparkle as he met each person's gaze, making them feel as though they were the sole focus of his attention in a world of infinite possibilities.

"Well, hello there!" he'd exclaim, his voice a rich baritone, smooth as aged whiskey. "Come to admire our little slice of heaven, have you? Don't blame you one bit. We've got some real beauties today, wouldn't you agree?"

He had an uncanny knack for anticipating needs, for articulating desires that people themselves hadn't quite managed to put into words. To Agnes Walker, who had timidly approached the navy-blue sedan, he'd leaned in conspiratorially, his voice dropping to a confidential murmur. "Ah, the 'Aurora'! A woman of discerning taste, I see. You know, I was just telling my young man here," he gestured to the silver-haired salesman, who offered a polite nod, "that this particular vehicle has a certain... *je ne sais quoi*. It speaks to a desire for elegance, for quiet confidence. It's not just a car, madam, it's a statement. A statement that says, 'I have arrived, and I have done so with impeccable style.'"

Agnes, who had spent the last decade driving a car that sounded like a dying badger, felt a blush creep up her neck. "Well, I... I do like the color," she stammered, her hand instinctively reaching out to trace the car's perfect lines.

Earl chuckled, a warm, resonant sound that filled the space between them. "The color is merely the wrapper, my dear Agnes. It's what's inside, the feeling it evokes, that truly matters. Think of it. Driving through Redwater Crossing, turning heads, feeling the road beneath you with a smoothness you haven't experienced in years. This car isn't just transportation; it's a restoration of pride, a whisper of the life you deserve." He paused, letting his words settle like gentle rain. "And at this price? It's practically a gift from the universe, wouldn't you say? A little nudge from fate, encouraging you to embrace the joy that's been waiting for you."

He repeated this performance with each person who ventured onto the lot, adapting his approach with chameleon-like skill. For young Tommy Miller, gazing longingly at the motorcycle, Earl's demeanor shifted. The conspiratorial whisper became a knowing wink, the shared secret now one of youthful rebellion and the open road.

"That's a fine machine, son," Earl said, clapping Tommy on the shoulder with a surprising amount of force. "A real spirit lifter. I see the fire in your eyes, the longing for freedom. This isn't just about getting from point A to point B, is it? This is about the wind in your hair, the rumble of the engine beneath you, the feeling of being truly alive. This is about escaping the ordinary, about carving your own path. And believe me," he lowered his voice, leaning closer, "this beauty is the perfect steed for such an adventure. Earl believes in giving young men like you a chance to chase their dreams. No need to wait years, scraping by. This can be yours, today, for a price that'll make your jaw drop."

He didn't just sell cars; he sold dreams, packaged in gleaming metal and vibrant paint. He sold the illusion of a better life, a life free from the persistent anxieties that plagued Redwater Crossing. His words were woven with threads of empathy, carefully crafted to resonate with the unspoken frustrations and buried aspirations of each individual. He'd subtly acknowledge their struggles – a mention of the rising cost of living, a nod to the limited opportunities – only to present his vehicles as the immediate, miraculous solution.

"I know times have been tough," he'd say, his brow furrowing with feigned concern. "We all feel the pinch, don't we? But that's precisely why Earl is here. He believes that everyone deserves a bit of good fortune, a chance to feel good about themselves again. He sees the potential, the inherent worth in every single person who walks onto this lot."

His benevolence was almost theatrical; a grand gesture designed to disarm and delight. He'd sometimes offer a free cup of coffee from a small, pristine cart that seemed to have appeared as magically as the cars themselves, or a complimentary air freshener, emblazoned with the 'Earl's Honest Rides' logo, in a scent described as "Essence of Prosperity." These small tokens, seemingly insignificant, added another layer to his carefully constructed persona, reinforcing the idea that he was not just a businessman, but a benefactor, a benevolent force descending upon their weary town.

Sheriff Brody, observing from the perimeter, noted the subtle shifts in Earl's interactions. He saw the way Earl's eyes would momentarily glaze over, a fleeting flicker of something unreadable, just before he launched into his most persuasive pronouncements. He noticed the way Earl's smile, while unwavering, sometimes felt a touch too bright, too fixed, like a mask that had been painted on and was beginning to crack. There was a calculated warmth, an almost aggressive sincerity, that felt manufactured, like the perfectly polished chrome of the vehicles themselves.

"He's got a way with words, that one," Martha muttered to Ned, who had ventured out of his hardware store, drawn by the unusual crowd. "Makes you want to believe him, even when your gut's telling you something's off."

Ned grunted, his gaze fixed on Earl as he embraced a middle-aged woman, his arm slung around her shoulders with an easy familiarity. "He's selling them hope, Martha. And in this town, hope's a rare commodity. People will pay a high price for it, even if they don't realize it yet."

Earl's charm offensive was a masterful display of psychological manipulation, a carefully orchestrated symphony of flattery, empathy, and audacious generosity. He wasn't just selling cars; he was selling a temporary escape, a glimmer of a brighter future, and in Redwater Crossing, a town starved of both, his performance was proving to be incredibly, and unsettlingly, effective. The townsfolk, eager to believe in this sudden windfall, were falling under his spell, their skepticism eroded by the sheer force of his captivating charisma and the irresistible allure of his impossibly honest rides. The ground beneath their feet might be crumbling, but Earl Maddox was offering them a chance to drive on solid gold, and for now, that was more than enough to make them forget the cracks.

The polished chrome of Earl's Honest Rides gleamed under the Redwater Crossing sun, reflecting a distorted, elongated image of the curious onlookers. While Earl Maddox, a symphony of bespoke tailoring and dazzling smiles, commanded the front lines of his burgeoning empire, a different kind of presence was beginning to seep into the town's collective consciousness – the whispered legend of his partner. He was a phantom, a silhouette glimpsed in the periphery, a rumor given form by the sheer unlikelihood of Earl's success. No one had seen him clearly, not really. He was more of an impression, a rumor that coalesced in the hushed conversations between customers, the furtive glances from the windows of the adjacent businesses, the uneasy silence that fell over a group when Earl's uncanny salesmanship seemed just a little too perfect.

They called him "the tall man." The moniker was less a description and more an acknowledgment of an absence, a void that spoke volumes. He was the shadow to Earl's blinding light, the silent partner in a dance of audacious commerce. Some said he was the brains, the architect of the impossibly low prices and the suspiciously generous financing. Others imagined him as the muscle, the silent enforcer who ensured that Earl's "honest rides" remained precisely that, and that no one dared question the integrity of the operation. His presence, or rather, the *idea* of his presence, was becoming as integral to the mystique of the car lot as Earl's own practiced charm.

Connie Howard, proprietor of the Redwater Crossing Gazette, found herself increasingly drawn to this unseen figure. She'd been observing Earl's meteoric rise with a mixture of professional curiosity and a prickle of unease. Her newspaper, once a reliable chronicle of bake sales and town council meetings, felt increasingly inadequate in the face of this flamboyant intrusion. The articles she'd written about Earl, filled with his own carefully curated anecdotes and manufactured humility, felt hollow. There was a missing piece, a darker hue in the vibrant tapestry Earl was weaving. And she suspected that missing piece was the tall man.

One afternoon, while attempting to capture a candid shot of Earl charming a particularly skeptical-looking farmer, Connie's lens caught a flicker of movement at the edge of the lot, near the back fence that bordered the overgrown woods. It was a figure, impossibly tall, silhouetted against the late afternoon sun. He was dressed in dark, nondescript clothing, and as he turned his head, Connie caught a fleeting glimpse of a sharp, angular profile, a feature that seemed too severe, too predatory, to belong to a simple business partner. He disappeared as quickly as he'd appeared, melting back into the shadows of the trees, leaving Connie with a rapidly beating heart and a sudden, chilling conviction.

She shared her observation with Ned Croft, the owner of Croft's Hardware, a man whose pragmatic nature was a rare anchor in Redwater Crossing's increasingly surreal atmosphere. Ned, ever the stoic observer, had also noticed the subtle shifts, the undercurrents beneath Earl's dazzling surface.

"He's not just selling cars, Connie," Ned had said, his voice low and gravelly, as they'd watched Earl from the relative safety of his store's entrance. "He's selling... something else. Something people want or think they want. And that partner of his... well, there's a reason he stays in the shadows."

Ned described a brief encounter he'd had a few days prior, while attempting to retrieve a misplaced delivery truck from the back of Earl's lot. He'd been startled by a sudden, guttural sound, a cough that seemed to vibrate through the very air. Looking up, he'd seen the tall man standing on the loading dock, his form an imposing shadow against the setting sun. Ned swore the man hadn't blinked, his eyes – if they could even be called eyes – seeming to bore directly into Ned's soul. There was an intensity there, a silent, unnerving power that had sent a shiver down Ned's spine. The man hadn't spoken, hadn't moved, but Ned had felt an unspoken command to retreat, to leave him undisturbed. He'd backed away slowly, the image of that towering, unnervingly still figure seared into his memory.

The whispers grew louder, more insistent. Teenagers dared each other to sneak onto the lot after dark, hoping for a glimpse of the tall man, a chance to boast about a fleeting encounter with the town's resident phantom. Stories began to circulate, embellishing the limited sightings with terrifying details. He had eyes like chipped obsidian, some said, or hands that were unnaturally long and skeletal. He moved with a preternatural silence, capable of appearing and disappearing without a sound. He was rumored to be a creature of the night, a guardian of secrets, his very existence tied to the shadowy dealings that fueled Earl's prosperity.

Even Earl, in his most unguarded moments, seemed to acknowledge the man's existence, albeit obliquely. One evening, as a particularly persistent reporter from the county paper pressed him about his business acumen, Earl had chuckled, a sound that didn't quite reach his eyes.

"Oh, I have a partner, certainly," he'd said, his gaze drifting towards the dark perimeter of the lot. "A very... *dedicated* individual.

He handles the more... *sensitive* aspects of our operation. You could say he's the foundation upon which this whole enterprise is built. Without him, well, none of this would be possible. He's a man of few words, but immense... capability." The reporter had pressed for a name, a description, but Earl had merely smiled, a tight, enigmatic curve of his lips, and changed the subject back to the gleaming virtues of a pre-owned minivan.

The townsfolk, starved for excitement, for anything to break the monotonous cycle of their lives, began to weave the tall man into the very fabric of Redwater Crossing. He became a local legend, a boogeyman for children, a source of morbid fascination for adults. He was the dark mirror to Earl's effervescent charm, the silent, imposing force that underpinned the glittering face of Honest Rides. His unseen hand guided the impossible deals; his silent vigilance ensured the smooth operation of Earl's carefully orchestrated deception.

There was a growing, unspoken understanding among those who felt the unease, the gnawing suspicion that something was fundamentally wrong with Earl's sudden success. They understood that the tall man was more than just a business partner. He was an enigma, a symbol of the unseen forces at play, the hidden depths beneath the sun-drenched surface of Redwater Crossing. And as the car lot continued to flourish, as more and more townsfolk succumbed to the allure of Earl's impossible offers, the shadow of the tall man grew longer, darker, and infinitely more compelling. The whispers of his existence were no longer just idle gossip; they were the first tentative breaths of a truth that was slowly, inexorably, taking shape in the heart of their unsuspecting town. The mystery surrounding him was a magnet, drawing in the curious, the desperate, and the fearful, all eager to catch a glimpse of the silent power that seemed to hold

Redwater Crossing in its enigmatic grasp. The very air around Earl's Honest Rides seemed to hum not just with the promise of a good deal, but with the palpable presence of something ancient, something unseen, something that moved in the shadows and cast a long, disquieting silhouette over their lives.

The gleaming promise of Earl's Honest Rides had become the town's new obsession, eclipsing even the annual pie-baking contest in its fervor. Conversations at the diner, the post office, and the barber shop inevitably circled back to the impossible prices, the impossibly low-down payments, and the sheer, intoxicating abundance of vehicles that seemed to materialize overnight on Earl Maddox's meticulously maintained lot. For a town long accustomed to the gentle rhythm of predictable scarcity, this sudden influx of affordable dreams was nothing short of a miracle. Entire families, their old jalopies sputtering their last breaths, converged on Redwater Crossing, their eyes wide with a desperate hope that felt both exhilarating and a little bit dangerous. These were people who had long ago resigned themselves to making do, to patching up, to scraping by. Earl's lot offered them an escape, a tangible symbol of a brighter future, a future where they could finally afford to be seen, to be mobile, to be... normal.

Among these hopefuls was the Henderson family, their ancient pickup truck wheezing its final days on the dusty backroads. Mr. Henderson, a man whose hands bore the permanent grime of years spent coaxing life from stubborn machinery, had arrived at Earl's with a budget that wouldn't even cover a decent set of tires a year ago. Yet, by lunchtime, he was driving away in a gleaming, cherry-red sedan, a vehicle that looked like it had rolled off the showroom floor that very morning, not spent years collecting dust in some forgotten corner. His wife, a woman whose weary smile usually held the faint scent of desperation, beamed with a joy that was almost jarring. Their two teenage children, usually sullen and withdrawn, were already planning a trip to the county fair, a trip that had been a distant, impossible fantasy just days before. They represented the burgeoning success story, the tangible proof that Earl's claims were not just hot air, but solid, drivable reality.

Yet, not everyone was swept up in the tidal wave of enthusiasm. Beneath the surface of collective excitement, a subtle undercurrent of disquiet began to stir, a quiet hum of unease that resonated with those who had seen enough of life to recognize the tell-tale signs of a trap. Sheriff Mason Brody was one of them. A man whose pragmatism was as ingrained as the lines etched around his weary eyes, Mason approached the situation with a healthy dose of skepticism that bordered on suspicion. He wasn't a man prone to flights of fancy; his world was one of tangible evidence, of observable facts, of the predictable ebb and flow of everyday life in Redwater Crossing. And Earl Maddox's sudden, dazzling success defied all logic.

Mason had seen businesses come and go in Redwater Crossing, some thriving, most struggling, but none had exploded onto the scene with the sheer, unadulterated velocity of Earl's Honest Rides. The prices were, to put it mildly, ludicrous. He'd heard the hushed conversations, the astonished whispers in the grocery store aisle. He'd seen the sheer volume of vehicles that seemed to appear and disappear on the lot with bewildering speed. It wasn't just a good deal; it felt... wrong.

His patrol car, a utilitarian machine built for the mundane realities of law enforcement, often found itself cruising past Earl's lot, Mason's gaze lingering on the endless rows of cars. He'd begun to notice peculiar things, subtle inconsistencies that pricked at his seasoned instincts. For one, the lot seemed to operate on a different kind of clock. Even late into the evening, long after other businesses had shuttered their doors, the lights on Earl's lot remained ablaze, the cheerful jingle of his advertised jingle echoing through the twilight. He'd seen customers leaving at all hours, their faces alight with triumph, their newly acquired vehicles leaving trails of dust in their wake. It was a constant, almost unnatural, level of activity that felt less like commerce and more like a carefully orchestrated illusion.

Then there was the distinct lack of any visible inventory process. Cars arrived, cars were sold, all with a seamlessness that defied the typical chaos of a used car lot. No haggling, no desperate sales pitches, just a quiet, efficient transaction that left both parties seemingly delighted, and the cash register ringing with an unnerving regularity. Mason had even made a few discreet inquiries, posing as a potential buyer with a list of questions that skirted the edges of genuine interest. Earl, of course, was a master of deflection, his smile as polished as the chrome on his prize vehicles, his answers always smooth, always plausible, yet somehow... hollow.

"Just a knack for finding good deals, Sheriff," Earl had said with a disarming chuckle, his eyes twinkling as he gestured to a practically new SUV. "I know where to look, that's all. And these folks... they deserve a break, don't they?"

But Mason wasn't buying it. He'd seen the desperation in the eyes of some of the buyers, a hunger that went beyond the desire for a reliable mode of transportation. It was a hunger for escape, for a change, for something more. And he couldn't shake the feeling that Earl was feeding that hunger with something far more complex, and potentially far more dangerous, than just cheap cars.

He also noticed the absence of paperwork, or at least, the *visible* absence of it. While other dealerships would have towering stacks of contracts, financing applications, and title transfers, Earl's seemed to operate with a surprising minimalism. He'd seen Earl signing documents, of course, but they were always brief, almost perfunctory. And he'd never seen a single finance manager, no anxious loan officers, no frantic phone calls to credit bureaus. It was as if the entire financial aspect of the business was handled with an almost ethereal efficiency, a smooth, silent operation that bypassed the usual bureaucratic hurdles.

One particular incident had cemented Mason's unease. He'd been called to the lot late one Tuesday night, a routine disturbance call about a car alarm going off. When he arrived, the lot was bathed in the eerie glow of the overhead lights, the jingle still playing its cheerful, incessant tune. He'd found the alarm silenced, the vehicle seemingly undisturbed. But as he'd circled the lot, his flashlight beam sweeping across the polished surfaces of the cars, he'd felt it – a strange, almost electric energy emanating from the very ground beneath his feet. It was a subtle thrum, a palpable vibration that seemed to be more than just the residual warmth of the asphalt. It was an unsettling sensation, as if the lot itself was alive, humming with a hidden power.

He'd also seen him then, or rather, he'd caught a fleeting glimpse. At the far edge of the lot, near the dark, imposing tree line that separated the car dealership from the dense woods, a figure had stood for just a moment, a tall, dark silhouette against the night sky. It was the briefest of apparitions, a mere flicker in his peripheral vision, but it had been enough. The sheer stillness of the figure, the unnatural stillness, had sent a chill down Mason's spine that had nothing to do with the cool night air. It was the stillness of something waiting, something watching.

He'd approached the area cautiously, his hand instinctively resting on the butt of his service weapon. But the figure was gone, vanished as if it had never been there. The only evidence of its presence was a faint disturbance in the dew-kissed grass, a subtle imprint that suggested something heavy, something tall, had stood there for a while.

"Anything out of the ordinary, Sheriff?" Earl had asked, appearing as if from nowhere, his smile as bright and artificial as the lot lights.

Mason had shaken his head, the unsettling sensation still clinging to him like a damp shroud. "Just a car alarm, Earl. Seemed to have stopped on its own."

"Ah, yes," Earl had said, his gaze sweeping over the lot, his expression unreadable. "Sometimes things just... resolve themselves here."

The phrase had stuck with Mason. "Resolve themselves." It implied an agency, a force beyond human intervention. And it was this growing suspicion, this gut feeling that something was fundamentally amiss, that prompted him to begin his own quiet investigation. He started by cross-referencing recent sales records, looking for patterns, for anomalies. He discreetly interviewed a few of the more recent buyers, gently probing for details about the financing, the origin of the vehicles, the overall experience. Most of them, caught up in the euphoria of their new possessions, offered vague, enthusiastic affirmations of Earl's honesty. But a few, the ones who seemed to possess a slightly sharper edge of desperation, offered hesitant, almost fearful, accounts. They spoke of a feeling, a pressure, a sense that they *had* to buy, that the opportunity was too good to pass up, that there was an unspoken urgency attached to every deal.

He also began to pay closer attention to the man himself, to Earl Maddox. He observed him interacting with customers, his charm, a carefully crafted weapon. He noticed the way Earl's eyes never quite met theirs directly, always darting, always scanning. He saw the subtle tension in his jaw when he thought no one was looking, the fleeting flicker of something cold and calculating that would pass across his face before being replaced by his practiced smile. Mason, a man who had spent years reading people, saw through the veneer. Earl was not just a salesman; he was a performer, and his stage was this impossibly bright, impossibly profitable car lot.

And then there was the partner. The phantom, the legend. Mason had heard the whispers, of course. The townsfolk, in their hushed tones, spoke of a tall, shadowy figure, a presence that seemed to haunt the edges of the lot. Mason, a man of facts, had dismissed it as local folklore, the product of overactive imaginations fueled by too much gossip. But that night, on the lot, he'd seen something. Or rather, he'd *felt* something. A presence, undeniable and unnerving.

He started making regular, unscheduled visits to the lot, not just during business hours, but in the early morning, late at night, whenever his patrol route took him past. He'd park his car a little further down the road, observing the comings and goings, the unnatural quiet that sometimes fell over the place, the almost predatory stillness that seemed to emanate from its depths. He noticed that the police scanner, usually a constant source of noise and activity, seemed remarkably silent when it came to Earl's Honest Rides. No complaints, no disturbances, no reports of any kind. It was as if the lot existed in a vacuum, untouched by the usual dramas of small-town life.

The seeds of hope were blooming vibrantly in Redwater Crossing, manifesting in the gleaming chrome and the joyous laughter of families finally able to afford their dreams. But for Sheriff Mason Brody, those same vibrant blooms were being choked by the insidious tendrils of suspicion, each impossible deal, each fleeting shadow, each unnerving hum of energy serving as a stark reminder that in the sun-drenched landscape of Earl's Honest Rides, something dark and unknown was taking root. He knew, with a certainty that settled deep in his bones, that this was more than just a car dealership. It was a mystery, and he was determined to uncover the truth, no matter how deeply it was buried beneath the polished surfaces and the carefully constructed smiles. The prosperity of Redwater Crossing felt increasingly fragile, built on a foundation that Mason was beginning to suspect was far more treacherous than anyone could imagine. The seeds of hope, he feared, were already being poisoned by something far more sinister.

CHAPTER 2
The Illusion of Prosperity

The air in Redwater Crossing, once thick with the quiet resignation of scarcity, now buzzed with an almost palpable excitement. It was a heady aroma, a potent cocktail of relief and possibility, and Earl Maddox's Honest Rides was the undeniable source. The first wave of buyers, those who had been the most immediate and perhaps the most desperate to embrace the improbable miracle, were now proudly piloting their newfound treasures through the familiar streets. These weren't just cars; they were chariots of escape, gleaming symbols of a future that, for so long, had seemed as distant and unattainable as the stars. For families who had spent years making do, their lives measured by the sputtering coughs of aging engines and the gnawing anxiety of mounting repair bills, these vehicles represented a seismic shift. They were tangible proof that their endured hardships had not been in vain, that a brighter horizon was not just a fantasy, but a purchasable reality.

Take, for instance, the Millers. Sarah Miller, a woman whose hands bore the perpetual faint redness of dishwater and whose eyes held the weary wisdom of a thousand sleepless nights, had driven her ancient, rust-flecked minivan for nearly a decade. Its once-vibrant blue had faded to a dull, patchy grey, and its interior perpetually smelled of stale Cheerios and damp dog. Her husband, David, a construction worker whose back protested with every dawn, had always promised her a newer car, a safer car, a car that didn't make their two children flinch every time they hit a pothole. But promises, in Redwater Crossing, often remained just that – whispers lost to the wind of economic reality. Then came Earl. With a down payment that felt like a mere pittance and a monthly payment that seemed almost ludicrously low, Sarah was now behind the wheel of a spacious, immaculate SUV. The cherry-red paint gleamed under the afternoon sun, reflecting a sky that suddenly seemed bluer, more full of promise. Her children, usually subdued in the back of their cramped, rattling vehicle, were now leaning forward, their faces pressed against the cool glass, pointing out landmarks they'd never bothered to notice before. It wasn't just a car; it was a declaration. It said, "We are here. We are moving forward. We are not stuck anymore."

Similarly, old Mr. Abernathy, who had a small family farm and ran the town's only pharmacy store, had finally traded in his wheezing pickup truck, the one with the perpetually foggy windshield and the driver's side door that required a specific, practiced jiggle to open. He'd always prided himself on his self-sufficiency, his ability to fix anything with a bit of wire, bubble gum, and a lot of ingenuity. But the repairs had become more frequent, more costly, and the truck's reliability was becoming a liability for his business. He'd been skeptical at first, eyeing Earl's lot with the same suspicion he reserved for unsolicited flyers. But the lure of a practically new, sleek black sedan, a vehicle that whispered of professionalism and efficiency, had been too strong to resist. He'd signed the papers with a flourish, a rare smile creasing his weathered face. Now, he found himself enjoying the drive to those housebound, the hum of the engine a soothing counterpoint to the usual clatter and rattle. He even found himself looking forward to his commute, a thought that would have been laughable just weeks prior. The sedan wasn't just a mode of transport; it was an upgrade to his identity, a subtle but significant elevation in his standing within the community.

The ripple effect was undeniable. The mood in Redwater Crossing began to shift, subtly at first, then with an accelerating momentum. The hushed conversations at the diner, which had once been dominated by complaints about the weather and the rising cost of living, now revolved around horsepower, fuel efficiency, and the sheer joy of a smooth ride. The laughter, once a rare and precious commodity, seemed to echo more frequently from the open windows of newly acquired vehicles. It was an intoxicating blend of relief and newfound pride. These weren't extravagant purchases; they were practical necessities, made suddenly, miraculously attainable. They were the tools that would allow people to reconnect with distant families, to seek out better job opportunities in neighboring towns, to simply escape the suffocating familiarity of their own struggles for a weekend.

There was Martha, who hadn't visited her ailing mother in the next county for over a year, the distance and the unreliable state of her old car a constant barrier. Now, with a comfortable, spacious minivan, she was planning a trip, her voice brimming with a long-suppressed joy. There was young Warren Rodgers, who had dreamed of becoming a mechanic but had always been held back by the lack of reliable transportation to get to the technical college in the city. Earl's lot, with its astonishing array of vehicles, had provided him with not just a car, but a pathway to his future. He'd chosen a sturdy, no-nonsense pickup truck, a tool of his aspiring trade, and his eyes now held a spark of ambition that had been absent before. These were not frivolous expenditures; they were investments in life itself, in relationships, in personal growth, in the simple, fundamental human desire for progress and betterment.

The sheer psychological impact of these transactions could not be overstated. For years, the residents of Redwater Crossing had been conditioned to expect disappointment, to brace themselves for the inevitable "no" or the prohibitive "too expensive." The constant barrage of financial setbacks had eroded their optimism, leaving a residue of cynicism that clung to them like the dust on their old cars. Earl's Honest Rides, with its seemingly endless supply of affordable vehicles, had shattered that paradigm. It was a place where the answer was always "yes," where the price was always within reach, where the dream was always on the table. This radical departure from their lived experience was, for many, disorienting, even unbelievable. They had to see it to believe it, and once they saw it, they had to possess it. The act of driving away from Earl's lot in a vehicle that was far beyond their previous financial reach was more than just a purchase; it was an act of defiance against the limitations that had defined their lives.

The intoxicating euphoria of these first purchases was a powerful, almost tangible force. It spread through Redwater Crossing like a benevolent contagion, infectious and irresistible. The scarcity that had once been a defining characteristic of the town was being replaced by an illusion of abundance, and the people were reveling in it. They pointed out their new cars to neighbors, shared photos on the community bulletin board, and recounted their experiences with the ease and efficiency of Earl's sales process with wide-eyed wonder. The narrative was simple: Earl Maddox was a miracle worker, a man who understood the struggles of ordinary people and had found a way to provide.

Even the town's perpetual cynics found themselves softening, their resistance eroded by the sheer, undeniable evidence of transformed lives. The sheer volume of cars moving in and out of Earl's lot was staggering, a constant churn that defied logic and fueled the growing belief that this was indeed a genuine economic boom. People who had been struggling to make rent were now cruising down Main Street in vehicles that looked like they belonged in a magazine.

The contrast was stark, and the emotional uplift was profound. The fragile hope that had been flickering in the hearts of many was now burning bright, a testament to the transformative power of a dream realized, even if that dream was delivered on four wheels and a powerful engine. This initial wave of buyers, emboldened by their own success and eager to share their good fortune, became the unwitting evangelists of Earl's Honest Rides, their beaming faces and gleaming cars the most persuasive advertisements imaginable. They were the proof, the living, breathing testimonials to the unbelievable promise that had suddenly materialized on the edge of town.

The gleam of polished chrome and the scent of new car polish, once so intoxicating, began to lose their allure. The initial elation that had swept through Redwater Crossing, a tide of relief and possibility, was starting to recede, revealing a stark and unforgiving shoreline of reality. It was a subtle shift at first, a barely perceptible tremor beneath the surface of newfound prosperity. Drivers who had once sung the praises of Earl Maddox's Honest Rides found their anthems faltering, replaced by hesitant questions and anxious glances at their gleaming dashboards. The improbable affordability that had drawn them in was now revealing its shadowy counterpart: a labyrinth of hidden costs and predatory terms.

Sarah Miller, who had so joyfully navigated her cherry-red SUV through town, was the first to feel the sharp pinch of this new reality. The impossibly low monthly payment, which had felt like a gift from the heavens, had inexplicably crept upwards. It wasn't a dramatic leap, but a series of small, insidious increments, each added with a justification that sounded plausible in isolation – a "documentation fee," an "administrative charge," a "service enhancement." Individually, they were minor annoyances. Collectively, they were a slow, steady drain on her already stretched budget. David, whose construction work provided their primary income, had noticed it first. He'd always kept a sharp eye on their finances, meticulously budgeting for every cent. When he saw the latest statement, his brow furrowed. "Sarah," he'd said, his voice heavy with a familiar weariness, "this payment's gone up again. By almost fifty dollars this month."

Sarah had initially dismissed his concern. "Oh, it's probably just one of those little fees Earl mentioned. He said there might be a few extra things now and then." But the "few extra things" began to accumulate, transforming the manageable payment into a source of gnawing anxiety. The initial shock turned to a quiet dread as she realized the true extent of what she had signed. The contract, a multi-page document filled with dense legal jargon and legalese, now seemed like an intricate trap. She'd skimmed it, eager to drive away in her new vehicle, trusting in Earl's seemingly benevolent demeanor and the honest-sounding name of his business.

Now, poring over the fine print under the dim glow of her kitchen lamp, she discovered clauses that seemed designed to obscure rather than clarify. An escalating interest rate, tied to an obscure economic index she'd never heard of, meant that the promised low rate was merely a fleeting introductory offer. A clause detailing "contingent service charges" allowed for fees to be levied at Earl's discretion, without prior notification.

The vehicles, once symbols of freedom, were rapidly transforming into gleaming shackles. Old Mr. Abernathy, who had been so proud of his sleek black sedan, found himself increasingly wary of the mail. The statements from Honest Rides were no longer just bills; they were harbingers of financial dread. His initial excitement over a professional image had curdled into a sick feeling of being exploited. The savings he'd anticipated from a more reliable vehicle were being entirely consumed by the escalating payments and the bewildering array of fees. He discovered that the advertised "low APR" was only applicable for the first six months, after which it ballooned to an astronomical rate, far exceeding anything he could have obtained from a traditional bank. He'd tried to speak to Earl, to seek clarification, but Earl was rarely available. When he did manage to corner the salesman, he was met with a practiced smile and a dismissive wave. "Standard practice, Mr. Abernathy," Earl would say, his voice smooth as polished glass. "It's all in the contract you signed. You read it, didn't you?"

The insidious nature of the debt was that it wasn't immediately catastrophic. It was a slow bleed, a gradual erosion of financial stability. For many in Redwater Crossing, accustomed to living on the edge, these incremental increases were easily masked, at first. They would cut back elsewhere – fewer groceries, no new clothes, postponing essential home repairs. But the demands of the car payments were relentless, and the underlying mechanics of Earl's financing were designed to ensnare. The goal wasn't simply to sell cars;

it was to ensnare buyers in a cycle of debt from which escape seemed increasingly impossible.

Martha, who had been so thrilled about visiting her ailing mother, found her minivan payments growing with each passing month. The joy of planning her trip had been replaced by the grim reality of the mounting bills. She'd always been a careful saver, but her meager savings account was being steadily depleted to cover the ever-increasing installments. The distance to her mother's house, once a simple hurdle, now felt like an insurmountable chasm, widened by the crushing weight of her financial obligations. She realized with a chilling certainty that the car that was supposed to reconnect her with her family had, in fact, become the very thing that was isolating her, trapping her in a tightening financial noose.

Young Warren Rodgers, whose pickup truck was supposed to be his ticket to a career in mechanics, discovered that the cost of ownership extended far beyond the monthly payment. While the truck itself was solid, the financing was anything but. The interest rates, once he delved deeper, were staggering. He found himself working extra shifts, taking on side jobs that ate into his study time, all to keep up with the payments that seemed to multiply inexplicably. The dream of a better future, once so bright and clear, was becoming shrouded in a fog of financial worry. He'd overheard conversations among other buyers, hushed whispers of being "underwater" on their loans, meaning they owed more on the car than it was actually worth. This realization hit him with the force of a physical blow. His truck, his tool of ambition, was becoming a financial black hole.

The illusion of prosperity, so carefully crafted by Earl Maddox, was beginning to unravel thread by thread. The initial euphoria had been a potent, almost narcotic, effect. It had dulled their senses, made them overlook the warning signs, and embrace the unbelievable. But as the bills continued to climb and the justifications for the increasing costs became more opaque, the veil of deception began to lift. The gleaming vehicles, parked proudly in driveways, were no longer just sources of pride; they were constant, physical reminders of the debt they carried. They were heavy, tangible symbols of a financial trap that had been sprung with deceptive ease.

Earl's Honest Rides, once a beacon of hope, was now perceived by many as a predatory enterprise. The charm of the sales process, the easy approval, the low initial payments – all were re-evaluated in the harsh light of mounting debt. The "honest" in the business name felt like a cruel, bitter joke. The smiles and assurances of the sales staff now seemed like calculated manipulations, designed to lure unsuspecting customers into a financial abyss. People who had been the proudest owners just weeks before were now exhibiting a newfound reticence. They no longer boasted about their vehicles; instead, they spoke in hushed tones, their faces etched with worry, sharing their escalating financial nightmares with a growing community of the disillusioned.

The community bulletin board, which had once been adorned with photos of happy families with their new cars, now featured desperate pleas for advice, anonymous warnings about hidden fees, and even outright accusations. The narrative had shifted from one of miraculous affordability to one of crippling debt. The dream of a better life, delivered on four wheels, was turning into a recurring nightmare. The physical manifestation of this financial ruin was everywhere – in the strained faces of neighbors, in the hushed arguments heard through open windows, in the growing number of cars parked on the street, their owners perhaps unable to afford the rising payments for their own driveways.

The psychological toll was immense. The hope that had been so carefully nurtured was being systematically crushed, replaced by a profound sense of betrayal and despair. The very things that were meant to improve their lives – the cars – were now the source of their deepest anxieties. They had traded one form of scarcity for another, a scarcity of resources now replaced by a scarcity of peace of mind. The weight of their obligations was not just a financial burden; it was an emotional one, a constant cloud of worry that overshadowed their daily lives. The illusion of prosperity had shattered, revealing the stark, unforgiving landscape of financial ruin beneath. The gleaming chariots of escape had become anchors, dragging them down into a depth of debt they had never imagined, a darkness far more pervasive and terrifying than the economic hardship they had sought to escape. The story of Earl Maddox's Honest Rides was no longer a tale of a benevolent benefactor; it was becoming a chilling testament to the devastating power of financial deception; a cautionary tale whispered in the shadowed corners of Redwater Crossing.

The air in Redwater Crossing, once thick with the scent of damp earth and pine, now carried a faint, metallic tang, like old blood and desperation. It clung to the peeling paint of the general store, seeped into the very fabric of the community center, and coiled around the gleaming hoods of the cars that were no longer symbols of freedom but gilded cages. This was the insidious work of the 'tall man,' a figure who had arrived in town with the same quiet inevitability as the changing seasons yet brought with him a chilling disruption to the natural order. He was more than just Earl Maddox's silent business partner; he was the physical manifestation of the Master, a malevolent entity whose existence was predicated on the slow, agonizing decay of human hope.

His presence was not announced by thunderous pronouncements or spectral apparitions. Instead, it was a subtler, more pervasive influence, like a creeping frost that withered the soul before it could even feel the bite. He moved through Redwater Crossing like a shadow, his gaunt frame and perpetually downturned gaze making him seem perpetually out of sync with the town's forced cheerfulness. Yet, wherever he went, a palpable shift occurred. Conversations would falter, laughter would die prematurely, and a prickling unease would settle over those around him. It was as if he carried a pocket of intensified gloom, a localized vortex of despair that subtly amplified the latent anxieties of the townsfolk.

He would observe, his eyes – dark, fathomless pools – scanning the faces of those ensnared by Earl's predatory schemes. He saw not just financial hardship, but the deeper, more profound desperation that fueled it. He saw the gnawing envy in a neighbor's glance, the suffocating fear of failure in a parent's tight jaw, the hollow ache of unfulfilled dreams in a young man's slumped shoulders. These were the raw materials of his existence, the psychic sustenance that allowed the Master to thrive. The tall man was the conduit, the earthly anchor for a power that fed on the spiritual corrosion of its victims.

He didn't need to speak, for his mere presence was a sermon of doom. When he stood near Earl Maddox's dealership, the whispers of impending financial ruin seemed to coalesce into a deafening roar. The anxieties of those signing contracts, their hopes already frayed, would stretch to a breaking point. The tall man would stand at the edge of the lot, a silent sentinel, and the barely suppressed panic within the hearts of buyers would bloom, nurtured by his unblinking gaze. He was the silent conductor of their spiraling anxieties, his unseen influence twisting their desires into destructive obsessions. The craving for a better life, the initial hopeful impulse that had driven them to Earl's lot, was subtly reshaped into a desperate, all-consuming need, a frantic scramble for an escape that would only lead them deeper into the mire.

Consider old Mrs. Anderson, a widow who had dreamed of a reliable car to visit her grandchildren in the next state. The gleam of the sedan, coupled with the promise of manageable payments, had felt like a second chance. But with each passing week, as the payments crept higher and the justifications became more convoluted, a gnawing fear replaced her initial excitement. She would see the tall man sometimes, standing across the street from the post office, his silhouette stark against the fading light. Each sighting would coincide with a fresh wave of dread, a feeling that her small world was shrinking, her options dwindling. It wasn't just the car; it was the entire edifice of her independence that seemed to be crumbling. The tall man's silent observation was a catalyst, amplifying the whispers of doubt that had begun to surface in her own mind. He didn't need to threaten; the despair he cultivated was a far more potent weapon. He was the embodiment of the Master's patience, his strategy not of swift annihilation, but of prolonged, agonizing erosion.

He would often be seen in the periphery of town gatherings, a dark stain on the fabric of community life. At the potluck supper, where once there had been boisterous laughter and shared stories, his quiet presence at the edge of the clearing cast a pall. Conversations would noticeably quieten as he approached, a subconscious acknowledgment of the palpable aura of negativity he exuded. The tall man was the living embodiment of the Master's grim satisfaction, his form a constant, unsettling reminder of the unseen forces at play. He savored the discord, the subtle fracturing of bonds as neighbors began to eye each other with suspicion, wondering if their own financial woes were somehow exacerbated by the tall man's proximity.

His influence was not limited to the direct victims of Earl's schemes. He seemed to have a parasitic relationship with the entire town, drawing strength from its collective anxieties. Even those who had managed to avoid the trap of Honest Rides found themselves unsettled. A vague sense of foreboding permeated the air, an intangible dread that seeped into everyday life. The children spoke of nightmares, of a tall, shadowy figure lurking at the edges of their dreams. The elders muttered about a "darkness" settling over Redwater Crossing, a spiritual malaise that had no easy explanation. The tall man, in his silent, spectral way, was orchestrating this pervasive sense of unease, subtly guiding the narrative towards the inevitable downfall of his victims, relishing their spiritual decay with a detached, ancient hunger.

Earl Maddox, of course, was merely a pawn, a willing participant in a game that was far larger and more sinister than he could comprehend. He saw the tall man as a business associate, a silent partner whose presence seemed to bring a certain... effectiveness to his operations. He attributed the heightened desperation of his clients, the almost feverish intensity with which they signed their lives away, to his own salesmanship, his astute understanding of human weakness. He never once considered that the true architect of their despair was the gaunt figure who stood so often in the background, a phantom conductor of their ruin. The Master, through his avatar, reveled in this ignorance, the ultimate irony being that the perpetrator of the immediate suffering was himself a victim, albeit one who willingly embraced the darkness.

The tall man's modus operandi was a chilling testament to the Master's ancient understanding of human nature. He didn't force; he tempted. He didn't destroy; he corrupted. He would appear at moments of peak desperation, a silent observer of the unfolding tragedy. When Sarah Miller, her face etched with worry, sat poring over her escalating car payments, the tall man might be seen walking his slow, deliberate path down the street outside her window, his presence a silent affirmation of her worst fears. He was the whisper of temptation in the ear of the desperate, the subtle nudge that pushed them further into the abyss. He was the quiet affirmation of their darkest impulses – the impulse to give up, the impulse to despair, the impulse to embrace the destructive.

He was the embodiment of the Master's patience, a stark contrast to the frantic, often clumsy, machinations of human greed. While Earl was driven by a more immediate, earthbound desire for profit, the tall man operated on a geological timescale. He was content to sow seeds of discord, to nurture the roots of despair, knowing that eventually, the rot would consume everything. He orchestrated the town's descent not through overt acts of malice, but through the subtle amplification of existing flaws, the intelligent exploitation of the cracks already present in the foundation of their lives. He was the whisper of the void, the silent promise of oblivion, a promise he was meticulously, patiently, fulfilling. His power was not in force, but in insidious suggestion, in the chilling certainty that whatever dark path one chose, there was always a silent, gaunt figure watching, approving, feeding. The illusion of prosperity, so carefully woven by Earl, was the initial lure, but it was the tall man who ensured that the unraveling would be complete, leaving behind only the tattered remnants of shattered lives and the echoing silence of spiritual decay.

The metallic tang in the air, once a subtle anomaly, had begun to assert itself, a persistent undertone to the forced cheerfulness that still clung to Redwater Crossing like a stubborn stain. Sheriff Mason Brody, a man who'd seen his share of human folly and desperation in his twenty years patrolling these woods, found himself increasingly unsettled. It wasn't the usual fare – petty theft, domestic squabbles, the occasional bar brawl. This was different. This was a pervasive sickness, a slow unraveling that seemed to emanate from the polished chrome and gleaming paint of Earl Maddox's car lot, Honest Rides.

He'd started noticing the pattern weeks ago, a subtle shift in the town's rhythm. At first, he'd dismissed it as the natural ebb and flow of a small community. Economic downturns happened. People struggled. But then the whispers started, growing louder, more desperate. They spoke of crippling payments, of loans with invisible clauses, of a desperation that clawed at the edges of reason. He'd seen it in the eyes of the folks who came into his office, not to report a crime, but to seek a miracle, to beg for an extension on a mortgage that had somehow spiraled out of control, a mortgage tied, more often than not, to a brand-new vehicle.

Brody was a man of logic, of tangible evidence. He dealt with facts, with the observable. Yet, the circumstances surrounding Honest Rides defied easy explanation. Earl Maddox, a man similar to someone Brody had known since childhood, he was like this man who'd always been a bit too slick, a bit too eager, and now had suddenly transformed into a pillar of prosperity. Earl's dealership, once a modest affair, now boasted the latest models, a parade of gleaming sedans and powerful trucks that seemed to materialize out of thin air. And people, ordinary folks, were clamoring for them, signing contracts with a feverish urgency that Brody found deeply disturbing.

He remembered stopping by the lot a few weeks back, ostensibly to check on a noise complaint about a particularly loud muffler.

Maddox had been beaming, surrounded by a gaggle of eager buyers. Brody's gaze had drifted to the edge of the lot, where a figure stood, almost blending into the shadows cast by a towering oak. It was the tall man; the silent associate Maddox had brought into the business. Even from a distance, there was something unnerving about him. His stillness was unnatural, his presence like a void, sucking the warmth out of the bright afternoon. He hadn't moved, hadn't spoken, yet Brody felt a prickling sensation on the back of his neck, a primal instinct screaming that something was fundamentally wrong.

Since then, he'd seen the tall man around town, always on the periphery, a silent observer. He'd be standing across the street from the post office as old Mrs. Gable, her face a roadmap of worry, collected her mail. He'd be a dark silhouette against the fading light outside the diner, his presence coinciding with hushed, tense conversations spilling out onto the sidewalk. He was a ghost in the machine of Redwater Crossing, an anomaly in the otherwise predictable landscape.

Brody started making discreet inquiries, leaning on his network of informants, the people who always knew what was going on in town. The stories he heard were disturbing. People were selling off assets, dipping into retirement funds, taking out second mortgages – all to keep up with payments for vehicles they could barely afford. The initial excitement of a new car had soured, replaced by a gnawing dread. He heard about arguments, hushed and bitter, echoing from homes that had once been bastions of peace. He saw the strain on faces that had always been open and friendly. The illusion of prosperity, meticulously crafted by Earl, was beginning to crack, revealing the desperation beneath.

One evening, while reviewing the town's financial records, a disturbing pattern emerged. A disproportionate number of foreclosures, bankruptcies, and debt consolidations had occurred in the past six months, all directly correlating with the surge in sales at Earl's Honest Rides. It wasn't just a few unlucky individuals; it was a wave, a tide of financial ruin washing over Redwater Crossing. And at the center of it all, like a spider at the heart of its web, was Earl Maddox and his silent partner.

Brody paid another visit to Honest Rides, this time unannounced. Maddox, his smile a little too wide, his eyes a little too shifty, greeted him with forced joviality. "Sheriff! To what do I owe the pleasure? Looking for a new set of wheels?"

"Just passing by, Earl," Brody said, his gaze sweeping across the lot. The same glinting rows of cars, the same eager customers. But this time, he noticed the tall man, standing by the service bay, his back to them, his silhouette stark and unmoving. A chill snaked down Brody's spine. "Heard you're doing real well, Earl."

"Business is booming, Mason," Earl said, clapping him on the shoulder. "People need reliable transportation. Honest Rides, that's the name of the game."

Brody didn't miss the subtle emphasis on "honest." It sounded hollow, a mockery. "Funny, though," Brody said, his voice low, "the paperwork coming across my desk tells a different story. A lot of folks are struggling to keep up with those "honest" payments."

Earl's smile faltered for a fraction of a second before snapping back into place. "That's just life, Mason. Sometimes people overextend themselves. We offer them a chance, and they take it."

"A chance at what, Earl?" Brody pressed, his gaze fixed on the tall man, who still hadn't turned around. "A chance at losing everything?"

Earl's jaw tightened. "You're not suggesting anything, are you, Mason?"

"I'm just asking questions, Earl," Brody replied, his voice even. "And the answers I'm getting are making me uneasy."

He tried to get a closer look at the tall man, but Earl subtly steered him towards a display of floor mats, his practiced patter a shield against Brody's scrutiny. As they walked, Brody kept his eyes on the periphery. He saw the tall man finally turn, his head moving with a slow, deliberate motion. His eyes, when they met Brody's, were devoid of any warmth, any discernible emotion. They were like polished obsidian, reflecting nothing, revealing less. It was a gaze that felt ancient, predatory, and utterly alien.

Brody felt a cold dread settle in his gut. This wasn't about predatory lending practices, not entirely. There was something else at play, something darker, something that whispered of forces beyond his understanding. He'd dealt with criminals who were driven by greed, by rage, by desperation. But the tall man... he was something else entirely. He radiated an aura of profound emptiness, a chilling indifference to the suffering he seemed to engender.

He began to investigate Earl's finances, digging deeper than he ever had before. He found shell corporations, offshore accounts, and a labyrinth of transactions that led to a dead end. The money was there, immense and untraceable, flowing in from sources unknown. It was as if Maddox was a conduit, a businessman acting as a front for something far more powerful, something that operated in the shadows, beyond the reach of the law.

Brody found himself spending late nights at his desk, poring over case files, his mind racing. He revisited the stories of the townsfolk, piecing together fragments of fear and despair. He heard about nightmares, vivid and terrifying, of a tall, shadowy figure lurking just beyond the edge of sleep. He heard the hushed pronouncements of the elders, their voices laced with a fear that went beyond economic hardship, a fear of a "darkness" that had settled over Redwater Crossing.

He tried to talk to Earl again, to confront him directly about the tall man. But Earl had become elusive, his phone calls going unanswered, his usual haunts suddenly empty. It was as if he and his silent partner had evaporated, leaving behind only the wreckage of shattered lives.

The unease in Brody had solidified into a grim certainty. He was no longer dealing with a common criminal. He was facing something that preyed on the soul, that fed on despair. The tall man was not merely a business associate; he was an instrument, a vessel for a malevolent force that thrived on the slow, agonizing decay of hope. Brody, the man of logic and law, found himself staring into an abyss, realizing that the laws he enforced were powerless against this encroaching darkness. The illusion of prosperity was just that – an illusion, a carefully constructed facade designed to lure the unsuspecting into a trap from which there was no earthly escape. And he, Sheriff Mason Brody, was left to witness the unraveling, a silent, helpless observer to the encroaching despair.

The gleam of chrome and the scent of new leather, once symbols of a brighter future, now seemed to cast long, unsettling shadows across Redwater Crossing. The initial euphoria that had swept through the town like a warm breeze, carried on the promise of affordable, reliable transportation from Earl's Honest Rides, had begun to curdle. What had started as hushed murmurs of fortunate bargains and clever financial maneuvering had, in a terrifyingly short span, devolved into a cacophony of hushed anxieties, desperate whispers, and outright fear. The polished surfaces of the vehicles, so carefully curated to represent success and stability, now felt like the cold, indifferent faces of adversaries, silently bearing witness to the ruin they had facilitated.

Sheriff Mason Brody felt the shift acutely, a physical manifestation of the town's unraveling. It wasn't just the increased volume of distraught calls to his office, though those had become a constant, wearying drumbeat. It was the palpable change in the very air of Redwater Crossing. The forced smiles that had once greeted him on Main Street were now strained, etched with worry lines that hadn't been there weeks ago. The casual greetings were shorter, the eye contact more fleeting, as if the townsfolk were too preoccupied with their own burgeoning nightmares to engage. Even the boisterous gatherings at the local diner, usually a hub of communal life, had taken on a somber hue, conversations abruptly halting and faces turning away whenever a new, grim tale of financial woe was shared.

He'd seen it in the eyes of Kara Anderson, an elderly woman who'd scrimped and saved for years, her retirement nest egg painstakingly built, only to see it vanish. She'd come into his office clutching a sheaf of papers, her hands trembling so violently he'd feared she might drop them. The car, a modest sedan she'd bought to finally feel secure, to perhaps take that long-promised trip to see her grandchildren, had become an insurmountable burden. The monthly payments, once presented as manageable, had somehow ballooned, fueled by interest rates and fees that seemed to materialize out of thin air, or perhaps, out of the slick, unreadable clauses in the contracts Earl's people had so readily had her sign. Her voice, usually so clear and steady, had cracked with despair as she recounted how she'd had to sell her antique piano, a cherished family heirloom, just to cover the last payment, and how even that wasn't enough. Her eyes, once sparkling with the quiet pride of a life well-lived, now held a haunting emptiness, mirroring the void left in her bank account.

Then there was young Warren Rodgers, a hardworking mechanic who'd always dreamed of owning a truck that could haul his tools and supplies without complaint. He'd been one of the first to take the plunge at Honest Rides, lured by the impossibly low introductory rates and the promise of a vehicle that would "put him on the road to success." Brody had seen Warren a week ago, looking haggard, his usual easygoing demeanor replaced by a gnawing anxiety. Warren had confessed, his voice barely above a whisper, that he was working eighteen-hour days, juggling two jobs, and still barely making ends meet. He'd spoken of sleepless nights, of the gnawing fear that the truck would be repossessed any day now, a fear that had driven him to the brink of exhaustion and despair. He'd even admitted to considering... options, options that made Brody's gut clench with a grim understanding of the desperation brewing beneath the surface of this once-peaceful town. The truck, once a symbol of freedom and opportunity, had become a gilded cage, trapping Warren in a cycle of debt and exhaustion.

The cars themselves seemed to have undergone a subtle transformation. Where once their gleaming exteriors had promised reliability and aspiration, they now appeared to loom with a sinister presence. When Brody drove past the houses of those who'd fallen prey to Earl's schemes, he'd see the vehicles parked in the driveways, no longer objects of pride but stark monuments to financial folly. Their polished surfaces seemed to mock the worried faces peering from behind drawn curtains. The vibrant colors, once so appealing, now felt garish, out of place against the backdrop of the town's growing unease. He'd seen a gleaming red pickup truck, the kind that had made Warren Rodgers' eyes light up, parked forlornly in front of a "For Sale" sign that was riddled with bullet holes, a testament to a desperation that had gone beyond mere financial hardship.

The ripple effect was undeniable. The hardware store reported a slump in sales of home repair materials, as people were now prioritizing car payments over fixing leaky roofs or mending broken fences. The local grocery store saw a decline in purchases of higher-end items, as families tightened their belts, opting for cheaper, more basic fare. Even the town's single movie theater reported a drop in attendance; entertainment was a luxury few could now afford. Redwater Crossing, once a community that prided itself on its resilience and neighborly spirit, was beginning to fracture under the strain. The shared optimism that had briefly characterized the town had been replaced by a pervasive sense of isolation, each household grappling with its own mounting crisis, too ashamed or too afraid to speak openly about the true extent of their predicaments.

Brody found himself returning to Earl's Honest Rides with increasing frequency, his unease a constant companion. The lot, once bustling with eager customers, now had a more subdued atmosphere. While some still milled about, their faces a mixture of hope and trepidation, many seemed to linger, their expressions etched with a dawning realization of the trap they had sprung. Earl Maddox, however, remained an unruffled island in the rising tide of discontent. His smile, though still present, had taken on a harder edge, his eyes scanning the lot with a calculating intensity that had nothing to do with customer satisfaction and everything to do with... something else. He moved with a restless energy, a constant orchestrator of deals, his voice a smooth, persuasive hum that seemed to soothe the anxieties of some while, Brody suspected, further ensnaring others.

And then there was the tall man. He was always there, a silent sentinel at the periphery. Brody had seen him observing a young couple, their faces alight with excitement as they discussed financing options with Earl. The tall man stood at the edge of the lot, his form a stark silhouette against the setting sun, his stillness unnerving. He didn't interact, didn't speak, yet his presence was a heavy, suffocating weight, a silent promise of consequences that the optimistic buyers seemed incapable of perceiving. Brody had tried to engage him once, approaching him with a casual "Afternoon" as he walked past. The tall man had merely turned his head, his obsidian eyes meeting Brody's with an unsettling blankness, an utter lack of recognition or response that sent a shiver down the sheriff's spine. It was a gaze that offered no reflection, no hint of humanity, only an impenetrable void.

The whispers had intensified, evolving from tales of slightly burdensome payments to outright accusations of predatory practices. Old Mrs. Anderson's story was not an isolated incident. Brody heard similar accounts from across town: a single mother forced to take out a payday loan to cover a car payment, a young couple on the verge of losing their home because their vehicle expenses had spiraled beyond control, a retired farmer who had dipped into his children's inheritance to keep his truck on the road. The common thread was always Earl, always Honest Rides, and always the invisible hand of that unnervingly silent associate. The illusion of prosperity was not just cracking; it was shattering into a thousand jagged pieces, revealing the stark, unforgiving reality beneath. The gleaming vehicles, once symbols of freedom, were now perceived as chains, binding the residents of Redwater Crossing to a future of financial servitude. The air, once thick with the optimism of new beginnings, was now heavy with the suffocating scent of despair and the metallic tang of fear.

CHAPTER 3
The Spiral of Despair

The jubilant hum that had once permeated Redwater Crossing, fueled by the allure of gleaming chrome and improbable deals from Earl's Honest Rides, had long since faded, replaced by a discordant symphony of strained silence and choked sobs. The promise of a new beginning, embodied in the sleek lines of a pre-owned sedan or the rugged utility of a pickup truck, had morphed into a suffocating noose, tightening with each passing day around the necks of its trusting residents. The initial euphoria, a potent elixir of hope and perceived financial acumen, had given way to the bitter, acrid taste of regret, a flavor that now lingered in every corner of the town, from the hushed whispers in the aisles of the struggling grocery store to the drawn curtains that shielded homes from the prying eyes of fate.

For Kara Anderson, the polished hood of her "reliable" sedan, purchased with the last vestiges of her retirement savings, had become a mirror reflecting her deepest fears. The monthly payment, initially presented as a manageable ebb in her predictable cash flow, had become a ravenous beast, devouring her meager income with insatiable hunger. Each morning, as she sipped her weak, lukewarm coffee, the dread would coalesce in her stomach, a cold knot of anxiety that tightened with the dawning realization of the astronomical sum that would be due in mere days. The antique piano, her solace, her connection to a more graceful past, had been the first sacrifice on the altar of Earl's "Honest Rides." Its absence in the living room was a gaping wound, a constant reminder of the Faustian bargain she had unwittingly struck. But the piano, as painful as its sale had been, had been a single, albeit agonizing, incision.

Now, the doctor's visits were becoming more frequent. She found herself foregoing her regular prescription refills, the cost of the car payment a tyrannical overlord dictating her health choices. The ache in her joints, once a mild annoyance, was becoming a persistent throb, a physical manifestation of the financial pain that gnawed at her from within. She'd even started rationing her groceries, the carefully curated meals that once graced her table now reduced to meager portions of the cheapest staples. The car, meant to provide freedom, had instead become a gilded cage, its monthly installments a cruel sentence to financial servitude. The whispers of her neighbors, once sympathetic murmurs of shared hardship, now felt like judgments, the unspoken question hanging heavy in the air: *How could she have been so foolish?*

Warren Rodgers, once the embodiment of Redwater Crossing's industrious spirit, now looked like a ghost haunting his own life. His hands, calloused and strong from years of honest work as a mechanic, now trembled with fatigue. The eighteen-hour days, the juggling of two jobs, the constant, gnawing fear of repossession – it had all taken a brutal toll. He would sit in the dimly lit garage after his second shift, the smell of oil and exhaust fumes clinging to him like a second skin, staring blankly at the truck that had once represented his dreams. It loomed in the bay, its imposing frame now a symbol of his undoing. He'd heard the hushed conversations at the diner, the stories of neighbors facing foreclosure, of families having to choose between keeping a roof over their heads and making a car payment. The truck, with its seemingly bottomless fuel tank and its powerful engine, was the albatross around his neck.

He'd taken out a second mortgage on his small house, the only asset he truly owned, to keep the truck's payments current. Now, the bank was calling about the mortgage. The foreclosure notices were starting to appear on doorsteps, stark white flags of surrender in the escalating war against debt. He'd seen the desperation in the eyes of his friends, the same desperation that was beginning to take root in his own soul. The thought of losing his house, the only home he'd ever known, sent a cold wave of nausea through him. He'd even found himself lingering outside pawn shops, the glint of gold and silver, a desperate, shimmering temptation that he fought with every fiber of his being. The truck, once a symbol of his ambition, had become a monument to his ruin, its very presence a constant, agonizing reminder of how close he was to losing everything.

The ripple effect, insidious and far-reaching, was now transforming the very fabric of Redwater Crossing. The local hardware store, usually a hub of activity for DIY enthusiasts and those tending to their homes, reported a dramatic drop in sales. Tools lay gathering dust, paint cans remained sealed, and the cheerful banter of customers discussing renovation projects had been replaced by the somber shuffling of feet as people came in to buy only the absolute essentials – duct tape for temporary fixes, light bulbs to ward off the encroaching darkness. The grocery store, once filled with the aroma of freshly baked bread and the vibrant colors of fresh produce, now echoed with the clatter of carts filled with budget brands and bulk staples. The luxury items, the occasional treat, the special occasion meals – these were now distant memories, sacrifices made to appease the insatiable appetite of their automotive debts. Even the town's single movie theater, a beloved local institution, saw its attendance dwindle to a trickle. The joy of shared laughter and escapism had become a luxury too expensive to afford. People were hoarding their meager savings, meticulously counting every penny, their lives reduced to a grim calculus of survival. The once-vibrant community spirit was fracturing, replaced by a pervasive sense of isolation. Each household became an island, battling its own tsunami of debt, too proud, too ashamed, or too terrified to reach out for help. The shared dream of a prosperous Redwater Crossing had dissolved, leaving behind a landscape of broken lives and shattered aspirations.

The air in Redwater Crossing had grown heavy, not just with the oppressive summer heat, but with the palpable weight of desperation. The casual wave from a passing car had been replaced by the anxious glance of a driver scanning the road for a tow truck. The once-common sight of children playing freely on their front lawns was now a rarity; parents kept them indoors, the looming threat of repossession casting a shadow over their youthful exuberance. The town's social calendar, once dotted with Friday night football games and Saturday afternoon farmers' markets, had become starkly barren.

Even the local church, usually a beacon of hope and community support, was overwhelmed. Reverend Thornton, a man known for his unwavering faith and gentle counsel, found himself spending more time mediating disputes over car payments and offering solace to families on the brink of eviction than he did leading services. His collection plate, once overflowing with the generous offerings of a prosperous community, was now thin, the coins rattling with a hollow, mournful sound. He'd seen families who had always been pillars of the congregation now struggling to make their tithes, their faces etched with a worry that transcended spiritual matters. He'd even heard whispers of families selling off their heirlooms, the tangible memories of happier times sacrificed to the relentless demands of the automotive financiers. The once-comforting stained-glass windows of his church now seemed to cast a somber, muted light, a reflection of the town's collective despair.

The gleaming vehicles themselves seemed to have acquired a sinister sentience. When Sheriff Mason Brody drove through the residential streets, he no longer saw them as symbols of aspiration. Instead, they appeared as predatory beasts, parked in driveways, their polished surfaces glinting mockingly in the sun, bearing silent witness to the ruin they had wrought. A vibrant blue convertible, once a symbol of youthful freedom, now sat idle, its tires slowly deflating, a stark monument to a broken dream. A sturdy family minivan, purchased with the hope of accommodating a growing brood, was now perpetually shrouded in a thin layer of dust, its windows tinted so darkly they seemed to hide a secret shame. Brody had noticed a chilling trend: the "For Sale" signs, once carefully placed at the end of driveways, were now appearing more frequently, their bright colors a stark contrast to the muted hues of despair that enveloped the town. And more disturbingly, some of these signs were defaced, scrawled over with angry graffiti or bearing the tell-tale signs of being ripped down and discarded in anger. The vehicles were no longer just possessions; they were burdens, anchors dragging their owners down into a sea of financial quicksand.

The mental toll was perhaps the most devastating consequence. Sleep was a luxury few could afford, replaced by the gnawing anxiety of late-night phone calls from creditors or the sheer mental exhaustion of trying to stretch meager resources to cover impossible obligations. The stress manifested in countless ways: increased irritability, a rise in domestic disputes, and a pervasive sense of hopelessness that clung to the town like a suffocating fog. Brody had seen it in the vacant stares of the people he encountered, the forced smiles that masked a deep well of despair, the way conversations would abruptly halt when he approached, as if the townsfolk were afraid of revealing the true extent of their financial ruin. The initial promise of freedom from Earl's Honest Rides had devolved into a suffocating trap, the weight of their ill-advised purchases crushing their spirits and, in many cases, their very futures. The dream of a better life had become a waking nightmare, and Redwater Crossing was slowly, irrevocably, being consumed by its own despair.

He was the whisper in the back of the mind, the subtle nudge towards a decision that would lead to ruin, the phantom hand that guided the pen signing away futures. The Master, as Earl had referred to him, was known in the shadowed corners of this escalating tragedy, was a parasite of the soul, an entity that fed not on blood or flesh, but on the raw, corrosive despair of the living. He required no physical form, no tangible presence to enact his will. His dominion was the ethereal plane, a vast, interconnected web of consciousness that he subtly manipulated, weaving his influence through the threads of human desperation. Redwater Crossing, in its current state of financial cataclysm, was a veritable feast for him, a fertile ground where the seeds of ruin had been sown and were now yielding a bountiful, agonizing harvest.

Each broken dream was a succulent morsel, each lost home a rich, satisfying bite that sustained his spectral existence. The collective anguish of the townsfolk was the sustenance that fueled his power, a potent elixir that amplified his reach and solidified his unseen control. He was the unseen conductor of this symphony of misery, his spectral baton orchestrating the dissonant chords of financial collapse, drawing energy from the town's collective suffering, his unseen presence growing stronger with every downward spiral of hope. The more broken the spirit, the deeper the despair, the more vibrant and potent the energy he absorbed. He didn't need to see the tears, hear the sobs, or witness the physical manifestations of their suffering. He felt it, tasted it, breathed it in through the very air that now felt thick with resignation and dread.

Consider Kara Anderson, her meager retirement funds dissolving like mist in the morning sun, her antique piano a ghost in her once-cherished living room. The Master didn't have to convince her to buy the car; he merely amplified the whispers of hope that Earl had so expertly manufactured. He didn't have to exert direct pressure to make her ration her food or skip her medication. He simply fanned the flames of her fear, the cold knot of anxiety in her stomach tightening with his subtle, unseen influence. He savored the moment she realized the piano, her sanctuary, was gone, a tangible symbol of her capitulation. He felt a subtle surge of power as she stared at the empty space, the absence a testament to his growing strength. He was the phantom breath on her neck as she rationed her meager groceries, the unseen hand that pressed down on her heart when she contemplated the growing ache in her joints, a physical manifestation of the abstract agony he so readily consumed. The car, a gleaming symbol of misplaced trust, became his chariot of suffering, its monthly payments a relentless drumbeat of her despair, a rhythm he orchestrated with exquisite cruelty.

Then there was Warren Rodgers, the once-proud mechanic, his hands now shaking, his days a blur of exhaustion and dread. The Master found a particular delight in the downfall of the industrious.

Warren's truck, once a symbol of his ambition, was now a monstrous debt, a hulking monument to his ruin. The Master didn't need to force Warren to take out the second mortgage. He merely amplified the fear of repossession, the gnawing dread of losing not just the truck, but his home, the last bastion of his security. He reveled in the slow erosion of Warren's spirit, the way the once-strong hands trembled, the vacant stare that replaced the sharp, intelligent glint in his eyes. The Master would linger in the shadows of Warren's garage, a spectral observer of his slow descent, feeding on the silent curses, the choked sobs of frustration that punctuated the long, lonely nights. He was the reason Warren found himself lingering outside pawn shops, the desperate allure of quick cash, a siren song amplified by the Master's insidious whispers, a temptation that chipped away at his resolve. The very air Warren breathed, thick with the smell of oil and despair, was a nourishing miasma for the Master.

The ripple effect, so devastating to the human inhabitants of Redwater Crossing, was the Master's greatest masterpiece. He didn't need to directly cause the hardware store's sales to plummet, or the grocery store to fill with budget brands. He simply intensified the underlying anxieties that led to these choices. He fed on the collective sigh of resignation that swept through the town as people began to prioritize survival over comfort, necessity over desire. The fracturing community spirit, the isolation, the pervasive sense of hopelessness – these were the very foundations upon which he built his power. Each silent fear, each unvoiced worry, was a brick in the growing edifice of his influence. He was the unseen force that turned friendly neighbors into wary strangers, the subtle agent that transformed shared dreams into individual nightmares. He was the darkness that crept into the aisles of the struggling stores, making the purchase of anything beyond the barest necessities feel like an extravagant indulgence, a risk too great to bear.

Reverend Thorton's plight was a particularly poignant source of sustenance. The Master relished the sight of a man of faith struggling to provide spiritual comfort in the face of overwhelming material hardship. He fed on the desperation that led families to neglect their tithes, on the quiet shame of those who had once been generous pillars of the congregation, now unable to contribute. He amplified the worry that etched itself onto their faces, a worry that transcended the purely spiritual. The Master even found a dark humor in the dwindling collection plate, the hollow rattle of coins, a mocking echo of a community's former prosperity. He was the unseen presence in the hushed conversations about foreclosures, the spectral hand that guided the pen signing away heirlooms, the tangible memories of happier times sacrificed to the insatiable demands of the financiers. The somber light cast by the church's stained-glass windows, a reflection of the town's collective despair, was a comforting glow for the Master, a testament to his pervasive influence.

Sheriff Mason Brody, with his weary eyes and his ingrained sense of duty, saw only the tangible symptoms of the town's disease. He saw the cars parked like predatory beasts, the defaced "For Sale" signs, the drawn curtains and the anxious glances. But he couldn't see the true architect of this destruction. He couldn't comprehend the parasitic entity that thrived on the very despair he was witnessing. The Master found a particular, almost perverse, satisfaction in this disconnect. He was the unseen hand that had orchestrated this entire spectacle, and the human agents of law and order were merely struggling to contain the fallout. He was the ghost in the machine, the unseen puppeteer pulling the strings of financial ruin, his power growing with every vehicle repossessed, every home lost, every dream irrevocably shattered. The shiny surfaces of the cars, so offensive to the Sheriff's eyes, were simply the polished shells of a devastating harvest, a harvest that nourished the Master immeasurably.

The mental toll, the sleepless nights, the gnawing anxiety, the irritability, the domestic disputes, the pervasive sense of hopelessness – these were the most potent sources of the Master's power. He didn't need to cause these things directly; he merely fanned the embers of existing anxieties, amplified latent fears, and nurtured the seeds of despair until they bloomed into a suffocating, all-encompassing fog. He was the unseen force that amplified the late-night phone calls from creditors, the spectral presence that intensified the exhaustion of trying to make impossible ends meet. He was the subtle poison that seeped into the very fabric of their thoughts, clouding judgment, fostering suspicion, and eroding the will to resist. He was the reason for the vacant stares, the forced smiles, the abrupt silences when the Sheriff's cruiser passed by. He fed on the very essence of their suffering, the raw, unadulterated anguish that was now the prevailing currency of Redwater Crossing. The initial promise of freedom from Earl's "Honest Rides" had indeed devolved into a suffocating trap, but it was a trap meticulously constructed and expertly maintained by the unseen hand of the Master. The dream of a better life had become a waking nightmare, and Redwater Crossing, in its slow, agonizing spiral into despair, was providing a feast for a darkness that thrived on their every loss. He was the unseen harvest, the predator that fed on the broken spirits, growing ever stronger in the fertile soil of their ruin.

The first tremor was almost imperceptible, a faint tremor in the foundations of Redwater Crossing's already precarious equilibrium. Kara Anderson, the woman whose nimble fingers had once danced across ivory keys, her retirement funds now a ghost of their former glory, was found in her silent, piano-less living room. The official cause was a heart attack, a sudden, swift end to a life that had been systematically stripped bare. But those who knew her, those who had witnessed the slow erosion of her spirit, the deepening shadows beneath her once-bright eyes, felt a prickle of unease. The whispers started then, quiet at first, like the rustling of dead leaves. A heart attack, yes, but had it been brought on by something more than mere stress? Had the gnawing fear, the relentless pressure of mounting bills, the shame of losing her cherished Steinway finally broken her? The Master, a silent observer from his ethereal vantage point, felt a subtle hum of satisfaction. Martha's quiet capitulation, the slow surrender of her dreams, had been a rich, lingering taste.

Then came Warren Rodgers. The strong, capable mechanic, the man whose hands could coax life back into any sputtering engine, was discovered slumped over his workbench, a single, stark red stain blooming on his faded work shirt. The lingering scent of oil and despair was a heady perfume for the unseen entity that now considered Redwater Crossing its hunting ground. A gunshot wound, the sheriff's report would later state, self-inflicted. The shame was what many whispered about. The shame of losing his home, of the repossession notices tacked to his door like predatory insects, of the gnawing fear of being unable to provide for his family. The weight of the second mortgage, a crushing burden he'd taken on in a moment of desperate optimism, had proven too much to bear. The Master savored the raw, metallic tang of Warren's final moments, the agonizing release of a spirit that had been ground down to its absolute breaking point. The tremor grew, a seismic shift in the town's fragile psyche.

The news spread through Redwater Crossing like wildfire through dry timber. Two deaths in as many weeks, both of respected, if struggling, townsfolk, both seemingly driven to desperate acts. The initial reactions were a mixture of shock, grief, and a desperate attempt to rationalize. Heart attacks happened. People fell into despair. These were tragedies, yes, but isolated incidents in a town already grappling with hardship. Sheriff Mason Brody, his face a roadmap of weariness, ran himself ragged, trying to find logical explanations, to soothe the growing unease that was beginning to weave its way through the community. He interviewed neighbors, family members, anyone who might have seen something, anything, that could shed light on these sudden, tragic ends. But his investigation, bound by the tangible, the observable, was blind to the true architect of this unfolding horror. He saw the symptoms, but he could not perceive the disease. The Master found a dark, unsettling amusement in Mason's efforts, a futile struggle against an enemy he couldn't even comprehend, let alone confront. The more Mason searched for rational causes, the more the Master's influence deepened, feeding on the very fear and confusion that his actions engendered.

The third death, however, could not be so easily dismissed. It was Rebecca Heath, a young woman barely out of her teens, whose bright, hopeful face had been a beacon of optimism just months before. She'd been a bright spark at the diner, her laughter infectious, her dreams of opening her own bakery a constant topic of excited conversation. But the lure of Earl's "Honest Rides" had proven too tempting, the promise of a gleaming, affordable car too hard to resist. The monthly payments, initially a manageable whisper, had grown into a deafening roar, drowning out her hopes and extinguishing her youthful exuberance. She'd started skipping shifts, her eyes hollow, her usual effervescence replaced by a dull, pervasive sadness. She was found in her small apartment, a bottle of pills clutched in her hand, a note scrawled on a napkin beside her: "I can't do this anymore." This was not a heart attack. This was not a moment of sudden, overwhelming despair. This was a deliberate act, a final, desperate escape from an unbearable reality.

The carefully constructed facade of normalcy in Redwater Crossing began to crumble. Rebecca's death shattered the illusion of isolated tragedies. A pattern, dark and insidious, was emerging. Kara, Warren, Rebecca – their lives had all been touched, ensnared, by the deceptive promises emanating from Ear's lot. The cars, once symbols of freedom and aspiration, were transforming into instruments of their destruction. The Master's influence, once a subtle undercurrent, was now a palpable force, a suffocating presence that settled over the town like a shroud. He fed on the collective gasp of horror, on the widening eyes that began to connect the dots, on the dawning, chilling realization that these were not mere coincidences. They were the direct consequences of a systematic plundering of hope, a deliberate dismantling of lives.

A profound and terrifying silence descended upon Redwater Crossing. The usual chatter in the general store, the friendly waves between neighbors, the boisterous laughter spilling from the local tavern – all of it faded, replaced by hushed conversations and averted gazes. The town had always been prone to hardship, to economic downturns, but this was different. This was a pervasive, soul-crushing despair that seeped into every home, every interaction. The funerals, once opportunities for community support and shared remembrance, became somber affairs, laced with an unspoken fear. People looked at each other, their eyes filled with a newfound wariness, a dawning understanding of their shared vulnerability. The question hung heavy in the air, unspoken but deeply felt: who would be next?

The Master reveled in this escalating terror. He thrived in the fertile ground of collective dread. He amplified the existing anxieties, turning everyday worries into paralyzing fears. The whispers that had once been dismissed as idle gossip now held a terrifying weight. People spoke of the cars, of the impossibly high payments, of the relentless calls from debt collectors. They spoke of Earl Maddox, his slick smile and his smooth words, and a chilling suspicion began to take root. He was not merely a businessman; he was a predator, and his prey was the very soul of Redwater Crossing. The Master, unseen and unfelt, nudged these suspicions further, fanning the embers of resentment into a slow-burning inferno of fear and mistrust. He savored the taste of their burgeoning terror, the way it sharpened their senses and amplified their despair.

Sheriff Brody found himself caught in a tightening vise. The tangible evidence pointed towards Earl Maddox and his car lot. The timing of the deaths, the financial distress of each victim, all seemed to converge on that single source. But the evidence was circumstantial, the connections tenuous. How could he prove that Earl's business practices had directly led to these deaths? It was a question of financial ruin, of predatory lending, of overwhelming debt – not murder. Yet, the palpable sense of dread that permeated the town, the undeniable feeling that something deeply sinister was at play, weighed heavily on him. He saw the fear in the eyes of his constituents, the way they flinched at the sight of a Earl's car driving down the street, the hushed accusations that followed Earl wherever he went. He was witnessing the unraveling of his community, and he felt powerless to stop it. The Master found Mason's struggle particularly satisfying. The Sheriff was a man of law, a man of order, and the Master was chaos personified, an entity that operated outside the bounds of human comprehension. Mason's frustration, his mounting sense of inadequacy, was a potent delicacy.

The town began to retreat into itself. Businesses that had once thrived now struggled to stay afloat as people hoarded their meager resources, terrified of making any purchase that wasn't an absolute necessity. The once-bustling Main Street became eerily quiet, the sounds of foot traffic replaced by the mournful sigh of the wind and the distant rumble of a Earl car. The fabric of the community, already strained, began to fray further. Neighbors who had once shared meals and laughter now eyed each other with suspicion, each fearing that their own circumstances might soon mirror those of the departed. The shared sense of community, the very thing that had always been Redwater Crossing's strength, was being systematically dismantled. The Master amplified these feelings of isolation, of mutual distrust, relishing the way it further cemented his grip on the town.

The stained-glass windows of Reverend Thorton's church, once bathed in the hopeful glow of Sunday mornings, now seemed to cast a somber, melancholic light upon the pews. The congregation dwindled with each passing week. Those who did attend sat in stony silence, their prayers tinged with a desperation that transcended the spiritual. They prayed for relief, for an end to the suffocating despair, but their pleas felt hollow, lost in the overwhelming weight of their material woes. Reverend Thorton, his voice cracking with emotion, tried to offer comfort, to preach hope, but even he felt the insidious tendrils of despair creeping into his own heart. He saw the vacant stares, the profound weariness, and he knew that his words, however heartfelt, were no match for the pervasive darkness that had enveloped his flock.

The Master found a particular resonance in the dwindling collection plate, the meager offerings a testament to the town's fractured faith and deepening desperation. He savored the silent prayers, the unspoken cries for help that went unanswered, knowing that their true solace lay not in divine intervention, but in the utter collapse of their worldly concerns.

The first suicides were a devastating blow, a stark and terrifying testament to the Master's insatiable hunger. They were the initial harvest, the first fruits of a ruin meticulously cultivated. The shock and disbelief that had initially rippled through Redwater Crossing were slowly giving way to a grim, chilling understanding. These were not isolated incidents of personal despair; they were the direct, undeniable consequences of a predatory scheme that had systematically targeted the town's most vulnerable. The Master, from his unseen perch, observed the deepening spiral, the encroaching darkness, and knew that his feast had only just begun. The despair was not just a symptom; it was the very nourishment he craved, the essence of his power, and Redwater Crossing was providing it in abundance. The town was no longer just struggling; it was drowning, and he was the invisible tide that pulled them under.

The weight of Redwater Crossing pressed down on Sheriff Mason Brody like a physical entity. Each morning, as he stepped out of his modest home, the air felt thicker, charged with a despair that seeped into his bones. He'd always considered himself a man of logic, of tangible evidence. His career had been built on the bedrock of facts, on the meticulous piecing together of clues. But the events of the past few weeks had thrown his entire world into disarray, forcing him to confront the limitations of his understanding. Kara Anderson's quiet demise, Warren Rodgers' self-inflicted wound, Rebecca Heath's tragic overdose – these were not random acts of desperation. Not anymore. A pattern, as undeniable as the bloodstain on Warren's shirt, was emerging, and it led directly to Earl's gleaming lot of "Honest Rides."

Mason had spent sleepless nights poring over old case files, not just from Redwater Crossing, but from neighboring counties, even across state lines. He was searching for echoes, for whispers of similar circumstances – towns crippled by economic hardship, marked by a sudden, inexplicable surge in suicides and despair-driven deaths, all seemingly linked to a predatory lending scheme. He found isolated incidents, of course. Cases of financial ruin leading to tragic ends were not unheard of. But nothing mirrored the insidious, pervasive nature of what was happening here. There was a chilling uniformity to the victims' circumstances, a shared vulnerability that seemed to have been deliberately exploited. His gut, a notoriously reliable compass in his line of work, screamed that this was no ordinary criminal operation. It was something far older, far darker, something that fed on the very fabric of a community's hope.

The oppressive weight of the town's despair was becoming a tangible adversary. Mason felt it in the way his chest tightened as he drove down Main Street, the once-familiar buildings now seeming to sag under an invisible burden. He felt it in the averted gazes of his neighbors, the hushed conversations that ceased whenever he approached. It was a suffocating blanket, woven from fear, regret, and a gnawing sense of helplessness. This wasn't just the natural consequence of economic hardship; it felt like a deliberate draining, a systematic siphoning of the town's very lifeblood. He found himself staring out his office window for long stretches, the swirling dust motes in the afternoon sun seeming to coalesce into ephemeral, whispering shapes that mocked his efforts. He was fighting a ghost, an entity that reveled in the shadows, that thrived on the very fear he was trying to combat.

His investigation into Earl Maddox had yielded a mountain of paperwork, but little in the way of concrete proof for murder. Earl was a businessman, a smooth operator who operated within the letter of the law, even if his practices skirted the edges of morality. The contracts were ironclad, the interest rates astronomical, but legal. Mason had brought in the state's financial crimes unit, but even they, with their expertise in predatory lending, could only shake their heads. They could identify the exploitation, the crushing debt, but they couldn't connect it directly to the deaths. "It's financial ruin, Sheriff," one of the agents had told him, his voice tinged with a weary resignation. "Tragic, yes. But not a crime in the way you're looking for."

Mason slammed his fist on his desk, the sound echoing in the unnervingly silent office. "But it *is* a crime!" he muttered, his voice raw. "These people are being driven to their deaths! It's murder, just a slower, more insidious kind." He ran a hand over his face, the stubble rough against his skin. He was a man trained to find the smoking gun, the concrete evidence that would stand up in court. But here, in Redwater Crossing, the gun was invisible, and the smoke was the collective breath of a dying town. He felt like he was drowning, the currents of despair pulling him under, the demands of his office a constant, draining pull against his weakening resolve.

He revisited the scene of Rebecca Heath's death, the small, sparsely furnished apartment. The lingering scent of cheap air freshener and stale sadness still hung in the air. He looked at the napkin with her desperate note, the bottle of pills that had been her final escape. He imagined her, young and full of dreams, trapped by insurmountable debt, her hopeful future reduced to a desperate plea for oblivion. He tried to channel her desperation, to understand the sheer, soul-crushing weight that would lead someone to such an act. It was then, standing in the stillness of her tragedy, that he felt it – a subtle shift in the atmosphere, a whisper of cold that had nothing to do with the draft from the window. It was a feeling of being watched, not by a human eye, but by something ancient and malevolent, something that fed on the very essence of her pain.

This feeling, this intangible presence, had become a constant companion for Mason. It was there in the hushed whispers of the townsfolk, in the way shadows seemed to deepen and writhe at the periphery of his vision, in the unnerving stillness that often descended upon the town, a silence so profound it felt like the absence of life itself. He'd started sleeping with his service weapon under his pillow, a futile gesture against an enemy he couldn't even define. His thoughts were a chaotic swirl of unanswered questions, his once-sharp mind dulled by exhaustion and the pervasive dread. He'd always believed in the good of people, in their inherent resilience. But now, he was witnessing the systematic dismantling of that resilience, the erosion of their very will to live.

He spent hours at the town archives, a dusty, forgotten room in the back of the library, sifting through brittle newspaper clippings and faded town records. He was looking for anything, any anomaly, any historical precedent that might offer a clue. He found accounts of hardship, of economic downturns, of families leaving in droves, but nothing that resonated with the specific, terrifying signature of the events unfolding now. It was as if Redwater Crossing had been singled out, targeted by a force that operated outside the normal ebb and flow of human misfortune. He felt a desperate urgency, a race against an unseen clock. How many more lives would be extinguished before he found the answer? How many more families would be shattered?

The weight of the town's collective sorrow was a physical burden, making every step an effort, every breath a struggle. It was more than just empathy; it was an insidious, draining force that seemed to sap his own strength, his own hope. He felt it when he visited the grieving families, the hollow-eyed parents clutching faded photographs, their voices choked with unshed tears. He felt it when he saw the empty storefronts, the "For Lease" signs a stark testament to the town's declining fortunes. He even felt it in the silence of his own home, his wife, Helen, her usual cheerful disposition replaced by a quiet, anxious weariness that mirrored his own.

He found himself questioning everything he'd ever known, his faith in the rational world wavering like a candle flame in a hurricane. He'd always dismissed talk of curses, of dark forces, as the fanciful ramblings of the superstitious. But now, faced with the undeniable reality of a town being systematically consumed by despair, he couldn't afford to dismiss anything. He remembered old Mrs. George, Kara's neighbor, a woman known for her cryptic pronouncements, muttering about "old debts" and "hungry shadows" when he'd first interviewed her. He'd brushed it off as the ramblings of an elderly woman, but now, her words echoed in his mind, carrying a chilling new significance.

The oppressive atmosphere of Redwater Crossing was not just a metaphor; it was a tangible presence, a suffocating miasma that seemed to cling to everything and everyone. Mason felt it most acutely when he was near Earl was the visible face of the problem, the conductor of this destructive orchestra, but Mason was beginning to suspect that

Earl was merely a pawn, a willing instrument for something far more sinister.

His investigation had become a desperate battle of attrition. Each dead end, each unanswered question, chipped away at his resolve. The sheer volume of work was overwhelming, but it was the gnawing certainty that he was missing something fundamental, something beyond the scope of conventional police work, that truly wore him down. He replayed conversations, scrutinized financial records, traced the ownership of the vehicles, all with a growing sense of futility. He was a bloodhound on the trail of a phantom, his senses attuned to the physical world, utterly blind to the spectral predator that was orchestrating this tragedy.

The Master, observing Mason's increasingly frantic efforts, felt a perverse sense of amusement. The Sheriff's struggle was a performance, a desperate dance against an unseen force, and the Master was the silent audience, savoring every moment of his futile exertion. The more Mason looked for tangible culprits, the more he inadvertently amplified the Master's influence, deepening the despair that was his very sustenance. The town's unraveling was a symphony of dread, and Mason Brody was merely a discordant note in its grand, terrible composition. He was fighting a war on two fronts: against the tangible, elusive threat of Earl's predatory practices, and against the intangible, soul-crushing presence that was slowly, inexorably, consuming Redwater Crossing. And on both fronts, he was losing.

The threads of community in Redwater Crossing, once woven together by shared histories and common aspirations, were beginning to fray, revealing a ragged, discolored underside. The initial shock of Kara Anderson's quiet passing, followed by Warren Rodgers' violent outburst and Rebecca Heath's tragic end, had morphed from collective grief into something far more corrosive: suspicion. Neighbors who had once shared garden fences and backyard barbecues now exchanged guarded glances, their familiar faces contorted with unspoken accusations. The town square, the very heart of Redwater Crossing where children's laughter once echoed and town meetings buzzed with civic engagement, had transformed into a stage for whispered anxieties and fearful murmurs. It was no longer a gathering place, but a somber testament to the encroaching darkness.

The air itself seemed to carry a charge of unease. Every averted gaze, every hushed conversation that fell silent as Sheriff Mason Brody or any of his deputies approached, was a palpable manifestation of the town's unraveling psyche. It was as if an invisible specter had settled over Redwater Crossing, its chilling touch eroding trust and planting seeds of paranoia. The simple act of walking down Main Street had become an exercise in navigating a minefield of veiled judgment. The baker, Mrs. Henderson, who worked at Cherry's Bakery, whose sourdough loaves had been a staple of the town for decades, now served her customers with a nervous tremor in her hands, her usual warm smile replaced by a tight-lipped apprehension. She'd catch herself watching her customers' faces, trying to decipher their thoughts, wondering if they harbored resentment for her quiet resilience, or perhaps something worse. Had she, in her own way, been complicit by simply continuing to exist, by not succumbing to the same despair that had claimed others?

The blame, a volatile commodity in times of crisis, began to splinter and scatter. Some, blinded by their own fear and a desperate need for an explanation, turned their ire towards the victims themselves. They whispered about recklessness, about poor choices, about those who had "let themselves go." These were the voices of individuals clinging to a fragile sense of order, terrified that such a fate could befall them if they faltered, even for a moment. They sought refuge in the comforting illusion that the victims were somehow different, somehow deserving of their tragic ends, thereby insulating themselves from the terrifying possibility that this darkness could consume anyone. This defensive rationalization, however, only deepened the chasm between neighbors, transforming empathy into a dangerous liability.

Others, their righteous anger simmering just beneath the surface, focused their accusations squarely on Earl and his "Honest Rides" empire. Earl, with his slicked-back hair and too-white teeth, had become the tangible embodiment of their suffering. His gleaming dealership, once a beacon of prosperity, was now seen by many as a den of thieves, a place where dreams were bought and sold at a ruinous price. They pointed to the impossibly low prices, the predatory financing, the sheer desperation etched on the faces of those who drove away from his lot in their new, yet ultimately crushing, possessions. Mason himself had heard the hushed, venomous pronouncements in the diner, the angry accusations leveled against Earl's name. But the absence of hard evidence, the legal loopholes Earl so expertly navigated, left these accusations hanging in the air, unresolved and fueling further distrust. They knew he was the cause, but they couldn't prove it, and that impotence was a bitter pill to swallow.

Even the smallest interactions were now tainted. A chance encounter at the post office, once an opportunity for a friendly chat, devolved into strained pleasantries and quick escapes. The usual camaraderie that had characterized Redwater Crossing for generations was dissolving like sugar in rain. People began to second-guess their own neighbors, to question long-held friendships. Was old Mr. Abernathy, who always had a kind word, now secretly judging them for their financial struggles? Did Mrs. Gable's sister, who had always been so reserved, harbor a hidden resentment that festered into something darker? These were not rational thoughts, Mason knew, but the pervasive atmosphere of dread had infected the town's collective consciousness, breeding a potent strain of paranoia.

The town's children, usually a barometer of its overall health, became withdrawn and unnerved. Their games in the park grew quieter, their imaginations no longer filled with heroic adventures but with hushed tales of shadows and unseen dangers. Parents found themselves struggling to explain the unexplainable, to comfort anxieties that stemmed from a darkness that even the adults couldn't fully grasp. The usual carefree exuberance of youth was being overshadowed by a premature understanding of loss and fear, a stolen innocence that was as heartbreaking as any of the adult tragedies.

Mason felt this fracturing most acutely in his own investigations. People who had once been eager to offer information, to share their observations, now hesitated. They looked over their shoulders before speaking, their voices dropping to a near-inaudible whisper. Fear had become a more powerful deterrent than any plea for justice. He saw it in the eyes of the young waitress at the diner, who stumbled over her words when he asked about Rebecca Heath's last few days, her gaze darting towards the corner booth where a group of men were engaged in a heated, hushed discussion. He saw it in the hesitant responses from Warren Rodgers' former colleagues, their faces a mask of strained neutrality as they spoke of his sudden, inexplicable depression. It was as if the entire town had been collectively gagged, their voices stolen by an unseen entity.

The once-vibrant community notice board outside the general store, usually plastered with flyers for bake sales, church picnics, and local events, now bore a sparse collection of "For Sale" signs and the occasional somber obituary. The colors seemed muted, the paper brittle, as if even the printed word had lost its vibrancy. It was a visual representation of the town's fading spirit. The local newspaper, the Redwater Crossing Chronicle, once a source of town news and community pride, was now filled with articles detailing the economic downturn, interspersed with carefully worded reports on the recent tragedies. But even the reporting felt hollow, lacking the punch, the urgency, that Mason felt was so desperately needed. The editor, a man named Thomas Finch, a lifelong resident with a deep love for Redwater Crossing, confessed to Mason that he felt a chilling restraint, a sense of being watched, that made him hesitant to delve too deeply into the darker currents flowing beneath the town's surface.

The pervasive sense of dread wasn't just an emotional state; it was a physical presence. Mason felt it every time he walked past the Miller apartment, a phantom chill that had nothing to do with the ambient temperature. He felt it in the unsettling stillness that often descended upon the town, a silence so profound it felt like the world holding its breath, waiting for the next shoe to drop. It was a silence that swallowed sound, that amplified the frantic beat of his own heart, that seemed to vibrate with an unspoken menace. He'd found himself increasingly seeking solace in the familiar, in the mundane routines of his job, but even those were now tinged with an unshakeable sense of foreboding. The siren call of the unknown was no longer a distant hum; it was a constant, maddening thrum in the background of his life.

The unraveling of Redwater Crossing was not a sudden cataclysm, but a slow, insidious rot. It was the erosion of trust, the fracturing of community bonds, the subtle, yet devastating, shift from shared hope to pervasive despair. Each suicide, each act of desperation, was not an isolated incident, but a stone thrown into a carefully constructed dam, each one widening a crack, weakening its foundation. Mason could see the inevitable flood approaching, a tide of darkness that threatened to engulf the entire town, and he was struggling to find the strength, the insight, to build a bulwark against it. The town's psyche was not just fractured; it was shattering, and the shards of what was left were sharp, dangerous, and capable of inflicting further, irreparable harm. The collective dread was no longer a passive observer; it was an active participant, a suffocating blanket woven from the fears of every man, woman, and child in Redwater Crossing, a testament to the insidious power of a darkness that fed on their very souls.

CHAPTER 4

The Vanishing Act

T he silence that descended upon Redwater Crossing after the sudden disappearance of Earl Maddox and his taciturn associate, the man everyone had started referring to, in hushed, fearful tones, as simply 'the Tall Man,' was a silence different from any Mason Brody had ever known. It wasn't the pregnant pause before a storm, or the somber quiet after a funeral. This was an empty silence, a void where something substantial had been, however abhorrent that substance might have been. The 'Honest Rides' car lot, once a garish splash of misplaced optimism against the muted tones of the town's growing despair, was now shuttered. Its brightly painted, almost neon, front, which had seemed to mock the town's financial woes with its veneer of prosperity, was now an opaque, unnerving testament to their abrupt departure. The colorful balloons that had once bobbed jauntily on strings, promising dreams of affordable mobility, were gone. The pennants that had fluttered in the breeze, designed to catch the eye and lure the hopeful, hung limply or had been torn away by the wind, leaving only the faded ghosts of their presence.

Sheriff Mason Brody stood across the street, leaning against the weathered brick of the old bakery, the scent of stale yeast and something faintly metallic – perhaps the lingering exhaust fumes from countless test drives – doing little to comfort him. The lot was still, unnervingly so. No gleaming chrome, no slick advertisements, no eager salesmen with their practiced smiles. Just rows of empty asphalt, punctuated by a few forlorn vehicles that hadn't been sold, their paint dulled by the elements, their windows opaque with dust and neglect. It was as if the entire operation had evaporated, leaving behind only the residue of broken promises and shattered finances. Mason had dispatched deputies, of course. Young Gilman, eager but green, had reported back with a shrug, his face reflecting the bewilderment that seemed to have settled over the entire town. The main office, a small, pre-fabricated building that had been trucked in and assembled with questionable haste, was locked tight. No sign of forced entry, no indication of a hasty departure, beyond the sheer, unadulterated *absence* of Earl Maddox and the Tall Man. Their personal effects, if any were significant, were presumably gone with them. The files, the ledgers—the tangible evidence of their predatory practices—were a mystery. Had they been meticulously cleared out, or had they vanished along with their architects?

The questions, once a manageable stream, now threatened to become a deluge. Where had they gone? And more importantly, *how* had they gone? There were no witnesses. No one saw them pack their bags, no one saw them load a U-Haul, no one heard the rumble of a departing eighteen-wheeler. It was as if they had simply stepped out of their gaudy office, perhaps to grab a quick lunch or a breath of stale air and had been swallowed by the very emptiness they had cultivated in the hearts of Redwater Crossing. The narrative that had been building, the growing certainty that Earl was at the heart of the town's unraveling, was now thrown into disarray. He was the villain, the tangible representation of their collective misfortune. And now, he was gone. The void he left was not one of relief, but of renewed confusion, of a deeper, more unsettling uncertainty. It was the feeling one got when a nightmare abruptly ends, not because the hero has triumphed, but because the dreamer has simply woken up, leaving the monstrous entity suspended in an impossible state of non-existence.

Mason ran a hand over his tired face. The deputies had scoured the premises, their flashlights cutting through the gloom of the empty offices. They found a half-eaten sandwich on a desk, a coffee mug still holding the dregs of cold, bitter liquid, a scattering of business cards bearing the 'Honest Rides' logo. It spoke of an ordinary end to an ordinary day, except that the ordinary had been irrevocably shattered. There were no signs of struggle, no blood, no hurried scribbles on notepads hinting at a desperate escape. It was as if they had simply ceased to be. The official reports would detail a sudden closure, a business that had packed up and left town. But Mason knew, with a bone-deep certainty that chilled him more than any winter wind, that this was no ordinary business closure. This was a vanishing act, orchestrated by hands that dealt in something far more sinister than car sales.

The immediate aftermath was a mixture of shock and a strange, almost morbid curiosity. People gathered in hushed groups, their whispers carrying on the autumn breeze. The general store buzzed with speculation. Mrs. Gable, her grief for her late husband still a raw wound, found herself drawn into the vortex of hushed theories. She'd always harbored a quiet resentment for Earl, for the way he preyed on the town's desperation, but she'd never imagined *this*. "Just... gone?" she'd murmur, her voice raspy. "Like smoke?" Old Man Percy, who'd sold a substantial portion of his retirement savings for a clunker from 'Honest Rides' that had promptly died on his driveway, scoffed, his voice a gravelly rasp. "Good riddance to bad rubbish," he declared, though his eyes, when Mason met them, held a flicker of something akin to fear. "But it ain't right, Sheriff. It ain't natural."

The town's collective narrative, so carefully constructed around Earl as the focal point of their woes, now fractured. Some saw it as divine intervention, a cosmic justice finally catching up to the unscrupulous dealer. Others, the more pragmatic or perhaps the more jaded, simply saw it as a clever escape, Maddox having foreseen the inevitable collapse of his empire and absconded with whatever ill-gotten gains remained. But for Mason, and for a growing number of others, the disappearance felt like another turn of the screw, another layer of an unfathomable darkness being revealed. It wasn't just about financial ruin anymore; it was about an unseen force that could pluck individuals from existence, leaving behind only unanswered questions and a chilling sense of vulnerability.

The Tall Man, a figure who had never uttered more than a handful of words, and those in a voice like grinding stones, became an even more spectral presence in their imaginations. He was the silent enforcer, the shadow behind the flashy smile. His disappearance alongside Maddox only amplified the enigma. He was the embodiment of the unknown, the silent, looming threat that had been a constant undercurrent in Redwater Crossing for the past year. Now, he too had vanished, leaving behind no trace, no footprint, no whispered legend. He was a phantom, and his departure was as silent and inexplicable as his arrival.

Mason found himself revisiting the few conversations he'd had with Earl, the man's oily charm and carefully constructed disguise now seeming even more grotesque in retrospect. Had there been clues? Had the glint in Earl's eye, the too-wide smile that never quite reached his eyes, been a sign of a man playing a much deeper, more dangerous game? Mason remembered Earl's almost dismissive attitude towards the town's misfortunes, his unwavering confidence, his serene detachment. It hadn't seemed like arrogance; it had seemed like... foresight. As if he knew something others didn't, as if he was privy to a secret that insulated him from the fallout.

The closure of 'Honest Rides' sent a fresh wave of panic through the town. For those who still had outstanding loans, for those who had traded in their old vehicles and now found themselves without transportation, the situation was dire. The few remaining dealerships in neighboring towns, already wary of Redwater Crossing's reputation, were quick to turn them away. The carefully constructed, if ultimately illusory, path to a better life that Earl had peddled was now a dead end, leading only to further destitution. The 'Honest Rides' lot, once a symbol of their desperate hope, was now a stark monument to their collective folly.

Mason stood in the deserted lot, the wind whistling through the skeletal frame of an unsold pickup truck. He looked at the closed office, the darkened windows like vacant eyes. He thought of the families he would have to inform that their pleas for recourse were now, at least for the moment, moot. The anger that had been simmering in the town was now a roiling tempest, directed not just at Earl, but at the entire system that had allowed him to operate so freely, and now at the universe that had simply allowed him to disappear. But beneath the anger, Mason sensed something else, something more profound and disturbing: a creeping realization that the problems of Redwater Crossing might not have been solely the product of one man's greed. Earl and the Tall Man might have been part of the decay, but they were not the source. Their vanishing act had not solved anything; it had merely exposed the hollowness that remained, a deeper, more insidious emptiness that the flashy promises of 'Honest Rides' had only managed to mask.

He kicked a loose stone, watching it skitter across the asphalt. The silence of the lot was profound, a tangible presence that seemed to press in on him. It was the silence of a stage after the play has ended, the actors gone, the audience dispersed, leaving only the empty sets and the lingering scent of manufactured drama. But this was no manufactured drama. This was real. And the real horror, Mason suspected, was just beginning to dawn on the people of Redwater Crossing. Their villain had fled, but the darkness he had brought with him seemed to have taken root, its tendrils now reaching into every corner of the town, leaving behind a chilling void that no amount of sunlight or hopeful platitudes could ever hope to fill. The absence of Earl Maddox was not an end; it was a terrifying, pregnant pause, a moment of stillness before the next, perhaps even darker, act began. He could feel it in the air, a prickling sensation on his skin, a whisper in the back of his mind that this was not the end of the story, but merely a terrifying prelude. The Tall Man, and Earl Maddox, had vanished, but what they had left behind, the fear, the desperation, the gnawing uncertainty, was more potent than ever. It was a specter that refused to be exorcised.

The town of Redwater Crossing was left to grapple with the wreckage. The financial devastation was not a localized event; it had spread like a contagion, infecting nearly every household, leaving a trail of ruin in its wake. The cars, once symbols of newfound freedom and hope, now sat idly in driveways, rusting hulks that served as constant, bitter reminders of their folly. They were monuments to misplaced trust and crushing debt, vehicles that had promised a better future but had delivered only deeper despair. Each dent, each scratch, each faded coat of paint seemed to whisper tales of broken dreams and insurmountable burdens. For many, the cars were no longer a means of transportation; they were anchors, dragging them further down into a sea of financial ruin. The down payments, the monthly installments, the inflated interest rates – they were debts that now hung over families like a guillotine, threatening to sever them from any semblance of financial stability. The very act of looking at these vehicles, of seeing them parked outside their homes, was a fresh stab of pain, a reopening of wounds that had barely begun to scab.

The suicides, a grim tally that had been steadily climbing in the months leading up to Earl's disappearance, had left gaping, irreparable holes in the fabric of the community. Families were shattered, children orphaned, and the collective grief of the town was a heavy, suffocating blanket. Each loss was a stark testament to the corrosive power of desperation, a chilling consequence of the relentless pressure exerted by Earl's predatory schemes. These weren't just statistics; they were neighbors, friends, loved ones, whose lives had been extinguished by the suffocating weight of debt and despair. The empty chairs at dinner tables, the silenced laughter in homes, the vacant stares of those left behind – these were the true, enduring scars left by 'Honest Rides.' The town's spirit, once characterized by a resilient, if quiet, pride, was now irrevocably broken, its future a bleak and uncertain landscape. The brief, destructive presence of Earl Maddox and his ilk had not just altered the town's economic trajectory; it had fundamentally reshaped its soul, leaving behind a legacy of fear, mistrust, and profound loss.

Mason found himself fielding calls from distraught citizens on a daily basis. The official channels for recourse had, with Maddox's vanishing, effectively evaporated. There was no one to sue, no one to hold accountable, no tangible entity to pursue. The paperwork that had once promised some semblance of legal protection now felt like a cruel joke, a collection of meaningless ink on paper. He listened patiently, his voice a low, steady rumble of reassurance, even as he knew the hollowness of his words. He was the sheriff, sworn to uphold the law, but the law, in this instance, seemed to have been rendered impotent. The very act of disappearing had been Earl's ultimate victory, a final, audacious act of defiance that had left the town defenseless and adrift.

The atmosphere in Redwater Crossing had shifted, the camaraderie that had once defined the community replaced by a pervasive sense of suspicion and isolation. Neighbors who had once shared porch swings and friendly waves now eyed each other with distrust, each fearing that the other might have been complicit, or worse, that they might become the next victim. The shared trauma had, paradoxically, driven them further apart, creating a mosaic of individual suffering rather than a unified front of collective resilience. The sense of community, already weakened by years of economic decline, had been all but obliterated.

The once-proud community, a place that had prided itself on its resilience and neighborly spirit, was now decimated. The vibrant tapestry of small-town life had been shredded, leaving behind only tattered remnants. The local businesses, already struggling, suffered further as residents, stripped of their disposable income, cut back on all but the most essential purchases. The bakery, the diner, the hardware store – they all felt the ripple effect of the car lot's ruin. The economic ecosystem of Redwater Crossing, already precarious, had been dealt a fatal blow. The town was slowly, inexorably, starving.

Children, too, bore the brunt of the devastation. The carefree innocence of youth was replaced by a gnawing anxiety, a palpable fear that permeated their homes. They overheard hushed arguments, saw the worried lines etched on their parents' faces, and felt the unspoken stress that hung heavily in the air. Schools reported an increase in behavioral issues, in withdrawn students who struggled to concentrate, their young minds burdened by the weight of their families' financial struggles. The future, once a landscape of boundless possibility, had shrunk to the immediate, the desperate need to simply survive.

Mason drove through the town, the familiar streets now appearing alien, imbued with a new, somber aura. He saw the abandoned cars, the shuttered businesses, the downcast faces of his constituents. He saw the ghost of what Redwater Crossing had once been, and he mourned the loss of its spirit. The problem, he realized with a sinking heart, was far more complex than just the disappearance of one unscrupulous man. Earl had merely been a catalyst, a festering sore brought to a head. The rot, he knew, went deeper, reaching into the very foundations of the town, a testament to years of neglect, economic hardship, and a pervasive sense of hopelessness that had made them so vulnerable to Earl's insidious promises in the first place.

The sheer audacity of the vanishing act, the complete erasure of Earl and the Tall Man from the face of the earth, left a void that was not just financial or emotional, but existential. It raised questions about the very nature of reality, about forces beyond comprehension that could operate in the shadows, unseen and unaccountable. It was a terrifying prospect, a notion that challenged the fundamental order of the world as they knew it. The absence of tangible proof, of a body, of a confession, left a wound that could never truly be healed, a festering question mark hanging over the town's collective consciousness.

The town's collective memory was now indelibly marked by the specter of 'Honest Rides.' It had become a cautionary tale, a dark legend whispered in hushed tones, a stark reminder of the dangers of unchecked greed and the fragility of hope. The bright, optimistic facade of the car lot, now shuttered and silent, served as a constant, grim reminder of the brief, destructive storm that had swept through Redwater Crossing, leaving behind only devastation and despair. The future of the town, once a path that held the promise of gradual recovery and rebuilding, now seemed like a treacherous, uncharted wilderness, fraught with uncertainty and the lingering echoes of ruin. The vanishing act had not been an escape for Earl Maddox; it had been an execution of Redwater Crossing's spirit, a final, devastating blow from which it was unclear if it would ever truly recover. The silence, once filled with the hum of commerce and the hopeful chatter of neighbors, was now a heavy, oppressive entity, a constant reminder of all that had been lost.

Sheriff Mason Brody felt the weight of Redwater Crossing pressing down on him, a physical burden as heavy and suffocating as the humid summer air had once been. Now, with the crisp, unforgiving bite of autumn, the town's despair felt even more pronounced, etched into the very landscape like frost on a windowpane. The 'Honest Rides' lot, a gaping wound in the heart of their already ailing town, remained stubbornly empty. His deputies had combed it over, their boots kicking up dust motes that danced in the weak afternoon sun, but they'd found nothing. Not a single dropped button, not a scuff mark that spoke of struggle, not a stray hair to offer a DNA sample. It was as if Earl Maddox and his silent, unnerving companion, the 'Tall Man,' had been raptured, plucked from existence by a force that defied earthly logic and the jurisdiction of the Redwater Crossing Sheriff's Department.

Mason's frustration was a bitter, coppery taste in his mouth, mingling with the stale coffee he'd been nursing for hours. He'd interviewed everyone. Neighbors who lived within earshot, shopkeepers who'd seen them come and go, the few desperate souls who'd been the last to interact with Earl at 'Honest Rides.' Their accounts were a frustrating tapestry of the mundane and the inexplicable. People remembered Earl's oily pronouncements, the Tall Man's unnerving silence, the gleam of a freshly polished fender, the rumble of an engine that sounded too good to be true. But no one saw them leave. No one heard a car start, no one saw a truck pull away. It was as if they had simply stepped behind the curtain of reality and never emerged. He'd even ordered a deeper dive into their backgrounds, running checks through every database available, chasing down whispers from neighboring counties. Earl Maddox was a ghost in the system, his past a carefully constructed void that offered no solid purchase. The Tall Man was even less. He'd appeared in Earl's orbit like a shadow taking form and vanished just as silently.

The legal ramifications alone were a nightmare. He'd spent the better part of the morning on the phone with the county prosecutor, a man whose patience was as thin as his receding hairline. "They're gone, Mason," the prosecutor had stated, his voice laced with a weary resignation. "There's no crime here, not one we can prove. Business closes and owners vanish. It happens. You've got no bodies, no ransom notes, no evidence of foul play. What do you want me to do, issue a warrant for their non-existence?" Mason had clenched his jaw, the words feeling like sawdust in his throat. He wanted justice. He wanted to explain to the families who'd lost everything that their tormentors hadn't simply skipped town but had been *erased*. But the law, as always, demanded tangible proof, and the universe, it seemed, had decided to withhold it.

He drove past the shuttered 'Honest Rides' lot again, the late afternoon sun casting long, skeletal shadows across the cracked asphalt. The few remaining cars on the lot, the ones that hadn't been repossessed or sold off in a desperate, last-ditch effort by Earl, sat like decaying relics. Their paint was dull, their tires flat, their once-gleaming chrome dulled by dust and neglect. They were monuments to broken promises, silent witnesses to the town's unraveling. Mason's gaze drifted to the small, prefabricated office building. Locked from the inside, just as his deputies had found it. He'd had it opened, of course. A thorough, painstaking search had yielded a half-eaten sandwich, cold and congealed, a coffee mug with the dregs of bitter liquid, a scattered assortment of business cards bearing the ubiquitous 'Honest Rides' logo. It spoke of an abrupt, but not necessarily violent, departure. It was the ordinariness of the scene that was so profoundly unsettling, the sheer *lack* of anything extraordinary in the immediate aftermath of something so extraordinary.

He thought of the letters he'd received. Piles of them, some tear-stained, some scrawled in angry, desperate script. Letters from elderly couples who'd sunk their life savings into a vehicle that had sputtered and died within a week. Letters from young families who'd taken out loans they could never hope to repay, their dreams of a stable future now shattered. Letters from single mothers who'd relied on those clunkers to get to work and now faced the terrifying prospect of unemployment. Each letter was a testament to Earl's predatory nature, a detailed account of his systematic dismantling of their lives. And now, with Earl gone, with the Tall Man vanished into the ether, these letters represented a plea for help that Mason could not answer. There was no one to arrest, no one to prosecute, no one to hold accountable.

The town's collective psyche was as fractured as the pavement on the car lot. Some clung to the notion of a divine intervention, a karmic retribution that had finally claimed the unscrupulous dealer. Others, the more cynical, simply saw it as a shrewd business move, Earl having pulled off the ultimate escape. But for Mason, and for many others, it was far more sinister. It was the chilling realization that forces beyond their comprehension were at play, forces that could simply erase individuals from existence, leaving behind only a void and a profound sense of helplessness. This wasn't just a financial disaster; it was a metaphysical one.

He remembered his last, brief encounter with Earl. The man had been all smiles and false platitudes, his eyes darting around with a peculiar, almost anticipatory glint. Mason had pressed him about the rising number of repossessions, the increasing desperation in the town. Earl had merely waved a dismissive hand, his smile widening. "The market's tough, Sheriff," he'd said, his voice smooth as polished chrome. "But 'Honest Rides' always finds a way. We believe in giving folks a chance, and sometimes, well, chances don't always pan out. That's just life." Mason had felt a prickle of unease then, a sense that Earl was not just a greedy businessman, but a man who understood something fundamental about the town's vulnerability, something he was actively exploiting. Now, looking back, that unease had blossomed into a terrifying certainty. Earl hadn't just been selling cars; he'd been cashing in on something far deeper, something rooted in the town's despair. And whatever that "something" was, it had clearly been powerful enough to spirit him and his silent partner away.

The silence that had descended upon the 'Honest Rides' lot was not the peaceful quiet of a town at rest, but the heavy, pregnant silence of a battlefield after the fighting has ceased, the wreckage still strewn about, the lingering scent of smoke and fear in the air. Mason could feel the fear permeating Redwater Crossing, a palpable entity that clung to the residents like a second skin. It wasn't just the fear of financial ruin, though that was rampant. It was a deeper, more primal fear. The fear of the unknown, of forces that operated outside the realm of human control, forces that could snatch people away without a trace.

He slammed his hand against the steering wheel, the sudden jolt of it echoing in the quiet car. His deputies were good men, honest men, but they were men bound by procedure, by the tangible. They could investigate a burglary, track down a hit-and-run driver, mediate a domestic dispute. But they couldn't hunt phantoms. They couldn't file charges against an absence. And neither could he. The sheer frustration of it gnawed at him. He was the sheriff, the man sworn to protect and serve, and he was utterly powerless. The very act of their disappearance, the perfect execution of their vanishing act, was their ultimate victory, a final, mocking testament to their superiority.

He thought about the implications. If Earl and the Tall Man could simply cease to exist, what did that say about the reality they inhabited? Were there cracks in the fabric of existence that allowed such things to happen? Was their town, Redwater Crossing, a place where such breaches were more common? The questions circled his mind like vultures, picking away at his resolve. He was trained to deal with the concrete, the rational. This was... other.

The pressure from the town council was mounting, too. They wanted answers, wanted to know what the sheriff's department was doing, what recourse the citizens had. Mason had met with them, trying to explain the impossible. He'd been met with skepticism, with accusations of incompetence, with the desperate pleas of people who had nowhere else to turn. He'd felt the familiar sting of their anger, their disappointment, and he'd carried it with him, adding to the ever-growing weight on his shoulders. He knew, with a certainty that chilled him to the bone, that the disappearance of Earl Maddox and the Tall Man was not the end of their story, but a chilling, terrifying prelude. They had vanished, but the darkness they had brought with them, the insidious rot they had sown, remained. And it was Mason's job to try and salvage what he could from the wreckage, even if the architects of that wreckage were now beyond his reach, beyond the very laws he was sworn to uphold. The silence of the empty lot was a deafening roar, a constant reminder of his failure, of the insurmountable forces that had swept through his town and left him standing alone in the ruins, with nothing but unanswered questions and a profound, soul-crushing sense of helplessness. He was a sheriff without a crime, a lawman without a law to enforce, tasked with managing the fallout of a phenomenon that defied explanation, and that, more than anything, was the true source of his gnawing frustration.

The Master's hunger was an ancient, gnawing thing, a void that consumed light and hope with equal ferocity. Redwater Crossing, with its festering wounds of broken dreams and shattered finances, had been a particularly ripe field. For weeks, he had subtly woven himself into the fabric of their despair, a silent conductor orchestrating a symphony of regret. Earl Maddox, that oily purveyor of false promises, had been his instrument, his desperate need for solvency a perfect conduit for the Master's influence. The Tall Man, a silent sentinel, had been the manifestation of that influence, a chilling embodiment of the unfulfilled desires and the suffocating weight of debt.

The act of vanishing had not been a panicked flight, but a deliberate, almost ritualistic withdrawal. It was the culmination of a harvest meticulously gathered. As the last of the "Honest Rides" vehicles had been spirited away, each transaction draining a sliver of hope from the buyers, so too had a corresponding measure of vitality flowed into the Master. He had absorbed the palpable despair, the gnawing anxiety that clung to the town like the persistent humidity. It was a sustenance far richer than any mortal meal, a draught of pure, unadulterated misery.

Now, revitalized, the Master moved on. The echo of Redwater Crossing's desolation was a faint hum in his awareness, a satisfied sigh after a prodigious feast. He had plucked the very essence of their broken spirits, leaving behind only the hollow shells of their former lives. The lingering regret, the whispers of 'what if' and 'if only,' were the faint traces of his passage, a subtle perfume of despair that would cling to the town, a silent testament to his power. It was a lure, almost imperceptible, for the unwary, a whisper in the wind that might beckon others into the same cycle of disillusionment.

He left behind a vacuum, not merely of people, but of spirit. The 'Honest Rides' lot was more than just an empty space; it was a scar upon the town's landscape, a physical manifestation of the spiritual void that had been created. The spectral emptiness that now permeated Redwater Crossing was the Master's signature, a chilling reminder that his influence was not always measured in tangible losses, but in the erosion of the very will to hope.

The cycle was an eternal one, a ceaseless rhythm of consumption and renewal. Redwater Crossing had served its purpose, providing the nourishment needed to sustain his existence, to fuel his continued presence in the mortal realm. He did not linger, for lingering invited scrutiny, and scrutiny was a threat to his insidious work. His existence was predicated on the unseen, the unacknowledged. To be seen was to be vulnerable, to be questioned was to risk exposure.

As he moved, the residue of Redwater Crossing clung to him, not as a burden, but as a successful conquest. The memory of Earl's desperate ambition, the Tall Man's unnerving stoicism, the collective anguish of the townspeople – these were not memories in the human sense, but reservoirs of energy. He drew upon them, a constant, low-grade hum that sustained him, allowing him to perceive the subtle vibrations of despair in other places, in other lives.

He was a force of nature, not of sun and rain, but of doubt and disillusionment. He did not create these emotions, but rather amplified them, nurtured them, and finally, harvested them. Redwater Crossing had been a particularly fertile ground because the despair had been so deeply ingrained, so willingly cultivated by its own circumstances and the predatory nature of men like Earl. The town had been ripe for his influence, a perfect storm of economic hardship and personal vulnerability.

The townsfolk, left behind to grapple with the aftermath, would experience a peculiar kind of emptiness. It wasn't just the absence of Earl and the Tall Man, or the financial ruin that had befallen so many. It was a deeper, more existential void. The realization that their problems, their very ruin, had been orchestrated by something beyond their understanding, something that fed on their misery, would be a profound and terrifying blow. It would leave them adrift, questioning the very nature of reality, wondering if the darkness that had consumed them was an external force, or a reflection of something intrinsically flawed within themselves.

The Tall Man known as The Master, however, felt no remorse, no empathy. These were human emotions, irrelevant to his purpose. He was an entity of sustenance, of perpetuation. His existence was tied to the ebb and flow of human suffering. He was the shadow that followed hope, the chilling whisper in the quiet moments of desperation. Redwater Crossing had been a particularly sweet vintage, a concentrated essence of all that he craved.

As he receded from the town, the faintest wisps of residual despair would remain, like the scent of decay after a storm. These would act as subtle beacons, calling to others who were susceptible, others who were teetering on the brink of their own personal precipices. It was an insidious form of propagation, a silent sowing of seeds for future harvests. The Master was not a destroyer in the conventional sense; he was a consumer, a transformer. He took the raw material of human misery and transmuted it into the energy that allowed him to persist.

The memory of his passage would be like a recurring nightmare for those who had been touched by it. Not a clear, defined memory, but a vague, unsettling feeling of loss, of something profound having been taken. They would look at the empty 'Honest Rides' lot, and a shiver would run down their spines, a phantom chill that had nothing to do with the autumn air. They would recall Earl's too-bright smile, the Tall Man's unnerving silence, and a sense of dread would wash over them, a premonition of darkness that they couldn't quite articulate.

This residual dread was, in itself, a form of sustenance, a low-level hum that the Master could still tap into, even from a distance. It was the echo of his power, a subtle reverberation that confirmed his presence and his efficacy. He was the unseen hand that guided the descent, the silent architect of their downfall. And in the emptiness he left behind, in the hollow ache of what was lost, lay the true measure of his success. Redwater Crossing had been a testament to his power, a monument to the insidious nature of despair, and a prelude to whatever darkness he would orchestrate next. He was the Master, and his sustenance was the very essence of human sorrow. The town had been drained, but its sorrow would linger, a ghost that whispered of his reign. He was a hunger that could never be truly sated, a void that would forever seek to fill itself with the misery of others. His work here was done, for now, but the legacy of his passage was etched into the very soul of Redwater Crossing, a testament to a hunger that transcended the mundane, a darkness that fed on the light of hope itself.

The silence that descended upon Redwater Crossing after the vanishing act was not the peaceful quiet of a town at rest, but the strained hush of a room after a violent argument, pregnant with unspoken accusations and lingering dread. The grand pronouncements of prosperity, once boisterous and full of bluster from Earl Maddox's booming voice, were now replaced by a gnawing emptiness. The gleaming chrome and polished paint of the "Honest Rides" vehicles, symbols of a brighter future just weeks before, had evaporated, leaving behind only the stark, muddy imprint of where they once stood, like phantom limbs on the landscape of the town's hopes. The empty lot, once a beacon of opportunity, now served as a gaping maw, a stark reminder of the insatiable hunger that had swept through their lives. It was a scar, deep and ragged, etched not onto skin, but onto the collective consciousness of Redwater Crossing.

The story of "Earl's Honest Rides" transformed with terrifying speed from a local success saga into a hushed, whispered cautionary tale. It became the ghost story parents told their children, not of spectral figures or ancient curses, but of something far more chillingly familiar: the predator that wore a human face, the con artist who peddled dreams with the same ease he peddled lies. Children, once captivated by the shiny new cars their neighbors brought home, now pointed with a nervous tremor towards the deserted lot, their young minds conjuring images of the smiling man, Earl Maddox, and his unnervingly silent companion, the Tall Man, as harbingers of something dark and unknowable. The tales were embellished with every retelling, the details growing more macabre, the inherent horror amplified by the absence of concrete answers. Had they simply fled? Had they been taken? Or had something far worse, something that fed on their very desperation, consumed them and their ill-gotten gains? The ambiguity itself was a form of torment.

The economic fallout was immediate and brutal. Families who had poured their life savings into these "honest" deals found themselves not just without a vehicle, but without the means to secure their livelihoods. The local banks, once eager to lend to the burgeoning clientele of "Honest Rides," now bore the grim faces of financial ruin. Mortgages went unpaid, businesses faltered, and the carefully constructed edifice of Redwater Crossing's newfound prosperity crumbled into dust. The veneer of respectability that Maddox had so expertly cultivated shattered, revealing the rot beneath. The town, so eager to shed its image of quiet desperation, now found itself mired in a deeper, more profound despair, a desolation born not of economic stagnation, but of betrayal.

Rebuilding was not merely a matter of economic recovery; it was an act of psychological resuscitation. The very fabric of trust had been torn asunder. Neighbors who had once shared dreams of a better life now regarded each other with suspicion, wondering who had been in on the deception, who had been a victim, and who, perhaps, had been a willing accomplice in their own downfall. The camaraderie that had briefly bloomed in the fertile soil of perceived success withered under the harsh glare of reality. Every smile from a stranger, every too-good-to-be-true offer, now carried a dark undertone, a phantom echo of Earl Maddox's glib assurances.

The scar on Redwater Crossing's memory was not a singular event, but a festering wound. It manifested in subtle ways: the averted gaze of a former "Honest Rides" customer, the nervous laugh of someone recounting the tale, the almost imperceptible flinch when the name "Earl" was mentioned. The empty lot became a pilgrimage site for the disillusioned, a place where they would stand, hands shoved deep in pockets, staring at the void, trying to reconcile the vibrant promises with the desolate present. Some would come at dusk, when the shadows stretched long and distorted, feeling a perverse kinship with the lingering sense of loss, a sense that something vital had been drained from the very air they breathed.

The insidious entity that had preyed on their hopes, the "Master" as he was later whispered about in hushed, terrified tones, had left a void that no amount of money could fill. It was a spiritual vacuum, an erosion of the very will to believe. The town had been a fertile ground, not because it was inherently weak, but because it had been yearning for something more, a chance to escape the mundane, to grasp at a brighter future. And in that yearning, they had been vulnerable. Earl, the oily purveyor of false promises, had been the perfect bait, his charisma a shimmering lure cast into the murky depths of their collective desire. The Tall Man, a silent, imposing shadow, had been the physical manifestation of the threat, the unspoken consequence of stepping too close to the precipice.

The whispers began not as accusations, but as confused murmurings. People would talk of a feeling, an atmosphere, a sense of unease that had settled over the town even before the full extent of the disaster became apparent. Some recalled fleeting glimpses of the Tall Man, not just at the "Honest Rides" lot, but lurking in the periphery, a silent observer in the burgeoning prosperity. Others spoke of Earl's increasingly erratic behavior in the final days, his smiles seeming a little too tight, his reassurances a little too frantic. These fragmented memories, once dismissed as the anxieties of people caught in a financial downturn, now took on a sinister new light. They were the glimmers of truth, the faint phosphorescence of a predator moving in the dark.

The notion of a singular, malevolent force, an entity that fed on despair and disillusionment, was a terrifying leap for a town that had always prided itself on its grounded, practical nature. Yet, the sheer completeness of the "vanishing act" defied conventional explanation. It wasn't just about stolen money; it was about stolen futures, stolen dreams, and a stolen sense of security. It was as if the very soul of the town had been siphoned away, leaving behind only the hollow shells of their former lives. This abstract horror, the idea of an unseen force orchestrating their downfall, was a burden far heavier than the tangible loss of their savings. It was the crushing weight of realizing their misfortunes were not just bad luck, but the result of a deliberate, almost supernatural predation.

The local historian, a retired schoolteacher named Mrs. Dillons, found herself increasingly sought after. Her knowledge of Redwater Crossing's past, once a quaint curiosity, now became a desperate search for answers. She spoke of the town's cycles of boom and bust, of previous economic downturns and local scandals, but none of it seemed to explain the profound, almost existential emptiness that now permeated the air. "There's a difference," she'd say, her voice trembling with a mixture of fear and profound sadness, "between a town that's fallen on hard times, and a town that's been *hollowed out*. This... this feels like the latter." Her words, spoken with the authority of years spent chronicling Redwater Crossing's story, only deepened the sense of dread.

The townsfolk, once eager to discuss their new vehicles and the opportunities they represented, now spoke in hushed tones, their conversations punctuated by nervous glances at the empty lot. The "Honest Rides" saga became a dark folklore, a legend whispered around campfires and over backyard fences. It was the story of how easily dreams could be twisted into nightmares, how a charismatic smile could mask a predatory intent, and how sometimes the most devastating losses were not of money, but of faith. The scar was not just on the land; it was on their hearts, a permanent reminder of their vulnerability.

The rebuilding efforts were slow, arduous, and often fraught with renewed anxiety. Every new business that opened, every new family that moved in, was met with a cautious optimism, tinged with the ever-present fear that history might repeat itself. The ghost of "Earl's Honest Rides" loomed large, a specter of what could go wrong, a constant whisper of doubt in the ear of hope. The prosperity that had seemed so tangible, so within reach, now felt like a mirage, a cruel trick of the light that had dissolved the moment they reached out to grasp it. Redwater Crossing was left to grapple with a wounded memory, a town forever marked by the day its honest aspirations were so ruthlessly, so inexplicably, made to vanish. The silence that remained was not an absence of noise, but a presence of fear, a testament to the invisible predator that had left its indelible mark. The town's scar was a story, and that story was far from over. It was a narrative that would be passed down, a somber inheritance for generations to come, a chilling reminder that some voids are not meant to be filled, but endured.

CHAPTER 5

122 Days Before the Vanishing Act Rinse and Repeat

edwater Crossing. The name itself conjured images of a rushing torrent, a vibrant lifeblood, but the reality was a slow, sluggish trickle. Like Redwater Crossing had before the unsettling gleam of Earl's chrome, Redwater Crossing wore its desolation like a threadbare coat. The grand old brick factory, once the pulsing heart of the town, stood as a monument to a bygone era, its windows like vacant eyes staring out at a landscape of boarded-up storefronts and weed-choked lots. The hum of machinery, the clatter of production, the very sound that had once defined the rhythm of life here, had long since faded into an oppressive silence, punctuated only by the mournful sigh of the wind through broken panes.

The economic malaise had settled over Redwater Crossing like a persistent fog, dampening spirits and leaching the color from everyday life. Jobs were a scarce commodity; prizes fiercely contested amongst a population dwindling in number and spirit. The young, with the restless energy of their years, saw little future in the stagnant air of their hometown. They packed their bags, their dreams, and their dwindling hopes, heading for the promise of brighter horizons, leaving behind an aging population who spoke with weary nostalgia of a time when Redwater Crossing had been a place of opportunity, a place where futures were forged, not forgotten. Their laments were a constant soundtrack to the town's slow decay, a mournful chorus to the fading glory of their once-thriving home.

This pervasive atmosphere of listlessness, this quiet resignation to a diminished existence, was precisely the kind of fertile ground the Master sought. He was a connoisseur of despair, a hunter who tracked the scent of economic ruin and the subtle, insidious aroma of a community losing its will to thrive. Redwater Crossing, with its hollowed-out core and its palpable sense of loss, was not just a town in decline; it was a community ripe for the plucking, its residents yearning for a flicker of hope, a chance to escape the suffocating grip of their present reality. The silence here wasn't just an absence of noise; it was a palpable presence, a vacuum waiting to be filled.

The narrative of Redwater Crossing was a familiar one, a lament sung by countless towns across the industrial heartland. The factory, the mill, the mine – whatever its specific function, it had been the bedrock upon which families built their lives, the engine that powered the community's growth. But as global markets shifted, as technology advanced, or as resources dwindled, these once-mighty pillars began to crumble. The downsizing wasn't a sudden collapse, but a slow, agonizing amputation. First, a department was shed, then another. Layoffs became a regular, grim ritual. The payroll shrunk, and with it, the town's purchasing power. Small businesses, dependent on the steady stream of wages from the factory floor, began to wither. The diner that served lunch to the hungry workers, the hardware store that supplied their tools, the pharmacy that dispensed their prescriptions – all felt the chill of the economic wind.

This economic contraction was more than just numbers on a ledger; it was a profound societal shift. The ingrained work ethic, the pride in providing for one's family through honest labor, began to erode. When the factory doors finally closed, or when its operations were reduced to a skeletal crew, it wasn't just jobs that were lost, but identity. The rhythm of life, dictated by the shift whistle, was gone. Weekends stretched into endless, purposeless voids. The camaraderie forged in shared labor was replaced by the solitary struggle against mounting bills and dwindling prospects.

The departure of the young was a particularly poignant symptom of Redwater Crossing's decline. They were the town's future, its vital force, and their exodus was a clear signal that the well had run dry. High school graduation ceremonies, once occasions of pride and celebration, now felt tinged with an elegy. Parents watched their children pack away their diplomas, their dreams of staying, of contributing to the town that had nurtured them, giving way to the stark reality of a job market that offered little more than minimum wage at the local struggling supermarket, or the prospect of a lifetime of underemployment. The roads leading out of Redwater Crossing became arteries of escape, carrying away the very lifeblood the town desperately needed to survive.

For those who remained, the days were often marked by a quiet resignation. They had weathered storms before, but this felt different, more permanent. They would gather at the few remaining public spaces – the park, the laundromat, the perpetually half-empty coffee shop – and their conversations would inevitably drift to the "good old days." They would reminisce about the bustling factory, the vibrant Main Street, the sense of shared purpose. These memories, while offering a bittersweet comfort, also served to highlight the stark contrast with their present reality, amplifying the feeling of loss and stagnation.

The older generation, those who had spent their entire lives in Redwater Crossing, bore the heaviest burden of this collective memory. They had witnessed the town's zenith and its subsequent decline, and the erosion of their home felt like a personal betrayal. Their pronouncements were often laced with a weary fatalism, a belief that the best days were behind them, and that no amount of effort could rekindle the lost spark. "This town's just a ghost of what it used to be," they'd say, their voices heavy with the weight of experience. And it was this pervasive sense of hopelessness, this ingrained belief in an inevitable downward spiral, that made Redwater Crossing so uniquely susceptible to the Master's insidious influence. He didn't need to manufacture despair; he simply needed to amplify what was already there, to offer a twisted salvation from a fate that the town's inhabitants already seemed to have accepted.

The physical landscape of Redwater Crossing mirrored this internal decay. The paint on the houses peeled like sunburnt skin, revealing the weathered wood beneath. Lawns that had once been meticulously manicured were now overgrown, surrendered to the persistent march of weeds. The once-proud town square, with its gazebo and its war memorial, was now a place of cracked pavement and faded glory. A single, flickering lamppost cast long, distorted shadows, making the familiar seem alien and unsettling, especially as dusk began to gather. Children's laughter, once a common sound, was now a rare, almost startling intrusion, often quickly silenced by an unseen hand, as if the very act of joy was an unwelcome disruption to the prevailing somber mood.

The absence of opportunity created a unique kind of desperation. It wasn't the frantic, grasping desperation of someone on the verge of immediate collapse, but a slow, grinding hunger, a constant ache for something more. It was the quiet desperation of a parent who couldn't afford new shoes for their growing child, the gnawing worry of a homeowner facing foreclosure, the quiet shame of a man who had once been a foreman now struggling to find work as a janitor. This was the undercurrent of Redwater Crossing, a silent, steady pressure that wore down the spirit over time.

The local businesses that still clung to existence operated in a state of perpetual fragility. The general store, a relic from a time when it had served as the town's everything-shop, now primarily catered to a dwindling elderly clientele, its shelves stocked with a curious mix of necessities and nostalgia-laden trinkets. The diner, its Formica countertops scared and its neon sign perpetually buzzing, served up comfort food that tasted of memory rather than fresh ingredients. Even the local bar, once a hub of social activity, now felt like a waiting room, the patrons nursing their drinks in a quiet contemplation of what might have been. Each establishment, in its own way, was a testament to the town's resilience, but also a stark indicator of its arrested development.

The town's infrastructure, too, reflected its neglect. Potholes pockmarked the roads, some so deep they threatened to swallow tires whole. The streetlights, where they worked at all, offered a dim, unreliable illumination, casting more shadows than light. The once-clear waters of the nearby creek, from which the town drew its name, now ran sluggish and clouded, an oily sheen often visible on its surface, a silent testament to decades of industrial runoff and a general lack of environmental stewardship. Even the air seemed to carry a faint, metallic tang, a constant reminder of the factory's presence, even in its diminished state.

This was the town that felt the first stirrings of a change, not a positive one, but a subtle shift in the atmosphere, a faint tremor beneath the surface of their placid despair. It was the kind of shift that most would dismiss, an instinctual unease, a prickling on the back of the neck that suggested something was amiss, even if nothing had tangibly changed. For the Master, this was the precisely the moment he had been waiting for. Redwater Crossing, with its muted suffering and its quiet yearning, was ready. It was a town that had already begun to hollow itself out, and all it needed was a catalyst, a charismatic figure to promise it a new soul, a borrowed brilliance, before it was ultimately consumed. The cycle, it seemed, was not just repeating; it was preparing to find its next unsuspecting victim. The stillness of Redwater Crossing was not a sign of peace, but of a deep, unsettling dormancy, a slumber that was about to be brutally awakened.

The air in Redwater Crossing, thick with the dust of forgotten industry and the scent of damp, decaying leaves, had a way of settling into your lungs, into your very bones, a constant reminder of stagnation. For months, that oppressive stillness had been the town's only companion. The boarded-up storefronts on Main Street seemed to gape like missing teeth, and the hulking silhouette of the defunct textile mill cast a permanent shadow, not just over the physical landscape, but over the collective psyche of its inhabitants. Hope had become a currency so scarce, most residents no longer bothered to check their wallets. They'd seen it before, this slow bleed of a town, and had learned to expect little beyond the predictable ache of disappointment.

Then, like a garish, unexpected bloom in a field of grey, it appeared. On the edge of town, where the last scraggly strip mall surrendered to overgrown weeds and the rusting skeleton of an old gas station, a splash of color erupted. It was a billboard, impossibly bright, emblazoned with a sunburst of primary hues – vibrant yellows, defiant blues, and a red so startling it seemed to vibrate. And on it, in bold, friendly lettering, the words: ***EARL'S HONEST RIDES - WHERE DREAMS GET THEIR WHEELS!***

The sight of it sent a ripple through the hushed arteries of Redwater Crossing. Whispers, tentative at first, then gathering momentum, spread like wildfire. It was the same billboard, the same slogan, the same unnerving cheerfulness that had graced Redwater Crossing a few years prior. The memory was still raw for some, a scar that hadn't quite faded. They remembered the initial surge of disbelief, the cautious optimism, the almost feverish scramble to see what this Earl's Honest Rides had to offer.

Within days, the lot itself materialized. It wasn't built, not in any conventional sense. It simply... appeared. One morning, where yesterday there had been nothing but an expanse of parched earth and discarded tires, stood row upon row of gleaming automobiles. Sedans, SUVs, even a few sporty coupes – all polished to a mirror finish, reflecting the pale, indifferent sky. They were a stark contrast to the rust-bucket pickups and faded family sedans that usually dotted the town's meager parking lots. These cars looked new, impossibly so, their chrome trim catching the sunlight like a thousand tiny diamonds.

And then came the prices. Displayed on individual, brightly colored signs attached to each vehicle, they were, quite frankly, absurd. A pristine, late-model minivan listed at a price that would barely cover a month's rent for a modest apartment. A sleek, black sedan, the kind that looked like it belonged in a city dealership's showroom, was marked with a figure that made people do a double take, then check their eyeglasses. It was too good to be true. Everyone knew it.

But the gnawing desperation that had become Redwater Crossing's default setting was a powerful counterweight to logic. The factory had been shuttered for five years, its silence a deafening testament to lost livelihoods. The jobs that remained were either minimum wage at the struggling grocery store or precarious, day-labor gigs that barely kept body and soul together. For families struggling to keep their heads above water, for individuals yearning for a sliver of independence, for the young dreaming of escape, Earl's Honest Rides wasn't just a sale; it was a mirage in a desert of despair, and sometimes, in the heat of your thirst, you're willing to believe in anything.

Martha Pike, whose days were a monotonous cycle of caring for her ailing mother and tending to their small, weed-infested garden, was one of the first to see it. She'd driven into town for her weekly pilgrimage to the pharmacy, her ancient Ford coughing and sputtering like a dying beast. As she passed the lot, the sheer incongruity of the scene hit her like a physical blow. She slowed the Ford to a crawl, her eyes wide. The cars shimmered. They *sang* with a silent promise of movement, of freedom, of a life not dictated by the creak of her mother's wheelchair or the gnawing anxiety about the next utility bill.

She saw a woman she vaguely recognized from the town's infrequent social gatherings, a Mrs. Fairlane, standing by a cherry-red convertible, her hand tentatively reaching out to touch its impossibly smooth surface. Mrs. Tori Fairlane's husband had lost his job at the mill two years ago, and since then, their world had shrunk to the four walls of their modest home. Tori imagined the joy, the sheer, unadulterated exhilaration, of feeling the wind in her hair, of escaping the suffocating familiarity of Redwater Crossing, even for an afternoon.

Martha pulled over leaving her sputtering Ford by the roadside. "Can you believe it, Tori?" Martha's voice was a hushed, almost reverent whisper. "Look at these prices. It's... it's a miracle."

Tori could only nod, her throat tight. A miracle felt like the only word for it. But a seed of unease, small and tenacious, had already begun to sprout within her. She'd heard the stories from King George a number of years back. She knew that miracles rarely came without a cost, and the price of these cars, so ridiculously low, felt like a down payment on something far more significant than a monthly payment.

"They're... beautiful," Tori managed, her gaze sweeping across the rows of vehicles. "But... how? How can they afford to sell them like this?"

Mrs. Pike shrugged, a gesture that was more bewilderment than explanation. "Who knows? Maybe Earl just likes helping people out. He's supposed to be a real honest guy, from what I hear."

"Honest Earl," Tori murmured, the name feeling strangely hollow on her tongue. There was something in the perfection of it all, in the unnatural vibrancy of the colors against the town's muted backdrop, that felt... staged. It was like a scene from a movie, too perfect, too clean, too good to be true.

As the days passed, the initial shock and disbelief gave way to a palpable buzz of excitement. More and more people were drawn to the lot, their skepticism warring with a desperate, hopeful curiosity. Small groups gathered, pointing, discussing, their voices a welcome change from the usual quiet hum of resignation. The diner, usually a sleepy outpost serving lukewarm coffee and stale donuts, found itself with a steady stream of customers eager to trade gossip and speculation about Earl's Honest Rides.

"Saw old man Peterson down there today," whispered Joe Miller, the owner of the diner, as he poured Betty another cup of coffee, his brow furrowed. "He's been talking about getting a new truck for years, ever since his old one finally gave up the ghost. Said he saw a Ford F-150, almost brand new, for less than he paid for his first car back in '78."

Betty stirred her coffee, the spoon clinking against the ceramic mug. "And did he buy it?"

Joe shrugged, his gaze distant. "He was looking at it like a man in a trance. Said he'd have to think about it. But you could see it in his eyes, Betty. He wanted it. We all want it, don't we? A way out. A way to feel like we're not stuck in this... this rut."

He was right. Redwater Crossing was a rut. A deep, wide, soul-crushing rut. And Earl's Honest Rides, with its impossibly shiny cars and its fairy-tale prices, was shimmering at the edge of that rut, a beacon of false promise, a siren song designed to lure the weary and the desperate.

The owner himself, Earl, was a curious figure. He wasn't the burly, grease-stained mechanic one might expect. Instead, he was a man of indeterminate age, with an unnervingly smooth face, bright, intelligent eyes that seemed to miss nothing, and a smile that never quite reached them. He wore crisp, clean overalls, always in a cheerful shade of blue, and his hands, Betty noticed, were remarkably clean for someone who supposedly dealt with cars all day. He spoke with a smooth, almost melodious voice, full of folksy charm and an uncanny ability to make each customer feel like they were his only priority.

He'd set up a small, brightly painted trailer on the lot, which served as his office. Inside, it was as meticulously organized and clean as his cars. There were no stacks of paperwork, no overflowing ashtrays, just a gleaming desk, a comfortable-looking chair, and a single, framed photograph on the wall – a picture of a smiling family, impossibly happy, standing in front of a perfectly manicured house. It was the image of an idealized American dream, a dream that felt impossibly distant for most of Redwater Crossing's residents.

Martha Pike, despite her reservations, found herself drawn to the lot again a few days later, under the guise of picking up some mail that had been misdelivered to her house. The air was alive with a nervous energy. Several people were test-driving cars, their faces a mixture of exhilaration and disbelief. A young man, no older than eighteen, was beaming as he steered a sporty coupe down the dusty road, his arm slung around his girlfriend, who looked equally thrilled.

Earl himself was orchestrating the scene with an almost invisible hand. He'd greet each potential customer with that same disarming smile, lead them to the car of their dreams, and then, with a few carefully chosen words, seal the deal. The financing, he explained, was incredibly simple. No credit checks, no lengthy applications. Just a small down payment, a few surprisingly low monthly installments, and the car was theirs. He made it sound so easy, so straightforward, so... honest.

But as Martha watched, a chill began to creep up her spine. She noticed the way Earl's eyes would linger on certain customers, the way his smile would widen just a fraction when someone seemed particularly vulnerable, particularly desperate. It wasn't the warmth of a businessman eager to make a sale; it was the predatory gleam of a hunter spotting his prey.

She saw Tori Fairlane again, this time sitting behind the wheel of the cherry-red convertible, her face alight with a joy Martha hadn't seen in years. Earl stood beside the car, his hand resting on its polished hood, his voice a low murmur. Martha couldn't hear the words, but she could read the body language. It was the language of persuasion, of seduction.

Later that day, she overheard a conversation between two men near the diner.

"He practically gave me the keys," one of them, a man named Mike who used to work in the mill's accounting department, said, his voice still a little shaky. "I've been trying to get a decent car for months, but every time I went to the dealerships in the next town, they'd laugh me out of the place when they saw my credit report. Earl... he didn't even ask. Just looked at me, smiled, and said, 'You look like a man who needs a ride.' And then he showed me this beauty." He gestured vaguely in the direction of the lot. "The payments are almost nothing. I don't know how he does it, but I'm not questioning it."

The other man, a younger fellow named Kevin who had been struggling to find consistent work since he was laid off at the mill, nodded in agreement. "My sister, she got a minivan from him last week. Said it's perfect for her and the kids. She was so worried about getting around, taking them to school, to their appointments. Now? She's like a new person."

Martha felt a knot tighten in her stomach. The same story. The same impossibly good deals. The same underlying current of something... not quite right. It was the echo of Redwater Crossing, the unsettling familiarity that screamed a warning.

She decided to walk past the lot again that evening, just as dusk was settling, painting the sky in bruised shades of purple and orange. The cars still gleamed under the harsh glare of temporary floodlights that had been erected overnight. Earl was still there, his silhouette sharp against the light, talking to a young couple who looked like they'd just graduated high school. Their faces, even from a distance, were etched with a hopeful excitement that was almost painful to witness.

Martha remembered the stories she heard as a teenager about what happened in Cave City, Arkansas when a strange used car lot, *Benny's Bright Roads* opened up. That was some 40-years ago, but she remembered how her uncle had talked with disdain about Benny and his dark sidekick, who never spoke, and the used car lot and what it did to the town. Her uncle in hushed tones would speak about how after the initial euphoria of getting their impossibly cheap cars, things had started to unravel. The cars themselves, while initially pristine, began to develop strange, inexplicable problems. Minor glitches at first – a radio that wouldn't turn off, a headlight that flickered erratically. Then, more serious issues. Engines would sputter and die without warning. Brakes would fail on quiet, country roads. And always, the payments, though low, were due on time, with astronomical penalties for even a single day's delay.

She remembered the whispered tales around the kitchen table of the people in Cave City who had lost their homes, their meager savings, everything, to the seemingly benevolent financing. The cars, it turned out, were merely bait, a meticulously crafted lure to ensnare the unwary. The real profit, the real purpose, was something far more sinister.

As she stood there, a phantom wind – for there was no actual breeze – seemed to whisper around her. It carried with it the faint scent of something metallic, something acrid, a scent that was disturbingly reminiscent of the lingering industrial fumes that still clung to the air around the old mill.

She looked at the gleaming cars, at the hopeful faces of the people gathered around them, and a profound sense of dread washed over her. Redwater Crossing, in its quiet desperation, was walking headfirst into the same trap that had ensnared Cave City all those years ago. The cycle was not just repeating; it was beginning anew, and the same insidious force that had preyed on one town was now casting its hungry gaze upon another. *Benny's Bright Roads* had reappeared as Earl's Honest Rides, a wolf in sheep's clothing, its bright colors and enticing prices a thinly veiled promise of ruin. The dreams it offered were not dreams of freedom, but dreams that would ultimately consume them.

The Master, a being whose rejuvenation was not measured in years but in the deepening of his ancient hunger, surveyed Redwater Crossing with a keen, almost paternal, satisfaction. The desolation of the town, the palpable air of weary resignation, was a canvas he knew intimately, a landscape ripe for his particular brand of cultivation. He moved amongst the townsfolk not as a predator, but as a benevolent shepherd, his aura radiating a calm, benevolent authority that belied the churning darkness within. His physical manifestation, the 'tall man' as he was known, remained a silent sentinel, a figure sculpted from shadow and an unnerving stillness, his presence a potent amplification of the unspoken fears and burgeoning desires that festered beneath the surface of Redwater Crossing's fragile hope.

He had always been a collector, not of trinkets or treasures, but of essence. The essence of a town's despair, the intoxicating aroma of desperation – these were his sustenance, his very lifeblood. He had observed the predictable ebb and flow of human frailty in countless settlements, watching as hope, like a flickering candle in a storm, was inevitably extinguished. Redwater Crossing was no different, yet it possessed a peculiar resonance, a depth of despair that promised a particularly rich harvest. He saw the way the eyes of the townsfolk would widen at the sight of the impossible cars, the way their hands would tremble as they reached out to touch the gleaming chrome. It was a symphony of longing, a prelude to the inevitable descent.

His role as the charismatic buyer for Earl's Honest Rides was merely a carefully orchestrated disguise, a stage upon which he could conduct his subtle orchestra of manipulation. He did not need to overtly command; his power lay in suggestion, in the art of unveiling the hidden desires that people themselves were too ashamed or too weary to acknowledge. He was the whisper in their ear, the subtle nudge towards the precipice. He saw the young couple, their faces alight with the naive joy of newly acquired freedom and felt a surge of something akin to pride. They were so eager, so utterly unaware of the intricate web being spun around them. Their dreams of open roads and boundless futures were the very threads he used to bind them.

"Isn't she a beauty?" Earl murmured, his voice a low, resonant hum that seemed to vibrate in the very air around the young man, a recent graduate named Connor. The car was a sporty red convertible, its polished surface reflecting the fading sunlight like a captured sunset. Connor, his eyes glued to the sleek lines of the vehicle, could only nod, a breathless gasp escaping his lips. "My... my whole life, I've dreamed of something like this," he stammered, his voice thick with emotion. "Something to get me out of here, you know? To see something more."

Earl's smile widened, a slow, deliberate unfolding that held no trace of genuine warmth. "And here it is, Connor," he said, his gaze sweeping over the young man, taking in the raw yearning etched onto his features. "Sometimes, all it takes is the right opportunity, the right honest deal. Here at Earl's we believe in giving folks a chance. A real chance to get their dreams rolling." He placed a gentle hand on the car's hood, his touch lingering as if imprinting his will upon the metal. "This car... it's more than just metal and rubber, isn't it? It's a promise. A promise of adventure, of escape."

In the distance, behind him, the 'tall man' remained a statue of silent observation. He was the Master and his physical presence was the anchor that tethered his ancient power to this mortal realm. His stillness was profound, a void that seemed to absorb the sounds and sights of the bustling car lot, drawing the attention of those nearby with an almost magnetic pull. His gaze, though seemingly unfocused, seemed to penetrate the surface of things, to see the hidden anxieties and desires that the Master so expertly exploited. He was the unspoken threat, the palpable weight of consequence that hung over every transaction, a silent amplification of the burgeoning unease that even the most hopeful of Redwater Crossing's residents could not entirely shake.

Earl's attention then shifted to a woman, Heather, her face etched with a familiar weariness, clutching a worn handbag as she eyed a sensible, yet impossibly affordable, minivan. Heather was a single mother, her days a relentless struggle to provide for her two young children. The dilapidated state of her current vehicle was a constant source of anxiety, a potential barrier to everything from grocery runs to doctor's appointments.

"This one," Earl said, his voice softening, a carefully crafted paternal concern coloring his tone, "this is a fine choice, Heather. Practical. Reliable. Exactly what a mother needs." He opened the sliding door, revealing a pristine interior, smelling faintly of new car polish. "Think of the ease, Heather. No more worrying about breakdowns. No more missed school plays or doctor's visits. Just smooth sailing." He met her gaze, his eyes holding a depth that seemed to understand her every struggle. "Here at Earl's we know that family is everything. That's why we make these deals. Our benefactor," Earl leaned in, his tone lowered as if imparting a secret that no one should overhear. "The Master, that's what I call him, believes everyone deserves a safe, dependable ride for their loved ones."

Heather's eyes welled up, a tear tracing a path through the dust on her cheek. "It's... it's just so much more than I could ever afford," she whispered, her voice choked. "I don't understand how..."

"Here at Honest Earl's," Earl finished for her, his smile returning, bright and reassuring. "The Master has a good heart. And he believes in the good of people. He sees your hard work, Heather. He sees you trying your best. And he wants to help." He gently closed the van door, the sound a soft thud that seemed to seal her fate. "A small down payment, a few easy payments, and this is all yours. Imagine the peace of mind."

The Master stood a little distance away, his shadow stretching long and distorted across the asphalt. A group of teenagers, drawn by the inexplicable aura of power surrounding him, had gathered at a safe distance, whispering amongst themselves. They didn't dare approach, but their eyes were fixed on him, a mixture of fear and morbid fascination evident in their young faces. He was the embodiment of the unknown, the silent testament to the ancient forces that lurked beneath the veneer of normalcy. He was the shadow that accompanied the light, the unseen consequence that clung to every seemingly benevolent offer.

Earl continued his rounds, a maestro of manufactured generosity. He spoke with an elderly couple, Mr. and Mrs. Henderson, whose worn-out sedan had finally coughed its last breath. They had been contemplating walking to the next town for groceries, a grim prospect in the dwindling daylight. He presented them with a practically new, fuel-efficient compact car, its price point so ludicrously low it felt like a hallucination.

"This little beauty will save you a fortune on gas," Earl assured them, his hand resting on the car's roof. "And think of the ease, Mr. Henderson. No more struggling with that old clunker. You'll be zipping around town like you were twenty again." He winked, a gesture that was both charming and deeply unsettling. "Earl's Honest Rides. We get you where you need to go, without breaking the bank."

Mr. Henderson, his hands gnarled with age and hard work, reached out and touched the car's pristine paint. "It's... it's a miracle," he breathed, his voice raspy with disbelief. "We didn't think we'd ever be able to afford anything like this again."

"Miracles happen when you're honest, Mr. Henderson," Earl replied smoothly, his gaze lingering on the couple's hopeful, albeit slightly bewildered, faces. "And the Master is the most honest man I know." He didn't need to force them; their own desperation did the work for him. He merely provided the exquisite temptation, the shimmering bait that would draw them inevitably into his snare.

The 'tall man' in the distance shifted his weight, a subtle movement that nonetheless sent a ripple of unease through the onlookers. It was a gesture that spoke of immense, barely contained power, a silent promise of something far beyond human comprehension. He was the unseen hand guiding the unfolding drama, the silent witness to the meticulous plan. His presence was a constant reminder that this was no ordinary sales event, that the seemingly benign transactions were merely a prelude to something far more profound, far more terrifying.

As the sun dipped below the horizon, casting long, eerie shadows across the lot, the Master stood on a small, raised platform, a beam of the dying light illuminating his face. The sounds of excited chatter and the roar of engines being test-driven filled the air. He surveyed the scene, his expression unreadable. The desperation in Redwater Crossing was a potent elixir, a potent fuel for his ancient rejuvenation. He had planted the seeds, watered them with false promises and impossibly low prices, and now he watched, with a predator's patience, as they began to sprout.

One could almost feel the surge of energy within him, a vibrant hum that resonated with the collective yearning of the town. This was his art, his domain. To witness the unraveling of hope, to orchestrate the descent from fragile optimism to utter despair. The Master stood as a silent monolith against the twilight sky, his presence casting a long, dark shadow over the jubilant scenes unfolding below. Redwater Crossing was now firmly ensnared in the Master's web, and the cycle, as it always did, was beginning anew, painted in the vibrant, deceptive hues of Earl's Honest Rides. The true cost, the real price of these dreams, remained unseen, a chilling promise whispered only in the rustling leaves of the encroaching night, a promise that would soon echo through the very soul of this unsuspecting town. The Master could almost taste it, the potent essence of their impending downfall, a flavor more exquisite than any he had savored in millennia.

Sheriff Mason Brody felt the familiar prickle of unease crawl up his spine the moment he drove past Earl's Honest Rides. It was a sensation he hadn't experienced with such intensity since Redwater Crossing, a town he'd once sworn he'd never revisit in his mind, let alone in the grim reality of his duty. But here it was again, this same unsettling tableau: a gleaming, impossibly well-stocked car lot blooming like a poisonous flower in the heart of Redwater Crossing, radiating an aura of too-good-to-be-true promises. The 'tall man,' that unnerving sentinel of silent observation, was present, a dark, unmoving statue against the vibrant chaos of polished chrome and eager faces. And then there was the man himself, Earl. The charmer, the purveyor of dreams wrapped in steel and affordable payments – Earl, where everyone in Redwater Crossing by now knew him by that name. Mason knew this type of person. He knew the scent of it, the cloying sweetness of desperation masking something far more sinister, something ancient and predatory.

He'd seen it before. The way the townsfolk, worn down by the relentless grind of their lives, their faces etched with the permanent lines of worry and unmet needs, gravitated towards the impossible deals. He was seeing it now, how the lure of a new start, a shiny escape vehicle, had blinded good people to the gaping maw of the abyss that lay just beyond the gleaming tires. He remembered the frantic, futile warnings he'd issued then, how he'd been dismissed as a man haunted by his own demons, too steeped in tragedy to see the simple, benevolent truth of the situation. And he remembered, with a cold dread that seeped into his bones, how wrong he had been to let them dismiss him.

Mason pulled his cruiser over to the side of the road, the tires crunching on the gravel shoulder. He watched the scene unfold with a heavy heart. A young couple, faces alight with a joy that felt almost defiant against the backdrop of Redwater Crossing's usual gloom, were practically swooning over a sporty convertible. A harried-looking mother, her eyes scanning the rows of minivans, clutched her worn handbag like a shield, her desperation a palpable thing in the humid afternoon air. An elderly couple, their gait slower than Mason's own weary pace, were being ushered towards a fuel-efficient sedan, their disbelief evident in their hesitant smiles. It was a repeat performance; a chilling echo of a nightmare he had hoped was confined to the scared landscape of his memory.

He sighed, the sound a ragged breath against the growing hum of excitement emanating from the car lot. He knew his words would likely fall on deaf ears. The people of Redwater Crossing were not foolish; they were simply... hopeful. And hope, when nurtured by desperation, could be a blinding force. They saw an escape from their immediate struggles, a tangible solution to their financial woes, a ticket to a brighter future that had always seemed just out of reach. Who was he, a tired sheriff with a past that clung to him like damp earth, to burst their fragile bubble?

Yet, he had to try. He'd learned that lesson at a terrible cost. He couldn't stand by and watch history repeat itself, not when he carried the ghosts of those who had been consumed by similar promises. He had to at least plant a seed of doubt, a sliver of caution, however small. He gripped the steering wheel, his knuckles white. He would go over there. He would speak to them. He would try to make them see what he saw, even if they chose not to believe him.

He got out of his cruiser, the familiar weight of his service weapon a cold comfort against his hip. As he approached the lot, the Master's gaze, sharp and unnervingly perceptive, flickered towards him. A subtle shift in the Master's posture, a tightening around the eyes that was almost imperceptible, but Mason caught it. The Master recognized him. Or, at least, he recognized the obstacle. The charmer's smile widened, a practiced, benevolent expression that did nothing to mask the predatory glint in his eyes.

Mason walked onto the lot, the smell of new car polish and something else, something faintly metallic and unsettling, filling his nostrils. He nodded curtly to the Master, his expression grim. The townsfolk, caught in the intoxicating thrall of their potential purchases, barely registered his presence.

"Beautiful day for a drive, Sheriff," Earl said, his voice smooth as polished obsidian. He gestured with a sweep of his hand, encompassing the dazzling array of vehicles. "We're doing some wonderful business today. Helping folks get into dreams they thought were out of reach."

Mason's gaze swept over the lot, taking in the eager faces, the way their hands lingered on the sleek surfaces of the cars. He saw the same hunger he'd seen before, the same desperate yearning for something more, something better. He focused on the young couple, Connor and his girlfriend, Sarah, their faces flushed with excitement as they admired a cherry-red convertible.

"Connor, Sarah," Mason began, his voice deliberately casual, though a knot of tension tightened in his gut. "That's a fine-looking car. Looks fast."

Connor, his eyes still sparkling, turned to Mason. "Sheriff! Yeah, it's amazing. I've never seen anything like it for this price. Earl here... he's a magician."

Earl chuckled, a low, resonant sound that didn't quite reach his eyes. "Just honest business, Sheriff. The Master believes in the power of a good deal to lift people up."

Mason met Earl's gaze, his own expression unyielding. "I've seen 'good deals' before," Mason motioned towards the Master. "Mr. ...?" He paused, deliberately letting the question hang in the air. No one knew his name, and Mason wasn't going to ask for a pseudonym.

"Just call him the Master," Earl replied smoothly, his smile unwavering. "It's what I've called him for years. And the Master... well, the Master is a legend in his own right."

"Right," Mason said, his tone flat. He turned his attention back to Connor and Sarah. "Connor, you're looking to get out of Redwater, right? See the world?"

Connor nodded eagerly. "That's the plan! This car... it's the first step."

"That's good," Mason said, forcing himself to keep his voice even. "But make sure you understand what you're getting into. These prices... they're almost unbelievable." He glanced at the Master, a subtle challenge in his eyes. "What's the catch?"

Earl's smile didn't falter. "No catch, Sheriff. The Master believes in giving people a chance. He takes a risk; we offer a dream. It's a simple exchange." Earl turned his attention to Heather, the single mother he'd seen earlier, now standing beside a pristine minivan, her face a mixture of hope and trepidation. "Heather," he said, his voice taking on a solicitous tone, "you were looking at this beauty. Imagine the freedom, Heather. No more worrying about breakdowns. Just peace of mind for you and the kids."

Heather looked from Earl to Mason, a flicker of confusion in her eyes. "It... it is a dream, Mr. Earl. I don't know how I can afford it."

"The Master makes it possible," Earl said, his hand resting gently on the minivan's door. "The Master scours the nation for the best deals. That's why I refer to him as the Master." Earl explained and leaned in. "A small down payment, a few manageable installments. It's designed for families like yours." He then met Mason's gaze again, a silent message passing between them.

You can't stop this. They want it.

Mason ignored the unspoken taunt. He stepped closer to Heather, lowering his voice. "Heather, I don't want to scare you, but I've seen situations like this before. Where the deals seem too good to be true, and they usually are. You need to be careful. Read everything. Understand every single word in that contract." He looked pointedly at the Master. "And make sure you know exactly what you're signing away."

Heather's brow furrowed. "Signing away? What do you mean, Sheriff?"

"I mean," Mason said, choosing his words carefully, "sometimes the 'payments' aren't just about money. Sometimes there are other... obligations. Things that aren't clearly written down." He glanced at the Master, who stood at the edge of the lot, an impassive figure, his silence more unnerving than any threat. Mason felt a chill cascade down his spine as the Master's head slowly turned, his gaze, or what felt like it, fixing on Mason. It was a gaze that felt ancient, alien, and utterly without warmth.

Earl chuckled again, a sound that was growing increasingly irritating to Mason. "Sheriff, you're letting your past cloud your judgment. These are honest folks, making honest deals. We're not here to trick anyone. We're here to help." He clapped Mason on the shoulder, a gesture that felt both patronizing and subtly menacing. "Redwater Crossing needs a little bit of good fortune, and Earl's Honest Rides is here to deliver it."

Mason stiffened under Earl's touch. He pulled away, his jaw tight. "I'm just doing my job as the Sheriff. Looking out for the people of this town."

He saw the subtle shift in the crowd. Some of the townsfolk were starting to look uneasy, their initial excitement tempered by Mason's somber warnings. They exchanged glances, a murmur of doubt rippling through them. But the allure of the cars, the dream of escape, was a powerful force. Earl, sensing the wavering, moved quickly to reassert his control.

"Let's not let a little skepticism dampen everyone's spirits," Earl announced, his voice carrying across the lot. He clapped his hands together, a sharp, decisive sound. "Who's next? Who wants to drive away in a brand new life today?"

He pointed to a family who had just arrived, their faces a picture of weary hope. Mason watched as Earl, with his practiced charm and disarming smile, drew them in, weaving his web of promises around them. He saw the flicker of indecision in their eyes, the struggle between caution and desire, and he knew, with a sickening certainty, that desire would win.

He turned and walked back towards his cruiser, the unease in his gut deepening into a gnawing dread. He had said what he could. He had tried to sow seeds of doubt, to remind them of the lessons he'd learned the hard way. But the pull of the Master's influence, the intoxicating promise of instant gratification, was too strong. He had seen it before, this cycle of desperation and false hope, and he knew, with a certainty that chilled him to the bone, that Redwater Crossing was now caught in its deadly embrace. The 'tall man' remained at the edge of the lot, a silent, ominous sentinel, his shadow lengthening as the sun began its descent, a harbinger of the darkness that was already beginning to seep into the heart of the unsuspecting town. He had warned them. Now, all he could do was watch and wait, praying that the cost of their dreams wouldn't be too high. But deep down, he feared he already knew the answer. The patterns were too familiar, the allure too potent. The cycle, once set in motion, rarely deviated from its tragic course. He could almost hear the whispers of the wind, carrying the echoes of past mistakes, a mournful lament for the souls soon to be ensnared.

Harmony Jakes found herself instinctively recoiling the moment her eyes landed on Earl's Honest Rides. It wasn't a conscious decision, more like a primal flinch, a deep-seated warning echoing from some buried corner of her being. The air around the car lot felt thick, cloying, like cheap perfume trying to mask a stench that was undeniably foul. Unlike the throngs of Redwater Crossing residents who seemed to be drawn to the gleaming chrome and impossibly low prices like moths to a flame, Harmony felt only a profound sense of unease, a visceral revulsion that curdled in her stomach.

She'd heard the buzz, of course. Whispers and excited chatter about the new car lot that had sprung up overnight, offering deals too good to be true. People were ecstatic, their faces alight with a desperate hope that Harmony found more disturbing than any overt threat. They spoke of Earl, a charismatic man who seemed to possess an uncanny ability to make dreams tangible, to bridge the chasm between meager paychecks and the desire for a better life. But Harmony saw something else. The Master and the way his smile never quite reached his eyes, the unsettling stillness of the impossibly tall man who stood sentinel at the periphery of the lot, a shadow carved from granite.

From her vantage point across the dusty street, tucked away in the relative anonymity of the bakery's side entrance, Harmony watched the unfolding spectacle with a keen, critical eye. Sheriff Brody had been there earlier, his presence a grim counterpoint to the carnival atmosphere. She'd seen him speak to a few people, his body language radiating a weary concern. She'd even seen him interact with Earl, a brief, tense exchange that had ended with Earl's infuriatingly smooth smile and a patronizing clap on the Sheriff's shoulder. Harmony had felt a surge of something akin to loyalty towards the Sheriff, a fellow traveler in this town's quiet desperation, but she also sensed that his warnings, however well-intentioned, were likely to be drowned out by the intoxicating siren song of instant gratification.

Earl was a performer, Harmony realized. He moved through the crowd with an effortless grace, his words weaving a tapestry of promises, each thread meticulously chosen to appeal to the deepest desires of his audience. He spoke of freedom, of escape, of a fresh start. He addressed them by name, remembered details about their lives, creating an illusion of personal connection that was as potent as any drug. Harmony, however, saw the strings being pulled, the masterful manipulation of manufactured scarcity and manufactured desire. She saw the predatory gleam in his eyes when he focused on a particularly vulnerable target, the way his head tilted slightly, like a hawk spotting its prey.

And then there was the tall man, the Master. He was a constant presence, an unnerving anomaly. He never spoke, never moved with any discernible purpose beyond his silent vigil. He was simply *there*, an immoveable object against the backdrop of a town constantly in motion, however sluggishly. His sheer physical presence was disquieting, his proportions seemingly stretched and distorted, making him appear less human and more like a grotesque monument to something ancient and unsettling. Harmony found her gaze drawn to him repeatedly, a morbid fascination taking root. There was a stillness about him that suggested immense power, a coiled tension that spoke of capabilities far beyond human comprehension. It was the kind of stillness that precedes a storm, or a predator's strike.

Unlike the other residents, Harmony didn't feel the intoxicating allure of the cars. She saw them for what they were – pieces of metal and plastic, conduits for a dream that felt inherently false. The 'honest deals' struck Harmony as an oxymoron. There was nothing honest about the palpable hunger she saw on the faces of the people flocking to the lot, a hunger that went far beyond a desire for a new vehicle. It was a hunger for validation, for escape, for a tangible symbol of success in a town that offered little of either.

She remembered her own past, a tapestry woven with threads of hardship and a quiet, gnawing desperation. She'd learned early on to trust her instincts, to listen to the small, persistent voice that whispered caution when things felt too good to be true. She'd seen people get what they wanted, only to find themselves trapped in a different kind of cage, the bars forged not of steel, but of unforeseen consequences and escalating debts. This situation at Earl's Honest Rides had that same acrid scent of impending disaster.

Harmony's gaze lingered on a young woman, no older than herself, animatedly discussing a sleek, black sedan with Earl. The woman's eyes sparkled with an almost feverish excitement, her hands gesturing wildly as she spoke. Harmony saw the desperation etched around her eyes, the faint lines of worry that even Earl's practiced charm couldn't entirely erase. It was the look of someone clinging to a lifeline, someone who had perhaps been told their entire life that they were destined for less, and who now saw a chance to defy that fate. Harmony felt a pang of sympathy, but it was overshadowed by a deeper, more chilling dread. She knew, with a certainty that settled heavily in her chest, that this young woman was not just buying a car; she was signing away something far more precious.

Earl's attention shifted, his attention snagged by a middle-aged man who approached him hesitantly, clutching a worn piece of paper. Earl's smile widened, his body language shifting subtly, becoming more inviting, more reassuring. Harmony watched as he took the paper, scanned it with an almost imperceptible flick of his eyes, and then made a show of nodding, a gesture of understanding and approval. The man's shoulders seemed to relax, a small smile of relief breaking through his worried frown. Harmony felt a cold dread coil in her gut. She recognized that look of relief. It was the look of a cornered animal that had just been offered a seemingly safe path out of its trap, only to be led further into the snare.

She thought about the stories that circulated in Redwater Crossing, hushed tales of unexplained disappearances, of people who had simply... vanished. Most dismissed them as gossip, the product of a small town's overactive imagination. But Harmony had always felt a disquieting resonance with those stories, a sense that they were not mere fiction. Now, watching the smooth maneuverings of the car lot unfold, those whispers seemed to gain a new, terrifying significance. The 'honest deals' and the 'fresh starts' felt less like opportunities and more like bait.

Harmony felt a sudden urge to intervene, to step out from her hiding place and shout a warning. But what could she say? How could she articulate the formless dread that gripped her? "Be careful, he's a predator?" "That tall man is a bad omen?" They would look at her with pity, perhaps with suspicion, just another eccentric resident of Redwater Crossing. They wouldn't see what she saw. They couldn't. They were blinded by the dazzling promise of something better, something more.

She noticed the Master glancing in her general direction. His eyes, sharp and intelligent, swept over the street, a flicker of something unreadable crossing his face as they passed over her. It was a fleeting moment, but Harmony felt a prickle of awareness. He had seen her. Or at least, he had registered her presence, her stillness, her apparent lack of engagement with the intoxicating spectacle. She instinctively pulled back further into the shadows, a sense of being observed settling upon her.

The Master seemed to shift. His head, which had been facing outward, towards the main road, slowly, deliberately, turned towards the bakery. Harmony couldn't make out his features from this distance, but she felt the weight of his attention, an ancient, alien gaze that seemed to bore through the brick and mortar. It was a gaze that held no curiosity, no judgment, only a profound, unsettling stillness. It was the gaze of something that was not meant to be here, something that was profoundly *other*.

Harmony shivered, a chill that had nothing to do with the late afternoon heat. This wasn't just about cars and money. This was something else. Something darker. She watched as a group of teenagers, their faces flushed with youthful bravado, approached a row of sporty, low-slung vehicles. Earl greeted them with an even wider, more effusive smile, his voice taking on a tone of playful camaraderie. Harmony recognized the predatory gleam again. Earl wasn't just selling cars; he was preying on the youthful desire for rebellion, for independence, for the thrill of the open road. He was offering them an escape from the perceived monotony of their lives in Redwater Crossing, an escape that would undoubtedly come with a price far exceeding the sticker value of the car.

She saw Connor, the young man Sheriff Brody had spoken to earlier, now back on the lot with Sarah. They were standing by a sleek, red convertible, their heads bent close together, lost in their shared dream. Harmony felt a pang of sorrow for them. They were so young, so full of hope, so vulnerable. They saw a means of escape, a ticket to a new life. Harmony saw a gilded cage. She understood the allure, the desperate need to break free from the confines of a small town that offered limited opportunities and even fewer horizons. But she also knew that some cages, no matter how beautifully adorned, were still cages.

Harmony realized that her revulsion wasn't just about the perceived dishonesty of Earl or the unnerving presence of the Master. It was a deeper, more intuitive understanding of the forces at play. It was the recognition of a pattern, a cycle that she had perhaps glimpsed before, in different forms, in different places. It was the predatory nature of desperation, the seductive power of false promises, and the ancient hunger that lurked beneath the veneer of civilization. Redwater Crossing, in its quiet, unassuming way, had become a fertile ground for such forces, and Earl's Honest Rides was the perfect Trojan horse.

As the sun began to dip below the horizon, casting long, distorted shadows across the car lot, Harmony knew she couldn't simply stand by and watch. Her instincts, honed by a lifetime of navigating treacherous emotional and social landscapes, screamed at her to do something. She didn't have the Sheriff's authority, nor his experience. But she had her intuition, a keen sense of observation, and a growing certainty that the 'honest deals' offered at Earl's were anything but. She would have to find a way to make others see, to pry open their eyes to the danger lurking beneath the polished chrome and persuasive smiles. The cycle, she suspected, was only just beginning, and she was determined to disrupt it, even if it meant stepping out of the shadows and into the perilous glare of the Master's attention. The Master's gaze, she felt, was still fixed in her direction, a silent, chilling promise of what was to come.

CHAPTER 6

The Master's Grip
Tightens

T he hum of the town, usually a low thrum of predictable routines, had escalated into a feverish buzz around Earl's Honest Rides. It was a sound that resonated with a primal chord in Redwater Crossing, a collective yearning for something more, something *better*. Earl, with his practiced charisma and an uncanny knack for mirroring the unspoken desires of his audience, had struck gold. His words, slick as polished chrome, painted vivid landscapes of financial freedom, of lives unburdened by the perpetual weight of want. The cars, gleaming under the relentless sun, weren't just vehicles; they were chimeras, tangible manifestations of dreams long deferred, promises whispered in the quiet desperation of countless evenings.

Each gleaming fender, each impossibly low-price tag, was a carefully calibrated lure. Earl and the Master understood the psychology of need, the insidious way desperation could erode judgment. Earl spoke not just of transportation, but of escape routes, of social mobility, of the sheer, unadulterated joy of possessing something that signified success in a town where success felt like a mirage. He wove a narrative of empowerment, positioning himself as the benevolent facilitator, the one who had the key to unlock the gilded doors of prosperity for those who dared to believe. This wasn't just a sales pitch; it was an expertly crafted illusion, designed to resonate with the deepest wells of hope and ambition within each individual.

He'd seen the weariness etched into the faces of the people who shuffled through Redwater Crossing, the quiet resignation that settled in the bones after years of scraping by. He understood the gnawing dissatisfaction, the unspoken desire to prove their worth, not just to themselves, but to a world that had seemingly overlooked them. The cars at Earl's were the antidote, the tangible proof that they, too, could have nice things, that they, too, deserved a slice of the good life. The Master played on this with a surgeon's precision, his every word, every gesture, a deliberate stroke designed to bypass rational thought and appeal directly to the heart's deepest yearnings.

Consider Amy Baker, for instance. A widow for five years, her life had shrunk to the confines of her small, meticulously kept home and the part-time job at the diner. Her children, grown and moved far away, rarely called. The rumble of her aging sedan was the soundtrack to her isolation. When Earl spoke of freedom, of the open road, of visiting grandchildren without the nagging fear of a breakdown, something inside Amy shifted. The Master saw the way her eyes lit up when he casually mentioned a compact, fuel-efficient model that practically ran on hope and good intentions, a car so reliable it would practically drive itself to the bank. He saw the flicker of a long-dormant desire for independence, for the ability to simply *go*, to break the monotony. Earl didn't mention the astronomical interest rates or the predatory clauses tucked away in the fine print. He spoke only of possibility, of a renewed sense of agency, and Amy, like so many others, was captivated. The deal, she was told, was practically a gift, a gesture of goodwill from the Master to the good people of Redwater Crossing.

Then there was young John Conway, fresh out of high school, working at the lumber yard for just above minimum wage. His dreams were as big as the sky, but his reality was the same dusty streets he'd grown up on. He yearned for respect, for a symbol of his arrival, of his potential. The sleek, black muscle car on display, the one with the roaring engine and the impossibly low-down payment, spoke directly to that yearning. Earl, sensing John's ambition, positioned himself as a mentor, a man who understood the drive of youth. He spoke of turning heads, of commanding attention, of making a statement. He painted a picture of John, not as a lumber yard worker, but as a man of means, a man who had made it. The sheer audacity of the price, initially daunting, began to fade under Earl's persuasive onslaught. It wasn't a purchase; it was an investment in his future, a down payment on the man he was destined to become. The other patrons, caught in their own similar dreams, offered silent validation, their nods of approval further cementing John's conviction.

The Master's strategy was one of calculated empathy, a deep dive into the collective psyche of a town wrestling with its own perceived limitations. He understood that people didn't just want cars; they wanted solutions. They wanted to escape the judgment of their neighbors, the quiet pity of those who seemed to have more. They wanted to silence the nagging voice of self-doubt that whispered, *You'll never be more than this.* The Master offered a tangible rebuttal to those doubts, wrapped in gleaming paint and promising acceleration.

He'd also masterfully tapped into the inherent human desire for a good bargain. The phrase "honest deal" was a stroke of genius, a deliberate irony that, paradoxically, made the offers seem even more legitimate. It played on the deep-seated belief that everyone loves a bargain, and that if something seems too good to be true, it probably is – unless, of course, someone truly benevolent is offering it. The Master presented himself as that benevolent figure, a titan of industry with a heart of gold, dispensing his wealth and opportunities to the deserving denizens of Redwater Crossing. The fact that the deals were, in reality, predatory was a detail expertly obscured by the dazzling spectacle of supposed generosity.

Every interaction was a performance, a carefully orchestrated dance of persuasion. The Master had Earl who would touch shoulders, make direct eye contact, lean in conspiratorially as if sharing a profound secret. He'd praise their good fortune, compliment their discerning taste, and subtly reinforce the idea that they were among the chosen few to receive such an extraordinary offer. The tall, silent figure who stood sentinel at the edge of the lot served as a subtle, almost subliminal reinforcement of the Master's power. His sheer, imposing presence spoke of an authority, a gravitas that lent an undeniable weight to the Earl's pronouncements. He was the silent enforcer, the living embodiment of the unspoken terms of the deal.

The townspeople, in their collective yearning, were willing to overlook the slight inconsistencies. The fact that Earl's Honest Rides had appeared seemingly out of nowhere, that its inventory was impossibly vast and its prices astronomically low, these were merely details that spoke of the Master's extraordinary business acumen, not of anything sinister. The sheer volume of satisfied customers, the joyous honking of horns as people drove away in their new acquisitions, all served as powerful social proof, drowning out any nascent doubts. Skepticism, a luxury few in Redwater Crossing could afford, was quickly shed in the face of such overwhelming evidence of good fortune.

The Master had a particularly keen eye for those teetering on the brink of despair, those whose desperation made them most susceptible to his brand of salvation. He identified the individuals whose lives were a tapestry of frayed ends, whose hopes had been repeatedly dashed. To these individuals, he offered not just a car, but a lifeline, a symbol of resilience, a tangible victory against the tide of misfortune. Earl painted the Master as their champion, the one who saw their potential when no one else did, the one who believed in them enough to offer them a chance to rewrite their stories.

Patricia Summer, whose husband had left her with a mountain of debt and a broken spirit, was another such case. Earl noticed her lingering by a sensible, mid-sized SUV, her gaze distant, her shoulders slumped. He approached her not with a sales pitch, but with a quiet, understanding word. He spoke of reclaiming independence, of the freedom to move forward, of a vehicle that wouldn't just get her from point A to point B, but would propel her towards a new beginning. He didn't pressure her; he merely offered a possibility, a gentle nudge towards a brighter future. He alluded to special financing options, tailored just for those facing... *challenges.* The phrase hung in the air, a promise of understanding and leniency. He made her feel seen, validated, and empowered, all while subtly steering her towards a commitment that would bind her tighter than any debt ever could. The allure wasn't just in the price; it was in the promise of restoration, of reclaiming a life that had been stolen.

The Master was a master alchemist, transmuting raw desperation into unwavering loyalty. He understood that in a place like Redwater Crossing, where the promise of a better tomorrow was often just that – a promise – the tangible present, however illusory, held immense power. The cars were not just objects; they were artifacts of a perceived better life, badges of honor in a town that often felt invisible. And the Master, in his dazzling generosity, was the gatekeeper to this new reality, his every offer a testament to his magnanimity, and his grip on the town, ever tightening. The hum of excited chatter, the gleam of polished metal, the scent of new tires and manufactured dreams – it was all part of the intoxicating symphony that was drowning out reason and ushering in a deeper, darker melody.

The cacophony of Elmwood Drive had become a constant, a low-frequency thrum that vibrated in Harmony Jakes' bones. It wasn't the familiar soundtrack of Redwater Crossing—the distant rumble of trucks on the highway, the murmur of gossip from the diner, the occasional bark of a stray dog. This was something different, a pulsating energy emanating from the gaudy chrome and polished paint of Earl's Honest Rides. It was a seductive hum, a siren song that seemed to weave its way into the very fabric of the town, drawing everyone into its magnetic field. Everyone, it seemed, but Harmony.

From her perch behind the counter of the dusty antique shop, a space that smelled of old paper and forgotten lives, Harmony watched the spectacle unfold. She saw the glazed expressions on the faces of her neighbors as they drifted towards the dealership, their steps unnervingly light, their eyes fixed on the gleaming machines like moths to a flame. She heard Earl's voice, amplified by speakers strategically placed around the lot, a smooth, resonant baritone that dripped with a false sincerity. His words, carefully chosen, played on hopes and fears, painting visions of prosperity and escape. He spoke of freedom, of reinvention, of a life lived in the fast lane, a stark contrast to the slow, predictable churn of their existence.

Harmony felt none of it. Instead, a cold, sharp clarity settled in her mind, a stillness that stood in stark opposition to the town's collective frenzy. The Master's influence, which seemed to wrap around everyone else like an invisible, silken shroud, bounced off her as if she were made of Teflon. She'd tried, initially, to understand it. She'd lingered at the edge of the crowd, straining to catch the essence of the Master's allure, to feel the pull that had ensnared her friends, her customers, even Sheriff Brody, who, despite his initial reservations, had been seen test-driving a sedan that looked far too expensive for his modest salary. But for Harmony, it was like listening to static, a jumbled mess of promises that held no weight, no resonance.

It was more than just a lack of susceptibility; it was an active repulsion. When the Earl's pronouncements echoed through the air, Harmony felt a physical tightening in her chest, a subtle discord that grated against her senses. It was as if his carefully crafted optimism was a discordant note in the symphony of her own being, a jarring intrusion that she instinctively sought to silence. She found herself unconsciously clenching her fists, her jaw setting as she fought against a creeping nausea, a visceral rejection of the pervasive enchantment.

Her immunity wasn't a point of pride, but a source of growing dread. She felt like a lone lighthouse on a treacherous coast, its beam cutting through a fog that had swallowed everything else. While others saw salvation in the polished chrome of Earl's Honest Rides, Harmony saw only a deepening shadow, a subtle distortion of reality that she couldn't quite articulate. The smiles on people's faces seemed painted on, their laughter a little too loud, a little too forced. The newfound confidence in their steps felt like a borrowed swagger, an illusion they were desperately trying to maintain.

Sheriff Brody noticed. He noticed the way Harmony's brow would furrow, a silent question etched into its lines, as she watched the crowds at the dealership. He noticed the way she'd subtly steer conversations away from Earl's latest pronouncements, her gaze sharp and analytical, searching for something others seemed determined to ignore. He'd seen Earl's charm work its insidious magic on seasoned businessmen and hardened skeptics alike, but Harmony remained an island of unblinking clarity in a sea of willing delusion.

One sweltering afternoon, Sheriff Brody found himself nursing a lukewarm coffee as he headed towards Harmony's shop, the bell above the door tinkling a lonely welcome. The air was thick with the scent of aged paper and wood polish, a stark contrast to the cloying sweetness of cheap air fresheners that now seemed to permeate the rest of the town.

"Still holding out, Harmony?" He asked, his voice low, a hint of weariness in its tone. He gestured vaguely towards the street, where a small group of people were excitedly climbing into a newly purchased minivan.

Harmony offered a weak smile, her eyes tracing the intricate pattern on a faded Persian rug. "I don't think I ever signed up for the tune, Sheriff. It just doesn't... sound right to me."

Brody nodded, his gaze thoughtful. He understood the subtle nuances of Harmony's resistance. It wasn't defiance, not in the conventional sense. It was an innate, almost intuitive aversion to Earl and the Master's psychic manipulations. He'd felt it himself, a faint pressure behind his eyes, a subtle urge to agree, to embrace the rosy picture the Master painted. But Harmony's resistance was a solid wall, her mind a fortress that the Master's insidious whispers couldn't breach.

"You're like a... a radio tuned to a different frequency," he mused, swirling the coffee in his mug. "Everyone else is picking up his broadcast, but you're getting something else entirely. Something clearer."

"I just see what's there, Sheriff," Harmony replied, her voice barely above a whisper. "And what's there feels... off. The prices, the way people are acting, the way *he* acts. It's all too perfect, too... manufactured." She picked up a delicate porcelain doll from the counter, its painted smile eerily vacant. "It's like these dolls. They look pretty, but there's nothing behind the eyes."

Brody leaned back in a chair, the old wood groaning in protest. He'd been struggling to find a legal angle, a way to combat the Master's predatory practices without concrete evidence of fraud. The contracts were cleverly worded, the interest rates disguised, the promises vague enough to be deniable. But Harmony's immunity, her unwavering perception of the underlying falsity, was a more potent weapon than any law book. She was an anomaly, a glitch in the Master's meticulously designed system.

"That's what I'm afraid of," Brody said, his gaze meeting Harmony's. "He's preying on desperation, Harmony. And people are so eager for a way out, they're blind to the strings attached." He paused, a flicker of something akin to hope igniting in his eyes. "But you're not blind. You see the strings."

Harmony felt a tremor of fear, not for herself, but for what her awareness represented. She was an outsider now, a dissonant note in the town's increasingly harmonious tune. Her resistance made her conspicuous, a target. The Master's gaze, she felt, would eventually fall upon her, and she knew, with a chilling certainty, that he would not tolerate such defiance.

"What do I do, Sheriff?" she asked, her voice trembling slightly.

"You keep seeing what you see, Harmony," Brody said, his voice firm, laced with a newfound resolve. "You keep asking the questions no one else is asking. You're our eyes, Harmony. You're the one who hasn't fallen under his spell. And maybe," he added, a faint smile touching his lips, "maybe you're the only one who can help break it."

The weight of his words settled upon Harmony's shoulders. She was not just an observer anymore; she was a potential weapon, a beacon of resistance in a town slowly succumbing to an insidious darkness. The quiet clarity she had always cherished now felt like a heavy burden, a responsibility she hadn't asked for but couldn't ignore. The Master's grip was tightening on Redwater Crossing, but in Harmony Jakes, he had encountered an unforeseen, and perhaps insurmountable, resistance. Her immunity was not a passive state; it was an active defiance, a silent rebellion that was just beginning to stir. She was the discordant note, and she was determined to make herself heard, to shatter the illusion before it consumed them all. The antique shop, once a refuge, now felt like a strategic outpost, a place from which to observe and, when the time was right, to act. The hum of Elmwood Drive continued, but within Harmony, a different kind of sound was beginning to build—a low, steady rumble of defiance, waiting for its moment to roar.

Sheriff Brody's investigation had taken a turn he'd never anticipated, a sharp, unnerving descent into the realm of the uncanny.

The meticulously documented financial irregularities at Earl's Honest Rides, the suspicious testimonials, the subtle but pervasive shift in the town's collective mood – it all pointed to something far beyond mere predatory business practices. The Master, as he was so chillingly known, wasn't just a charismatic con man; he was a puppeteer pulling strings that seemed to vibrate with an unnatural energy. Brody, a man who prided himself on his grounded, logical approach, found himself grappling with a truth that defied rational explanation.

His office, once a sanctuary of order, now felt like a battleground. The fluorescent lights hummed with a new, oppressive intensity, and the familiar scent of stale coffee and worn leather seemed tainted by an unseen presence. He'd spent hours poring over case files, not just from Redwater Crossing, but from surrounding counties, and then further afield. He'd started with vague suspicions; whispers he'd picked up at county fairs and hushed conversations at regional police chiefs' conventions. Now, those whispers had coalesced into a chilling pattern.

There was the town of Oaklawn, a prosperous farming community that had inexplicably withered after a sleek, identical dealership, bearing the same ostentatious chrome and polished promises, had set up shop on its outskirts. Records indicated a sudden surge in bankruptcies, followed by a quiet exodus of its most industrious citizens. They'd vanished, leaving behind empty homes and fields that lay fallow, a stark testament to a vitality that had been inexplicably siphoned away. Then came King George, a mining town that had been revitalized, or so it had seemed, by a charismatic figure who promised riches and a new beginning. The prosperity was fleeting, a bright, ephemeral spark that quickly sputtered out, leaving the town in deeper desolation than before. The mining operations had shuttered, the workers' savings had evaporated, and a palpable despair had settled over the community like a shroud.

Brody meticulously charted these occurrences, linking them with dates and timelines that unnervingly overlapped with the arrival and subsequent departure of similar dealerships, all bearing the hallmarks of Earl's Honest Rides. The names of the proprietors varied, the local faces changed, but the underlying script, the insidious method, remained identical. Each town, in its turn, had been captivated by the allure of easy wealth and a promised escape from hardship. Each had succumbed, their vibrant spirit slowly extinguished, leaving behind hollow shells of their former selves.

He began to see the Master not as an individual, but as a force. It was a parasitic entity, a sophisticated predator that didn't hunt with fangs and claws, but with glittering promises and a sophisticated understanding of human desperation. It fed on the latent anxieties, the unspoken dreams of a better life, the gnawing dissatisfaction that festered beneath the surface of even the most placid communities. It was a malaise that settled over towns like a persistent fog, obscuring reason and fostering a blind faith in the impossible. The Master, Brody realized with a shiver, was the conductor of this symphony of ruin, his influence a chillingly effective contagion.

He started making discreet calls, using burner phones and encrypted channels to contact his counterparts in these affected towns. The conversations were fraught with a shared, unspoken dread. They spoke of the "salesman," the "evangelist," the "miracle worker," all descriptions that mirrored the townsfolk's current adoration of the Master. They recounted tales of neighbors who had become eerily detached, their conversations revolving solely around the dealership and its charismatic leader, their eyes holding a vacant, almost ecstatic sheen. The initial enthusiasm, they confirmed, always soured into a grim reality of debt, disillusionment, and ultimately, disappearance.

"He promised me the world," one sheriff in a town Brody couldn't even pronounce had confessed, his voice raspy with a grief that spanned years. "Said he'd set me up with a new life, a fresh start. I sold everything. My house, my truck... my wife's jewelry. And then... poof. He was gone. Took half the town's savings with him. Left us with nothing but the dust and the echoes of his lies."

The pattern was undeniable. The Master, or whatever entity he represented, was a seasoned entity, a creature of habit that refined its methods with each successive town it consumed. Brody felt a growing sense of urgency, a cold dread that tightened his chest with every new piece of information he uncovered. Redwater Crossing wasn't just another mark; it was another meal, another town destined to be hollowed out and discarded.

He started to see Earl's Honest Rides not as a business, but as a tumor, a malignant growth that had metastasized on the very heart of Redwater Crossing. The gleaming cars, the persuasive rhetoric, the increasingly fervent crowds – it was all a carefully orchestrated illusion, a stage set for a tragedy that was already in motion. He looked at the faces of his deputies, men he'd known for years, and saw the subtle shifts. The way Deputy Miller's eyes now seemed to linger on the glossy brochures scattered across his desk, the way Officer Davies had started humming a jingle he'd heard from the Earl's broadcasts. They were all susceptible, all dancing to the Master's tune, even if they didn't realize it.

Harmony Jakes, he thought, was the exception. Her unwavering clarity, her almost palpable resistance to the Master's influence, was becoming his most valuable asset. She was the only one who saw the strings, the only one who hadn't been lulled into a state of blissful ignorance. He felt a surge of protectiveness for her, and a grim determination to ensure her safety. She was a beacon in the encroaching darkness, and he couldn't let the Master extinguish her light.

He began to work late into the nights, the glow of his desk lamp the only illumination in the otherwise dark station. He documented every transaction, every interaction, every subtle anomaly he could find. He cross-referenced them with the information he was gathering from other towns, building a comprehensive profile of the Master's modus operandi. He wasn't just investigating a potential scam anymore; he was charting the movements of a supernatural predator, a force that thrived on despair and left a trail of ruin in its wake. The law books offered no solace, no precedents for the kind of enemy he now faced. He was venturing into uncharted territory, armed with little more than his intuition, a growing body of disturbing evidence, and the quiet, unyielding skepticism of an antique shop owner. The Master's grip was tightening, and Sheriff Brody knew, with a chilling certainty, that he was running out of time. He had to find a way to expose this entity, to sever its hold on Redwater Crossing before it was too late, before his town, like so many others, became just another forgotten footnote in a history of silent destruction.

The gilded promises of Earl's Honest Rides, once a siren song of prosperity, were beginning to warp into something far more sinister. The Master, a phantom in the guise of a benefactor, was orchestrating a symphony of discord, his invisible baton conducting a rising crescendo of unease that permeated every corner of Redwater Crossing. It wasn't enough to simply ensnare wallets; now, he was methodically dismantling the very bonds that held the community together, turning neighbor against neighbor, friend against friend, in a grotesque display of psychological warfare.

The initial euphoria, the collective gasp of wonder at the Master's seemingly boundless generosity, had begun to curdle. Beneath the veneer of shared optimism, old resentments, long buried beneath the dust of everyday life, were being unearthed and fanned into flames. Petty squabbles, once dismissed with a shrug and a shared laugh, were now magnified into bitter disputes. Mrs. Stevens, whose prize-winning roses had always been the envy of Elm Street, found herself in a shouting match with young Timmy Peterson's father over a fallen branch that had dared to encroach upon her meticulously manicured lawn. The argument, fueled by a new, raw edginess that clung to the air like static, escalated with astonishing speed. What had once been a minor inconvenience was now a declaration of war, their voices raw with an anger that seemed to spring from a deeper, more primal well. Brody, on his rounds, had overheard the venom in their exchanges, the way "Earl's Honest Rides" was carelessly woven into their accusations, as if the Master's influence had somehow granted them permission to unleash their accumulated frustrations. "He's showing us how to *truly* get ahead," Mrs. Stevens had shrieked, her face contorted, "by not letting anyone stand in your way!"

The dealership itself had become a focal point for this manufactured animosity. Conversations at the Saturday market, once filled with easy camaraderie and shared gossip about local happenings, were now punctuated by suspicious glances and hushed, accusatory whispers. Old Man Hennessy, a fixture at the farmer's market for forty years, found himself ostracized after he voiced his lingering doubts about the Master's rapid ascent. "He's too smooth," Hennessy had grumbled to anyone who would listen, his weathered face etched with a familiar skepticism. "Too good to be true, like a fresh coat of paint on a rotten barn." His pronouncements, once respected as the wisdom of experience, were now met with derision and outright hostility. The Master's devoted followers, their eyes glazed with an almost religious fervor, painted Hennessy as a bitter, jealous old fool, clinging to the past while the future, bright and gleaming like a new automobile, was passing him by. They would convene in hushed knots near the shimmering chrome of the displayed vehicles, their whispers laced with a venomous glee as they recounted Hennessy's supposed failings, their words sharper than any broken glass.

This pervasive paranoia began to seep into family units. Beyond the purchase of a car, Earl's Honest Rides offered simple investment opportunities in future car lots across the state. The financial incentives, the promises of lucrative "investment opportunities" and "early bird bonuses" at Earl's, created an invisible chasm within households. Fathers, eager to provide the lavish lifestyle dangled before them, began to pressure their wives and children to forgo even basic necessities, squirreling away every last penny in anticipation of a windfall that existed only in the Master's fervent pronouncements. Cindy Gerber, a usually pragmatic woman and the mother of two boisterous children, found herself in increasingly desperate arguments with her husband, Jerry. He had taken out a second mortgage on their modest home, convinced he would be able to pay it back tenfold within weeks thanks to a "special dividend" the Master's program had hinted at. Cindy, with her sharp mind and a grounding in practical economics, saw only the precipice of ruin. "Jerry, this is madness!" she had pleaded, her voice trembling, clutching a sheaf of papers that detailed their rapidly dwindling savings. "He's got you blinded! We have bills to pay; the kids need new shoes! This isn't prosperity, it's a delusion!" Jerry, his gaze fixed on a glossy brochure depicting luxury car lots, had simply waved her concerns away. "You don't understand, Cindy. This is our chance. The Earl said... we need to show faith in the Master. Those who are patient will be rewarded." His words, echoing the Earl's sermons about the Master, were a chilling testament to the insidious hold the man had on his mind, turning a loving husband and father into a blind devotee. The arguments became a nightly ritual, the air thick with unspoken accusations and the gnawing fear of what lay ahead.

Even the children were not immune to the Master's subtle manipulations. The dealership, with its bright lights and cheerful jingles, had become a tempting playground, a place where they were showered with small trinkets and saccharine compliments, their innocent minds easily swayed. They began to parrot the Master's slogans, their youthful voices innocent but their words echoing the growing divisiveness. Friendships fractured over perceived slights and stolen toys, with parents, their own anxieties amplified, often taking their children's childish disputes far too seriously, projecting their own insecurities and suspicions onto the innocent interactions. A game of tag in the park, once a joyous expression of childhood exuberance, could devolve into accusations of unfairness, of favoritism, as if the very fabric of playtime had been tainted by the Master's pervasive influence. Children would return home reporting playground gossip that mirrored the adult conversations, tales of how certain families were "wise" to invest, while others were "foolish" for holding back.

Sheriff Brody observed this slow, agonizing unraveling with a growing sense of dread. He saw the familiar faces of Redwater Crossing, faces he had known for years, contorted with suspicion and animosity. The warmth that had always characterized their interactions was being replaced by a chilling coldness, a wariness that made him deeply uneasy. He noticed how people avoided eye contact, how conversations abruptly ceased when he approached, replaced by nervous coughs and averted gazes. The town, once a tight-knit tapestry of shared experiences and mutual respect, was being systematically torn apart, thread by thread. The Master wasn't just selling cars; he was selling discord, trading in the currency of broken relationships and fractured trust.

He recalled the case files from Oaklawn and King George, the chilling echoes of similar social disintegration. The reports had mentioned a rise in domestic disputes, an increase in petty crime, a pervasive sense of isolation and mistrust. It was as if the Master's presence acted like a catalyst, bringing to the surface the latent anxieties and resentments that festered beneath the surface of any community, then amplifying them to a breaking point. He pictured the Master, not in the gleaming showroom, but in a dimly lit room, perhaps with charts and diagrams, meticulously planning the erosion of Redwater Crossing's social structure, understanding that a divided populace was a far more easily controlled populace. The financial ruin was the ultimate goal, but the psychological disintegration was the crucial, and perhaps more insidious, first step.

Harmony Jakes, with her keen observational skills and her inherent distrust of anything that felt too polished, had also noticed the shift. She spoke of it in hushed tones to Brody; her brow furrowed with concern. "It's like they're all walking on eggshells, Sheriff," she'd confided, her voice low. "One wrong word, one disagreement, and it explodes. People who have been friends for decades are suddenly avoiding each other. It's not just about the money anymore, is it? It's about something...deeper. Something meaner." She pointed out how conversations at the diner had become strained, how laughter felt forced, and how an undercurrent of tension was always present, like a low hum beneath a strained melody. She had witnessed a public argument between two long-time friends, a dispute over a trivial matter that quickly spiraled into accusations of betrayal and selfishness, their faces red with a fury that seemed out of proportion to the offense. They had stormed away from each other, their parting words laced with a bitterness that suggested the friendship, once so strong, might be irrevocably broken.

Brody understood. The Master was employing a classic tactic of oppression: divide and conquer. By fostering internal strife, he weakened the community's ability to resist him. When people were focused on their neighbors' perceived transgressions, their attention was diverted from the Master's own machinations. The paranoia he sowed created fertile ground for his ultimate control. Individuals, isolated by suspicion and fear, were less likely to band together, less likely to question his authority, and far more likely to seek solace and security in his charismatic embrace, believing he was the only constant in a world that had suddenly become unpredictable and hostile. He was turning Redwater Crossing into a house divided against itself, a strategy as old as time, and as devastatingly effective as ever. The psychological warfare was not a side effect of his scheme; it was the core of it, the unseen weapon that ensured his ultimate victory. He was not merely a con man; he was a master architect of social decay, and Redwater Crossing was his latest, most ambitious project.

The air in Sheriff Brody's office had always held a faint scent of stale coffee and the comforting, if slightly musty, aroma of aging paper. But lately, it felt different. A subtle, cloying sweetness, almost floral but with an unsettling undertone, had begun to permeate the space, like a perfume left too long in a closed room, its initial pleasantness curdled into something sickly. He'd tried to pinpoint its source, attributing it to an errant air freshener or perhaps a lingering trace from Mrs. Steven's aggressive rose fertilizer, but it persisted, a phantom scent that seemed to cling to the very walls. This olfactory disturbance was merely another layer in the increasingly disorienting reality of Redwater Crossing, a town that was subtly, insidiously, shifting beneath his feet.

He found himself spending more and more time poring over the old town archives, a collection of brittle, yellowed documents that were more often consulted for historical trivia than for any pressing investigative need. The Master's methods were so... *unconventional*. The financial persuasions and the psychological manipulation were textbook criminal enterprises, albeit executed with a chilling finesse. But there was an *otherness* to it all, a feeling that the Master was operating on a plane beyond mere avarice. Brody found himself drawn to the forgotten corners of Redwater Crossing's history, to the whispers and the folklore that the townspeople, in their current state of heightened suspicion and factionalism, had little patience for.

It was in a dusty, leather-bound volume, detailing local oral traditions and superstitions, that he first encountered the phrase: *the Rooms Between*. The passage was brief, almost an aside, couched in the kind of allegorical language that characterized much of early folklore. It spoke of a liminal space, a place not of this world and yet intrinsically connected to it, where things misplaced, forgotten, or intentionally hidden could find a peculiar form of refuge. The text described them as *thresholds of perception*, places where the veil between the tangible and the ethereal grew thin, allowing for the possibility of passage, though seldom return. Initially, Brody had dismissed it as fanciful nonsense, the kind of superstitious rambling that often accompanied periods of societal unease. Yet, the phrase snagged in his mind, a burr of curiosity he couldn't quite dislodge.

He began to notice other, similar allusions, scattered like breadcrumbs through the historical records. An old diary entry from a reclusive farmer spoke of *borrowed time spent in the quiet spaces where echoes reside*. A collection of folk songs, painstakingly transcribed by a long-dead folklorist, contained a verse about *the silent corridors where yesterday waits for tomorrow*. Each mention, vague and easily explainable away as metaphorical language, began to coalesce into a pattern, a subtle undercurrent of belief in something beyond the ordinary physical realm. These weren't just fanciful tales; they were threads woven into the very fabric of Redwater Crossing's collective unconscious, fragments of a shared understanding of a reality that possessed hidden depths.

The Master's influence was so pervasive, so all-encompassing, that it felt as though he had woven himself into the very fabric of the town's existence. The financial ruin he orchestrated was palpable, the broken relationships were undeniable, but Brody felt an intangible element at play, something that transcended mere greed and manipulation. He recalled the reports from Oaklawn and King George, the chilling accounts of how entire communities had been systematically dismantled. The official reports spoke of economic collapse, of psychological distress, but Brody sensed a missing piece, a reason for the sheer *completeness* of the Master's victory in those towns, a victory that felt too absolute, too... unnatural.

He remembered a particular detail from the King George investigation, a recurring mention of residents feeling "disconnected" from their own lives, as if they were observing themselves from a distance. It had been chalked up to mass hysteria and the stress of financial ruin. But what if it was more? What if these *Rooms Between* were not just theoretical concepts but actual places, accessible perhaps by someone with the Master's particular brand of... whatever it was he possessed?

He found himself drawn to the abandoned sections of town, the dilapidated buildings that had long been left to rot. The old Peterbilt Mill, its skeletal remains silhouetted against the bruised twilight sky, felt like a place that might hold such secrets. Locals whispered that it was haunted, that time itself moved differently within its crumbling walls. Brody had always dismissed such tales, grounding himself in the tangible evidence of his profession. But now, he saw a different possibility. Could these *hauntings* be echoes, remnants of individuals who had stumbled into these liminal spaces, their presence lingering like a forgotten scent?

He revisited the few remaining King George residents who had agreed to speak with him, their voices hollow with a despair that still clung to them years later. They spoke of a pervasive sense of loss, not just of material possessions, but of self. One woman, a Mrs. Lori Wilber, her face a roadmap of grief, had described her husband's descent into a fugue state. "He... he just wasn't *there* anymore, Sheriff," she'd said, her voice barely a whisper. "He'd stare at the wall for hours. Not seeing anything, but not blind either. Like he was... somewhere else. And when he did speak, it was like he was trying to remember words from a language he'd once known, but had forgotten."

Brody had initially attributed this to severe depression. But now, listening to her describe his vacant eyes, the way he would sometimes reach out as if to grasp something just beyond his reach, he saw a chilling parallel to the disconnectedness he'd heard about. Was it possible that the Master, through his machinations, was somehow... *accessing* these *Rooms Between*, drawing people into them, or perhaps isolating them within them? The thought sent a cold dread through him, a feeling of confronting an enemy far more ancient and terrifying than any he had ever imagined.

He recalled the incident at the Redwater Crossing quarry, the one where young Fred Tiller had claimed to have seen *a door that wasn't there* before vanishing for nearly two hours, only to reappear at the edge of town, disoriented and unable to recall anything of his disappearance. At the time, it had been written off as a child's vivid imagination, a story concocted to explain his being lost. But the mention of a door, a gateway, struck a new chord. Could Tiller have accidentally stumbled upon one of these *Rooms Between*? And if so, what had he experienced in that brief, unaccounted-for time?

The Master's rhetoric, so carefully crafted to inspire hope and financial prosperity, now seemed like a deliberate misdirection, a siren song designed to lure people away from recognizing the true nature of his domain. His sermons, delivered by Earl, were filled with promises of abundance and success, were also laced with veiled references to *finding your true place* and *unlocking hidden potential*. Brody began to dissect these sermons with a newfound intensity, searching for hidden meanings, for the subtle hints that pointed towards something far more sinister than a Ponzi scheme. He imagined the Master not in a brightly lit showroom, but in some clandestine space, perhaps within these very *Rooms Between*, orchestrating his symphony of despair from a vantage point that defied conventional understanding.

He found a tattered pamphlet, buried deep within the town's historical society archives, titled *Whispers from the Unseen: A Guide to*

Redwater Valley's Hidden Places. It was written by a local eccentric from the early 20th century, a woman named Ellen Abe. Ellen wrote extensively about places where the *mundane world frayed at the edges*, locations where the air felt thick with unseen presences and where shadows seemed to possess a life of their own. She described these as "portals," not in the sci-fi sense, but as liminal spaces where one could slip through the cracks of reality. She explicitly mentioned a specific cluster of locations within Redwater Crossing itself: the aforementioned Peterbilt Mill, the deep, still waters of Parker's Pond, and the ancient, gnarled oak tree at the crest of Whisperwind Hill. These weren't places of physical danger, according to Ellen, but places of profound spiritual and psychological risk, where the unwary could become lost, not just in space, but in time and self.

Brody looked out his office window at the distant silhouette of Whisperwind Hill. The ancient oak, a solitary sentinel against the sky, had always been a landmark, a silent witness to generations of Redwater Crossing life. He had never considered it anything more than a tree. But now, Ellen Abe's words echoed in his mind: *the silent corridors where yesterday waits for tomorrow.* Was it possible that these locations, these seemingly ordinary places, were in fact entrances, thresholds to the Master's true domain? If so, the implications were staggering. He wasn't just dealing with a criminal; he was dealing with someone who could manipulate reality itself, someone who operated within the very seams of existence. The financial ruin was a byproduct, a consequence of people being drawn into these *Rooms Between*, their lives and their sanity irrevocably altered, leaving them adrift in a psychic limbo from which the Master could then extract whatever he desired. The thought was terrifying, and yet, it was the only explanation that seemed to fit the sheer, pervasive, and increasingly surreal nature of the Master's grip on Redwater Crossing. The investigation had moved beyond the realm of human endeavor and into something far more ancient and unsettling. He was no longer just hunting a thief; he was chasing a phantom who dwelled in the spaces between moments, a master of illusions who had found his stage in the fractured reality of his town. The *Rooms Between* weren't just folklore; they were the Master's hunting grounds, and Redwater Crossing was his unsuspecting prey.

CHAPTER 7
The Unraveling

The palpable thrill that had gripped Redwater Crossing, a collective exhalation of newfound possibility, was rapidly morphing into a suffocating dread. It was the same insidious transition that Sheriff Brody had pieced together from the fragmented accounts of Oaklawn and King George, a chilling echo of economic devastation. The initial euphoria surrounding the "opportunity of a lifetime"—the gleaming new cars, the promises of rapid wealth, the rejuvenated sense of pride in their community—was now like a poorly cured stain, its bright surface peeling back to reveal the rot beneath. The Master's carefully constructed edifice of prosperity was not just cracking; it was crumbling with alarming speed, the very foundations of the town's economy dissolving into dust.

The new vehicles, once symbols of success and aspiration, had become metallic anchors, dragging their owners down into a maelstrom of debt. What had begun as manageable installments, easily swallowed by the projected returns from the Master's ventures, now loomed as insurmountable mountains. The local car dealership, a beacon of prosperity just weeks prior, was now a ghost town of repossessed vehicles, the once-bustling showroom eerily silent, its polished floors reflecting only the vacant stares of its former patrons. Brody received reports daily, each one a testament to the escalating crisis. Families who had mortgaged their homes to afford these luxury models found themselves staring at foreclosure notices, their dreams of a brighter future shattered by the stark reality of impending homelessness. The celebratory dinners, once held toasting the Master and his genius, had been replaced by hushed, desperate conversations in dimly lit kitchens, the clinking of glasses now a mournful dirge for lost savings and impending ruin.

The ripple effect was devastatingly swift. Businesses, reliant on the newfound disposable income of Redwater Crossing's citizens, found their customer base evaporating. The small boutique on Main Street, which had proudly displayed its "Sold Out" sign for a new shipment of designer handbags, now stood with empty shelves and a vacant gaze. The popular diner, once packed from breakfast through dinner, saw its tables dwindle from overflowing to sparsely occupied, the scent of sizzling bacon replaced by the more pungent aroma of desperation. Owners, their life savings invested in these establishments, were forced to make agonizing decisions: lay off loyal staff, drastically cut back on inventory, or face the inevitable closure. Each shuttered storefront was another wound inflicted upon the town, a stark visual representation of the Master's destructive artistry. The once vibrant Main Street, a symbol of Redwater Crossing's renewed spirit, was rapidly transforming into a gallery of despair.

The human cost was the most heartbreaking. Brody saw it in the eyes of the people who walked into his office, their shoulders slumped, their voices trembling as they confessed their inability to make payments, their fear of losing everything. He saw it in the tear-streaked face of Mrs. Cherry, the proud owner of the local bakery, who had invested heavily in new, state-of-the-art equipment to meet the surge in demand, only to find herself facing bankruptcy. Her hands, once dusted with the comforting flour of her craft, now trembled as she clutched a stack of unpaid invoices. "Sheriff," she'd choked out, her voice thick with unshed tears, "I... I don't understand. We were doing so well. Everyone was buying my cakes, my bread... He promised us such... such abundance." Her words, echoing the sentiment of so many others, underscored the profound betrayal, the shattering of faith that had accompanied this economic implosion.

The narrative of the "deal of a lifetime" had become a cruel, ironic punchline. What was once spoken with reverence, the Master's name uttered like a benevolent deity's, was now whispered with a mixture of fear and loathing. The initial fervor that had blinded them to any potential downside had evaporated, leaving behind a bitter residue of regret and recrimination. People who had once lauded the Master as their savior now spoke of him in hushed, fearful tones, their newfound financial ruin casting a dark shadow over their every thought. They felt trapped, ensnared by a meticulously laid trap, the glittering bait of prosperity now a cruel mockery. The sense of community, once a source of strength, was fractured by suspicion and blame, as neighbors turned on neighbors, questioning who had profited the most, who might have known more than they let on.

Brody found himself caught in the crossfire of this unraveling. He was the authority figure, the one people turned to in their desperation, yet he felt increasingly powerless. His hands were tied by the sheer scale and complexity of the Master's operations. The financial instruments were labyrinthine, designed to obscure the flow of money and to create an illusion of legitimate investment. He'd spent countless nights poring over bank statements, loan applications, and promissory notes, but the more he looked, the less sense it made. The numbers didn't add up, not in any conventional financial model. It was as if the Master was playing by a different set of rules, a set of rules that defied logic and gravity. This wasn't just a matter of predatory lending or simple fraud; it felt like something far more profound, something that was systematically dismantling the economic fabric of the town from the inside out.

The psychological toll was becoming as evident as the financial one. The initial optimism had given way to a gnawing anxiety, a constant thrum of worry that permeated every interaction. People who had once been jovial and gregarious were now withdrawn and irritable, their faces etched with the strain of sleepless nights and mounting fears. The promise of abundance had curdled into a specter of scarcity, and the townsfolk, stripped of their financial security, were left adrift in a sea of uncertainty. This rapid descent from perceived prosperity to abject poverty was a deliberate and brutal tactic, designed to break the spirit and sow seeds of despair. The Master wasn't just taking their money; he was systematically eroding their hope, their resilience, their very sense of self-worth. And Brody, watching this unfold, couldn't shake the feeling that the financial collapse was merely a symptom, a very visible and devastating consequence of something far more fundamental and disturbing that was happening just beneath the surface of Redwater Crossing. He had seen this pattern before, read about it in the hushed tones of discredited reports, and the chilling realization was dawning that the Master's methods were not just about financial ruin, but about the systematic dismantling of a community's very soul. The once-bright promise of the *deal of a lifetime* had indeed become a lifelong burden, a weight that threatened to crush the spirit of Redwater Crossing entirely.

The Master's hunger, an insatiable void that had been merely a gnawing emptiness at the outset, now swelled into a ravenous maw. It was a hunger not of the flesh, but of something far more primordial, a craving for the very essence of human despair. And Redwater Crossing, in its spectacular, agonizing unraveling, was proving to be an inexhaustible feast. The initial whispers of economic hardship had, under his unseen tutelage, crescendo into a cacophony of ruin. He did not merely observe the descent; he orchestrated it, a conductor of chaos, his unseen baton drawing forth the dissonant chords of desperation from every corner of the town.

Each dawn that broke over Redwater Crossing brought with it a fresh wave of misery, a new offering to the Master's growing appetite. The initial shock of financial ruin had begun to calcify into a bone-deep despair, a pervasive atmosphere that clung to the town like a shroud. Homes that had once echoed with laughter and familial chatter were now thick with a suffocating silence, punctuated only by the strained whispers of arguments born of unbearable stress. The children, too young to fully comprehend the magnitude of their parents' plight, sensed the shift. Their games grew quieter, their laughter less frequent, their wide eyes reflecting the fear and uncertainty that now permeated their homes. The playgrounds, once vibrant hubs of youthful exuberance, saw fewer small figures, their energy seemingly sapped by the pervasive gloom.

The Master, though physically absent, was a palpable presence. His influence was a chilling fog, seeping through the cracks in the town's foundation, not just of commerce, but of spirit. He reveled in the collective anguish, drawing strength from the bitter tears shed over empty tables, the gnawing fear that gnawed at the edges of sleep, the shattered dreams that lay scattered like so much broken glass. With each hope extinguished, with each carefully constructed future reduced to ashes, his power solidified. It was as if the town's very essence, its vibrant spirit, was being siphoned away, feeding an unseen entity, a dark heart that beat in time with Redwater Crossing's death throes.

The figure of the Master, the "tall man," once a fleeting, almost mythical image, began to solidify in the collective consciousness, an embodiment of the burgeoning dread. It was no longer just a rumor, a spooky tale to frighten children. It was becoming a tangible manifestation of the Master's consumption. As the town's despair deepened, so too did this spectral figure's imposing stature. The Master's "tall man" seemed to grow taller with every foreclosure, his shadow stretching further with every lost job. The weight of Redwater Crossing's misery was literally being absorbed, collected, and magnified within this phantom form. He was a living monument to their suffering, a terrifying testament to the Master's insatiable need.

The very air in Redwater Crossing seemed to thicken, heavy with the unspoken. Conversations were stilted, laced with a desperate need for normalcy that could no longer be sustained. Neighbors who had once shared coffee and gossip now eyed each other with a newfound suspicion. Who had managed to hold onto a semblance of their former lives? Who had been more susceptible to the Master's initial allure? These questions, born of fear and a desperate need to assign blame, fractured the already fragile bonds of community. The shared experience of ruin was not a unifying force; it was a catalyst for division, each person retreating into their own personal hell.

Sheriff Brody felt this shift most acutely. His office, once a sanctuary of order, was now a revolving door of shattered lives. He saw it in the haunted eyes of parents struggling to explain to their children why there would be no Christmas presents this year, no summer vacation. He heard it in the choked sobs of individuals facing the cold, impersonal reality of eviction notices. His own nights were no longer filled with the quiet vigilance of policing, but with the gnawing anxiety of helplessness. He was the shepherd of a flock being systematically devoured, and his crook was utterly ineffective against the predator.

The Master's influence wasn't confined to financial ruin. It was a psychological war waged on the very soul of the town. The initial promises of abundance had been a meticulously crafted illusion, designed not just to extract wealth, but to dismantle the very foundation of self-worth. When a person's livelihood is stripped away, when their carefully constructed future crumbles to dust, it doesn't just leave them financially destitute; it leaves them existentially adrift. The Master understood this. He understood that true power lay not just in controlling a person's resources, but in controlling their hope, their belief in themselves, their very sense of being.

And Redwater Crossing was capitulating. The proud, industrious spirit that had once characterized its residents was being systematically eroded. There was a weariness that settled upon them, a profound exhaustion that went beyond the lack of sleep. It was the weariness of fighting a battle that was unwinnable, of grappling with an enemy that was as pervasive as it was invisible. The Master's hunger was being sated, not just by the tangible loss of money and possessions, but by the intangible erosion of spirit. Each act of despair, each whispered curse, each tear of frustration was a drop of sustenance for his ever-growing power.

The Master's figure, the visual manifestation of this consumption, became an increasingly common hallucination, a shared delusion born of a shared trauma. People reported seeing him lurking at the edges of their vision, a gaunt silhouette against the setting sun, a shadow that deepened the encroaching darkness. He was the embodiment of the unspoken dread, the silent witness to their suffering. Some claimed to see him standing outside the boarded-up shops, a mournful sentinel guarding the ruins of their prosperity. Others swore they saw him on the deserted streets at night, his impossibly long legs carrying him with an unnerving grace, his form seeming to absorb the very shadows around him.

Brody found himself poring over old folklore, local legends, anything that might offer a clue to the nature of this pervasive dread. He was grasping at straws, but the logical explanations had all proven inadequate. The financial maneuverings were too complex, too opaque to be mere greed. There was a deeper malevolence at play, a deliberate act of spiritual and economic exsanguination. The Master wasn't just a businessman; he was a predator of the most insidious kind, feeding on the very lifeblood of a community.

The despair wasn't a singular event; it was a cascading waterfall, each failed attempt to claw back their losses only plunging them further into the abyss. The loans taken out to cover previous debts became a noose, tightening with each passing day. The pleas for help to external agencies were met with bureaucratic indifference or insurmountable paperwork, a stark reminder that they were alone in their fight. The Master had ensured this isolation, his machinations ensuring that no outside intervention could penetrate the suffocating grip he held on Redwater Crossing.

The Master's influence was like a psychic parasite, latching onto the town's collective consciousness and feeding on its negative energy. He didn't need to be physically present to exert his will; his power flowed through the veins of the town's despair, a dark, invisible current. The more people succumbed to hopelessness, the stronger he became. It was a self-perpetuating cycle of destruction, expertly designed. The initial lure of prosperity had been the bait, and the ensuing ruin was the hook, sinking deeper with every struggle.

The physical manifestations of the Master's consumption began to appear, not in his own form, but in the subtle, unsettling changes within Redwater Crossing itself. The vibrant colors of the town seemed to fade, as if a dimmer switch had been slowly turned down. The once-lush trees lining Main Street began to look gaunt, their leaves prematurely yellowed and brittle. The very air seemed to carry a faint, metallic tang, a subtle reminder of the draining that was occurring. It was as if the town itself was slowly being consumed, its vitality leached away to fuel the Master's insatiable hunger.

Brody found himself growing increasingly paranoid, seeing shadows in every corner, hearing whispers on the wind. He was not immune to the Master's influence, even as he fought against it. The constant exposure to the town's despair was a corrosive force, slowly eroding his own resolve. He felt the weight of it pressing down on him, the constant burden of responsibility for a community that was slipping through his fingers. He saw the Master in his dreams, a silent, imposing figure watching him from a distance, his presence a chilling promise of further devastation.

The Master's hunger was not a finite thing. It was a force of nature, a dark, unending void that sought to expand and consume. Redwater Crossing was merely the latest proving ground for his destructive artistry, a canvas upon which he painted his masterpiece of ruin. And as the town continued its agonizing descent, the Master, in his unseen dominion, grew stronger, more potent, his power a dark constellation born from the ashes of a community's shattered dreams. The unravelling was not just a financial collapse; it was a spiritual erosion, a systematic dismantling of hope, all for the insatiable appetite of a phantom master.

The townsfolk, once a proud and self-sufficient community, were now reduced to a state of perpetual anxiety. The days blurred into a monotonous cycle of worry and dwindling resources. The optimistic pronouncements of the Master's early days were now a bitter memory, a cruel joke that echoed in the hollow spaces of their lives. They had been promised a golden age, and instead, they had been plunged into a medieval darkness, stripped of their wealth, their security, and their very sense of self. The Master's consumption was a feast of despair, and Redwater Crossing was the sacrificial lamb, its spirit being slowly, deliberately devoured.

The insidious nature of the Master's influence was that it preyed on their very humanity. He didn't just steal their money; he stole their joy, their confidence, their belief in a brighter tomorrow. Each failed attempt to salvage their situation, each rejection from a financial institution, each hollow promise from a well-meaning acquaintance, served to deepen their despair and, in turn, to feed his growing power. The 'tall man' figure, a spectral manifestation of this growing power, became a recurring nightmare for many, a silent, looming presence that seemed to embody the all-consuming nature of their plight.

Sheriff Brody found himself staring at the same unsettling patterns in his investigations, the same threads of manipulation that seemed to originate from an unseen puppeteer. The financial instruments were designed to be indecipherable, a labyrinth of debt that ensnared anyone who dared to engage. But beyond the financial ruin, Brody sensed a deeper predation. He saw the psychological toll manifesting in the town's residents – the increased rates of depression, anxiety, and even domestic disputes. This wasn't just about economics; it was about the deliberate dismantling of a community's spirit, a feeding on their collective anguish.

The Master's hunger was not a passive state; it was an active force that compelled him to push Redwater Crossing further into the abyss. He actively encouraged the descent, subtly manipulating events to ensure that no ray of hope could penetrate the suffocating gloom. It was as if he derived a perverse pleasure from witnessing the erosion of their optimism, the shattering of their dreams. The more despair he sowed, the more potent he became, his power, a dark bloom nurtured by the tears and anxieties of the town's inhabitants. The 'tall man' was the visible manifestation of this growing power, a colossal shadow cast by the Master's insatiable need, growing larger and more imposing with each broken spirit. Brody felt the weight of this growing presence even in his waking hours, a constant, chilling reminder of the unseen force that was systematically consuming his town.

The vibrant hues of Redwater Crossing seemed to be leaching away with each passing day, a spectral pallor settling over the once-thriving community. Harmony Jakes watched it all unfold, a knot of dread tightening in her stomach with a ferocity that threatened to consume her own fragile peace. Her peculiar immunity, a shield against the Master's insidious whispers, allowed her to see the tendrils of manipulation weaving through the town with chilling clarity. It was like witnessing a slow-motion contagion, an unseen blight that was systematically turning her neighbors against themselves, against each other, and against any semblance of hope.

She saw it in Mrs. Cherry, her usually cheerful demeanor replaced by a pinched, anxious frown as she clutched a stack of overdue bills, her eyes darting nervously towards the imposing silhouette of the newly constructed "financial hub" on Main Street. Harmony had tried to speak to her, to offer a gentler perspective, to point out the predatory nature of the "investment opportunities" that had ensnared so many. But Mrs. Cherry had merely waved a dismissive hand, her voice tight with a defensive anger. "You don't understand, Harmony," she'd snapped, her gaze fixed on some distant point beyond the encroaching gloom. "This is our chance. You're just jealous you weren't smart enough to see it." The words stung, a sharp reminder of the Master's greatest weapon: the twisting of pride into blindness, of aspiration into delusion.

Then there was young Timmy Chiller, whose father, a proud craftsman, had poured every last penny into one of the Master's "guaranteed growth" schemes. Harmony had seen the subtle shift in Mr. Chiller's gaze, the way it had become unfocused, distant, as if he were perpetually looking past the present and into a shimmering, illusory future. His workshop, once a testament to meticulous skill and dedication, now stood silent and shuttered, the scent of sawdust replaced by a faint, musty odor of neglect. Harmony had approached Mr. Chiller, her heart heavy with a premonition of disaster. She'd mentioned the whispers she'd heard, the hushed conversations about sudden, unexplained disappearances of funds, the impossibly high interest rates that seemed designed to trap rather than enrich. Mr. Chiller's reaction was even more volatile than Mrs. Cherry's. His face had contorted with fury, his voice a low growl. "You're spreading lies, Jakes! Trying to undermine everything I've worked for! The Master is helping us, and you're just a bitter single mother who can't stand to see anyone succeed." The accusation, so patently false, hung in the air between them, a thick, suffocating blanket of the Master's influence.

It wasn't just individual losses that gnawed at Harmony; it was the erosion of the very fabric of their community. The neighborly bonds, once as strong and reliable as the old oak tree in the town square, were fraying, snapping under the strain of suspicion and whispered accusations. She saw it in the way people no longer gathered on their porches in the evenings, sharing stories and laughter. Instead, they retreated behind closed doors, their faces illuminated by the cold glow of screens displaying cryptic financial reports or, worse, staring blankly into the encroaching darkness, consumed by their own private anxieties.

Harmony felt a growing sense of responsibility, a heavy mantle settling upon her shoulders. Her immunity, once a source of quiet relief, now felt like a burden, a constant reminder of the vulnerability of those around her. She was the sole observer of the game being played, the only one who could truly see the strings being pulled by the unseen Master. This awareness, however, brought with it a profound helplessness. Her warnings, her attempts to pry open the eyes of her neighbors, were consistently met with a wall of defensiveness, a hardened resolve born from the Master's subtle reprogramming of their minds. They were so deeply invested, not just financially, but emotionally, in the narrative the Master had spun, that any attempt to challenge it was perceived as a personal attack.

She tried reasoning with Willow Vargas, a young mother who had eagerly signed up for the Master's "future investment fund," a scheme that promised astronomical returns with minimal risk. Harmony had pointed out the sheer impossibility of such returns, the statistical improbability, the lack of any tangible asset backing the supposed investments. Willow, her eyes wide and almost feverish, had simply smiled thinly. "You're stuck in the past, Harmony. This is the new way. The Master knows what he's doing. He's giving us a chance to escape this town, to finally get ahead. Don't you want that?" The question was laced with an accusation, a subtle implication that Harmony's reluctance was a sign of her own personal failure, her inability to embrace progress. It was a clever tactic, turning Harmony's concern into a character flaw, her caution into a lack of ambition.

The more Harmony tried to intervene, the more she encountered this impenetrable barrier. It was as if the Master had inoculated his followers against any dissenting voice, their minds so thoroughly saturated with his ideology that logic and reason could no longer penetrate. The anger that flared when she voiced her concerns was not the natural frustration of a community facing hardship; it was a manufactured rage, a defensive posture designed to protect the Master's carefully constructed illusion. They clung to his promises like drowning sailors to a phantom raft, unwilling to acknowledge the truth of the ocean's icy depths.

Even Sheriff Brody, a man Harmony had always respected for his grounded nature and clear-headedness, seemed to be grappling with the subtle shifts in the town's collective psyche. While he was undoubtedly investigating the financial irregularities, Harmony sensed his struggle to comprehend the sheer malevolence at play. He was looking for financial fraud, for evidence of greed and mismanagement, but he was missing the deeper, more insidious predation – the systematic dismantling of spirit, the siphoning of hope. He was trying to catch a ghost with a conventional net, his efforts hampered by the Master's elusiveness.

Harmony recalled a conversation she'd had with him just a week prior. She'd found him hunched over his desk in the dim light of his office, a thick stack of foreclosure notices spread before him. "Sheriff," she'd begun, her voice barely above a whisper, "it's not just about the money, is it? It's... something more." Brody had looked up, his eyes tired and etched with a weariness that went beyond lack of sleep. He'd run a hand over his stubbled chin. "Harmony, I've got families losing their homes, businesses going under. It's a disaster, plain and simple. The economy..." He'd trailed off, his gaze drifting back to the stark white paper, as if searching for an answer within the printed words. "But it feels different," Harmony had pressed gently. "It feels... deliberate. Like someone is *enjoying* this." Brody had sighed, a deep, weary sound. "Everyone's under a lot of pressure, Harmony. People say things, do things they wouldn't normally do when they're desperate." He'd spoken of financial mismanagement, of market fluctuations, of external economic forces. He'd acknowledged the speed and severity of the collapse, but the idea of a deliberate, malicious orchestrator seemed to elude him, or perhaps, he was simply unwilling to confront such a terrifying possibility.

This resistance to the truth was the most unnerving aspect of the Master's influence for Harmony. It wasn't just about financial ruin; it was about the psychological chains that bound the townsfolk. They were so eager to believe in a savior, in a path to prosperity that required so little effort on their part, that they willingly surrendered their critical thinking, their common sense, their very autonomy. The Master offered a siren song of effortless wealth, and Redwater Crossing, blinded by its own desperate yearning, had sailed headlong towards the rocks.

Harmony found herself walking the quiet, increasingly desolate streets, observing the subtle signs of decay. The once-proud storefronts were boarded up, their windows opaque with dust and neglect. The vibrant murals that had once adorned the walls of the community center were now faded and peeling, like forgotten memories. Even the air seemed heavier, imbued with a palpable sense of resignation. She saw the Master in her peripheral vision, a fleeting shadow at the edge of her awareness, a phantom presence that seemed to grow more distinct with each passing day, a silent testament to the Master's ever-expanding dominion. He was the embodiment of their collective despair, the looming manifestation of the unseen entity that was feasting on their hopes and dreams.

The weight of her knowledge pressed down on her. She was an outsider looking in, a reluctant witness to a tragedy she couldn't prevent. The more she tried to warn people, the more isolated she became. Their anger, their disbelief, their outright hostility, served only to reinforce the Master's hold. They saw her as an obstacle, a harbinger of bad news, a threat to the fragile hope they desperately clung to. Her efforts to break the spell only seemed to strengthen it, pushing them further into the Master's embrace. She felt a chilling realization dawn: perhaps, for some, the illusion was more comforting than the stark, brutal reality. And in that comfort, the Master found his greatest strength.

The persistent drizzle that had become Redwater Crossing's unwelcome soundtrack seemed to mirror the deepening gloom in Sheriff Mason Brody's heart. His office, usually a sanctuary of ordered files and the faint scent of stale coffee, now felt like a cage. Stacks of reports, each detailing another financial ruin, another shattered family, another instance of uncharacteristic irrationality, lay scattered across his desk like fallen dominoes. He'd chased every lead, interviewed every victim, and the common thread was as chilling as it was inexplicable. The numbers didn't add up, the motives were too perverse, and the sheer speed of the town's descent was unlike anything his years of law enforcement had prepared him for. He was a man who dealt in tangible evidence, in observable facts, but what he was facing felt like a phantom limb, a presence that was undeniably there, yet impossible to grasp.

He'd dismissed Harmony Jakes' earlier warnings as the ramblings of an eccentric woman, a product of isolation and an overactive imagination. But the events of the past few weeks had chipped away at his skepticism, replacing it with a gnawing unease. He'd witnessed her interactions, her calm demeanor amidst the rising hysteria, her unnerving ability to see through the veil of panic that had descended upon his town. While others were consumed by suspicion and fear, Harmony seemed to possess an almost serene clarity, a detachment that wasn't born of apathy, but of something else entirely. He'd seen it in her eyes when she spoke of the "Master," a word she uttered with a conviction that sent a shiver down his spine. He'd initially dismissed it as a delusion, a metaphor for the financial predator he was desperately trying to unmask. But the pervasive, almost supernatural dread that clung to the town, the way people spoke of an unseen influence guiding their decisions, began to lend credence to her unsettling pronouncements.

He'd even sent deputies to investigate the derelict estate on the outskirts of town; the place Harmony had alluded to as the "Master's domain." They'd found nothing but overgrown weeds, a crumbling manor house, and an unsettling silence. No opulent headquarters, no visible operations center, just decay and an oppressive stillness that sent even his hardened deputies back with a sense of profound disquiet. It was as if the entity they were searching for didn't exist in the physical realm, but rather in the collective consciousness of Redwater Crossing, a parasitic consciousness feeding on their hopes and vulnerabilities.

It was the sheer, unshakeable faith of the townsfolk that truly unnerved him. They clung to the Master's promises with a religious fervor, dismissing any evidence of financial ruin as temporary setbacks, minor glitches in an otherwise flawless system. When he'd tried to explain the predatory nature of the "investment schemes," the impossible interest rates, the lack of regulation, he was met with blank stares or, worse, outright hostility. They saw him not as their protector, but as an impediment, a relic of an outdated way of thinking, unwilling to embrace the future the Master had so generously offered. The fear of being left behind, of being deemed foolish by those who had embraced the Master's gospel, was a powerful, invisible force, binding them tighter to his will.

He'd even found himself subtly altering his approach. Instead of focusing solely on financial fraud, he'd begun looking for patterns of manipulation, for psychological coercion. He'd consulted with experts, psychologists, even a retired FBI profiler in Percy, but their insights, while valuable, felt incomplete. They spoke of cult-like behavior, of groupthink, of charismatic leaders preying on the vulnerable. But none of them could explain the palpable sense of dread that permeated the air, the whispers of shadows moving in the periphery, the chilling synchronicity of the town's descent. It was as if a malignant intelligence was at play, an entity that operated beyond the realm of human understanding.

It was this gnawing, unanswerable question that had finally driven him to seek out Harmony Jakes. He'd found her tending her small garden, her movements deliberate and unhurried, a stark contrast to the frantic energy that now characterized the rest of the town. The late afternoon sun cast long shadows across her face, highlighting the lines etched by years of quiet observation, but her eyes, when they met his were clear and steady, devoid of the frantic desperation he saw everywhere else.

"Ms. Jakes," he began, his voice rougher than he intended, the formality feeling absurdly out of place. "Sheriff Brody. I... I need to talk to you."

Harmony straightened, wiping her hands on her apron. There was no surprise in her expression, only a quiet acknowledgment. "Sheriff," she replied, her voice calm and measured. "I've been expecting you."

Her words, delivered with such certainty, sent another ripple of unease through him. "Expecting me? How could you possibly...?"

"Because," she interrupted gently, "you're the only one left who's still trying to see the truth. The others... they've made their choice." She gestured towards the town, a subtle sweep of her hand encompassing the quiet streets and shuttered businesses. "They've chosen the illusion."

He walked with her to her small porch, the scent of damp earth and fading roses filling the air. He sat on the worn wooden steps, feeling the weight of his badge, the futility of his uniform, pressing down on him. He opened his mouth, then closed it again, struggling to articulate the formless dread that had taken root in him.

"It's not just about the money, is it?" He finally managed, echoing her earlier sentiment. "These losses... they're too systematic, too... complete. It's like something is actively *draining* this town, not just its wealth, but its spirit."

Harmony sat beside him, her gaze fixed on the distant, mist-shrouded hills. "It is, Sheriff. It's feeding. It feeds on desperation, on greed, on the longing for something more without the willingness to work for it. It's the Master."

He flinched at the name. "Harmony, I've investigated every angle. Financial malfeasance, organized crime, even white-collar fraud. But there's no paper trail, no clear perpetrator. Just... this." He gestured vaguely, encompassing the pervasive sense of despair. "People are losing everything, their homes, their businesses, their sanity. And they blame everyone but him. They defend him."

"Because he's promised them everything," Harmony said, her voice barely a whisper. "And he delivered just enough to make them believe. He's a master manipulator, Sheriff, but not in the way you understand it. His influence isn't just financial; it's psychological, spiritual. He whispers what people want to hear, amplifies their deepest desires, and then twists them into chains."

Mason ran a hand over his face, the stubble rough against his palm. "I've heard the whispers too. About shadows, about a presence. My men have reported... oddities. Lights in the woods, unexplained noises. I dismissed it, of course. Paranoia. Stress. But now..." He looked at Harmony, a dawning realization in his eyes. "You're not afraid of him, are you?"

A faint, almost imperceptible smile touched her lips. "I feel him, Sheriff. I feel his influence, his hunger. But it doesn't touch me. Not in the way it touches others. It's like... I'm immune."

The word hung in the air between them, heavy with implication. Mason stared at her, his mind racing. Immunity. It explained so much. Her clarity, her lack of fear, her ability to see what others couldn't. He'd always sensed something different about Harmony Jakes, a quiet strength that set her apart. He'd attributed it to her solitary life, her connection to the land. But now, he wondered if it was something far more profound.

"Immune," he repeated, the word feeling foreign on his tongue. "How?"

"I don't know," she admitted honestly. "It's always been this way. The whispers, the temptations... they pass through me. They find no purchase." She looked at him, her gaze penetrating. "But you, Sheriff. You're trying to fight him with the tools of this world, with logic and evidence. He's not bound by those things."

"Then what *is* he?" Mason demanded, the frustration boiling to the surface. "A ghost? A demon? Vampire? Some kind of... cosmic parasite?"

"He is what we allow him to be," Harmony said softly. "He is the embodiment of our darkest impulses, amplified and given form by our collective despair. He is the Master of our own making, as much as he is an entity unto himself."

Mason stood up, pacing the small porch. The drizzle had intensified, plastering his hair to his forehead. He felt a desperate need for concrete answers, for something tangible to hold onto, but all he found was an abyss of the unknown. "So, what do we do? How do we fight something that feeds on our own weaknesses? How do we fight an enemy that lives inside our heads?"

Harmony rose as well, her gaze unwavering. "We start by understanding, Sheriff. You've seen the financial ruin, the desperation. I've seen the underlying cause, the subtle corruption of minds. You look for the tangible evidence, the footprints. I feel the ethereal presence, the shadow. Perhaps, together, we can see the whole picture."

He turned to her, a flicker of hope igniting within him. It was a fragile thing, born from the abyss of his despair, but it was there. For the first time since this nightmare had begun, he felt a sense of possibility, not of victory, but of understanding. "You mean... you'll help me?"

"I've been trying to help this town for a long time, Sheriff," she said, a hint of weariness in her voice. "But I couldn't do it alone. My words were dismissed, my warnings ignored. But you... you're listening. You're looking beyond the obvious. And you have a power of your own. You have the authority, the reach, the respect of some. You can investigate, you can gather information, you can expose the outward manifestations of his influence."

"And you?" Mason pressed, eager to define their roles.

"I can see what he is," Harmony stated, her voice resonating with a quiet power. "I can feel his presence, anticipate his moves. I can be your eyes and ears in a realm where your badges and firearms are useless."

He looked at her, this unassuming woman who held a truth that seemed to transcend the ordinary. She was the key, the missing piece of the puzzle he hadn't even known he was searching for. Her immunity was not a curse, but a gift, a beacon in the encroaching darkness.

"This Master," Mason began, his voice low and steady, "he's not just interested in money, is he? He's interested in... control. In breaking us."

"He is interested in consumption, Sheriff," Harmony corrected gently. "He consumes hope, he consumes peace, he consumes the very essence of what makes us human. And he does it by preying on our failings, our vulnerabilities. He turns neighbor against neighbor, friend against friend, all while promising unity and prosperity."

"I've seen it," Mason admitted, the memory of the escalating tensions, the bitter arguments, the sudden betrayals, flashing through his mind. "The way people have turned on each other. It's like they're being puppeteered."

"They are," Harmony confirmed. "But the strings are invisible, woven from their own fears and desires. He offers them a shortcut, a way to bypass the struggle, the hard work, the inherent risks of life. And in return, he asks for their autonomy, their discernment, their very souls."

He felt a surge of anger, cold and sharp. "And he's succeeding. Redwater Crossing is dying, Harmony. And I'm watching it happen, powerless."

"Not entirely powerless, Sheriff," Harmony countered, her gaze steady. "You have the capacity for reason, for action. You are a force for order in a world that is being consumed by chaos. And you have me." She extended a hand, her palm open and inviting. "We may not have the weapons he understands, but we have something he cannot comprehend: shared purpose, and a resistance born not of immunity, but of a desperate, unyielding love for this town."

Mason looked at her hand, then back at her face. The rain had begun to subside, leaving behind a world washed clean, yet still shrouded in an unsettling mystery. He knew, with a certainty that chilled him to the bone, that Harmony Jakes was not just a witness, but a warrior. And in her quiet strength, in her unshakeable resolve, he found the first glimmer of true hope he had felt in months. He took her hand, his grip firm.

"Alright, Harmony," he said, the formality shed, replaced by a newfound camaraderie. "Tell me everything. Tell me what you feel. Tell me what you see. We'll face this Master together."

As their hands clasped, a silent pact was forged. The Sheriff, grounded in the tangible world of law and order, and Harmony, attuned to the spectral currents of the supernatural, stood on the precipice of a battle that transcended the ordinary. The unraveling of Redwater Crossing had begun, but now, for the first time, there was a chance, however slim, that it could be unraveled, not by destruction, but by understanding and a courageous stand against the encroaching darkness. The fight for Redwater Crossing had just found its unlikely champions.

Harmony Jakes had been right. The town wasn't just suffering from economic collapse; it was undergoing a spiritual famine. The Master was feeding, not on their bank accounts, but on their despair, their regret, their festering resentments. It was a parasitic entity, thriving on the disintegration of hope and community. Mason remembered Harmony's words about the Master amplifying their deepest fears and regrets, and he saw it playing out with horrifying clarity. Old grudges, long buried, were resurfacing with venomous intensity. Neighbors who had once shared barbecues were now locked in bitter disputes over perceived slights, their conversations laced with accusations that echoed the Master's insidious whispers of betrayal and inadequacy.

He'd seen the physical manifestations too, subtle but undeniable. The once-vibrant flower beds outside the town hall were choked with weeds. The paint on many of the houses was peeling, neglected. A pervasive sense of decay seemed to permeate everything, a physical mirroring of the town's inner rot. Even the stray dogs that roamed the streets seemed thinner, their eyes carrying a hunted look. It was as if the entire ecosystem of Redwater Crossing was being starved, its vitality leached away by an unseen force.

The psychological toll was perhaps the most devastating. Mason had witnessed individuals he knew to be rational, level-headed people behaving erratically, their judgment clouded by an almost fanatical devotion to the Master's promises. They clung to the phantom hope of recovery, dismissing any evidence of their ruin as temporary setbacks, convinced that a windfall was just around the corner. This denial was a powerful shield, but it was also a cage, preventing them from seeing the precipice they were teetering on. They were so blinded by the allure of instant wealth that they couldn't see the invisible strings pulling them towards their own destruction.

He recalled a conversation with Julie Cherry, the owner of the local bakery, a woman whose kindness had always been as abundant as her bread. She had lost her life savings, her business on the brink of collapse. Yet, when Mason had tried to offer solace, she had waved him away with a strange, almost vacant smile. "Don't worry, Sheriff," she'd said, her voice unnervingly calm. "The Master has a plan. We just have to have faith." Her eyes, however, held a flicker of something else, a deep, unsettling fear that she quickly masked. It was that fear, Mason knew, that Harmony Jakes could sense, the fear that was being expertly exploited.

The isolation extended beyond the interpersonal. The outside world, once a source of news, information, and potential aid, had become a distant, almost irrelevant entity. The internet, which had once connected them to the wider world, was now a source of further anxiety, with news of market crashes and global instability only serving to reinforce the town's sense of impending doom. But even that external pressure seemed to pale in comparison to the internal rot. Redwater Crossing was consuming itself; its inhabitants trapped in a self-perpetuating cycle of paranoia, despair, and a desperate, misguided faith.

Mason felt the weight of this isolation pressing down on him. He was the Sheriff, the supposed protector of this town, yet he felt utterly alone in his fight against this insidious force. His deputies, once loyal and capable, were becoming increasingly demoralized, their own families affected by the unfolding disaster. He saw the weariness in their eyes, the dawning realization that their badges and their firearms were useless against an enemy that operated in the shadows of the mind. They were a town cut off, not just by geography, but by an unseen, malevolent will, its tendrils tightening around their collective psyche. The world outside no longer seemed like a place where help could be found; it felt like a realm of forgotten dreams, a stark contrast to the suffocating reality of Redwater Crossing's self-imposed exile. The town, once a community, was now a collection of isolated souls, each one a potential victim, each one a pawn in a game they didn't understand, played by a master they could not see.

CHAPTER 8

The Surge of Suicides

The whispers started subtly, like the first crack in a frozen pond. A hushed mention at the general store, a sidelong glance exchanged over a cooling cup of coffee. Then, the whispers gained a morbid momentum, like a snowball rolling downhill, gathering size and terror. The first confirmed loss was old Mr. Hector Abernathy, a man who had farmed the same land his father and grandfather had before him. His property, once the pride of the county, was now a ghost of its former glory, burdened by loans that had ballooned into monstrous entities. Mason had found him in the barn, the smell of hay and despair thick in the air, a scene so utterly devoid of life it felt like a deliberate tableau of defeat. It was the quietness of it that struck Mason – the absence of struggle, the resigned surrender. He had always believed the darkest of deeds were born of frantic passion, of a mind pushed beyond its breaking point. But Mr. Abernathy's end felt different, a chillingly calm exhalation of a life that could no longer bear the weight of its own crushing reality.

The official reports were clinical, sterile attempts to impose order on chaos. An overdose of sleeping pills. A self-inflicted gunshot wound. A fall from the old water tower, a landmark that had once been a symbol of community pride, now a grim monument to individual despair. Each incident chipped away at Redwater Crossing's already fragile soul. The town, once characterized by its bustling Main Street and the cheerful greetings of its residents, now felt like a gathering of mourners. The faces that had once been etched with the honest lines of hard work now bore the deeper furrows of sleepless nights and gnawing fear. The collective trauma was a palpable thing, a suffocating blanket that settled over the town, making each breath a conscious effort.

Mason found himself performing a grim new ritual, visiting homes not to offer comfort in the face of loss, but to document the very act of loss itself. He saw the hollowed eyes of widows and widowers, the bewildered stares of children who no longer understood why their parents had simply... gone. He spoke with parents who had outlived their own children, a reversal of nature that felt like a profound cosmic error. The justifications offered were always the same, variations on a theme of inescapable ruin. "The debts were too much," they'd murmur, their voices raspy with unshed tears. "There was no way out." "He couldn't bear the shame anymore." The shame. That was a recurring word, a poison seeping into the very core of their identities. The Master's promises of prosperity had not only failed to materialize, but their absence had bred a new, more insidious kind of failure – the failure to provide, the failure to protect, the failure to simply *be* enough.

The surge in suicides wasn't confined to any particular demographic. It wasn't just the farmers losing their land, or the small business owners watching their livelihoods evaporate. It was teachers, their pensions wiped out. It was the young couple who had poured their savings into a dream home, only to find its mortgage unpayable. It was even Julie Cherry, the baker whose smiles had once been as warm as her ovens. Mason had found her note tucked beneath a cooling rack, a few lines of elegant script that spoke of a profound weariness, of a love for her craft that had been extinguished by the relentless pressure of financial ruin. Her bakery, a place that had once filled the town with the comforting aroma of fresh bread, now stood silent, its windows dusty, its doors locked. The loss of Julie, a woman so intrinsically linked to the town's sustenance, felt like a particularly cruel blow, a sign that even the most cherished institutions were not immune to the Master's blight.

The fear intensified with each passing day. It wasn't just the fear of losing money anymore; it was the primal, gut-wrenching fear of death, of the unknown that awaited those who chose to end their suffering. And with each suicide, the Master seemed to grow stronger. Mason felt it – a subtle shift in the atmosphere, a deepening of the oppressive gloom. The whispers of the Master, once faint and easily dismissed, now seemed to echo in the very air. Harmony Jakes had warned him about this, about how despair was a fuel, a potent energy source for the entity she called the Master. It thrived on broken spirits, on the extinguishing of hope. And Redwater Crossing was becoming a veritable feast.

He saw it in the eyes of the living, too. A new kind of desperation had taken root. It wasn't the desperate hope for a quick fix anymore, but a desperate clinging to anything that offered a momentary distraction from the encroaching darkness. People became reckless, their judgment further clouded. Some turned to alcohol, seeking oblivion in the bottom of a bottle. Others engaged in increasingly dangerous behaviors, as if tempting fate was the only way to reclaim some semblance of control over their lives. The town was unraveling, its social fabric torn to shreds by the relentless pressure. Neighbor turned against neighbor not out of malice, but out of a desperate need to find someone, anyone, to blame for their own agonizing circumstances. Scapegoats were sought with a fervor that bordered on religious zeal, each accusation a desperate attempt to deflect the unendurable weight of personal failure.

Mason tried to maintain order, to offer a steady hand in the swirling chaos. He increased patrols, tried to be visible, to project an image of calm authority. But he knew it was a disguise. His own resources were stretched thin, his deputies as weary and frightened as the townsfolk. They were law enforcement officers, trained to deal with crime, with tangible threats. But how do you arrest despair? How do you handcuff hopelessness? The Master operated on a level that defied their training, their understanding of the world. It wasn't about breaking laws; it was about breaking people.

The town council meetings, once routine affairs, had devolved into shouting matches, accusations flying like poisoned darts. Greg Bottoms, the former mayor, who had been instrumental in the town's ill-fated financial ventures, was now the most frequent target. His pleas for patience, for continued faith in the future, were met with jeers and demands for his resignation. But even in his desperation, Bottoms seemed to possess a strange, almost defiant resilience, a chilling echo of the Master's own manipulative charm. He spoke of unseen forces, of external manipulators who had targeted Redwater Crossing, deflecting blame with practiced ease. It was a performance Mason found both sickening and terrifying.

The grief in Redwater Crossing became a constant companion. It hung in the air like a perpetual fog, muffling laughter, dimming smiles, and casting long shadows even on the brightest of days. The local cemetery, once a quiet place of remembrance, now saw a steady stream of new arrivals. The fresh earth piled atop graves became a stark visual representation of the town's ongoing hemorrhage of life. The sense of community, which had been slowly eroding, now seemed to have fractured entirely, replaced by a profound and terrifying loneliness. Each death was a private tragedy, experienced in isolation, with few resources left to offer solace or support.

The weight of it all began to press down on Mason, a physical ache in his chest. He saw the faces of the deceased in his sleep, their eyes wide with the silent question: *Why?* He saw the desperate hope that had flickered in their eyes before it was extinguished, the misguided faith that had ultimately led them to their doom. And he saw the Master, a formless, insidious presence, feeding on their extinguished light, growing stronger with each flicker that died out. He understood, with a bone-chilling clarity, that this was not merely an economic crisis. This was something far older, far more malevolent, and Redwater Crossing was its chosen ground, its unwilling sacrifice. The grim toll mounted, each life lost a testament to the Master's growing power, and a chilling harbinger of what was yet to come. The silence left by each departed soul was not an empty void, but a space that the Master eagerly filled, its whispers becoming louder, more insistent, preying on the hearts of those left behind, ensuring the grim toll would continue to climb.

The silence that descended upon Redwater Crossing was not the peaceful quiet of a town at rest, but the suffocating stillness of a tomb. Each new headline in the local paper, each hushed conversation overheard on the street, confirmed what Mason already felt in his gut: this was no mere economic downturn. This was a calculated culling, orchestrated by an unseen hand. The Master. The word itself, once a phantom conjured from Harmony Jakes' frantic warnings, now felt like a palpable entity, a shadow that clung to the very fabric of the town.

Mason found himself haunted by the spectral presence of the "tall man," a figure Harmony had described with a chilling blend of dread and awe. He was not a man in the conventional sense, but an avatar, a physical manifestation of the Master's growing influence. His stoic demeanor, once perceived as a sign of quiet strength, now seemed to carry an immense weight, as if he were a vessel absorbing the very essence of the despair that bled from Redwater Crossing. Mason envisioned him standing on the periphery of each tragedy, a silent, stoic observer, his form subtly shifting, darkening, as if drawing strength from the extinguishing of each life. He was the Master's grim testament, a sentinel of sorrows, his very existence a chilling promise of the entity's insatiable hunger.

The Master, Mason realized, was not content to merely watch. He was the conductor of this macabre symphony, the puppeteer pulling the strings of desperation. The subtle nudges, the whispered suggestions that preyed on pre-existing anxieties, the insidious amplification of perceived failures – these were his tools. He didn't create the cracks in their lives; he widened them, expertly, patiently, until the foundations crumbled. A farmer, already burdened by crop failure and mounting debt, might suddenly recall a forgotten childhood promise of a better life elsewhere, a promise that, in his current state, felt like a mocking taunt of what he was missing. A small business owner, facing foreclosure, might fixate on a single, dismissive comment from a customer, twisting it into a damning indictment of their entire existence. The Master didn't need to shout; his whispers were far more potent, lodging themselves in the darkest corners of the mind, festering like unseen wounds.

Mason often found himself retracing the final steps of the departed, a grim investigative ritual that offered little comfort. He stood in the empty rooms, the air still holding the faint scent of lives lived and tried to pinpoint the exact moment the Master's influence had tipped the scales. Was it the day the bank foreclosed? The day the factory closed its doors? Or was it a far subtler moment, a fleeting thought, a flicker of doubt amplified into an insurmountable dread? He saw it in the eyes of the grieving – a desperate plea for understanding, a silent question that echoed his own: *How could this happen?* And the answer, he was increasingly certain, lay in the insatiable appetite of the entity they had unknowingly invited into their lives.

The wave of despair washing over Redwater Crossing was, for the Master, a veritable feast. Each life extinguished, each hope crushed, was a morsel of potent energy, fueling his power, expanding his reach. Harmony had described him as an entity that fed on broken spirits, on the absence of light. And Redwater Crossing, once a beacon of small-town resilience, was now a sprawling buffet. The collective trauma wasn't just an emotional contagion; it was a psychic nourishment, a spiritual sustenance for this ancient, malevolent force. The more they suffered, the stronger he became. The more they despaired, the more he thrived.

Mason's own resolve began to fray under the relentless onslaught. He felt the oppressive weight of the town's collective misery pressing down on him, a physical burden that made each breath an effort. He saw the faces of the deceased in his dreams, their eyes wide with a vacant horror, their spectral forms accusing him of his helplessness. He would wake in a cold sweat, the whispers of the Master seeming to slither into his subconscious, mocking his efforts, feeding his own burgeoning doubts. Was he truly making a difference, or was he merely a futile figurehead, a symbol of a law and order that was rapidly becoming irrelevant?

The 'tall man' became a recurring phantom in Mason's mind, a disturbing embodiment of the Master's pervasive influence. He imagined him moving through the town like a phantom wind, his presence marked by a subtle ripple in the oppressive atmosphere, a deepening of the shadows, a chilling silence that fell over conversations. He saw him, not with malice, but with a profound, unnerving detachment, as if he were merely a conduit, a vessel through which the Master's will was enacted. The stoic facade of the tall man was not indifference; it was a chilling reflection of the Master's own vast, alien perspective, a perspective that viewed human lives not as precious sparks, but as transient flickers to be extinguished when they ceased to serve a purpose.

Mason's investigation into the suicides became less about uncovering foul play and more about understanding the insidious mechanisms of despair. He meticulously documented the notes left behind, the final desperate cries of souls pushed beyond their limits. These weren't always eloquent pleas; sometimes they were fragmented sentences, scrawled in haste, expressing a profound exhaustion, a sense of being utterly overwhelmed. "Can't take it anymore." "It's too much." "Forgive me." Each note was a small, dark testament to the Master's efficient harvesting of misery. He saw a pattern emerging, not of a single perpetrator, but of a pervasive influence that preyed on individual vulnerabilities, amplifying them until they became unbearable.

The Master's satisfaction was a tangible thing, Mason felt it in the increasingly oppressive atmosphere, in the way the very air seemed to thicken with a suffocating dread. Harmony had spoken of how despair was a form of power, an energy that the Master could harness and amplify. Redwater Crossing was providing him with an unprecedented surge of it. The carefully constructed face of community life was crumbling, replaced by suspicion, fear, and a desperate scramble for individual survival. Neighborly trust had eroded, replaced by a gnawing suspicion. Each person looked at the other, wondering if they, too, were succumbing, or worse, if they were somehow complicit in the spreading darkness.

He thought of Greg Bottoms, the former mayor, whose platitudes about perseverance now seemed hollow, almost mocking, in the face of such widespread devastation. Bottoms's own transformation from a respected figure to a pariah was a stark illustration of how quickly fortunes could turn, how swiftly hope could curdle into despair. Mason suspected Bottoms, in his own desperate attempts to salvage his reputation, might have inadvertently become a pawn, a voice that, while trying to offer reassurance, was ultimately amplified by the Master to spread a false sense of security that only made the eventual fall more devastating. The Master thrived on such ironies, on the perversion of good intentions into instruments of ruin.

The sheer volume of the suicides was overwhelming Mason. He felt like a man trying to bail out a sinking ship with a teacup. Each successful intervention, each person he managed to pull back from the brink, felt like a minor victory, but it was dwarfed by the relentless tide of despair that continued to claim victims. He knew the Master wasn't acting in isolation; he was working through the subtle societal pressures, the economic anxieties, the inherent human fears that were already present within Redwater Crossing. He merely fanned the flames, turning embers of discontent into raging infernos of self-destruction. The tall man, in Mason's increasingly disturbed imagination, was not just an observer; he was the embodiment of this destructive force, his silent presence a chilling promise of more souls to come. The Master was not a distant deity; he was an intimate predator, whispering his temptations directly into the ears of the vulnerable, feeding on the deepest insecurities until they became an unbearable weight. And Redwater Crossing, broken and bleeding, was his banquet.

The escalating toll of lives lost in Redwater Crossing was a brutal forge, and within its searing heat, Harmony Jakes' fragile apprehension began to crystallize into something far more formidable: resolve. Each whispered account of another tragedy, each vacant stare of profound grief that met her on the streets, was a fresh strike of the hammer against the anvil of her spirit. It wasn't just fear that coursed through her veins anymore; it was a molten fury, a visceral need to shield her daughter, Lily, from the encroaching darkness. Lily, with her innocent eyes and laughter that was slowly being muted by the pervasive gloom, represented everything the Master sought to extinguish. She was the fragile bloom in a poisoned garden, and Harmony was her fierce, unyielding guardian.

The initial helplessness, the gnawing uncertainty that had plagued her since she first sensed the insidious presence, had begun to recede, replaced by a steely clarity. Harmony understood, with a chilling certainty that settled deep in her bones, that the conventional defenses of law, reason, and communal support were utterly impotent against this foe. The Sheriff's department, bless their earnest efforts, were like men trying to dam a tsunami with buckets. The town council's pronouncements of hope and resilience were hollow echoes in the face of the Master's silent, devastating efficacy. This wasn't a problem that could be solved with budgets or task forces. This was a spiritual war, waged in the shadowed corners of the human psyche, and it demanded a different kind of fight.

She started to see the Master not as a distant, abstract evil, but as an intimate predator, one who had learned the subtle rhythms of Redwater Crossing, who knew its vulnerabilities, who whispered directly into the ears of its most desperate souls. The suicides were not random acts of despair; they were calculated assassinations, each one a meticulously planned maneuver designed to weaken the collective spirit, to sow discord, and to feed the Master's insatiable hunger. The "tall man," that spectral sentinel Harmony had glimpsed on the fringes of Mason's own troubled investigations, was no longer a mere hallucination or a figment of her heightened senses. He was the embodiment of the Master's will, the silent enforcer of his morbid decrees. Harmony pictured him not as a man, but as a silhouette against the dying light, a figure carved from the very despair he oversaw, his stoicism a chilling reflection of the Master's vast, inhuman perspective.

This realization brought with it a profound sense of isolation. Who could truly understand the nature of this threat? Mason, for all his dedication and his growing awareness, was still operating within the framework of a world that was rapidly becoming irrelevant. The townspeople, consumed by their own fear and grief, were too caught in the undertow to grasp the true architect of their suffering. Harmony was alone in her understanding, burdened by a knowledge that set her apart, a terrible clarity that offered no comfort, only the stark imperative to act.

Her preparation began in the quiet sanctuary of her own mind. She spent hours in silent meditation, not seeking solace, but fortifying her inner defenses. She visualized a shield of pure, unwavering love, an impenetrable barrier around herself and Lily, an energy that pulsed with defiance against the encroaching darkness. She revisited the memories of Lily's birth, of those first tender moments of motherhood, drawing strength from the sheer, primal power of that bond. It was a love so potent, so absolute, that it felt like a force of nature in itself, a counterpoint to the Master's nihilistic void. She needed to become a conduit for that love, to channel it into a weapon.

Harmony also began to study the patterns, the subtle shifts in the town's atmosphere that preceded each wave of suicides. She noticed how the air would grow heavy, how a peculiar stillness would settle over the streets, how even the birds seemed to fall silent. These were not meteorological phenomena; they were the psychic tremors of the Master's proximity, the subtle atmospheric shifts that signaled his influence was tightening its grip. She started keeping a secret journal, not of events, but of feelings, of sensations, of the almost imperceptible changes in the town's energetic field. She was learning to read the Master's mood, to anticipate his next move, to discern the subtle currents of his malicious intent.

She began to subtly shift her interactions with Lily. While maintaining a disguise of normalcy, she infused every hug, every shared story, every gentle touch with a heightened intensity, a silent promise that she would never let go. She taught Lily simple affirmations, not as rote repetition, but as mindful declarations of inner strength. "I am brave," Harmony would whisper, her voice firm and resonant. "I am loved. Darkness cannot touch me." Lily, sensing the shift in her mother, would echo the words, her young voice a fragile counterpoint to the encroaching dread. It was a subtle battle, waged in the quiet spaces of their home, a testament to Harmony's unwavering commitment.

The more Harmony delved into the nature of the Master's influence, the more she realized its insidious nature. It didn't manifest as overt coercion, but as a subtle amplification of existing anxieties. A whispered doubt about one's worth, a fleeting thought of failure, a moment of profound loneliness – these were the seeds the Master cultivated. He didn't create the pain; he nurtured it, watered it with despair, and coaxed it into a monstrous bloom of self-destruction. This understanding fueled her determination. If the Master exploited weaknesses, then her strength lay in reinforcing them, in building emotional resilience, not just for herself and Lily, but for anyone she could reach.

She started taking longer walks, not just for the fresh air, but to observe. She would linger near the edges of town, near the abandoned mill, near the dense woods that bordered the eastern ridge. These were places where the veil between worlds felt thinnest, where the Master's presence seemed to hum with a low, persistent energy. She wasn't looking for a physical confrontation, not yet. She was seeking to understand the source, the anchor point of his power, if such a thing existed. She was mapping the territory of her enemy, preparing for a battle that would require more than just courage; it would require a profound understanding of the dark forces at play.

The thought of confronting the Master directly was a terrifying prospect, a chilling abyss that beckoned with its own dark allure. Yet, the alternative – to stand by and watch Redwater Crossing be consumed, to see Lily's light extinguished – was infinitely more terrifying. Her resolve hardened with each passing day, each fallen soul. She knew, with an unshakeable conviction, that she was no longer a passive observer. She was a bulwark, a defiant flame against the encroaching night, and she would not be extinguished. The love she held for her daughter was not just an emotion; it was a weapon, a shield, and a guiding star, and she would wield it with every fiber of her being. The Master had underestimated the power of a mother's love, and in that underestimation, Harmony Jakes knew, lay his ultimate undoing.

Her nightly rituals became increasingly focused. She would sit by Lily's bedside, not just to ensure she slept soundly, but to project a silent, unwavering shield of protection. She visualized tendrils of pure, white light extending from her own heart, weaving a protective cocoon around her sleeping daughter. This wasn't mere fantasy; it was an act of spiritual warfare, a conscious effort to imbue Lily with an inherent resistance to the psychic pollution seeping into their lives. She saw the Master as a psychic parasite, and her love was the potent antidote, the immune system of the soul.

Harmony began to experiment with different forms of spiritual defense, drawing from obscure texts and forgotten lore she had stumbled upon in her quiet research. She wasn't seeking arcane rituals or dark incantations; her focus was on strengthening her own energetic field, on purifying her intentions, and on creating a sanctuary of light within herself. She discovered that grounding herself, feeling the deep, steady pulse of the earth beneath her feet, provided a crucial anchor against the Master's disorienting influence. She learned that affirmations, spoken with genuine conviction and focused intent, could indeed create subtle shifts in her immediate environment, pushing back against the encroaching gloom.

She also found herself drawn to the places where the suicides had occurred. Not to mourn, but to observe, to feel the residual energy, to try and discern the precise moment the Master's influence had become overwhelming. She stood on the bridge where old Mr. Abernathy had jumped, feeling the cold, despairing emptiness that still clung to the air. She walked through the overgrown field where Candi Prince had ended her life, sensing the ghost of a hope that had curdled into utter despair. These were not morbid pilgrimages; they were reconnoitering missions, attempts to understand the enemy's modus operandi on a visceral level. She was learning the language of despair, and in doing so, she was slowly learning how to speak its opposite: hope.

The weight of this knowledge was immense, a constant pressure that threatened to buckle her shoulders. There were nights when sleep offered little respite, when her dreams were haunted by the spectral figures of those lost, their eyes wide with an unseeing terror, their silent accusations a heavy burden. But each morning, the sight of Lily, her innocent face buried in her pillow, would reignite the fire within Harmony. Her daughter was her north star, the tangible reason to push forward, to resist, to fight.

She began to notice subtle shifts in her own perception. Colors seemed brighter, sounds sharper, her senses attuned to a frequency that had previously been beyond her awareness. It was as if the constant exposure to the Master's influence, coupled with her own determined resistance, was awakening latent abilities within her. She could feel the emotional states of others with a new clarity, sensing the subtle currents of fear and despair that rippled through the town. This heightened awareness was both a gift and a curse, a constant reminder of the battle being waged all around her, but also a tool that would prove invaluable.

Harmony understood that a direct confrontation with the Master was inevitable, a terrifying certainty that loomed on the horizon. She knew she couldn't defeat him through conventional means, through force or trickery. His power was too vast, too insidious. Her only hope lay in overwhelming his influence with a force that was its antithesis: pure, unadulterated love and unwavering hope. It was a formidable weapon, one he could not comprehend, one he could not corrupt. Her resolve had not just hardened; it had transformed into a radiant, unyielding core of defiance, a beacon of light in the encroaching darkness, fueled by the fierce, primal love of a mother for her child. She was ready to face whatever came, for Lily, and for the soul of Redwater Crossing.

Sheriff Brody's office, usually a hub of contained chaos, had become a monument to weary helplessness. The usually stern lines of his face were etched deeper, permanent shadows under eyes that had seen too much, too soon. Stacks of paper, once meticulously organized, now lay scattered like fallen leaves, each report a stark testament to another life extinguished, another family shattered. The sheer volume of it all was a suffocating weight. He'd spent his career dealing with the tangible evils of the world – petty thieves, drunk drivers, the occasional violent crime born of human frailty or rage. But this... this was different. This was a poison seeping through the very foundations of Redwater Crossing, invisible, insidious, and utterly relentless.

He'd worked himself to the bone, a phantom himself, flitting from one grieving household to another, offering words of comfort that felt hollow even as they left his lips, extending a hand that could offer no tangible solace. He'd seen the vacant stares, the choked sobs, the sheer, soul-crushing weight of loss that had settled over the town like a shroud. Each death was a fresh wound, and the town was bleeding out. He'd dispatched his deputies, sent them on futile patrols, hoping against hope that a visible presence, a show of authority, might somehow deter the darkness. But the darkness didn't care about patrols. It thrived in the quiet corners of the mind, in the hushed whispers of doubt, in the suffocating blanket of despair.

The "tall man" Harmony had spoken of, that spectral sentinel of despair, had become a chilling reality for Brody too. He'd seen him, or thought he'd seen him, on the periphery of his vision, a fleeting shadow at the edge of a crime scene, a dark silhouette against the stark winter sky. He'd dismissed it as exhaustion, the tricks of a mind pushed too far. But now, with each successive tragedy, with the eerily similar patterns emerging from the chaos, he couldn't shake the feeling that they were not alone in their fight, and that their adversary was not of this world.

His focus had narrowed, his relentless energy now channeled into a single, desperate hope: Harmony Jakes. He didn't fully understand the scope of what she was facing, the profound spiritual battle she seemed to be waging, but he recognized the steel in her eyes, the fierce protectiveness that burned beneath her fear. He saw a kindred spirit, someone else who refused to be swallowed by the encroaching despair, someone who was fighting back with a ferocity he could only admire. He felt a desperate need to support her, to be her anchor in this storm.

He'd started leaving anonymous notes for her, tucked into her mailbox, left on her doorstep, or discreetly passed to her during their increasingly rare encounters. These weren't just reports of sightings or statistical data; they were fragments of the Master's pattern, pieced together from the hushed confessions of the bereaved, from the subtle anomalies his deputies had noticed but couldn't explain, from the eerie coincidences that screamed of a malevolent design. He'd documented the specific timings of the suicides, noting the uncanny correlation with certain astrological alignments that even he, a man of science and logic, couldn't ignore. He'd detailed the locations, highlighting the unsettling proximity to areas that had long been rumored to hold a dark history, places where the veil between worlds was said to be thin.

"Harmony," one note read, scrawled in his hurried, illegible hand, "the wind chimes at the old Miller place. They were silent all day before Tammy jumped to her death. Not a breath of air, and those things usually sing. Something is *wrong* with the air itself." Another offered a chilling observation: "The creek behind the old mill. Deputy Byers found footprints there the morning after young Danny drowned. Not his. Too big. And they just... stopped. Like whoever made them vanished." He'd also included his own growing list of superstitions, things he'd never admit to anyone else, but which he felt Harmony would understand. "The town clock stopped at 3:17 AM on the night of Mrs. Valentine's death. Same time the lights flickered at the station. It's not just bad luck. It's... coordinated."

He was sharing what little he had, a desperate offering to a cause he believed in, even if he couldn't fully articulate its nature. He was a man bound by the law, by the tangible world, and yet he found himself increasingly reliant on the intuition of a woman who saw beyond the veil. He provided her with access to any town records she needed, any old maps or historical documents that might shed light on the Master's influence. He ensured his deputies, those who were not completely consumed by their own fear, were on the lookout for anything unusual, anything that echoed Harmony's descriptions of the Master's presence. He steered them away from asking too many questions about her activities, framing her interest as that of a concerned citizen, a mother trying to protect her child.

He knew he was overstepping his bounds, bending the rules, but the conventional methods of law enforcement were failing. The town was a powder keg, and he was watching it explode, one soul at a time. Harmony, he believed, was the only one with a chance to defuse it, to understand the spark that ignited the flames. His role, he realized with a heavy heart, was to be her unseen support, her silent accomplice in a war that was being fought on a battlefield far more treacherous than any he had ever known. He could offer her resources, protection of a sort, and most importantly, his unwavering belief. He was the sheriff, the man sworn to protect his town, and if that meant fighting an enemy he couldn't see, an enemy that preyed on the very essence of human spirit, then he would do it, even if it meant stepping into the shadows himself.

Brody would spend hours poring over Harmony's cryptic notes, trying to decipher the underlying patterns. He'd visit the sites she mentioned, not with the authority of his badge, but with a quiet reverence, a desperate hope that he might catch a glimpse of what she saw. He learned to recognize the oppressive stillness that preceded a tragedy, the way the birds would fall silent, the unnatural quiet that descended upon the usually bustling streets. He started to trust his own gut instincts, a sense that had been dulled by years of rational thinking, but which now screamed a warning whenever the Master's presence felt heavy in the air.

One particular incident stood out, a young man named Roger, known for his bright spirit and his love of photography. He'd been found in the woods, a single, perfectly framed photograph clutched in his hand – a shot of the moon, stark and beautiful, taken just hours before his death. Brody had visited the site, a dense thicket of pines where the air was unnaturally cold, even on a warm spring day. He'd found no struggle, no evidence of foul play in the traditional sense. But he'd felt it – a profound, suffocating emptiness, a void that seemed to suck the very life out of the air. He'd remembered Harmony's words about the Master amplifying existing anxieties, and he'd wondered if Roger's quiet perfectionism, his artistic yearning, had been twisted into a fatal obsession. He'd scribbled a quick note about the cold, the silence, and the photograph, leaving it where he knew Harmony would find it. He felt a desperate kinship with her, a shared burden of knowledge that isolated them from the rest of the town, even from their own colleagues.

He began to notice his own deputies becoming more withdrawn, their usual bravado replaced by a hushed fear. They'd whisper about feeling watched, about seeing things out of the corner of their eyes, about a pervasive sense of dread that clung to them like a damp chill. Brody found himself having to reassure them, to pull them back from the brink of their own despair, while simultaneously wrestling with his own growing conviction that their fears were not unfounded. He started keeping a separate, secret log of his deputies' observations, anomalies that might seem insignificant to an outsider but which, to him, formed a chilling tapestry of the Master's influence. He noticed how certain phrases, uttered by those on the verge of suicide, echoed sentiments he'd heard in Harmony's hushed warnings. It was as if the Master was speaking through the town, a collective voice of despair.

The loneliness was profound. He was the Sheriff, the man expected to have answers, to be the unshakeable pillar of the community. But he was adrift in an ocean of uncertainty, clinging to the fragmented clues that Harmony provided, his faith in her growing with each passing day. He felt a desperate need to protect her, not just from the Master, but from the weight of her own knowledge. He knew she was carrying an immense burden, and he wanted to alleviate it in any way he could. He started making small gestures of support – leaving bags of groceries on her porch, ensuring her car was always topped up with gas, making discreet inquiries about her daughter Lily, wanting to know that she was safe, that her innocence remained untainted.

He even began to research the town's history himself, digging through dusty archives in the back of the town hall, looking for any mention of similar phenomena, any old legends or folklore that might offer a clue. He was a man of logic and evidence, but this situation demanded more. It demanded faith, intuition, and a willingness to believe in the unbelievable. He found unsettling accounts of periods of intense despair in Redwater Crossing's past, brief, unexplained surges of madness that had always been attributed to mass hysteria or unfortunate coincidences. But now, with the benefit of Harmony's insights, he saw a pattern, a recurring darkness that had always lurked beneath the surface, waiting for the right conditions to erupt.

The weight of his responsibility was immense. He was not just fighting against individual acts of suicide; he was fighting against a force that sought to dismantle the very fabric of his community, to extinguish hope, and to plunge Redwater Crossing into an eternal night. He knew that Harmony was his best, perhaps his only hope. And so, he committed himself to being her steadfast ally, her silent protector, her unwavering support in a battle that would ultimately determine the fate of them all. He would offer her every resource, every piece of information he possessed, and his own hard-won understanding of the invisible enemy they faced. He would be the bulwark, the earthly shield for her spiritual war.

The weight of Redwater Crossing's unfolding tragedy pressed down on Sheriff Brody with a suffocating familiarity. He found himself poring over old newspaper clippings, yellowed and brittle with age, seeking solace or perhaps a grim validation in the documented sorrows of the past. His search had led him to the story of Batesville, a town nestled a hundred miles to the north, a place that had once been vibrant and prosperous before a series of inexplicable events had bled it dry, mirroring Redwater Crossing's current descent into despair. The archival articles spoke of a chilling epidemic of suicides that had swept through Batesville decades ago, a period of darkness that had nearly obliterated the small community. The parallels were not merely anecdotal; they were terrifyingly precise. The demographics of the victims, the methods employed, even the eerie silence that had descended upon the town in the days preceding each death – it all painted a picture of a hauntingly similar enemy at work.

Brody remembered Harmony mentioning the "tall man" with a chilling dread, a spectral figure that seemed to preside over the suicides. He now saw how that description echoed through the fragmented accounts of Batesville. Witnesses, their voices tinged with a fear that transcended time, spoke of a shadowy presence, a gaunt figure glimpsed at the edges of their vision, a silent observer of their collective unraveling. One particularly disturbing article detailed the experience of a Batesville resident, a Mrs. Vicki Yearn, who described seeing a "tall, gaunt man, like a shadow stretched too thin," standing by the town's old clock tower on the eve of her neighbor's sudden death. She recalled a profound sense of dread, a suffocating emptiness that had settled over her like a physical weight, making it difficult to breathe. The clock tower, the article noted, had stopped at precisely 3:17 AM, the same time Dr. Brock's lights had flickered in Batesville. The déjà vu was so potent, so visceral, it felt less like a historical record and more like a premonition.

The chilling realization settled over Brody like a shroud: the Master, or whatever entity Harmony was battling, was not a new threat. This was an ancient, parasitic force, a predator that fed on despair and vulnerability, a recurring blight that resurfaced in unsuspecting communities when the conditions were ripe. Batesville had been its previous hunting ground, and now Redwater Crossing was its current victim. This knowledge, while terrifying, also brought a desperate clarity. It meant they were not facing a random, isolated outbreak of mental illness. It meant there was a pattern, a malevolent intelligence behind the devastation, and if they understood its past actions, they might be able to predict and thwart its future ones.

He found himself spending late nights in his office, the only light the stark glow of his desk lamp, surrounded by the ghosts of Batesville's past and the immediate horrors of Redwater Crossing. He pieced together the timelines, cross-referencing the dates of the suicides in both towns, looking for any correlation, any subtle sign that might reveal the Master's rhythm. He noticed that the outbreaks in Batesville had occurred during periods of economic hardship and social unrest, times when fear and uncertainty were already gnawing at the community's edges. Redwater Crossing, too, had been grappling with the closure of the lumber mill, a significant blow to the town's livelihood, leaving many families on the brink of financial ruin. The Master, it seemed, was a shrewd opportunist, preying on the fractures already present in the societal fabric.

The details were unnervingly consistent. In Batesville, as in Redwater Crossing, there were reports of localized environmental anomalies preceding the suicides. Whispers of strange atmospheric conditions, unexplained silences in nature, and peculiar shifts in temperature. One article from Batesville Chronicle spoke of a period where the local creek, usually teeming with life, had inexplicably dried up for three days, only to return to its normal flow immediately after the last recorded suicide. Another detailed how the town's normally vocal birds had fallen eerily silent for weeks, their absence a deafening testament to the encroaching dread. Brody recalled the note he'd sent to Harmony about the silent wind chimes at the old Miller place, and the unnatural cold at the site where Roger was found. The Master's influence wasn't just psychological; it was a palpable, environmental manipulation.

He felt a growing sense of urgency, a desperate need to impress upon Harmony the full gravity of their situation. This wasn't a localized problem; it was a recurring nightmare, a monster that had claimed entire towns before and would likely do so again if left unchecked. He found himself rereading Harmony's descriptions of the Master, her intuitive understanding of its insidious nature, her struggle to articulate its ethereal presence. He saw how her descriptions of the "shadows that whispered" and the "cold that seeped into your bones" directly mirrored the experiences of those in Batesville. It was as if she was experiencing echoes of the past, or perhaps the Master was broadcasting the same oppressive aura that had plagued that other, forgotten town.

The historical accounts also hinted at a communal aspect to the Master's influence; a way it seemed to amplify existing anxieties and sow discord. In Batesville, before the suicides escalated, there had been a rise in petty squabbles, a noticeable increase in suspicion and mistrust among neighbors. Friendships soured, families fractured, and a general air of paranoia descended upon the town. Brody recognized this pattern in Redwater Crossing, too. The hushed gossip, the nervous glances exchanged in the grocery store, the palpable tension that hung in the air whenever two or more people gathered. It was as if the Master was deliberately isolating individuals, breaking down the bonds of community one frayed thread at a time, making them more susceptible to its fatal whisperings.

He looked at the photograph of the Batesville clock tower, its hands frozen at the tell-tale time. He superimposed it in his mind's eye over the image of Redwater Crossing's own clock tower, a structure that had also ceased to function at the precise moment of a tragedy. It was more than a coincidence; it was a signature. The Master was leaving its mark, a temporal and spatial imprint that spoke of its dominion. This recurring pattern was both a curse and a potential key. If they could identify the conditions under which the Master manifested, the environmental or emotional triggers that allowed it to gain a foothold, they might be able to disrupt its cycle.

The knowledge of Batesville's fate was a heavy burden. It solidified Brody's belief that the fight was not merely against despair, but against a specific, ancient entity that actively cultivated it. This was a spiritual war, waged in the hearts and minds of innocent people, and the stakes were far higher than he had initially understood. The fact that this had happened before, and would likely happen again, amplified the urgency of Harmony's mission. They couldn't afford to fail. The lives of Redwater Crossing's residents, and countless others in the future, depended on their success. He knew he had to share everything he'd found with Harmony, not to frighten her, but to arm her with the knowledge that she was not alone in this fight, and that their enemy, though ancient and powerful, was not invincible. He would ensure she had access to all the archived material, any and all information that could shed light on this recurring darkness, this spectral shadow that had haunted Batesville and now threatened to consume Redwater Crossing. The past was not just prologue; it was a roadmap, a chilling testament to what they were up against, and a desperate plea for them to find a way to break the cycle, to prevent the echoes of Batesville from becoming the final dirge of Redwater Crossing.

CHAPTER 9

Harmony Jakes, The Unyielding

Harmony Jakes moved through the suffocating miasma of Redwater Crossing like a lone star in a storm-choked sky. While the tendrils of despair, woven by the Master's insidious influence, wrapped around the hearts and minds of her neighbors, a strange, almost miraculous calm resided within her. It wasn't a manufactured stoicism, a forced smile plastered over an abyss of fear. It was a genuine clarity, a stubborn refusal to succumb to the encroaching darkness. This resilience, this unyielding core of her being, was not born of armor or any tangible defense, but from something far more profound, something that defied the Master's predatory logic.

The Master thrived on the rot, on the festering wounds of doubt and fear that weakened the spirit. It was a parasite that fed on the unraveling threads of sanity, exacerbating existing anxieties until they snapped. For most in Redwater Crossing, this meant succumbing to the overwhelming tide of dread, their thoughts becoming a fractured mirror reflecting the Master's darkest desires. They saw the shadows lengthen, heard the whispers of hopelessness, and their will to resist crumbled. Harmony, however, seemed to exist on a different plane, a frequency the Master's insidious broadcast couldn't quite tune into.

Sheriff Brody, observing her from the periphery of the town's collective madness, found himself constantly searching for an explanation. He had seen the glazed eyes of the afflicted, the vacant stares that spoke of an interior landscape stripped bare. He had witnessed the sudden, violent shifts in mood, the irrational bursts of anger or despair that signaled the Master's grip tightening. But Harmony remained an anomaly. Her gaze was sharp, her mind incisive, her actions deliberate and focused. When others stumbled, she stood firm. When fear threatened to paralyze, she moved forward.

He pondered the nature of her immunity. It wasn't a matter of brute strength; Harmony was physically no more formidable than many others in town. It wasn't a shield of faith, for while she possessed a quiet spirituality, it wasn't the fervent, evangelical kind that might theoretically ward off such an entity. What, then, was this unwavering bulwark within her? He began to suspect it was rooted in the very fabric of her being, in the quiet strength that had always characterized her, a resilience forged not in a single, cataclysmic event, but in a thousand tiny battles fought and won against the everyday trials of life.

He recalled conversations, fragments of her past that had seemed inconsequential at the time but now resonated with profound meaning. The way she spoke of her deceased mother, not with debilitating grief, but with a gentle, enduring love that seemed to warm even the coldest memories. The quiet determination with which she had cared for her ailing father, enduring long nights and mounting worries with a steady, uncomplaining resolve. These weren't grand gestures, but the quiet, persistent acts of love and duty that built an inner fortress, brick by invisible brick.

This inner strength, Brody theorized, was a potent counterforce to the Master's influence. The Master preyed on isolation, on the feeling of being utterly alone and unloved. It whispered that no one cared, that all efforts were in vain, that despair was the only logical response. But Harmony, Brody suspected, carried a reservoir of love within her – the love she had given, the love she had received, the enduring memory of love that transcended physical presence. This love, he believed, acted as a shield, a vibrant, living force that the Master's darkness could not extinguish. It was a connection to something pure and unwavering, something the parasitic entity could not comprehend or corrupt.

Her unique resilience also made her a puzzle to the Master. The entity likely operated on predictable algorithms of fear and desperation. It identified vulnerabilities, exploited weaknesses, and amplified negative emotions until they became overwhelming. Harmony, however, presented no such easy target. Her emotional landscape, while not devoid of sadness or worry, was anchored by a fundamental optimism, a deep-seated belief in the possibility of good, and an unwavering connection to those she loved. This made her unpredictable, a deviation from the Master's meticulously crafted patterns of destruction.

He saw it in her interactions with others, even those succumbing to the Master's influence. While others recoiled from the despairing, Harmony approached them with a quiet empathy, a refusal to judge. She didn't dismiss their fears or belittle their anguish. Instead, she offered a steady presence, a hand to hold, a listening ear. It was as if she understood, on some primal level, that the Master was the true enemy, and that those caught in its web were, in essence, its victims. This compassion, rather than weakness, was her strength. It allowed her to remain a beacon of clarity in a town drowning in confusion.

The sheer contrast between Harmony and the rest of Redwater Crossing was stark. While the townsfolk became increasingly withdrawn, suspicious, and prone to irrational outbursts, Harmony remained engaged, observant, and capable of clear thought. She navigated the town's descent into chaos with a sharp awareness, noticing the subtle shifts in behavior, the creeping paranoia, the hollowed-out expressions that signaled the Master's hand at work. She didn't dismiss these signs; she cataloged them, analyzed them, her mind working to unravel the mystery while others were being ensnared by it.

This ability to remain clear-headed was not a superpower in the traditional sense, but a testament to her inner fortitude. It was the quiet strength of a person who had learned to confront adversity without allowing it to consume her. The Master's influence was like a psychic virus, designed to infect and dismantle the mind. But Harmony's mind, perhaps hardened by life's subtler, yet persistent, challenges, possessed a natural immunity, an inherent resistance to the invasive whispers of despair.

Consider the way she dealt with the growing unease around the Miller's place. While others whispered of hauntings and bad omens and succumbed to the creeping dread that emanated from its decaying structure, Harmony approached it with a practical curiosity. She didn't deny the palpable sense of unease, the unnatural stillness that pervaded the air around it, but she didn't allow it to paralyze her. Instead, she sought understanding. She spoke to the few remaining neighbors, piecing together fragmented histories, looking for rational explanations before succumbing to supernatural interpretations. This methodical approach, this refusal to jump to fearful conclusions, was a direct defiance of the Master's manipulative tactics, which thrived on speculation and amplified fear.

Her love for her community, even in its current broken state, was another facet of her resilience. While some residents were turning inward, consumed by their own burgeoning despair, Harmony continued to look outward. She worried about Mrs. Conrad, about young Byran, about the fading light in Sheriff Brody's eyes. This concern for others was not a burden; it was a source of strength, a reminder of what was at stake, and a powerful motivator to fight back. The Master sought to isolate, to sever connections, but Harmony's deep-seated empathy acted as a continuous reassertion of those bonds, a constant affirmation that they were not alone, even in their suffering.

This unique immunity wasn't a passive state. It was an active, conscious choice. Harmony didn't just *not* succumb; she actively resisted. Her clarity of thought allowed her to question the insidious narratives the Master was weaving. When the whispers suggested futility, she focused on the small victories, the acts of kindness that still flickered in the darkness. When fear threatened to take root, she nurtured the seeds of hope. She was a gardener of the soul, tending to the delicate blossoms of resilience in a barren, poisoned land.

The Master, accustomed to predictable prey, likely found Harmony a frustrating enigma. It was like a predator encountering prey that, instead of fleeing in terror, turned to face it with a steady gaze, assessing its weaknesses. This defiance, this refusal to play by the Master's rules, must have been disorienting. Her very existence was a contradiction to its philosophy of despair. She embodied hope in a place where hope was being systematically extinguished. She represented clarity in a fog of confusion. She demonstrated love in an atmosphere of encroaching isolation.

This inner strength, this unyielding resilience, was not a gift bestowed upon her but a quality cultivated. It was the byproduct of a life lived with purpose and anchored by love. It was the quiet strength that emerged from facing challenges head-on, from caring deeply, and from refusing to let the darkness extinguish the light within. In the heart of Redwater Crossing's unfolding tragedy, Harmony Jakes stood as a testament to the enduring power of the human spirit, a solitary warrior whose greatest weapon was the unyielding sanctuary of her own indomitable soul. Her immunity wasn't a shield of invincibility, but a vibrant testament to the life force that the Master, in its ancient hunger for despair, could never truly understand, let alone conquer.

The Master, an entity woven from the very essence of despair, had grown accustomed to the predictable ebb and flow of human weakness. For centuries, it had orchestrated its insidious symphony of dread, drawing souls into its vortex of hopelessness with a practiced, almost weary, precision. Cities crumbled, empires withered, and individuals shattered under its unseen influence, each falling victim in their own unique, yet ultimately similar, fashion. Its methods were honed through countless ages, a vast repertoire of whispers and shadows, of amplifying anxieties and twisting truths until the foundations of sanity gave way. Redwater Crossing was merely another canvas, another quiet town ripe for the plucking, its inhabitants already burdened by the subtle anxieties that served as fertile ground for its growth.

But Harmony Jakes was different. She was a discordant note in its meticulously composed melody, a splash of vibrant color in a world it had carefully muted to shades of gray. Initially, her resilience registered as an anomaly, a statistical outlier that the Master might have dismissed as a temporary glitch in its otherwise flawless system. It was accustomed to the initial flicker of defiance, the brief surge of will before the encroaching darkness inevitably extinguished it. It had seen it countless times, the flicker of courage quickly overwhelmed by the suffocating weight of despair, the individual's spirit buckling under the relentless pressure. Yet, Harmony did not buckle. She did not falter. She merely... persisted.

This persistence, so alien to the Master's experience, began to shift from a mere curiosity to a gnawing fascination. It was like a skilled musician encountering a complex, unfamiliar rhythm that refused to resolve into its expected pattern. The Master, a connoisseur of broken things, found itself studying Harmony with an intensity it hadn't applied to any single soul in decades. It probed her mind, not with the brute force of terror, but with the subtle, almost surgical precision of an entomologist dissecting a rare specimen. It sent tendrils of doubt, insidious suggestions designed to unravel even the strongest of wills, but they seemed to slide off Harmony's inner core, dissipating like mist under the morning sun.

The entity could feel her thoughts, not in their entirety, but in their vibrant, unwavering essence. It sensed the calm that underpinned her daily existence, a profound quietude that no amount of external chaos could disturb. It observed her interactions, the way she met the increasingly erratic behavior of her neighbors not with fear, but with a gentle, steady concern. When Mr. Anderson, his eyes wide with a terror that no longer had a discernible source, accused her of conspiring with the shadows, Harmony didn't shrink away. She met his frantic gaze with a placid sincerity, her voice a low, steady anchor in his storm of delusion. "There are no shadows here, Mr. Anderson," she had said, her words imbued with a quiet certainty that, for a fleeting moment, seemed to pierce the fog in his eyes.

This was not the stoicism of the deeply repressed, nor the denial of the willfully ignorant. It was something deeper, more fundamental. The Master, which understood despair as a tangible force, a viscous, suffocating presence, found itself unable to categorize Harmony's inner landscape. It was a void, but not an empty one. It was a calm, but not a dormant one. It was a presence that defied its very nature, a vibrant, living lack of what it sought to impose. It was an affront, a silent, unwavering accusation that its power, so absolute in its dominion over the broken, was somehow incomplete.

The Master's fascination began to curdle into something akin to irritation. It was a sensation it rarely experienced, a flicker of something akin to wounded pride. Its existence was predicated on the universal truth of human frailty, on the inherent susceptibility of the soul to darkness. To have this fundamental law of its being challenged, to have an exception so boldly displayed, was not merely an obstacle; it was an insult. It was as if a master architect, who had built countless impregnable fortresses, suddenly found itself facing a single, stubbornly intact structure that defied all known principles of engineering.

The usual tactics, the carefully calibrated whispers that preyed on individual fears, seemed to lose their potency when directed at Harmony. When it nudged her towards the suffocating guilt over her mother's passing, it found not the expected despair, but a quiet, enduring love, a warm memory that served as a balm rather than a wound. When it tried to amplify the anxieties surrounding her father's illness, it encountered the resolute strength of a daughter who had already walked through the valley of that fear, emerging not broken, but tempered. The Master found itself probing for weaknesses that simply weren't there, or rather, weaknesses that had been transformed, transmuted into sources of resilience.

This realization was a turning point. The Master shifted its focus. No longer content with observing from a distance, it began to direct its immense, disembodied will with a singular, unyielding purpose: Harmony Jakes. It needed to understand this anomaly, to dissect its nature, and ultimately, to dismantle it. The entity began to weave more intricate illusions around her, not necessarily to break her, but to observe her reactions, to learn the precise mechanics of her immunity. It conjured fleeting glimpses of lost loved ones, distorted reflections of her deepest desires, hoping to find the seam in her composure, the single thread that, if pulled, would unravel the whole tapestry.

One evening, as dusk bled into the sky above Redwater Crossing, casting long, distorted shadows across the weary landscape, Harmony found herself walking along the edge of the woods, the air thick with the oppressive silence that had become the town's new normal. The Master chose this moment to intensify its focus. It didn't manifest as a monstrous form, or a terrifying sound. Instead, it presented itself as a subtle shift in the very fabric of her reality. The trees seemed to lean in, their branches like skeletal fingers reaching out. The familiar scent of pine needles was replaced by a cloying, sickly sweetness that hinted at decay.

Harmony paused, her breath catching not in fear, but in a keen, almost scientific observation. She recognized the unnatural stillness, the way the birdsong had abruptly ceased, the unsettling visual distortions that hinted at something beyond the ordinary. Most people would have turned back, their hearts hammering against their ribs, their minds already succumbing to the primal urge to flee. But

Harmony, with a quiet determination, took a step further into the altered perception.

The Master, sensing her willingness to engage, escalated its efforts. It projected an image into her mind – a vivid, heartbreaking scene from her childhood. Her father, younger, vibrant, laughing as he lifted her onto his shoulders. It was a memory so pure, so brimming with love and joy, that it felt as if she were reliving it. The Master's intent was clear: to twist this cherished memory, to inject it with a poisonous undercurrent of loss, to make her feel the agony of its passing with a renewed, soul-crushing intensity. It wanted to see her gasp, to hear her cry out, to witness the foundation of her emotional resilience crumble.

But as the image played out, Harmony did not weep. Instead, a soft smile touched her lips. She didn't see the impending loss; she saw the love. She felt the warmth of her father's embrace, heard the genuine joy in his laughter, and she allowed herself to bask in that memory, not as a prelude to grief, but as an enduring testament to the connection they shared. The Master, observing this internal reaction, felt a surge of something akin to disbelief. It was like a master alchemist attempting to transmute gold into lead, only to find the gold stubbornly resisting the transformation, retaining its inherent brilliance.

The Master's efforts became more focused, more personal. It began to whisper directly into her consciousness, not with the generic pronouncements of doom it unleashed upon others, but with tailored accusations, subtle manipulations designed to exploit the very foundations of her character. It insinuated that her steady nature was a form of emotional cowardice, that her quiet resilience was a denial of the suffering around her, that her refusal to succumb to panic was a selfish act. It tried to make her doubt her own strength, to convince her that her inner calm was a delusion, a fragile facade that would inevitably shatter.

"You pretend to be strong," the whispers hissed, a silken venom seeping into the edges of her awareness. "But you are merely afraid to feel. You see the pain, but you choose to ignore it, to insulate yourself in your false peace. You are no better than those who succumb, for you refuse to acknowledge the truth of despair."

Harmony, walking through the increasingly distorted woods, heard these insidious accusations. They were designed to isolate, to create internal conflict, to fracture her sense of self. But they did not take root. Instead, they seemed to bounce off a core of understanding. She knew her strength was not born of denial, but of acceptance. She had faced hardship, acknowledged loss, and found a way to carry it without being consumed. Her peace was not a denial of suffering, but a testament to the enduring power of love and hope *in spite* of it.

"Despair is a choice," she thought, her inner voice firm and unwavering. "And so is hope."

The Master found this internal retort particularly galling. It operated on the assumption that despair was an inevitable, almost natural, state. To be confronted with the notion that it was merely an option, a choice that could be refused, was profoundly unsettling. It was like a fundamental law of physics being challenged by a single, inexplicable phenomenon.

The entity began to weave more elaborate scenarios around her. It showed her visions of the townspeople turning on her, their fear and paranoia manifesting as accusations and outright hostility. It amplified the existing tensions, creating phantom arguments in her vicinity, projecting the sound of angry shouts where there was only silence. It wanted to isolate her, to strip away her support system, to leave her utterly alone with its suffocating presence.

Yet, even in these staged conflicts, Harmony's response was not one of fear or anger. When the phantom arguments swirled around her, she would pause, listen, and then calmly continue on her path, her mind analyzing the patterns of manipulation rather than reacting to the manufactured emotions. She saw the Master's hand in the distorted cries, the unnatural intensity of the phantom anger. She understood that these were not genuine reflections of her neighbors' feelings, but carefully crafted illusions designed to make her believe she was truly alone and reviled.

The Master, growing increasingly desperate, began to experiment with more direct forms of influence. It tried to subtly alter her perceptions of the physical world. Colors would momentarily shift to a duller hue, familiar objects would seem to warp and distort, and the very air would sometimes feel heavy, charged with an unseen malevolence. It was attempting to create a pervasive sense of unease, to make her environment itself feel hostile, to erode her confidence in her own senses.

Harmony would blink, her brow furrowed slightly, and then calmly re-focus. She would touch the surface of a tree trunk, its bark rough and familiar beneath her fingertips, or look at the distant horizon, its steady line a reassurance against the fleeting distortions. She acknowledged the strangeness but refused to be governed by it. Her grounding in reality, her connection to the tangible world, was a powerful countermeasure against the Master's illusory tactics.

The entity was perplexed. Its vast arsenal, honed over millennia of soul consumption, was proving remarkably ineffective against this one individual. It was accustomed to the gradual erosion, the slow breakdown of defenses, the inevitable capitulation. Harmony, however, presented a solid, unyielding wall. It was like trying to break down a mountain with a single drop of water.

The Master's fascination had morphed into a consuming obsession. Harmony Jakes was no longer just an anomaly; she was a challenge, a deeply personal affront to its very being. It began to dedicate more of its energy, more of its ancient power, to understanding and breaking her. It sensed that her resilience was not merely a passive state, but an active force, a constant, conscious resistance that it could not simply wait out. It had to actively engage, to find a way to dismantle the fortress that stood so defiantly in the heart of its encroaching darkness. The Master was accustomed to hunting prey, but Harmony was beginning to feel like a predator confronting an equally ancient, and far more subtle, hunter. The game had changed, and the Master, for the first time in a very long time, found itself on the defensive.

Sheriff Mason Brody felt the familiar weight of his badge settle against his chest, a comforting solidity in the increasingly surreal landscape of Redwater Crossing. For weeks, a creeping dread had settled over the town, a palpable shift in the atmosphere that defied logical explanation. Neighbors whispered behind drawn curtains, children's laughter had evaporated from the playgrounds, and a pervasive anxiety seemed to hang in the very air, thick and suffocating. Brody, a man built on the bedrock of procedure and common sense, found himself adrift in a sea of the inexplicable. His usual tools—a keen eye for detail, an understanding of human nature, and the authority of the law—felt woefully inadequate against the encroaching tide of fear.

But then there was Harmony Jakes.

He'd known her for years, of course. She was a fixture in Redwater Crossing, a quiet, steady presence that never sought the spotlight. He'd seen her navigate life's quiet storms with a grace and resilience that he'd always admired, but never truly fathomed until now. Now, as the town's collective sanity frayed at the edges, Harmony remained an island of calm in the escalating chaos. While others succumbed to paranoia, their eyes wide with nameless terrors, Harmony met the growing strangeness with an unnerving composure. She didn't deny the oddities; she observed them, analyzed them, as if she were a scientist studying a peculiar phenomenon rather than a victim of it.

Brody had initially approached her with a professional detachment, trying to find a rational explanation for the town's malaise. He'd spoken to her about the unusual number of disappearances, the increasingly erratic behavior of residents, the unsettling quiet that had fallen over the normally bustling streets. Harmony had listened patiently, her gaze steady, her responses measured. She spoke of the subtle shifts, the way shadows seemed to linger too long, the unnatural stillness that preceded the most disturbing events. It was the kind of talk that would have sent a lesser man to the nearest mental health professional, but in Harmony's calm pronouncements, Brody heard not madness, but a strange, unsettling truth.

He found himself drawn to her quiet strength, her unyielding core. She was, he realized, the only one in Redwater Crossing who seemed to understand that the darkness wasn't just a manifestation of fear, but something... active. Something that fed on it. And she, somehow, was immune. Brody, a pragmatist to his core, wasn't one for mystical explanations, but faced with the undeniable reality of what was happening, he found himself willing to entertain possibilities that lay far beyond the confines of his police academy training.

He started by offering practical assistance, a familiar anchor in the swirling uncertainty. He'd bring her coffee at her bookstore, not just as a neighbor, but as a fellow sentinel standing watch. He'd ask about her day, about any new observations, his notepad always at the ready. He ensured her shop's security systems were top-notch, doubling down on patrols around her block, a silent promise of protection. He listened to her theories, no matter how outlandish they might seem at first glance, always looking for the kernel of logic, the thread of evidence that might connect them to the tangible world.

"Anything new, Harmony?" he'd ask, his voice a low rumble, as he leaned against her counter, the scent of old paper and brewing coffee a welcome contrast to the metallic tang of fear that seemed to permeate the town. "Any... unusual visitors today? Strange conversations?"

Harmony would often offer a faint smile, a gentle acknowledgment of his concern. "Just the usual unease, Sheriff. People are jumpy. Mr. Henderson almost mistook his own shadow for something sinister this morning." She'd then recount a subtle anomaly, a fleeting scent of decay in the air that quickly vanished, or a peculiar pattern of silence that descended on the street for precisely five minutes at noon. Brody would meticulously jot down these details, his brow furrowed in concentration, trying to find a pattern, a correlation.

He began to see his role not just as a law enforcement officer, but as Harmony's strategic advisor, her tether to the mundane reality that was slowly slipping away from everyone else. He understood that her unique ability to resist the encroaching darkness came with a profound burden. She was alone in her clarity, surrounded by a town succumbing to a collective delusion. Brody recognized the immense pressure this must place on her, the isolation of being the only one who saw things as they truly were.

"You're doing a good job, Harmony," he'd say, his voice gruff with sincerity. "Keeping your head. That's more than most can do right now. If you need anything, anything at all, you know where to find me. My door's always open."

He meant it. He was willing to bend the rules, to stretch the boundaries of his authority, if it meant supporting Harmony. He'd authorize extra stakeouts, discreetly gather information on residents exhibiting particularly disturbing behavior, and even discreetly contact neighboring law enforcement agencies, framing it as an unusual epidemic of mass hysteria, a carefully constructed lie to explain away the unexplainable without raising further alarm. He used his network, his contacts, to try and find any logical explanations for the town's decline, delving into local history, old town records, anything that might offer a clue, a precedent, a reason for the darkness descending upon Redwater Crossing.

Brody found himself spending less time on routine patrols and more time at Harmony's bookstore. It had become his unofficial command center, a place where the whispers of fear could be muted by the steady hum of ordinary life and Harmony's unwavering presence. He'd bring her case files, maps of the town, anything that might help her visualize the patterns of the disturbances. He provided her with a secure communication line, a burner phone that was untraceable, for when she needed to relay information that might be too sensitive for public channels.

"I've been looking into the old quarry," he told her one afternoon, spreading a tattered map across her counter. "There are some... stories. Local legends about strange occurrences out there. Nothing concrete, mind you, just whispers from the old timers. But given what's happening..." He trailed off, his gaze meeting hers. He was no longer just a sheriff investigating a crime; he was a man trying to understand a force that defied all his training.

Harmony traced a finger over the map, her expression thoughtful. "The quarry. Yes, I've felt a... pull from that direction sometimes. A coldness that doesn't feel natural."

"I'll organize a search," Brody stated, his jaw set. "Discreetly. A few trusted deputies, under the guise of looking for a lost hiker. We'll see if we can find anything tangible. Anything that doesn't make us question our own sanity." He knew it was a long shot, a desperate measure, but he was prepared to chase every shadow, investigate every rumor, if it offered even the slightest possibility of helping Harmony, of helping Redwater Crossing.

He also began to discreetly gather information about the town's history, poring over dusty tomes in the local library's archives. He was searching for anything that might explain the phenomenon, anything that might offer a historical context for the supernatural intrusion. He found fragmented accounts of unexplained phenomena, local folklore filled with tales of entities that fed on despair, of a darkness that had periodically touched the edges of Redwater Crossing throughout its history, but never with such pervasive intensity. Each discovery, however obscure, was shared with Harmony, her insightful interpretation often shedding light on the cryptic passages.

"It speaks of a 'Shadow Weaver'," Brody read aloud from a brittle, leather-bound journal, his voice tinged with disbelief. "A being that draws sustenance from fear and despair, its influence growing with every soul it consumes. It mentions wards, ancient symbols meant to repel it, but these are described as 'fading' over time."

Harmony listened intently, her eyes wide but not with fear. "Fading wards... perhaps that's why this is happening now. The protection has weakened."

Brody nodded, his mind racing. "If that's the case, then we need to understand those wards. Find them. Reinforce them. It's a long shot, Harmony, a real long shot, but it's more than we had yesterday." He promised to dedicate resources to researching those ancient symbols, to see if any remained in local churches, old gravestones, or forgotten corners of the town. He would task his deputies with looking for any unusual markings or patterns, subtle clues that might lead them to these forgotten defenses.

He understood that Harmony was the key, the fulcrum upon which the town's fate would turn. His role was to ensure she had the strength, the resources, and the unwavering support to bear that burden. He was her shield, her sounding board, her link to the world of reason and order. He would ensure that the mundane mechanisms of law and order, however inadequate they felt, continued to function, creating a fragile bulwark against the encroaching madness. He would be the steadfast presence that reminded her that she wasn't entirely alone, that even in the face of the incomprehensible, there was still a man willing to stand by her side, to believe in her, and to fight for the dawn. He saw her as more than just a resident; he saw her as Redwater Crossing's last, unyielding hope, and he was committed to seeing that hope survive. His support was not just a professional obligation; it was a personal conviction, a quiet promise to the woman who, against all odds, was holding back the night. He would ensure that she had everything she needed, even if it meant venturing into realms far beyond his jurisdiction, realms where logic ceded to the unknown, and where the badge on his chest felt both a comfort and a stark reminder of the limitations of his earthly power. He would be her anchor, her confidant, her most loyal ally in the fight against the encroaching darkness, and he would do it all without question.

The scent of aged paper and brewing chamomile tea had always been a balm to Harmony's senses, a familiar comfort in the often-turbulent currents of life. But lately, even these accustomed fragrances seemed tinged with an underlying anxiety, a subtle discord that resonated with the growing unease of Redwater Crossing. Sheriff Brody's visits, once a welcome respite, now carried a weight of shared urgency, his earnest attempts to impose order on the encroaching chaos, a stark reminder of the battle they were collectively facing. He saw her as an island of calm, but he couldn't truly grasp the storm brewing within her. It was not a calm born of ignorance, but of a fierce, internal preparation.

Harmony Jakes, proprietor of "The Bound Tome" and, unbeknownst to most, a nascent guardian against the encroaching darkness, was no longer content to merely observe. The passive resistance she had offered thus far, the quiet fortitude that had so impressed the Sheriff, was becoming insufficient. The subtle shifts in the town's atmosphere, the unnerving silences, the fleeting glimpses of something fundamentally wrong – these were no longer mere observations; they were omens. The "Master," as she had come to think of the unseen architect of this malaise, was growing bolder. His tendrils of influence were tightening, not just around the town, but around the very souls of its inhabitants. Harmony felt it, a cold pressure against her own inner equilibrium, a subtle temptation to succumb, to let fear dictate her actions. But she resisted. She had to.

Her preparation wasn't about acquiring weapons or devising elaborate traps, though she'd considered such things in the desperate throes of sleepless nights. Sheriff Brody was focused on the tangible, the observable. He looked for patterns in disappearances, for physical evidence, for the logical progression of a crime. Harmony knew that the Master's game was far more insidious, played on a subtler battlefield: the human psyche. His power wasn't in brute force, but in the insidious manipulation of doubt, despair, and ultimately, fear. He didn't break his victims; he unraveled them from the inside out, feeding on their fractured selves.

She began by dissecting his methods, not as an investigator, but as a scholar of the human heart, albeit one facing an unprecedentedly corrupting force. She'd sit in her quiet study above the bookstore, the dim glow of a single lamp illuminating stacks of old journals, folklore collections, and texts on psychology she'd acquired over the years, hoping for some tangential insight. She revisited the moments of unease she'd felt in the town, the peculiar interactions, the subtle shifts in people's demeanors that had initially seemed like mere eccentricity or stress. Now, she saw them through a new lens, identifying the insidious artistry of his influence.

She'd recall Mrs. Cherry, the usually vibrant baker, suddenly consumed by a crippling self-doubt, convinced her bread was now tasteless, her cakes an insult to her customers. Harmony remembered the almost imperceptible way a shadow seemed to deepen around Mrs. Cherry's eyes in the days leading up to her breakdown, the way her voice had lost its usual rhythm, replaced by a hesitant, almost apologetic tone. It wasn't just sadness; it was a carefully cultivated erosion of self-worth, a whisper of inadequacy amplified into a roar of despair. The Master hadn't forced Mrs. Cherry to doubt herself; he had simply nurtured the seeds of doubt that already lay dormant within her, watering them with subtle suggestions and preying on her anxieties.

Then there was young Timmy Peterson, who had always been a boisterous, imaginative child. Harmony remembered seeing him a few weeks prior, sitting alone on the park bench, his shoulders slumped, his once bright eyes vacant. He'd been obsessed with stories of monsters and ghosts, but now, his fear had taken on a new, paralyzing quality. He'd spoken of a "darkness" following him, not as a game, but with a genuine, bone-chilling terror. Harmony had seen how the Master could twist innocence into abject dread, making the fantastical real and terrifying, not through apparition, but through insidious suggestion that preyed on a child's nascent fears. He'd likely fed on Timmy's vivid imagination, turning his creative spirit into a tool of his own torment.

Harmony realized that the Master's power lay in his ability to identify and exploit the deepest insecurities, the unspoken fears that festered beneath the surface of everyday life. He was a maestro of discord, orchestrating a symphony of suffering from the hidden corners of the human soul. She studied the subtle cues: the averted gazes, the sudden irritability, the irrational anxieties that began to plague the townsfolk. These weren't random occurrences; they were deliberate strokes of his malevolent brush, painting a picture of a town slowly being consumed by its own inner demons.

Her days were now a carefully orchestrated ritual. Mornings were dedicated to the bookstore, to maintaining the face of normalcy, to offering a quiet word of encouragement or a knowing glance to those who seemed most affected, a subtle counter-force against the pervasive gloom. She'd offer a warm drink, a listening ear, a gentle reminder of simpler, brighter times, knowing that these small acts of connection were a form of quiet defiance. She saw herself as a lighthouse, her steady presence a beacon in the encroaching fog.

Afternoons were reserved for deeper work. She'd retreat to her study, the door closed, the world outside muted. Here, she engaged in practices that felt both ancient and entirely new. Meditation, once a tool for simple mindfulness, now became a rigorous discipline of self-fortification. She'd sit for hours, focusing on her breath, on the sensation of her own being, pushing back against the intrusive whispers of doubt that the Master so expertly wove into the fabric of her thoughts. It was a constant, internal battle, a wrestling match with shadows that threatened to engulf her.

She learned to recognize the insidious tendrils of the Master's influence not just in others, but within herself. When a flicker of anger sparked over a misplaced book, she'd pause, breathe, and question its origin. Was it genuine frustration, or a subtle nudge from the darkness, amplifying a minor annoyance into a consuming rage? When a wave of despondency washed over her, she'd examine it closely. Was it born of her own weariness, or was it a carefully crafted despair, designed to weaken her resolve? This constant vigilance was exhausting, but essential.

Central to her preparation was her unwavering love for her daughter, Lily. Lily, a bright spark of pure innocence, remained largely shielded from the town's overt unraveling, her world still defined by school, playdates, and the comforting routine of home. But Harmony knew that Lily was not immune. The Master's influence, if unchecked, would inevitably touch her daughter's life. The thought of Lily succumbing to fear, to despair, was an unbearable prospect, a pain so profound it acted as an inexhaustible wellspring of strength.

Harmony would often hold Lily close, breathing in the scent of her clean hair, tracing the curve of her cheek, and in those moments, she felt a surge of power unlike anything she had ever known. It wasn't a violent, aggressive force, but a deep, unyielding fortitude, a primal instinct to protect. Her love for Lily wasn't just an emotion; it was a force field, a protective aura that the Master would find difficult to penetrate. She focused on this love, drawing it in, letting it fill her, fortify her. She would visualize it as a warm, golden light, expanding outwards from her core, a shield against the encroaching chill.

She began to understand that her strength, and the town's potential salvation, lay not in matching the Master's malice with her own, but in an unwavering inner fortitude. Violence would only feed the cycle. The Master thrived on chaos and fear, on the basest aspects of human nature. Harmony's path lay in cultivating the opposite: resilience, clarity, and an unwavering commitment to truth, even when that truth was terrifying. Her power was in her stillness, her resolve, her ability to stand firm in the face of overwhelming darkness without succumbing to its seductive despair.

She studied the lore that Sheriff Brody had been uncovering, the fragmented accounts of ancient defenses and forgotten rituals. While Brody focused on the tangible aspects – the symbols, the locations – Harmony delved into the underlying principles. She understood that these weren't just arbitrary markings; they were expressions of focused intent, of collective will channeled into protective energies. The *fading wards* weren't just decaying symbols; they were a manifestation of a forgotten vigilance, a collective belief that had waned over time.

She learned to recognize the Master's subtle manipulations in her own interactions. When a neighbor, usually kind and chatty, offered a curt, almost hostile response to a simple greeting, Harmony didn't retaliate with annoyance. Instead, she'd acknowledge the shift internally, understanding it as a sign of the Master's touch. She'd offer a gentle smile, a polite nod, and continue on her way, not out of weakness, but out of a conscious refusal to engage with the manufactured negativity. Each such interaction was a small victory, a reaffirmation of her control over her own emotional landscape.

Her preparation also involved a subtle redirection of energy. She began to practice a form of "spiritual housekeeping," clearing out old resentments, forgiving past hurts, and actively cultivating gratitude. It felt counterintuitive, focusing on personal well-being when the town was in such peril, but she understood that a fractured inner self was an open door for the Master. She needed to be whole, unassailable, to stand against him. She meticulously cataloged her own vulnerabilities, not to dwell on them, but to understand their potential triggers and develop strategies to counter them. If the Master sought to exploit her anxieties about Lily's future, she would counter it with a fierce affirmation of her love and her unwavering belief in Lily's innate strength. If he preyed on her fear of failure, she would remind herself of her purpose, her commitment, and the inherent value of her resistance, regardless of the outcome.

She spent hours studying the subtle patterns of the town's collective mood. She noted how certain areas seemed to emanate a heavier sense of dread, how specific times of day often coincided with a palpable dip in morale. These weren't random atmospheric shifts; they were echoes of the Master's presence, areas where his influence was strongest, where he had found fertile ground for his insidious work. She began to mentally map these zones of influence, understanding them not as physical locations, but as pockets of amplified despair.

The bookstore, ironically, became her sanctuary and her training ground. The familiar rhythm of customer interactions, the quiet rustle of pages, the comforting aroma of coffee – these elements of normalcy were her anchor. She would sometimes pause between serving a customer and observing the subtle changes in their expressions, the fleeting shadows of fear or doubt that crossed their faces. It was a constant, low-level training, honing her ability to perceive the Master's touch, to distinguish between genuine human emotion and his manufactured distortions.

She started to incorporate elements of nature into her practice. She would walk in the woods surrounding Redwater Crossing, not seeking out the quarry as Brody was, but finding pockets of undisturbed natural energy. She would sit by the creek, feeling the pulse of the earth beneath her, drawing strength from its ancient, enduring power. She believed that nature, in its uncorrupted state, held a resonance that was antithetical to the Master's decay.

Harmony knew that her confrontation with the Master would not be a physical one, at least not in the traditional sense. It would be a battle of wills, a clash of fundamental energies. She wasn't preparing to fight, but to *endure*, to *resist*, and ultimately, to *overcome*. Her strength would not come from aggression, but from an unyielding inner core, a commitment to truth, and an incandescent love that would serve as her shield and her sword. She was readying herself for a fight that raged not in the streets of Redwater Crossing, but within the deepest chambers of the human heart. The Master sought to break spirits; Harmony was preparing to mend hers, and in doing so, to perhaps, offer a flicker of hope to a town lost in the encroaching shadows.

The realization had dawned on Harmony not with a thunderclap, but with a quiet, insistent whisper, much like the Master's own insidious influence. She saw the Sheriff, a man of action and order, tirelessly pursuing tangible clues, meticulously documenting the outward manifestations of the town's decay. He was charting the physical symptoms, the disappearances, the subtle behavioral shifts, believing he was closing in on a culprit, a physical entity responsible for the encroaching madness. But Harmony understood, with a clarity that both terrified and empowered her, that this was not a battle that could be won with handcuffs or a search warrant. The Master was not a man with a hidden lair; he was a parasite of the soul, a weaver of illusions that fed on the fertile ground of human frailty.

To confront him with the blunt force of conventional conflict would be to misunderstand the very nature of his power. If she were to meet his manipulations with anger, his despair with righteous indignation, his fear-mongering with her own calculated terror, she would be handing him the very ammunition he craved. He thrived on the eruption of negative emotion, on the unraveling of reason, on the descent into primal fear. Harmony recognized, with a dawning certainty, that her arena was not the physical world, but the ephemeral, yet infinitely more potent, landscape of the mind and spirit. Her weapon would not be steel, but steadfastness. Her shield would not be wood or metal, but an unshakeable conviction.

She began to actively train herself in the art of non-reaction. It was a discipline far more demanding than any physical regimen. When a particularly unsettling thought, a dark premonition about Lily, would slither into her mind, she learned to acknowledge it without letting it take root. She'd observe it, like a strange cloud passing across the sky, and then gently, deliberately, redirect her focus. This was not about denial, which could fester into its own form of unease, but about a conscious choice of where to invest her mental and emotional energy. She would anchor herself to the tangible, the real: the warmth of Lily's hand in hers, the comforting weight of a beloved book, the enduring beauty of the ancient oak tree outside her window. These were the touchstones of her reality, the bulwarks against the Master's illusions.

She spent hours in contemplation, not just meditating in the traditional sense, but actively analyzing the Master's patterns of influence as she perceived them in the townsfolk. She saw how he would subtly amplify existing insecurities. Mr. Haverty, a generally jovial man, had recently become prone to fits of inexplicable paranoia, convinced his business dealings were being sabotaged. Harmony had noticed the shift began after a minor financial setback, a ripple of worry that the Master had skillfully inflated into a tidal wave of dread. He hadn't *created* Mr. Haverty's fear; he had merely found the crack in his confidence and widened it until it consumed him.

Harmony's strategy was to do the inverse. She would identify the seeds of positivity, the quiet acts of kindness, the moments of resilience, and consciously nurture them. Her interactions with her customers became micro-battles. A flicker of doubt in a young woman's eyes as she browsed a self-help section? Harmony would offer a gentle, encouraging word about her own journey of self-discovery, subtly reinforcing the idea of internal strength. A weary sigh from an older gentleman buying his weekly newspaper? Harmony would share a brief, pleasant anecdote, a reminder of shared joys and simpler times, a small beacon against the encroaching gloom. These were not attempts to manipulate, but to counter-manipulate, to introduce an opposing force of hope and light into the Master's encroaching darkness.

The Master's greatest weapon, she surmised, was his ability to distort truth, to present lies as undeniable realities. He whispered doubts into ears, painted shadows as monsters, and made despair seem like the only logical conclusion. Harmony's counter-weapon was an unwavering commitment to truth, not just objective facts, but the deeper, more profound truths of human connection, of inherent worth, of enduring love. This was the bedrock upon which she would build her defense. When she felt the insidious tendrils of the Master attempting to sow discord in her own mind, perhaps by preying on her fears of inadequacy as a mother or a business owner, she would consciously affirm her love for Lily, the pride she felt in her bookstore, the knowledge that she was doing her best. It was a constant, internal reassertion of her own foundational truths.

She understood that the Master's power was inherently parasitic. He did not create; he corrupted. He did not build; he dismantled. This meant that the most potent offense she could mount was not an attack, but a strengthening of her own core, and by extension, the cores of those she could reach. Her love for Lily was not just a shield; it was a source of infinite, generative power. It was the antithesis of the Master's destructive force. When she felt the chill of his influence attempting to seep into her consciousness, she would visualize Lily's laughter, her bright eyes, her innocent trust. This vivid remembrance would fuel her resolve, reminding her of what she was fighting for, and crucially, what she was fighting *against*. The Master fed on emptiness; she would fill herself, and her surroundings, with abundance of spirit.

There were moments, especially in the quiet solitude of her study, when the sheer weight of it all threatened to overwhelm her. The vastness of the Master's reach, the insidious nature of his power, the sheer exhaustion of constant vigilance – it was a daunting prospect. But then she would recall the image of Mrs. Gable, her vibrant spirit dulled by manufactured doubt, or Timmy Peterson, his imagination turned into a source of terror. These were not abstract tragedies; they were the lives of people she knew, people she cared for. And in their suffering, Harmony found not despair, but a fierce, unyielding determination.

She wasn't deluding herself into believing this would be an easy fight. It was, in fact, the hardest fight imaginable, a relentless battle fought on the most intimate of battlegrounds. But she was no longer merely an observer. She was an active participant, armed with an understanding that transcended the superficial. Her strength lay not in her ability to strike a blow, but in her capacity to stand firm, to radiate truth in the face of illusion, and to offer unwavering love in the abyss of despair. This, she believed, was a force the Master had never truly encountered, a power that could, in its quiet, unyielding way, ultimately prevail. She was a librarian of souls, and she would not let her collection be defaced.

CHAPTER 10

Confrontation at the Lot

The hum of the fluorescent lights in Earl's Honest Rides was a discordant counterpoint to the gnawing unease that had settled over Redwater Crossing like a suffocating blanket. Harmony Jakes stood across the street, the familiar, jarringly cheerful face of the used car lot a stark contrast to the shadow it now represented. The vibrant reds, blues, and yellows of the pennants, meant to evoke excitement and opportunity, now seemed garish, almost sickly, under the dull afternoon sun. This was the nexus, the place where the Master's influence felt most concentrated, a psychic leech disguised as a purveyor of second-hand dreams. Sheriff Brody's intel, pieced together through hushed confessions and unnerving patterns of behavior, pointed to this gaudy monument to desperation as a primary locus of the Master's power. He had shared his findings with Harmony in hushed tones, the worn maps spread across her antique table, highlighting the cluster of desperate transactions, the sudden reversals of fortune that had begun, unnervingly, around the time Earl's Honest Rides had expanded its lot.

Harmony's breath hitched, not from fear, but from a deep, resonant resonance with the palpable despair that seemed to emanate from the very asphalt of the lot. It was a sickness, a psychic residue of broken promises and shattered hopes, a stagnant pond of regret that the Master had so skillfully cultivated. She felt it as a physical pressure, a subtle yet insistent push against her resolve, a dark whisper attempting to sow doubt in her own mind: *You're just a bookseller. What can you possibly do against this? You're weak. You're alone.* The whispers were an old enemy, familiar echoes of her own deepest insecurities, amplified and weaponized by an unseen force. But the lessons of the past weeks, the rigorous mental and emotional discipline she had imposed upon herself, had forged a shield against such insidious assaults. She held onto the image of Lily, her daughter's innocent smile a beacon in the encroaching gloom, and the weight of her purpose settled, grounding her.

She clutched the worn leather strap of her satchel, her knuckles white. Inside, nestled amongst her notebook and a slim volume of poetry, was a small, smooth stone, a gift from Lily, found on one of their walks by the creek. It was nothing more than a simple river rock, but to Harmony, it was an anchor, a tangible piece of her daughter's unwavering belief in her. She drew a slow, measured breath, the scent of exhaust fumes and something vaguely metallic, the smell of desperation, filling her lungs. She wouldn't be met with physical violence, not directly. The Master's game was far more subtle, an insidious manipulation of perception and emotion. Her confrontation would be a psychic one, a test of wills waged in the intangible ether of intent and belief.

With a final, resolute glance at the street, the chipped paint of the curb beneath her sensible shoes, Harmony began to walk. Each step was a deliberate act of defiance, a measured stride towards the heart of the darkness. The air seemed to grow heavier with every yard she crossed, the vibrant colors of the lot pressing in on her, a sensory overload designed to disorient and overwhelm. She noticed the way the sunlight seemed to refract oddly around the edges of the buildings, the way the shadows cast by the parked cars seemed too deep, too still. These were not natural phenomena; they were subtle distortions, the Master's artistry in manipulating the mundane.

As she reached the entrance to the lot, a sales associate, a man with slicked-back hair and a smile that didn't quite reach his eyes, detached himself from a small cluster of idling vehicles. His gaze swept over Harmony, a practiced assessment that cataloged her as neither a serious buyer nor a troublemaker. He was a pawn, she knew, another soul ensnared by the Master's influence, his own desires and ambitions twisted into a desperate need to make a sale, to appease the unseen entity that dictated his livelihood. His smile widened, a practiced, oily sheen. "Looking for a good deal today, ma'am?" he called out, his voice carrying a forced joviality that felt hollow.

Harmony met his gaze, her own eyes steady, unwavering. She offered a polite, almost imperceptible nod, but did not respond verbally. Her silence was a deliberate choice, a refusal to engage with the manufactured disguise. To engage would be to invite the Master's tendrils to latch onto her, to begin the subtle erosion of her defenses. She saw the flicker of confusion, then annoyance, cross his face, a subtle crack in his practiced veneer. He was accustomed to predictable responses, to the easy acquiescence of those already susceptible to the lot's pervasive despair. Her stillness, her unresponsiveness, was an anomaly, a disruption to his carefully orchestrated routine.

She continued her walk, moving past the rows of vehicles, each one a silent testament to a different story of compromise. There were families with worn-out minivans, their faces etched with the weariness of endless commutes and the quiet desperation of needing reliable transportation on a shoestring budget. There were young couples, their hopeful eyes scanning the sporty coupes, dreaming of a future that seemed just out of reach. And there were older individuals, their postures conveying a quiet resignation, their choices dictated by necessity rather than desire. Harmony felt the weight of their collective hopes and disappointments, a heavy current of psychic energy that the Master fed upon.

She paused before a gleaming, cherry-red sedan, its paint impossibly bright, almost unnaturally so. It sat on a prominent display pad, drawing the eye like a siren's call. A small, laminated sign perched on its hood read: *Dream Machine! Drive home your aspirations today!* Harmony felt a prickle of recognition. This car was more than just metal and engine; it was a focal point, a tangible manifestation of the Master's promise of fulfillment, a glittering lure designed to ensnare the unwary. She could almost feel the insidious pull it exerted, a subtle whisper promising escape, a better life, all for a seemingly manageable price.

She extended a hand, not to touch the car, but to feel the subtle energetic disturbance that surrounded it. It was like stepping into a pocket of frigid air on a warm day, a tangible disruption in the natural flow of energy. The air around the sedan felt...thinner, somehow, as if the very vibrancy of the atmosphere had been leeched away to fuel its deceptive allure. She could sense the faint, almost imperceptible hum of desperation emanating from it, the silent pleas of those who had poured their hopes into its purchase, only to find their dreams turning to dust.

Sheriff Brody had spoken of Earl, the owner of the lot, a man who appeared out of now where. Earl's Honest Rides trajectory was an economic anomaly that defied market sense. The car lot had an inverse relationship that did not mirror the town's trajectory. As the town descended the car lot sales ascended. At first, Earls Honest Rides became a pillar of the community, and Earls business acumen was seemingly blessed. Yet, Brody had described his eyes that held a perpetual, haunted glaze that accompanied a boisterous laughter with almost a nervous, almost frantic energy. He was a puppet, Harmony realized, his strings pulled by an unseen hand. At one time, Earl must have been a man with a desperation for success, only to be twisted into a tool for the Master's insidious purposes. Earl's Honest Rides wasn't just a business; it was a hunting ground, a place where the Master preyed on the vulnerable, offering false promises in exchange for their very souls.

As Harmony ventured deeper into the lot, she observed the other salesmen, their movements stiff, their smiles too wide, their eyes vacant. They were extensions of Earl, and by extension, of the Master himself. Their desperation to make a sale was palpable, a primal need that overrode any semblance of genuine human interaction. She saw a young couple, their faces alight with hope, being ushered towards a small, sputtering hatchback by a salesman whose grin was stretched to its breaking point. The salesman was leaning in, his voice a low murmur, filling their ears with promises of low payments and incredible financing, drowning out the silent scream of the car's dilapidated engine.

Harmony felt a pang of sorrow for them, for their naive trust, for the inevitable disappointment that awaited them. This was the Master's cruel artistry: not to inflict pain directly, but to orchestrate its arrival, to ensure that the victims themselves led the way into their own despair. She understood then that her approach needed to be precise, surgical. She couldn't simply barge in, shouting accusations. The

Master thrived on chaos, on drawing attention to himself in a way that would only further disempower those around him. Her confrontation had to be subtle, a disruption of the psychic currents, a quiet assertion of a different, more resilient truth.

She reached the center of the lot, near a small office trailer that bore the lettering of "Earl's Honest Rides." The air here was thickest with the Master's influence, a cloying miasma of despair and unspoken regret. It felt like standing at the bottom of a well, the walls slick with the tears of broken dreams. She could sense the concentrated energy, the psychic residue of countless transactions, each one a tiny piece of a soul bartered for a fleeting sense of security.

Then, she saw him. Earl. He stood by the trailer's door, a tall, gaunt figure silhouetted against the dull interior light. His shoulders were hunched, as if carrying an invisible weight, and his gaze was fixed on the ground, a posture of perpetual defeat. Even from this distance, Harmony could sense the profound weariness that clung to him, the suffocating despair that had become his constant companion. He was the embodiment of the Master's ultimate victory: not in breaking his victims, but in convincing them that they deserved their fate.

Harmony took another deep breath, steadying herself. The fear was a cold knot in her stomach, but it was tempered by a growing sense of purpose. She was not here to fight Earl, but to confront the entity that had enslaved him. She was here to disrupt the cycle, to introduce a dissonant note into the Master's symphony of despair. She began to walk towards the trailer, her footsteps deliberately slow, each one a conscious act of reclaiming the ground that had been ceded to darkness. The sales associate who had first approached her watched her, his initial annoyance replaced by a flicker of something akin to unease. She was not behaving as expected, not cowering or pleading, but walking with a quiet, unnerving resolve.

As she drew closer to Earl, she could see the subtle tremors in his hands, the way his jaw was clenched tight. His eyes, when he finally lifted them to meet her gaze, were hollow, devoid of any spark of recognition or genuine emotion. They were the eyes of someone who had seen too much, endured too much, and finally, given up. "Can I help you?" he rasped, his voice rough, unused.

Harmony stopped a few feet away from him, the worn stone in her satchel a comforting presence against her hip. She could feel the Master's presence subtly shifting, a heightened awareness in the atmosphere around them. It was as if the very air crackled with a nascent tension, a primal predator sensing a challenge. She didn't flinch. Instead, she met Earl's gaze with a steady, compassionate look. "Earl," she said, her voice calm and clear, a stark contrast to the cacophony of despair that permeated the lot. "I'm here to talk about what's happening here."

Earl's eyes widened, a flicker of something – fear? surprise? – momentarily breaking through the dull haze. He took a step back, instinctively recoiling from her directness. "I... I don't know what you mean," he stammered, his gaze darting away from hers, towards the rows of cars, towards anything but her unwavering stare. The salesmen nearby had paused their predatory routines, their eyes now fixed on the unfolding interaction, a silent audience to a drama they did not fully comprehend.

"I think you do," Harmony continued, her voice gentle but firm. "This place... it's not honest. Not anymore. And it's hurting people." She gestured broadly, encompassing the entire lot, the faded paint, the gleaming false promises, the very air thick with unspoken regret. She saw the subtle tightening of Earl's features, the way his breath hitched. He was a man trapped, and she understood that her confrontation wasn't with him, but with the force that held him captive.

"It's... it's just business," Earl managed to choke out, the words sounding like a lie even to his own ears.

"Is it?" Harmony pressed, taking another deliberate step closer. She could feel the Master's influence attempting to cloud her mind, to whisper doubts, to amplify her own fears. She pushed them back, anchoring herself to the truth of her purpose. "Is it just business when people are losing their homes? When their hopes are being crushed? When their very spirits are being drained away?"

She saw the effect her words had. Earl flinched, a physical manifestation of the truth striking a nerve. His hands began to tremble more violently, and his gaze flickered towards the small, dark interior of the trailer, as if seeking an unseen protector. "You don't understand," he pleaded, his voice barely a whisper. "You can't understand."

"I'm starting to," Harmony said, her voice soft but unwavering. "I'm starting to understand the cost of what you're allowing to happen here. And I'm here to put a stop to it." She didn't raise her voice, didn't make any sudden movements. Her power lay in her stillness, her clarity, her refusal to be drawn into the Master's game of emotional manipulation. She was offering a different path, a silent counter-narrative to the despair that had become the lot's unofficial slogan.

The air grew noticeably colder. A palpable shift occurred, a tightening in the atmosphere that spoke of unseen forces stirring. The salesmen shuffled their feet, their predatory smiles faltering. They sensed the change, the disruption of the familiar, oppressive energy. Harmony felt it too, a prickling sensation on her skin, a deep thrumming beneath the surface of reality. The Master was aware, and it was not pleased.

"You should leave," Earl whispered, his eyes wide with a primal fear. "You don't know who you're dealing with."

Harmony didn't move. She held his gaze, her own filled with a mixture of sorrow and resolve. "I know what you are," she said, her voice a quiet assertion that cut through the palpable tension. "And I'm not leaving until you understand that this has to end." She didn't expect Earl to suddenly break free from his tormentor, but she knew that her presence, her refusal to be intimidated , was a disruption. It was a seed of doubt planted in the Master's carefully constructed domain, a whisper of resistance in the suffocating silence of despair. The confrontation had begun, not with a roar, but with a quiet, determined stand.

The slick, manufactured sheen of Earl's smile, usually so effective at lulling the desperate into a false sense of security, seemed to sputter and dim under Harmony's steady gaze. He had emerged from the shadowed doorway of the small office trailer, his movements no longer the confident stride of a successful businessman, but the jerky, uncertain steps of a man pulled by unseen strings. He straightened his already immaculate tie, a purely performative gesture that lacked any genuine conviction. "Well now, miss," he began, his voice adopting the practiced, honeyed tone that had once been the hallmark of Earl's Honest Rides, "I don't believe we've had the pleasure. Lost your way, perhaps? Or are you in the market for a truly exceptional vehicle? We've got some beauties on the lot today, real... honest value."

Harmony's lips curved into a faint, knowing smile. It wasn't a smile of amusement, but one of profound sadness, tinged with the grim satisfaction of seeing the truth laid bare. "I'm not lost, Earl," she stated, her voice calm, cutting through the thick, stagnant air. "And I'm not looking for a car. I'm looking for the truth." She let her gaze drift past him, towards the interior of the trailer. It was dark, cramped, and smelled faintly of stale cigarette smoke and something else... something acrid and unsettling, like old fear. She could sense a distinct presence within, a pulsing, malevolent energy that seemed to feed on the despair radiating from the lot. It was the Master, the entity that had twisted Earl's ambition into this grotesque mockery of honest trade.

Earl's disguise, so painstakingly constructed over years of calculated charm and carefully curated empathy, began to crack. His eyes, which had always held a peculiar, unsettling brightness, now seemed to recede into his gaunt face, shadowed by a weariness that went beyond mere fatigue. The practiced smile faltered, pulling at the corners of his mouth like ill-fitting mask. "The truth?" he echoed, his voice losing its silken edge, becoming rough, strained. He shifted his weight, his hands clenching and unclenching at his sides. The subtle tremors Harmony had noticed earlier were more pronounced now, betraying an internal struggle. "I... I don't know what you're talking about. This is a reputable establishment. We pride ourselves on our integrity." The words tumbled out, a desperate attempt to cling to the illusion, but the conviction was gone, replaced by a hollow echo.

Harmony took another step forward, her eyes never leaving Earl's. She could feel the psychic pressure intensify, a suffocating blanket of dread attempting to smother her resolve. The whispers, which had been a faint murmur at the edge of her awareness, grew louder, more insistent: *He's too strong. You're making a mistake. Run. This is beyond you.* But she held firm, drawing strength from the smooth, cool stone in her satchel, from the image of Lily's trusting face. "Reputable?" Harmony's voice was quiet but carried an undeniable weight. "Earl, I've seen the records. I've spoken to people who've bought cars from you. They came here hoping for a way out, a chance to make ends meet, and they left... ruined. Their savings gone, their hope extinguished. That's not reputation, Earl. That's predation."

The tremor in Earl's hands escalated into a full-blown shake. His gaze darted away from Harmony, flickering towards the rows of gleaming cars, their chrome reflecting the dull sky like mocking eyes. He seemed to be seeking refuge in the familiar, in the tangible symbols of his supposed success, but even they offered no solace. The desperation that clung to the lot, a tangible miasma of broken promises, was now a suffocating shroud around him. "You... you don't understand the pressures," he stammered, his voice barely audible. "The... the demands."

"Demands from whom, Earl?" Harmony pressed, her voice remaining steady, a beacon of calm in the rising storm of his distress. She saw it then, a fleeting glimpse behind the mask. It wasn't Earl's own fear she was witnessing, not entirely. It was the fear of something ancient and insatiable, something that had found a willing vessel in his ambition and his vulnerabilities. The entity that inhabited him was becoming agitated, its patience wearing thin. A subtle shift occurred in the atmosphere, a palpable drop in temperature, a prickling sensation on Harmony's skin. The very air seemed to thicken, charged with a raw, unfettered power.

Earl visibly flinched, his head snapping back as if struck. His eyes widened, and for a terrifying second, Harmony saw a flicker of something truly monstrous in their depths – a predatory gleam, ancient and cold, that was undeniably not Earl's. It was the Master, asserting its presence, its control. The jovial salesman who had first approached Harmony, and a few others who had been loitering nearby, suddenly stopped their feigned interest in the vehicles. They stood frozen, their vacant stares fixed on Earl, as if sensing the shift in power, the growing unrest within their employer. They were more than just employees; they were extensions of the Master's will, their own desensitized minds incapable of fully comprehending the subtle dance of psychic warfare unfolding before them.

"You should go," Earl choked out, his voice a ragged whisper. His gaze, however, was no longer directed at Harmony, but at some unseen point beyond her, his eyes filled with a terror that transcended his own personal fear. It was the primal terror of a creature realizing its domain had been infiltrated, its prey threatened. The vibrant pennants that adorned the lot, once symbols of aggressive salesmanship, now seemed to writhe in the slight breeze, their garish colors suddenly appearing sinister, like the flickering tongues of a predatory beast. The cheerful music that had been playing softly from a tinny speaker was abruptly cut off, leaving an unnerving silence that amplified the tension.

Harmony stood her ground, her resolve hardening. The Master's agitation was a confirmation of her presence, of her impact. It was a sign that the carefully constructed facade of Earl's Honest Rides was indeed a nexus of its influence. "I can't go, Earl," she said, her voice firm. "Not until this stops. Not until you understand that what you're doing... what *it's* doing through you... is wrong." She focused her intent, projecting a wave of calm, focused energy towards Earl, attempting to anchor him, to remind him of the man he once was, buried beneath the layers of manipulation and despair. "This isn't honest business, Earl. This is destruction. And I won't let it continue."

The entity within Earl seemed to lash out. The air around them grew colder, a biting wind swirling dust and debris across the asphalt, as if the very elements were being manipulated to create a disorienting, hostile environment. The cars on the lot seemed to gleam with an unnatural intensity, their metal surfaces reflecting the grim sky with an almost aggressive sheen. One of the salesmen, a man with tired eyes and a perpetually slumped posture, let out a soft whimper and took a hesitant step backward, his gaze fixed on Earl's contorted face. He was a pawn, Harmony knew, but even pawns could be rattled when the game master's sanity began to fray.

Earl staggered, his hand flying to his head as if warding off a physical blow. A guttural sound, a strangled cry that was not entirely human, escaped his lips. His carefully crafted persona, the one that had charmed and manipulated Redwater Crossing for months, was shattering completely. The mask had not just slipped; it had disintegrated, revealing the raw, writhing horror beneath. For a moment, Harmony saw not Earl Maddox, the used car salesman, but a grotesque vessel, his features stretched and distorted, his eyes glowing with an alien, malevolent light. The predatory entity was no longer content with subtle manipulation; it was asserting its dominance, its raw power.

"You... you're a fool," a voice rasped, not from Earl's lips, but seeming to emanate from the air around him, a layered, distorted sound that was chillingly devoid of human emotion. It was the Master's voice, a symphony of suffering and malevolence. "You think you can challenge me? Here? In *my* domain?" The air crackled with energy, and the cars on the lot seemed to hum with a low, resonant vibration, as if they were alive, participants in this unholy ritual. The pennants snapped violently, their cheerful colors now a mockery against the darkening sky.

Harmony felt a wave of pure dread wash over her, a chilling awareness of the vast, ancient power she was confronting. It was a force that fed on desperation, that thrived on broken spirits. But within that dread was a core of steel. "This is not your domain, Master," she countered, her voice resonating with a quiet, unwavering conviction. She could feel her own energy reserves being tested, the insidious tendrils of the entity attempting to pry into her mind, to sow seeds of doubt and fear. She tightened her mental grip, holding onto the purity of her purpose, the image of Lily her unbreakable shield. "This is a place where people come for hope, not for their souls to be devoured."

Earl, or rather, the entity inhabiting him, let out a ragged, rasping laugh that scraped against Harmony's nerves. "Hope is a commodity, little bookseller. And I am the ultimate purveyor." His body spasmed again, and this time, the movement was more violent. He lurched forward, not directly at Harmony, but towards the rows of cars, his arms outstretched as if embracing them, as if drawing power from their silent, desperate narratives. The salesmen recoiled, their faces pale with a dawning horror. They had always known Earl was... intense. Driven. But this was something else entirely. This was a perversion.

"Look at them," the layered voice commanded, echoing through the suddenly still lot. "Each one a dream purchased. A promise fulfilled, for a time. They came to me in their need, and I gave them what they desired. For a price, yes. But a price they willingly paid." Earl's gaunt face was contorted in a rictus of something that might have once been a smile but now resembled a predatory snarl. His eyes, no longer holding even a trace of Earl Maddox, burned with an ancient, cold fire. The asphalt beneath his feet seemed to ripple, as if the very ground was responding to his agitated state.

Harmony watched, her heart pounding, but her mind remained clear. She saw the way the entity fed on the lingering despair, on the psychic residue of broken promises. It wasn't just about selling cars; it was about consuming the very essence of hope, of aspiration. "They didn't know the true price, Earl," she said, her voice firm, resonating with an authority that surprised even herself. "They didn't know you were selling them pieces of themselves. They didn't know they were being used."

The entity seemed to recoil from her words, as if they were a physical blow. The malevolent light in Earl's eyes flickered, and a spasm of pain crossed his face. It was the first genuine sign of Earl's consciousness resurfacing, a brief struggle against the parasitic presence. The salesmen exchanged nervous glances, their fear a tangible thing in the charged atmosphere. They were trapped between the growing terror of the unknown and their own ingrained instinct for self-preservation.

"You... you cannot comprehend the hunger," the entity hissed, its voice laced with a chilling despair of its own, a reflection of the countless souls it had consumed. "The need for... sustenance. For purpose." Earl's body seemed to sag, the unnatural energy temporarily draining from him. He slumped against a gleaming, cherry-red sedan, his hands splayed on its hood. The car, which had seemed so vibrant moments before, now appeared dull, almost lifeless, as if the entity had drawn its radiance into itself.

Harmony saw her opening. This was not about brute force; it was about severing the connection, about starving the parasite. "Your purpose is to destroy, not to sustain," she stated, her voice ringing with truth. She focused her will, drawing on a deep well of inner strength, and projected a counter-frequency, a subtle resonance of peace and renewal, towards Earl. It was a whisper of the natural world, of the quiet strength of resilience, a stark contrast to the Master's cacophony of despair. "You prey on the vulnerable. You twist their hopes into chains. That is not purpose, Earl. That is a sickness."

Earl groaned, his body trembling violently. His eyes fluttered closed, and a single tear, a testament to the buried man, traced a path through the grime and despair on his cheek. The sales associates, sensing the shift, took another step back, their expressions a mixture of fear and dawning comprehension. They had been complicit, yes, but this... this was beyond their understanding, beyond their ability to rationalize.

The entity within Earl roared, a sound of pure, unadulterated rage that seemed to shake the very foundations of the lot. The pennants whipped violently, the cars emitted a discordant hum, and the air grew heavy with a palpable sense of menace. "You will not interfere!" the voice shrieked, no longer layered, but sharp and piercing, a venomous hiss. "I have consumed stronger than you! I have broken greater wills!" Earl's body spasmed, arching unnaturally, as if being torn apart from the inside.

Harmony did not flinch. She stood her ground; her gaze locked on the struggling man. She could feel the entity's power, its immense, ancient darkness, but she also felt the fragile spark of Earl's humanity fighting for survival. It was that spark she was appealing to, that flicker of decency she sought to reignite. "You feed on despair, Master," she said, her voice calm, yet carrying a steel edge. "But despair is not all there is. There is also resilience. There is also hope. And that is what I represent." She reached into her satchel, her fingers closing around the smooth river stone. She held it tightly, drawing strength from its simple, grounding reality.

The confrontation reached its apex. The entity within Earl thrashed, attempting to overwhelm Harmony with a torrent of psychic force, a bombardment of her deepest fears and insecurities. Images flashed through her mind: Lily in danger, her own failures magnified, the crushing weight of her isolation. But she held on, her focus unwavering, anchored by the stone, by her purpose. She projected a silent, powerful wave of defiance, a refusal to be broken, a steadfast belief in the inherent goodness that the Master sought to extinguish.

The struggle was not a physical one, but a war waged in the intangible realms of the mind and spirit. Earl's body became a battleground, his form flickering between the gaunt, tormented man and something far more ancient and terrifying. The salesmen watched, paralyzed by a terror they could not articulate, their carefully constructed apathy shattered by the raw, primal forces at play. The air grew thick and heavy, charged with a volatile energy that threatened to consume them all. The facade of Earl's Honest Rides, so long a symbol of deceptive prosperity, was now crumbling, revealing the monstrous truth that lay beneath. The confrontation had truly begun, and the outcome was far from certain.

The air around them grew heavy, thick with an unnatural stillness that pressed in on Harmony's eardrums. It was the silence that preceded a cataclysm, a vacuum of sound pregnant with unseen threat. Earl's body, still slumped against the gleaming sedan, began to twitch again, but this time, the movements were not the erratic spasms of internal conflict. They were deliberate, controlled, imbued with a terrifying grace. His spine seemed to lengthen, his limbs to stretch, his very frame elongating upwards. It was a subtle yet profound transformation, a disturbing origami of bone and sinew orchestrated by an unseen puppeteer. Harmony's breath hitched. This was not Earl. This was the manifestation.

He rose, unfolding himself from the semiconscious salesman like a predator shedding its camouflage. The transformation was not instantaneous, but a fluid, unnerving process, as if the very fabric of reality was being stretched and reshaped around him. His head tilted back, his neck cracking with a sound that was too loud, too sharp, in the oppressive silence. The skin on his face seemed to tighten, drawing taut over bone, his features becoming sharper, more angular, losing the last vestiges of Earl Maddox's weary humanity. His eyes, which had been dulled with despair and fear, now blazed with an ancient, predatory light, a cold, unwavering ember that fixed on Harmony. He towered over her, a silhouette against the bruised twilight sky, his presence a physical weight that threatened to crush her. He was the 'Tall Man,' a being sculpted from the shadows of greed and the echoes of broken dreams.

He was impossibly tall, his form stretching beyond the natural limits of a man, an unnatural extension that seemed to mock the very concept of human proportion. His silhouette was that of a man, yet distorted, stretched, as if viewed through a warped lens. His shoulders seemed broader, his frame impossibly lean and elongated, casting a shadow that seemed to writhe and deepen, consuming the meager light that dared to touch it. Harmony felt a prickle of primal fear crawl up her spine, a visceral reaction to the sheer wrongness of his presence. He was an anomaly, a disruption in the natural order, a living testament to the corrupting influence that had festered on this lot for so long.

His gaze, when it finally settled on her, was not merely intense; it was a physical assault. It bored into her, stripping away her defenses, probing the rawest nerves of her psyche. There was no flicker of recognition, no trace of Earl's lingering consciousness. This was pure, unadulterated malice, focused and absolute. He didn't speak, not at first. His silence was more potent than any threat, a vast, echoing chasm that amplified the terrifying stillness of the lot. The pennants, which had been writhing moments before, now hung limp and lifeless, as if intimidated by his sheer presence. The cars, their chrome surfaces reflecting the darkening sky, seemed to shrink away from him, their usual gleam muted.

Harmony, despite the tremor that ran through her limbs, held her ground. Her heart hammered against her ribs like a trapped bird, but her gaze remained locked on the imposing figure before her. She clutched the river stone in her satchel, its smooth coolness a grounding anchor in the swirling vortex of fear and dread. She could feel the entity's power radiating from him, a palpable force that warped the very air, making it feel viscous and suffocating. It was a power that fed on despair, that thrived on the crushing weight of broken hopes.

The 'Tall Man' took a step forward, his movement unnervingly smooth, silent. The sound of his feet on the asphalt was a muted scrape, devoid of the impact one would expect from such a large form. He moved with the predatory grace of a hunter, his intentions chillingly clear. He was not here to negotiate, not here to reason. He was here to assert dominance, to crush the intruder who dared to challenge his dominion. He was the embodiment of Earl's darkest impulses, amplified and unleashed by a force that existed beyond the realm of mortal comprehension.

"You... disturb my quiet," the voice finally came, a low, resonant rumble that seemed to emanate from the very depths of his elongated form. It was not Earl's voice, nor was it the layered, distorted sound Harmony had heard earlier. This was something else, something ancient and resonant, a voice that seemed to carry the weight of millennia of darkness. It was the voice of the Master, speaking through its most potent vessel, its physical manifestation. It was a voice that promised oblivion.

Harmony swallowed, her throat suddenly dry. "I'm not here to disturb you," she replied, her voice surprisingly steady, though it felt like a fragile thread in the face of his overwhelming presence. "I'm here to end this." She met his unnerving gaze, refusing to flinch, refusing to be intimidated. The raw, supernatural power emanating from him was immense, a suffocating blanket of dread designed to break her spirit before he even laid a hand on her. But she would not break. Not now. Not ever.

The 'Tall Man' tilted his head, a slow, deliberate movement that seemed to stretch his neck to impossible lengths. A sound that might have been a chuckle, but was more akin to the grinding of stone, emanated from him. "End this?" he echoed, the words laced with a chilling amusement. "You speak of ending that which is eternal. You are but a fleeting spark against an ancient night, little bookseller." His eyes narrowed, the predatory gleam intensifying. "You have trespassed where you do not belong. You have disturbed the balance. And for that, you will pay."

He raised a hand, long fingers that seemed to taper into sharp points, and pointed directly at Harmony. The gesture was slow, deliberate, each movement imbued with a chilling power. As he did, the air around Harmony grew noticeably colder, a frigid wind whipping up a dust devil that swirled around her ankles. The shadows seemed to deepen and writhe, stretching towards her like grasping tendrils. The cars on the lot emitted a low, discordant hum, a chorus of metallic misery that amplified the oppressive atmosphere. It was a display of raw, untamed power, a raw assertion of control over the very elements.

Harmony felt the psychic pressure intensify, the entity's attempt to overwhelm her with sheer force. It was a barrage of sensations: the chill of the grave, the suffocating weight of despair, the gnawing fear of absolute annihilation. Images flashed through her mind, not of her own fears, but of the victims – their hopeful faces contorted in agony, their dreams dissolving into dust. It was a deliberate attempt to break her, to force her to her knees with the sheer weight of suffering. But the image of Lily, of her radiant, innocent smile, flickered in her mind's eye, a beacon of pure light in the encroaching darkness.

"Your power comes from their suffering," Harmony stated, her voice resonating with a quiet, unyielding conviction. She focused her intent, projecting a shield of calm, resolute energy around herself. It was a subtle resistance, a refusal to be consumed. "You thrive on their despair. But their despair is not your strength; it is your weakness. It is proof that you are a parasite, not a creator." She met his unnerving gaze, her own eyes burning with a fierce determination. "And parasites can be eradicated."

The 'Tall Man' recoiled slightly, a subtle, almost imperceptible flinch that sent a ripple of energy through his elongated form. The raw power he exuded seemed to falter for a fleeting moment, as if Harmony's words had struck a hidden nerve. It was a testament to the fragile nature of his existence, a being that fed on negation, on the absence of hope.

"Eradicated?" the rumble of his voice took on a sharper edge, a hint of something akin to disbelief, or perhaps even outrage. "You speak as if you understand. As if you possess the knowledge to unmake me. You are a fool. I am the hunger that drives them, the void they seek to fill. I am the consequence of their wants, their needs, their failings." He gestured vaguely towards the rows of cars, his long fingers tracing invisible patterns in the air. "They come to me, willingly or not, seeking salvation, seeking a way to escape their meager lives. I offer them a chance, a fleeting illusion of prosperity, and in return, I take what is owed."

He took another step closer, his shadow engulfing Harmony completely. The temperature plummeted further, and a fine mist began to condense on the polished surfaces of the cars. The scent of ozone filled the air, a sharp, acrid smell that spoke of immense, volatile energy. "You cannot comprehend the depth of my existence, the vastness of my hunger. I am woven into the fabric of their desperation, a shadow in the heart of every unfulfilled desire." His gaze flickered, momentarily shifting from Harmony to a point beyond her, as if observing the spectral echoes of past transactions. "Each car on this lot," he continued, his voice dropping to a chilling whisper, "is a monument to a broken soul. A testament to their willingness to sacrifice everything for a taste of something more."

Harmony felt a surge of pity, not for the entity, but for Earl, trapped within its monstrous grip. She could see the faint vestiges of the man, the ambitious salesman, the one who had sought to provide for his family, now twisted into this instrument of pure consumption. But pity would not win this battle. Resolution would.

"But they don't understand the true cost, do they?" Harmony countered, her voice unwavering. "They don't realize that with each purchase, they're not just signing a contract; they're signing away pieces of themselves. Pieces of their hope, their dreams, their very essence. That's not a transaction. That's a ritual of consumption." She held the stone tighter, its solidity a grounding force. "And I won't let you consume any more."

The 'Tall Man' let out a low hiss, a sound like air escaping a ruptured pipe. His form seemed to flicker for a moment, as if the energy that sustained him was being momentarily disrupted. "You misunderstand," he rasped, his voice now a venomous serpent's whisper. "I do not consume. I *am* them. I am the manifestation of their deepest needs, their most desperate desires. When they want more than they have, when they crave what is just beyond their reach, they reach for me. And I answer."

He extended his hand again, this time palm up, as if offering something. In the center of his palm, a faint, ethereal light began to coalesce, shimmering and pulsing. It wasn't the warm glow of hope, but a cold, spectral luminescence, like moonlight on frost. "See this?" he hissed, his unnerving gaze fixed on the glowing light. "This is the essence of what they seek. A fleeting moment of triumph. A taste of power. A promise of a better tomorrow." The light pulsed brighter, and Harmony could feel its deceptive allure, a siren song designed to lure the unwary.

"That is not essence," Harmony stated firmly, her voice cutting through the illusions. "That is a reflection of their own trapped spirits, twisted and distorted. You offer them a hollow promise, a mirage born of their own desperation." She took a step forward, her intent clear. "You are a predator, feeding on the vulnerable. And I am here to stop you."

The 'Tall Man' let out a guttural roar, a sound that vibrated through Harmony's very bones. The cars on the lot groaned and shrieked, their metallic bodies contorting as if in agony. The asphalt beneath their feet cracked and buckled, fissures spreading outwards like spiderwebs. The sky above darkened further, the twilight giving way to an oppressive, starless night. This was the Master's true power unleashed, a raw, destructive force wielded through its chosen vessel.

"You cannot stop what is inevitable!" the voice boomed, no longer a whisper, but a thunderous declaration of dominance. "You cannot fight the hunger that drives them! You cannot extinguish the darkness that resides within! I am the consequence! I am the price! And you, little bookseller, are merely a fleeting annoyance!" He lunged, not with the speed of a physical being, but with the sudden, disconcerting motion of a shadow detaching itself from a wall. He moved with a terrifying fluidity, his elongated form blurring as he closed the distance between them.

Harmony braced herself, her hand tightening on the river stone. She felt the icy tendrils of the Master's power reach out, seeking to ensnare her, to drag her down into the abyss of despair. But she stood firm, her resolve a silent, unyielding bulwark. The confrontation had reached its zenith, and she would not falter. The fate of Redwater Crossing, and the souls caught in the Master's grasp, rested on her ability to withstand this monstrous manifestation. She met the 'Tall Man's' furious gaze, a silent promise in her own eyes: she would not break. She would not yield. She would fight.

Harmony's voice, though smaller than the monstrous rumble that emanated from the entity before her, carried a resonance that seemed to cut through the oppressive atmosphere. She didn't scream, she didn't plead, she simply stated. "You don't offer them salvation. You offer them a cage. A beautiful, shiny cage that promises freedom but delivers only servitude." She took a breath, her gaze unwavering, meeting the cold, ancient light in the Tall Man's eyes. "You prey on their weakness, on their desperate need to believe in something more, something better. And in return, you drain them. You leave them hollow, empty husks, just like Earl is now."

The words hung in the air, sharp and precise, like scalpel cuts dissecting the Master's carefully constructed mask. She wasn't accusing him of being evil; she was stating what he *was*. A parasite. A creature that fed on the unmet desires and broken dreams of others, offering a fleeting illusion of fulfillment in exchange for their very essence. "Every car on this lot isn't a monument to a fulfilled desire; it's a tombstone for a lost soul. Each gleaming hood, each polished chrome fender, is a memorial to what they sacrificed. Their savings, their peace of mind, their integrity... sometimes, even their hope."

She gestured subtly towards the rows of vehicles, their silent presence suddenly imbued with a profound sense of tragedy. "You don't answer their needs; you exploit them. You whisper promises of a life beyond their grasp, a life of comfort and status, and then you extract payment in the only currency that truly matters: their spirit. You make them believe they are buying their dreams, when in reality, they are selling their very selves. And what do they get in return? A piece of metal that rusts, a machine that breaks down, and a debt that haunts them until their dying day."

Harmony's words were not born of anger, but of a profound sadness for the victims, and a cold, hard understanding of the Master's true nature. She saw the desperation that drove people to this lot, the yearning for escape from mundane lives, the foolish hope that a new car could be a new beginning. And she saw how the Master, in its insatiable hunger, twisted that yearning into a tool of its own perpetuation.

"You call yourself a consequence, a price," she continued, her voice gaining a quiet strength. "But you are not a consequence of their actions; you are a sculptor of their downfall. You don't just take what is owed; you manufacture the debt. You create the desperation. You foster the discontent that drives them to your doorstep, blinded by promises you have no intention of truly fulfilling."

The Tall Man remained silent, but the air around him crackled with an unseen energy, a palpable tension that spoke of his growing irritation, his frustration with this unexpected resistance. His unnaturally long fingers twitched, and a low hum emanated from his being, a sound like an overloaded transformer.

"You speak of hunger," Harmony pressed on, her voice unwavering, "but your hunger is a void. It can never be satisfied. You consume, and consume, and yet you remain perpetually empty. That is not power; that is a sickness. A profound and terrible imbalance that you inflict on others to mask your own inherent lack." She looked directly into his blazing eyes. "You are not woven into their desperation; you are the thread that unravels it. You are not a shadow in the heart of their desires; you are the rot that sets in when those desires turn to obsession."

She took another step forward, her movement deliberate, reclaiming a small piece of the ground that had been swallowed by his encroaching shadow. "You offer them a taste of power, you say? What power is there in being controlled? What triumph is there in being hollowed out? The only triumph belongs to you, Master. The triumph of deception. The triumph of feeding on the innocent and the vulnerable."

The spectral light that had appeared in his palm flickered and died, a tiny supernova of illusion extinguished by the stark reality of Harmony's words. His form seemed to shift, the sharp angles of his elongated frame momentarily softening, as if the very illusion he presented was being challenged at its core.

"They seek to escape their meager lives," Harmony conceded, "but you trap them in a far more meager existence. You offer them a temporary escape, a fleeting illusion, but the chains you bind them with are eternal. They are shackled to regret, to debt, and to the gnawing knowledge that they were duped, that their deepest longings were used against them."

She could feel the entity's rage building, a dark storm gathering within its borrowed form. The cars around them groaned louder, their metal bodies vibrating with the sheer force of his suppressed fury. The ground trembled subtly beneath her feet. This was not a physical battle of strength, but a war of truths, a clash of realities. Her reality, grounded in empathy and consequence, against his reality, built on deception and consumption.

"You are not the manifestation of their deepest needs," Harmony declared, her voice ringing with conviction. "You are the embodiment of their greatest fear: the fear of being truly seen, of being truly known, and of being found wanting. You thrive because they are afraid of confronting that fear, so they turn to you, seeking an easy answer, a quick fix, a way to fill the void they perceive within themselves. But the void you fill is not their own; it is the one you create."

She paused, allowing the weight of her words to settle. The Master was a predator, yes, but a predator that depended on its prey's willing participation, however misguided. And Harmony's aim was to strip away that illusion of willing participation, to reveal the coercion, the manipulation, the sheer parasitic nature of his existence.

"You talk of answering their call," she said, her voice softening slightly, a hint of sorrow entering her tone. "But it is not a call for help you answer. It is a cry of weakness you exploit. It is the sound of their own self-doubt that you magnify and reflect back at them, telling them that *this*, this hollow shell, this servitude, is all they deserve. That is not an answer; it is a condemnation."

The Tall Man let out a sound that was less a roar and more a choked gasp, as if Harmony's relentless truth was physically constricting him. The shadows around him seemed to recoil, as if momentarily blinded by the light of her pronouncements. He was a being of illusion, of carefully crafted deception, and she was peeling back the layers, exposing the naked, consuming hunger beneath.

"You are a parasite, Master," Harmony stated, her voice firm and resolute. "And you thrive because people are afraid to acknowledge their own vulnerabilities. You offer them a way to pretend, to mask their imperfections with possessions, to buy a semblance of happiness instead of earning it. But it is a false happiness, a fragile facade that crumbles under the slightest pressure. And when it crumbles, all that is left is the ruin you leave behind."

She held his gaze, her own eyes, once filled with fear, now burning with a quiet, unyielding certainty. She saw the flicker of ancient malice, the immense power, but also, for the first time, she saw a desperate, gnawing emptiness that was the Master's true face. It was a being that existed only through negation, through the consumption of others. It had no substance of its own, no true being. It was a void made manifest, feeding on the light of others to create the illusion of its own existence.

"You cannot win," she declared, her voice resonating with the certainty of a truth revealed. "Because what you offer is not real. It is a shadow, a reflection, a distorted echo of what people truly desire. And no amount of consumption, no amount of preying on their weakness, will ever fill that void within you, because the void is all you are."

Harmony took another step, then another, closing the distance between them. The river stone in her satchel felt warm now, a comforting anchor against the icy tendrils of the Master's power. She wasn't fighting to destroy him, not in the physical sense. She was fighting to expose him, to strip away his power by revealing the hollowness of his promises, the destructive reality of his influence. She was speaking his truth, the truth of his existence, a truth he had tried so desperately to conceal behind a veneer of desire and fulfillment. And in speaking it, she was rendering him impotent.

The Tall Man recoiled, his elongated form shrinking back, as if the very air around him had become toxic. His blazing eyes seemed to dim slightly, the intense predatory light wavering, replaced by a look of something akin to shock, or perhaps even a primal fear. Harmony's words had not been an attack; they had been a mirror held up to his existence, reflecting back the grim, consuming reality of what he truly was. And for a being that existed solely through illusion and deception, that was the most terrifying weapon of all. The silence that followed was no longer pregnant with threat, but with the weight of an unveiled truth, a truth that was slowly, inexorably, unraveling the Master's reign of deception.

The spectral light in the Tall Man's hand sputtered, not with a dying ember's glow, but with the chaotic, unpredictable flicker of a failing circuit. Harmony's words, delivered with the quiet, unshakeable conviction of one who has nothing left to lose but everything to gain, were not simply words. They were a disruption. A discordant note struck against the carefully orchestrated symphony of desire and desperation that constituted the Master's domain. He was a maestro of manipulation, accustomed to the predictable ebb and flow of human frailty, the easy resonance with greed and fear. But Harmony sang a different tune, one of stark, unvarnished truth, a melody that refused to be drowned out by his seductive, hollow chorus.

Her pronouncements – that he was a parasite, a sickness, a void made manifest – were not just accurate; they were poisonous to his very essence. He fed on the illusion of control, on the whispered promise of fulfillment that masked an insidious emptiness. Harmony, however, had seen through the charade, had peered into the abyss of his being and named it. She had not offered him an argument to refute, but a mirror that reflected his own hideous, consuming hunger. This was not a challenge to his power, but a refutation of his existence, a denial of the very reality he imposed.

The Tall Man's form wavered, the sharp, angular silhouette momentarily losing its menacing definition. It was as if the carefully constructed edifice of his presence, built brick by brick from the unfulfilled aspirations of countless souls, was beginning to crumble under the sheer weight of Harmony's insight. The cars surrounding them, usually silent sentinels of his influence, seemed to groan in sympathy, their metallic husks vibrating with a subtle tremor. This was not the thunderous roar of an enraged deity, but the low, disquieting hum of something fundamental breaking. A tremor ran through the asphalt beneath Harmony's feet, not a violent upheaval, but a soft, almost imperceptible shift, like the earth sighing under a new burden.

Sheriff Brody, observing from the shadowed periphery of the lot, his hand resting on the cool, worn leather of his holster, felt it too. A subtle dissonance in the air, a brief silence that wasn't peaceful but pregnant with an unseen unraveling. He had spent months sensing the Master's presence, the heavy, suffocating blanket of despair that settled over Redwater Crossing, particularly on this lot. It was a familiar weight, a pervasive miasma that made the air feel thick and difficult to breathe. But now, for the first time, there was a lightness, a fleeting, almost imperceptible lifting of that oppressive atmosphere. It was as if a single, stubborn weed, stubbornly resisting the Master's dominion, had finally managed to push its way through the cracked pavement.

Harmony's voice, though soft, was a beacon, a sharp, clear note piercing the fog of manufactured desire. She wasn't railing against him; she was simply stating facts, observations distilled into truths so potent they acted as an antidote to the Master's venom. He offered illusions, she countered with reality. He promised freedom, she exposed the chains. He dealt in dreams, she revealed the nightmares. The sheer audacity of her clarity was the disruptor. He was a creature of darkness, of manipulation, of preying on weakness and fear. Harmony, however, stood in the light of her own courage, armed with a love that transcended the ephemeral promises of material possession and a truth that cut deeper than any manufactured desire.

The Tall Man's spectral hand, which had been beginning to reform, to gather the ethereal energy that fueled his illusions, faltered. The light within it dimmed, not in defeat, but in confusion, as if his internal mechanisms, finely tuned to exploit specific human vulnerabilities, were encountering an error code. Harmony's resilience was not born of strength, but of a different kind of power altogether, a power that the Master, in all his ancient, parasitic existence, had never truly encountered. He understood desperation, ambition, greed, and loneliness. He could weave a tapestry of these emotions, twisting them into the tempting lure of a gleaming automobile. But he did not understand the quiet, unyielding power of a heart that beat with love, that held onto truth even when surrounded by deception.

This was the crack. Not a gaping chasm, not yet, but a hairline fracture in the Master's meticulously constructed edifice of control. It was a subtle dissonance, a momentary lapse in the overwhelming influence he exerted over the souls drawn to this place. He was accustomed to a unified chorus of desire, a symphony of wants that he could easily conduct. Harmony, however, was a solo performance, a defiant aria that refused to conform to his score. Her voice, clear and true, was creating a ripple effect, a subtle vibration that was spreading outwards, touching the very foundations of his power.

The air around the Tall Man grew heavy, not with menace, but with a strange, almost static-like tension. It was the tension of a machine encountering an unforeseen variable, of a perfectly calibrated system thrown into disarray. The polished chrome of a nearby sedan seemed to gleam with a less alluring, more accusatory light. The paint, usually a vibrant advertisement of status and success, appeared duller, flatter, as if the very color was being leached away by the confrontation of opposing realities. Harmony's quiet defiance was, in a bizarre way, a form of resurrection for the victims, a reawakening of their dormant spirits. She was reminding them, not through accusation, but through her own unshakeable presence, that there was more to existence than the hollow promises of the Master.

Sheriff Brody shifted his weight, a barely perceptible adjustment. He had seen the way people's eyes glazed over when they walked onto this lot, the way their resolve seemed to dissolve like sugar in hot coffee. He had attributed it to the Master's insidious influence, a psychic vampirism that drained the will and replaced it with a craving for the unattainable. But Harmony was different. Her eyes, though filled with a fierce, protective fire, held no trace of that glazed-over emptiness. They were sharp, clear, and unyielding. And in her presence, he felt a faint stirring of something he hadn't felt in years on this lot: hope. A fragile, almost forgotten ember, fanned by the unexpected breeze of her courage.

The Tall Man's long fingers, usually so deliberate and unnervingly graceful, twitched. It was a minute imperfection, a flicker of involuntary movement that betrayed a disturbance within his carefully maintained composure. He was a being of absolute control, of subtle dominance, and Harmony's unwavering resistance was anathema to him. She was not cowering, not begging, not bargaining. She was simply standing her ground, her words like precision-guided missiles, hitting their targets with devastating accuracy. Each truth she spoke was a hammer blow against the gilded cage he had built, a cage that was now beginning to show its first, significant cracks.

He hadn't expected this. He had anticipated fear, desperation, and finally, a hollow acceptance of his terms. He had factored in every human failing, every yearning, every regret. But he had not factored in the power of genuine love, the unshakeable strength of a soul rooted in truth, the quiet rebellion of a spirit that refused to be extinguished. Harmony's love for the town, for the lost potential, was a force that could not be quantified, could not be corrupted, and certainly could not be controlled by his spectral schemes. It was a pure, unadulterated energy, and it was acting as a repellent to his insidious influence.

The very air seemed to vibrate with a nascent freedom, a subtle hum of possibility that had been absent for so long. The illusion that had permeated the lot, the intoxicating scent of new beginnings and limitless potential, was beginning to dissipate, revealing the stark, barren reality beneath. The cars were no longer symbols of aspiration, but monuments to broken promises, and Harmony's voice was the eulogy. She was not just speaking truth; she was unmaking him, word by word, by stripping away the veils of deception he had so carefully woven. And as those veils thinned, the true nature of the Master, a hungry, hollow entity, was beginning to become visible, not just to Harmony, but to any who might have the clarity to see.

This was more than a confrontation; it was a fundamental challenge to his very being. Harmony was not fighting him with force or aggression, but with an unwavering adherence to reality. She was demonstrating that his power was not inherent, but borrowed, derived from the willingness of others to believe in his lies. By refusing to believe, by seeing him for what he truly was, she was withdrawing the very sustenance he craved. And in that withdrawal, the Master's hold, which had seemed so absolute, began to fray. It was a subtle unraveling, a slow, almost imperceptible loosening of his grip, but it was happening. The crack was widening, and the light, the harsh, revealing light of truth, was beginning to pour in.

CHAPTER 11

The Master's Vulnerability

armony's pronouncements had not merely been statements; they had been seismic tremors, shaking the very foundations of the Master's power. He thrived on the predictable currents of human weakness – the gnawing anxieties, the avaricious desires, the gnawing emptiness that drove souls to his desolate lot. He was a connoisseur of despair, a collector of broken dreams, and he had always found them abundantly available, ripe for his parasitic harvest. Yet, in Harmony's presence, he encountered an anomaly, a profound deviation from the expected. Her unwavering will, forged not in the fires of ambition or greed, but in the quiet crucible of genuine love and an unyielding adherence to truth, was a force he could not comprehend, let alone manipulate.

He had anticipated a dance of deception, a predictable tango of enticement and desperation. He had plotted his steps meticulously, ready to exploit any flicker of doubt, any surge of longing. But Harmony refused to take his hand. She stood firm, her spirit a bulwark against his spectral influence, her gaze unwavering, seeing him not as a purveyor of dreams, but as the hollow void he truly was. He fed on the shadows that clung to humanity, the self-doubt, the regrets that festered in the dark corners of the heart. But Harmony was a being of light, her inner luminescence a stark contrast to his shadowy existence. Her resilience was not a shield he could shatter, but a solid, unyielding core that simply absorbed his spectral attacks, rendering them impotent.

The Master's usual tactics – the subtle whispers of unfulfilled potential, the seductive gleam of possessions, the phantom echoes of what might have been – bounced off Harmony like pebbles against granite. He could manipulate the fear of loss, the yearning for acceptance, the bitter sting of inadequacy. But Harmony possessed a different kind of wealth, a spiritual and emotional abundance that his spectral coffers could never emulate. Her connection to the town, the love that pulsed through her veins that had been consumed by the Master's machinations, was an anchor, grounding her in a reality that his illusions could not penetrate. This love was not a vulnerability to be exploited, but a source of profound strength, a wellspring of courage that sustained her, unyielding and pure.

He observed her closely, his spectral senses straining to find a chink in her armor, a whisper of the desperation he so readily preyed upon. He saw no trace of it. Instead, he saw a quiet determination, a resolute stillness that spoke of a deep well of inner peace. She was not fighting him with aggression, but with a passive resistance that was infinitely more destructive to his kind. By refusing to be drawn into his game of desire and fear, she starved him. He couldn't feed on her truth, her love, her unwavering conviction. These were the antitheses of his being, the very forces that repelled him.

The spectral light in the 'Tall Man's' hand flickered again, a more pronounced tremor this time. It wasn't just a failing circuit; it was a system overload. Harmony's presence was a paradox he couldn't resolve. He was a creature of manipulation; his power derived from the subtle art of twisting human frailty into tangible desire. But Harmony was unfettered by such frailties. Her will was a pure, unadulterated force, a testament to the enduring strength of the human spirit when unburdened by the very things he exploited. He was like a predator who had hunted the same prey for centuries, only to suddenly find himself facing a creature that was not only unappetizing but actively repelled him.

Sheriff Brody watched, his own unease beginning to morph into a nascent understanding. He had seen the Master as an insurmountable force, a pervasive darkness that was simply a part of Redwater Crossing's grim tapestry. But Harmony was unraveling that tapestry, thread by thread, not with violence, but with an unwavering clarity. She was not engaging in a battle of wills, but in a quiet affirmation of reality. The Master dealt in the ephemeral – promises, illusions, futures that would never come to pass. Harmony dealt in the concrete – truth, love, the unwavering present.

The 'Tall Man's' usual aura of intimidation, a palpable force that pressed down on the very souls of those who dared to look upon him, seemed to recede. It was as if Harmony's inner light was pushing back the shadows, carving out a space of clarity in the oppressive gloom. The cars, once symbols of intoxicating possibility, now seemed to stand as silent, desolate monuments to shattered dreams, their polished surfaces reflecting only the stark reality of Harmony's gaze. The Master, accustomed to drawing power from the collective longing of the lost and the desperate, found himself facing a singular, unyielding force that offered him nothing to consume.

He had always been able to sow discord, to amplify insecurities, to create an environment where his whispers of *what if* could take root and flourish. But Harmony's unwavering self-possession, her quiet confidence that stemmed from a place of deep inner truth, left no fertile ground for his seeds of doubt. She was not seeking validation, not yearning for what she lacked. She was simply *being*, and in her being, she negated his entire purpose. His power lay in the gap between what people were and what they desperately wanted to be. Harmony occupied no such gap; she was whole, complete in her own truth.

The Master, for the first time in what felt like an eternity, was at a loss. He could not manipulate her, could not corrupt her, could not even truly touch her with his spectral tendrils. She was like a solid object that absorbed and nullified his attempts to interact. His usual repertoire of temptations, his carefully crafted illusions of success and happiness, were like rain on a duck's back – they simply slid off, leaving her untouched and unmoved. This was not defiance born of anger, but a profound indifference to his methods, an indifference that was far more damning than any outward show of resistance.

He shifted, his spectral form rippling as if struggling to maintain coherence. The energy he drew upon, the ambient despair and ambition of countless souls, was not being effectively channeled. It was like trying to drink from a broken fountain; the water was there, but the vessel was faulty, unable to deliver its contents. Harmony's unwavering focus was the fault in the vessel. She was not giving him the feedback he needed, the desperate energy that fueled his existence. Her will was a constant, steady hum, a frequency that disrupted his ability to tune into the chaotic symphony of human frailty.

He attempted a new tack, a subtle redirection of his spectral energy. Instead of directly confronting Harmony, he tried to amplify the lingering desperation in the surrounding cars, hoping to draw attention away from their confrontation, to remind her of what was at stake, of the potential for loss that always lingered. He projected fleeting images into the minds of those still lost in the periphery of his influence: a gleaming sports car, a coveted promotion, the approval of a scornful parent. But Harmony remained unmoved. Her gaze was fixed on the Master, her understanding of his game absolute. She knew these were just echoes, phantoms of a life she refused to chase at the expense of her soul.

Her love for the town was not a weakness he could exploit; it was his ultimate undoing. He had always understood love as a possessive, transactional force – the love of a parent for a child they wished to control, the love of a spouse for the security they provided. But Harmony's love was different. It was a selfless, enduring force, a testament to the power of connection, of shared humanity. It was a love that transcended material gain, a love that saw the inherent worth in souls, even those that had been damaged. This was a concept entirely foreign to his parasitic existence, a currency he could not trade in, a resource he could not plunder.

The Master's form began to flicker more erratically. The carefully constructed face of power was crumbling, not under a barrage of attacks, but under the sheer weight of its own irrelevance in the face of Harmony's unwavering being. He was a master of illusions, but Harmony was the embodiment of reality. He fed on shadows, but she stood in the light. He preyed on desperation, but she was fueled by love and truth. And in this confrontation, the Master found himself not a predator, but a starved entity, facing a feast he could not partake in. His power was derived from the willing participation of his victims, from their desire to believe in his false promises. Harmony, by refusing to believe, by seeing him for what he was, was effectively starving him, withdrawing the very essence of his existence. He was a parasite in need of a host, and Harmony, with her unyielding will and her radiant spirit, was a host that actively rejected his infection.

The vulnerability wasn't in her, but in his own inability to comprehend or overcome such a profound, unassailable strength. He was a creature of the mind, of suggestion, of whispered doubt. Harmony was a creature of the spirit, of unwavering conviction, of solid, unshakeable truth. And in that fundamental difference lay the Master's ultimate, and most terrifying, vulnerability. He could not defeat what he could not understand, and Harmony, in her quiet, resolute strength, was utterly beyond his grasp. The spectral light in his hand dimmed further, a flicker of genuine bewilderment replacing the usual aura of menacing power. He was a force of nature, but Harmony was a force of spirit, and the latter, he was discovering, was far more enduring, far more powerful, and ultimately, far more destructive to his kind. The silence that fell between them was not the absence of sound, but the presence of a power that the Master, for all his ancient existence, had never truly encountered.

The Master's spectral form shimmered, a subtle ripple of frustration passing through his ethereal presence. Harmony's unyielding spirit, her unwavering truth, was not just an inconvenience; it was a void, an emptiness he couldn't fill, a sustenance he couldn't derive. He had spent millennia preying on the anxieties of the heart, the gnawing hunger of the soul, the desperate grasp for more. But Harmony offered nothing of the sort. She was a testament to a different kind of wealth, a currency his spectral economy could not comprehend. Her love for the town was not a weakness, as he had initially presumed, but a shield, an impenetrable fortress built of shared memories and an enduring connection that his illusions could not penetrate. His spectral tendrils, designed to ensnare and corrupt, merely dissipated against the sheer, unadulterated force of her conviction. He could weave dreams, craft visions of glittering futures, but Harmony saw through the cheap artifice, recognizing the hollow core of his promises. She was not a victim waiting to be broken; she was a bulwark, a living testament to a strength he could not replicate or subdue.

Yet, as the Master grappled with this unprecedented impasse, a new strategy began to coalesce in the barren landscape of his spectral mind. Harmony's unwavering resolve, while frustrating, was also a testament to a singular, potent anchor. It wasn't her own strength that was the problem, but rather what that strength was tethered to. He had attempted to sever the connection to the town, to chip away at the foundation of her love, but that had proven as futile as trying to drain the ocean with a sieve. But there were other ties, other vulnerabilities, threads of affection that, if tugged hard enough, might just snap. His ancient eyes, spectral and piercing, scanned the periphery of Harmony's consciousness, not for her own fears, but for the echoes of those she held dear. The spectral light in his hand, though dimmed, still pulsed with a malevolent energy, an energy now re-focused, refined, honed in on a singular, devastating objective.

His primary target was no longer Harmony's spirit, but her heart. And within that heart, he knew, resided a love far more potent, far more pure than any he had encountered before: the love for her daughter. Little Lily. The name itself was a whisper of innocence, a beacon of joy, a vulnerability the Master had not yet fully exploited. He had seen glimpses of her in Harmony's thoughts, a bright, laughing presence, the culmination of a love that had endured unimaginable hardship. This was it. This was the chink in the armor, the single, perfect point of leverage. Harmony's power stemmed from her truth and her love for the town, yes, but her deepest, most visceral connection, the one that would unravel her very being, was to the child who represented a future, a hope, a continuation of that love.

With a silent, almost imperceptible shift, the Master began to weave a new kind of illusion. It wasn't a grand spectacle designed to tempt or to terrify, but a subtle, insidious displacement. He reached out, not with physical force, but with a spectral probe, a tendril of his consciousness, seeking to locate the locus of this precious connection. He delved into the ambient psychic residue of Redwater Crossing, the lingering echoes of despair and desperation, searching for the faint, untainted signal of a child's innocent presence. He had always been adept at sensing the emotional currents of humanity, and the pure, unadulterated love radiating from Lily was a beacon in the spectral fog.

He found her. Not through sight, not through sound, but through the sheer, overwhelming resonance of her spirit. She was asleep, tucked away in her small room, a picture of untroubled innocence. Harmony, in her focus on the Master, had inadvertently let down her guard, believing her victory was imminent. The Master, however, knew that true victory lay not in defeating an opponent, but in breaking their will. And for Harmony, Lily was her everything.

A low, guttural hum emanated from the Master, a sound that vibrated not in the air, but in the very bones of those who could perceive it. He gathered his spectral energy, no longer attempting to overwhelm Harmony, but to subtly manipulate the fabric of reality around the child. It was a delicate operation, requiring precision and a deep understanding of the unseen forces that bound souls together. He couldn't simply snatch Lily away; such a crude action might alert Harmony too soon. Instead, he began to weave a disorienting fog, a psychic miasma that would cloud Lily's dreams, replacing them with images of fear and distress, subtly drawing her away from the safety of her slumber and into a state of vulnerability.

The air in Lily's room grew heavy, thick with an unseen presence. The shadows that danced in the corners seemed to deepen, to writhe with a life of their own. Lily stirred in her sleep, a soft whimper escaping her lips. Her small brow furrowed, her tiny hands clenching into fists. The Master watched, a predatory gleam entering his spectral eyes. He could feel the shift, the subtle tremor of unease rippling through Lily's innocent mind. He amplified it, coaxing forth phantom whispers, distorted echoes of familiar sounds twisted into something menacing. The creak of a floorboard became the scraping of claws, the rustle of leaves outside her window a sinister whisper, a call from the darkness.

He pictured Harmony's face, the unyielding strength that had defied him, the pure light that had repelled him. He imagined that light flickering, then extinguishing, replaced by the raw, primal terror of a mother facing the ultimate loss. This was his endgame. He would not claim Harmony's soul directly; that was a battle he was losing. Instead, he would claim it indirectly, by shattering the one thing she cherished above all else. He would watch as her strength dissolved, her resolve crumbled, her love transformed into a consuming grief that would leave her utterly broken, a vacant vessel ripe for his taking.

He intensified his spectral caress, drawing Lily further into a nightmare. The room seemed to shrink, the walls closing in. The familiar comfort of her blankets became a suffocating shroud. Her whimpers grew louder, more desperate. He saw it then, in the flickering psychic currents, the dawning realization in Harmony's awareness. A sharp intake of breath, a sudden surge of panic. She had sensed the shift, the dark tendrils reaching for her precious daughter.

Her eyes, moments before fixed on the Master with unwavering defiance, now darted towards the periphery, a new kind of terror igniting within them. The Master allowed himself a moment of spectral satisfaction. The tide was turning. The unwavering fortress of Harmony's spirit was about to be breached, not by direct assault, but by the devastating weapon of maternal love turned into unimaginable anguish. He would soon taste the exquisite despair of a mother's broken heart, and it would be the most potent sustenance he had ever consumed.

The spectral tendril, once a probe, now solidified, coiling around the very essence of Lily's innocent dreams. The Master's ancient, desiccated mind, a labyrinth of forgotten fears and harvested despair, began to construct its new theatre of operations. He wasn't merely dipping his toes into the ethereal; he was plunging headfirst into the churning, abyssal waters he had meticulously cultivated over millennia. This was his dominion, the unsung, unacknowledged reality that existed in the slivers of perception, the yawning gulfs between what was and what could be. He called them the *Rooms Between*.

They were not physical spaces, not in any conventional sense. Instead, they were constructs of perception, voids shaped by the echoes of existence, meticulously carved out of the collective subconscious. Imagine the phantom limb of a forgotten desire, the lingering regret of a spoken word never retracted, the gnawing emptiness left by a promise broken before it was even made. These were the building materials. The Master, with an architect's precision born of an eternity of observation and manipulation, harvested these emotional detritus, these psychic slivers, and wove them into tangible, albeit spectral, dimensions. Each Room was a unique prison, tailored to the individual soul it ensnared, a personalized hellscape designed to extract the deepest essence of their being.

Sheriff Brody, in his maddening quest to understand the pervasive blight upon Redwater Crossing, had stumbled upon the periphery of this spectral architecture. His disjointed notes, his cryptic ramblings about 'liminal spaces' and 'unseen pathways,' had been dismissed by most as the ravings of a man unhinged by the town's relentless despair. But he had been closer to the truth than anyone, save perhaps for the Master himself, could have imagined. Brody had felt the faint tremors of these dimensions, the subtle shifts in reality that betrayed their existence. He had sensed the pockets of profound dread, the inexplicable voids that seemed to swallow hope whole, and he had intuited, with a chilling accuracy, that these were not random occurrences. They were deliberate, curated spaces, and their architect was the very entity he had been hunting.

The Master's power wasn't derived from physical coercion or overt displays of terror, though he was capable of both. His true strength lay in his ability to exploit the unseen fractures within the human psyche, to lure souls into these self-created pocket realities where their essence could be slowly, methodically drained. Think of a seasoned fisherman casting his net into a calm sea, not realizing the depths below conceal a monstrous predator. Redwater Crossing was the surface, its inhabitants the unsuspecting fish, and the Master's insidious influence was the subtle lure that drew them towards the precipice of oblivion.

He had always preferred subtlety, the slow burn of despair that eventually led to capitulation. The allure of the material, the promise of wealth and status, the whispered temptations of power – these were merely the bait. Once a soul took the hook, their descent into his true domain began. They wouldn't be dragged screaming into a dungeon; they would be gently guided, almost willingly, into a Room Between.

For Harmony, this revelation was a brutal crystallization of her deepest fears. Lily was not simply lost in the mundane world, not a victim of a terrestrial abduction. She had been taken into the Master's absolute control, spirited away to a place where the very rules of reality were dictated by his malevolent will. The spectral light that had dimmed in his confrontation with Harmony now flared with a renewed, terrifying purpose. It was no longer a tool for intimidation; it was a beacon, guiding him through the intricate, labyrinthine pathways of his own creation.

He envisioned Lily's small room, not as it was, but as it was becoming through his influence. The familiar teddy bear on her bed contorted into a monstrous silhouette. The gentle moonlight filtering through the curtains twisted into skeletal fingers scratching at the glass. Her innocent slumber was being systematically replaced by a symphony of spectral dread, each note precisely orchestrated to maximize her terror and, by extension, Harmony's. This was not about breaking Harmony's spirit through her own despair; it was about shattering her through the anguish of her child's suffering.

The Master felt Lily's nascent fear bloom within the nascent Room Between he was constructing around her. It was a fragile seed, but potent, imbued with the untainted terror of a child suddenly confronted by the monstrous. He amplified it, fanning the flames of her unease. He didn't need to conjure phantoms from scratch; he merely needed to twist the existing architecture of her reality, perverting familiar objects and sounds into instruments of her burgeoning panic. The gentle hum of the refrigerator downstairs became the ominous thrumming of a monstrous heart. The rustle of leaves outside her window transformed into the whisper of unseen entities slithering just beyond the veil of her consciousness.

He saw Harmony's reaction, a raw, primal surge of awareness as the psychic tendrils of her daughter's distress reached her. It was a jagged spike of fear, a visceral alarm that bypassed her intellectual defenses and struck directly at the heart of her maternal instinct. This was the moment. The Master had meticulously planned this gambit, understanding that Harmony's strength, while formidable, was tethered to her love. And her love for Lily was an anchor so profound, so absolute, that its severance would not just wound her; it would fundamentally break her.

He retreated from Harmony's immediate psychic proximity, a strategic withdrawal that allowed her to focus on the unfolding horror concerning her daughter. His spectral form, now less defined and more fluid, began to traverse the unseen corridors of his domain. He needed to prepare the final destination, the ultimate sanctuary for his latest prize. The Rooms Between were not static; they were fluid, adaptable, morphing and shifting based on the essence of the souls they contained. Lily's Room would be a masterpiece of her own innocence twisted into a testament to her ultimate vulnerability.

He navigated through what could only be described as spectral dust motes, the lingering remnants of souls long since consumed, swirling in a perpetual twilight. There were other Rooms, vast and ancient, holding the psychic residue of lives that had flickered out centuries ago. He passed by a Room that resonated with the cold, calculating avarice of a Renaissance merchant, its walls lined with phantom gold coins that clinked with an ethereal, hollow sound. Another pulsed with the desperate ambition of a failed artist, its confines filled with canvases that depicted eternally unfinished masterpieces, shimmering with the ghost of unfulfilled genius.

These were the lesser chambers, the waiting rooms of his spectral purgatory. Lily's Room would be different. It needed to be a place of profound, suffocating isolation, yet also a place that reflected the purity of her essence, so that its corruption would be all the more devastating for Harmony. He envisioned a landscape of impossible innocence: a meadow of perpetual spring, where flowers bloomed with impossible vibrancy, their petals etched with the subtle, haunting familiarity of Lily's own laughter. The sky would be a flawless, ethereal blue, devoid of clouds, of any indication of change or passage of time. And in the center of this pristine, yet sterile, expanse, would be a single, impossibly fragile structure, a dollhouse made of pure light, within which Lily would be confined.

This dollhouse, he mused, would be the focal point of her prison. Not a cage of bars, but a prison of overwhelming beauty and crushing solitude. Within its luminous walls, the laughter of her imagined friends would echo, eternally just out of reach. The games she played would be endlessly replayed, the same joyous moments looping, devoid of any sense of progression or novelty, a perfect reflection of a life frozen in time, a soul slowly withering in gilded isolation.

As he solidified the architecture of this new Room, he felt a faint disturbance, a ripple in the fabric of his domain. It was Harmony. She was pushing against the periphery, her raw maternal instinct, a force he had underestimated. Her love for Lily was not just an emotional tether; it was a psychic beacon, a beacon that was now actively seeking out the source of her daughter's torment. He had intended to lure Harmony into his trap by focusing on Lily, but he hadn't anticipated the sheer, unyielding power of her maternal will.

He could feel her probing, her spectral touch, however weak compared to his own, seeking to unravel the illusion he had woven. She was fighting her way through the psychic fog, her desperation a potent fuel. He had anticipated her fear, her grief, but he had not fully accounted for her fierce, protective rage.

The Master solidified his own spectral form, no longer a fluid entity, but a towering silhouette against the impossible spring of Lily's future prison. He extended a spectral hand, not to Harmony, but to the nascent dollhouse. He needed to accelerate the process, to anchor Lily firmly within this nascent reality before Harmony could fully breach the veil. He channeled a portion of his power into the structure, imbuing it with a subtle, pervasive sense of permanence.

The flowers in the meadow began to wilt, their impossible vibrancy turning to a dull, sepia tone. The flawless blue sky fractured, revealing glimpses of a churning, inky blackness beyond. The dollhouse, once radiating pure light, now pulsed with a dim, sickly luminescence, its ethereal construction beginning to fray at the edges. He was accelerating the corruption, forcing the essence of the Room to solidify around Lily, to bind her to this decaying paradise.

He felt Lily stir within her actual room, her whimpers intensifying. She was sensing the shift, the fundamental alteration of her perceived reality. The playful whispers of imaginary friends were now morphing into disembodied taunts, the gentle lullabies into discordant shrieks. He could feel her small mind struggling to comprehend the distortion, the betrayal of her own senses.

Harmony's presence intensified, a burning comet of pure, unadulterated will. She was close, so close to breaching the threshold. The Master allowed himself a moment of spectral satisfaction. He had underestimated her love, yes, but he had also created a scenario where her love was her greatest liability. He had not just kidnapped her daughter; he had weaponized her daughter's innocence against her.

He directed his attention back to the dollhouse, pouring more of his spectral energy into its foundation. The toy walls began to shimmer, not with light, but with a sickly, internal decay. The phantom laughter within grew more frantic, more desperate. He needed to complete the anchoring ritual before Harmony could reach them. The Rooms Between were his sanctuary, his larder, his ultimate expression of power. And the most exquisite nourishment came not from the broken souls of the jaded and the greedy, but from the shattered spirit of a loving mother, broken by the ultimate despair: the loss of her child. He would not simply consume Lily's essence; he would make Harmony bear witness to its slow, agonizing corruption, forcing her to watch as the light of her daughter's soul was extinguished, one spectral ember at a time. This was not just about feeding his hunger; it was about breaking the unbreakable. And Lily, her innocent spirit trapped within the collapsing architecture of a corrupted paradise, was the key. The Master felt the final anchor solidify, a cold, spectral chain binding Lily to the heart of his constructed nightmare. He could feel Harmony's desperate attempts to break through, her psychic struggle a tangible force battering against the edges of his domain. But it was too late. Lily was now inextricably linked to this Room Between, and the more Harmony fought, the more she inadvertently fed the very power that held her daughter captive. The Master, for all his ancient malevolence, felt a flicker of something akin to anticipation. The true feast was about to begin.

The raw, unadulterated terror that had initially seized Harmony, a cold, paralytic dread that threatened to shatter her very being, began to recede. It was replaced, not by resignation, but by a roaring inferno. The image of Lily, her daughter's innocent spirit twisted and corrupted within the Master's spectral prison, was a brand seared into Harmony's soul. Yet, this searing pain did not break her; it tempered her. Her grief, a profound and bottomless chasm, became the fertile ground from which an unyielding fury sprouted. It was a righteous anger, a primal instinct honed by millennia of maternal defense, now unleashed with terrifying clarity. The Master had sought to exploit her love, to use Lily as a weapon against her, but he had miscalculated the resilience of that love. He had underestimated the incandescent power that could be forged in the crucible of a mother's desperate protectiveness.

Harmony's spectral senses, honed by her own nascent abilities and amplified by the sheer force of her will, strained against the veil separating her from her daughter. The Master's carefully constructed illusion of a decaying paradise, a place of corrupted innocence, shimmered and fractured under the relentless pressure of her focus. She could feel Lily, a faint, flickering ember of light desperately struggling against the encroaching darkness. The phantom laughter, the distorted lullabies – they were not the sounds of a child playing, but the desperate cries of a soul being systematically extinguished. And with each echo of that despair, Harmony's resolve solidified. The grief was a heavy cloak, but the fury was the sharpened blade she now wielded.

The Master had anticipated fear, despair, even a desperate, flailing struggle. He had prepared for the emotional outpouring of a grieving mother. But he had not prepared for this: a transformation. Harmony was no longer merely a mother searching for her lost child; she was a force of nature, a tempest of pure, protective will. The spectral chains that bound Lily, the psychic anchors the Master had so meticulously forged, began to strain. They were designed to withstand the subtle erosion of a soul, the gradual decay of hope. They were not designed to withstand the concentrated, explosive power of a mother's unleashed fury.

Harmony's awareness expanded, pushing beyond the immediate confines of her physical body. She could feel the ethereal tendrils the Master had woven, the threads of his spectral architecture. Where before there had been a terrifying void, now she saw pathways, albeit treacherous ones. The Master's domain, a labyrinth of harvested despair and twisted dreams, was no longer an impenetrable fortress. It was a structure with weaknesses, with points of ingress and egress that her sharpened senses could now perceive. Her grief was not a paralyzing weight; it was a fuel, igniting her awareness, sharpening her perception, and giving her the strength to push against the impossible.

She focused on Lily, on the faint, desperate pulse of her daughter's spirit. It was a beacon in the spectral storm, a single point of undeniable truth amidst the Master's illusions. Harmony's own spectral form, once a hazy outline, began to coalesce, to sharpen. The raw, untamed energy of her emotions was lending her a new substance, a new definition within the ethereal plane. She was becoming a more potent entity, a being capable of navigating the very spaces the Master had created to ensnare her. The Master had intended to break her by breaking her daughter, but he had inadvertently forged her into a weapon capable of dismantling his own carefully constructed reality.

The Master, for all his ancient power, felt the disturbance not as a mere ripple, but as a seismic shockwave. He had underestimated the generative power of Harmony's love, the sheer, unyielding force it could manifest when pushed to its absolute limit. He had seen her grief, and he had assumed it would be a passive, consuming force. He had not accounted for the fact that grief, when combined with a desperate love and a furious protectiveness, could become an active, aggressive power, capable of unraveling the very fabric of his dominion. He had woven a tapestry of despair, and Harmony was now beginning to pull at its threads, one by one, with a relentless, burning intensity.

Her spectral touch, once tentative and uncertain, was now a probing force, a precise instrument seeking out the vulnerabilities within the Master's spectral constructs. She could feel the decay within Lily's prison, the sickening rot at the heart of the corrupted paradise. The Master had accelerated the process, attempting to bind Lily irrevocably, but in doing so, he had made the prison more fragile, more susceptible to outside influence. The cracks he had created in his haste were now widening under Harmony's focused assault. She could feel the phantom laughter of Lily's imagined friends, no longer a comforting echo, but a desperate, distorted wail. And with each wail, Harmony's resolve deepened, her fury burning brighter.

The Master's control over the Room Between was absolute, but it was a control built on the foundation of deception and illusion. Harmony, driven by an unwavering truth – the love for her child – was beginning to expose those deceptions. She was not seeking to destroy the Master's domain through brute force; she was seeking to dismantle it from within, by peeling back the layers of his carefully crafted lies and revealing the hollow core beneath. Her grief, once a source of agonizing pain, was now a clear lens through which she could see the Master's manipulation for what it was: a desperate attempt to feed his own insatiable hunger by shattering the purest of bonds.

She could feel Lily's small spirit, flickering but not yet extinguished. It was a testament to her daughter's inherent resilience, a spark that Harmony was determined to fan back into a blazing inferno. The Master's spectral chains were designed to drain, to consume, to slowly erode. But they had not accounted for the possibility of a counter-force, a force born not of corruption and despair, but of an unwavering love that refused to be extinguished. Harmony was no longer just fighting for Lily; she was fighting to reclaim the very essence of what it meant to be a mother, a force the Master, in all his ancient malevolence, had never truly understood.

Sheriff Brody stood at the edge of the abyss, not of a physical chasm, but of a reality he had only dimly perceived until Harmony's ordeal had dragged him, kicking and screaming, into its terrifying depths. The abduction of Lily had not just been a criminal act; it had been a cataclysm, a tearing of the natural order that had left him reeling. He had seen the impossible, witnessed phenomena that defied every tenet of his lifelong understanding of the world. The spectral chains, the decaying paradise, the palpable aura of ancient malevolence emanating from the entity everyone called "the Master" – these were not figments of a distraught mother's imagination. They were the chillingly real manifestations of a power that dwarfed any earthly threat.

His initial reaction had been a primal, protective urge, a burning desire to marshal his resources, to organize a search party, to bring the full weight of his badge and his men to bear. But the stark truth, laid bare by Harmony's desperate whispers and the unsettling evidence she'd shown him, was that his conventional methods were utterly useless. How did one issue an APB for a being that existed, it seemed, between worlds? How did one track a predator that could snatch a child from her bed without leaving a single physical trace, only to imprison her in a realm spun from nightmares? The sheer, overwhelming helplessness of it all had threatened to crush him. He, a man who prided himself on his ability to maintain order, to bring solutions to chaos, was staring into a void where solutions ceased to exist.

Yet, it was precisely in this void that his true strength lay, and it was a strength Harmony had inadvertently awakened within him. If he couldn't chase the Master with a patrol car, he would chase him with knowledge. If he couldn't fight him with a badge, he would fight him with the accumulated wisdom of those who, perhaps, had encountered such horrors before. The devastation he felt for Lily, for Harmony, was a raw wound that wouldn't heal, but it had been cauterized by a burning need to *do something*. He refused to be a bystander in this cosmic horror. He refused to let this evil win, not if there was even a sliver of a chance he could contribute, however indirectly.

His office, once a sanctuary of order and procedure, now felt like a research station. The meticulously filed reports, the case binders stacked high – they seemed laughably inadequate against the backdrop of the Master's power. But Brody began to shift his focus. He bypassed the crime scene photos and the witness statements, instead pulling out dusty tomes from the county's historical society archives, old newspapers yellowed with age, and even some of the more esoteric texts he'd kept for personal curiosity, texts that spoke of local legends, of strange occurrences, of whispered tales that had been dismissed as folklore. He wasn't looking for evidence of burglary or assault; he was looking for echoes, for patterns, for anything that might resemble the "Room Between," the spectral prison, the Master's modus operandi.

He remembered stories his grandfather used to tell, tales of "thin places" in the woods, of houses where shadows lingered too long, of inexplicable disappearances that had never been solved. He'd always filed them away as fanciful ramblings, the product of an aging mind. Now, he reread them with a desperate intensity. He poured over local histories, searching for accounts of entities that operated in similar liminal spaces, beings that preyed on innocence, that fed on despair. He was hunting for lore, for mythological precedents, for any fragment of wisdom that might illuminate the Master's nature or, more importantly, his vulnerabilities.

Brody's approach was methodical, almost obsessive. He created a sprawling whiteboard, filling it with fragmented notes, sketches of symbols he'd found in obscure texts, and timelines that seemed to stretch into impossibility. He cross-referenced every snippet of information, no matter how obscure, trying to weave a coherent narrative from the scattered threads of ancient warnings and forgotten fears. He was looking for the commonalities, the recurring themes that might point to a consistent weakness in such entities. Was there a particular type of artifact that repelled them? A specific ritual that could disrupt their hold? A celestial alignment that rendered them vulnerable?

He spent hours poring over old maps, not for geographical features, but for anomalies. Were there places in the county with a history of unusual events, of unexplained phenomena, that might have served as focal points for such beings in the past? He wasn't expecting to find a direct map to the Master's lair, but he hoped to uncover clues about how these entities moved, how they established their domains, and, critically, how they could be hindered. He even delved into theological texts, looking for any mention of beings that existed outside the mortal coil, for discussions of their weaknesses and limitations. The sterile logic of law enforcement was being stretched to its absolute breaking point, replaced by a desperate scramble for any knowledge, however esoteric, that could offer a glimmer of hope.

The weight of his responsibility was immense. He was not just a sheriff; he was a guardian, and he had failed to protect Lily. This failure gnawed at him, a constant, dull ache beneath the surface of his desperate research. But he channeled that guilt, that agonizing remorse, into his work. He saw Harmony, her face etched with a grief so profound it was a physical entity, and he knew he couldn't give up. Her strength, her unwavering resolve in the face of unimaginable horror, was a silent challenge, an inspiration. If she could face the Master with such courage, then he, armed with the tools of knowledge, could at least try to find a way to help her.

He had reached out to contacts outside the usual law enforcement channels. He had contacted a retired anthropology professor from the state university, a man known for his unconventional theories on folklore and ancient belief systems. He had discreetly interviewed elderly residents, not about crimes, but about local superstitions, about the stories whispered around campfires generations ago. He learned to listen for the underlying truths in embellished tales, for the echoes of real fear in exaggerated narratives. He was learning a new language, the language of the uncanny, the language of the spectral.

His findings were sparse, often contradictory, and deeply unsettling. There were whispers of entities that fed on emotions, of realms that mirrored the mortal world but twisted and corrupted, of ancient beings that could manipulate perception and reality. Some texts spoke of "anchors," objects or places that tethered these entities to our world, and others of "keys," words or symbols that could disrupt their power. The idea of a "Room Between" resonated with several obscure passages, described as pocket dimensions, extra-dimensional spaces where these entities could operate with impunity, drawing power from the very essence of those trapped within.

One particular legend he had found in a crumbling journal belonging to a long-forgotten local historian, spoke of a being known only as "the Weaver," an entity that lured souls into a labyrinth of its own making, a place where memories became distorted and reality fractured. The Weaver, according to the legend, was weakened by pure, unadulterated truth, by the unwavering light of an uncorrupted spirit. Brody felt a tremor of recognition. Harmony's love for Lily, her fierce protectiveness – wasn't that the purest form of truth? Wasn't that an uncorrupted spirit shining brightly against the Master's darkness?

He began to meticulously document every detail about the Master's domain that Harmony had described. The decaying paradise, the phantom laughter, the sense of profound wrongness – these were not just sensory experiences; they were clues. He looked for patterns, for the underlying architecture of the Master's illusion. If the Master was a creator of illusions, then illusions had to have rules, however twisted. And if they had rules, then they had exploitable weaknesses. He started to theorize about the nature of the Master's power, whether it was inherent or derived, whether it was fixed or fluid.

The sheriff's office began to feel less like a hub of law enforcement and more like a den of occult investigation. The scent of old paper and dust mingled with the subtle, metallic tang of fear that Brody couldn't quite shake. He found himself staring at the shadows in the corners of his office, his imagination now a fertile ground for the horrors he was researching. He knew he was treading on dangerous ground, that delving too deep into these matters could be as perilous as the Master's power itself. But the image of Lily's stolen innocence, of Harmony's desperate plight, propelled him forward. He was a man of the law, but he was also a man of his word, and he had promised Harmony his full support. He was going to find a way to keep that promise, even if it meant venturing into realms beyond his comprehension. He was gathering his arsenal, not of bullets and handcuffs, but of forgotten lore and ancient warnings, hoping to find a crack in the Master's seemingly impenetrable facade, a weakness that Harmony could exploit. His role had evolved; he was no longer just the sheriff, but a scholar of the spectral, a desperate archivist of the damned, all in service of saving a child from a darkness that threatened to consume them all.

CHAPTER 12

The Kidnapping and the Wound

The air in Harmony's bedroom, moments before a sanctuary of slumber and innocent dreams, had curdled into a nightmare. It was a transition so abrupt, so violent, that the remnants of peace felt like a cruel mockery. One heartbeat, Lily was nestled in the familiar warmth of her blankets, her soft breaths a gentle rhythm in the quiet night. The next, the room was a vortex of impossible energies, the mundane fabric of reality rent asunder by a force that defied all earthly logic.

Harmony's scream was not merely a sound; it was a primal, guttural shriek of pure terror, ripped from the deepest wells of a mother's soul. It was the sound of a world imploding, of a universe tilting on its axis. Her eyes, wide and uncomprehending, had witnessed the unthinkable. Not a shadowy figure, not a mundane burglar, but something far more ancient, far more terrifying. The Master, a being whose very presence seemed to leach the color and life from the air, had manifested. And in his grasp, Lily was not merely held, but *absorbed*.

298

It was as if the air itself had congealed, forming phantom tendrils, chains of shimmering, spectral energy that latched onto Lily's small form. Harmony had lunged, her motherly instincts a desperate, futile surge against an unstoppable tide. She had felt the oppressive, chilling aura of the Master, a palpable wave of malice that seemed to suck the very breath from her lungs. His eyes, if they could be called eyes, were pits of malevolent intelligence, devoid of any warmth or empathy, reflecting only a chilling, alien purpose.

And then, with a speed that defied perception, Lily was gone. Not carried, not thrown, but *pulled*. It was as if the very space around her had folded in on itself, drawing her into an unseen abyss. The ethereal chains tightened, not with a snap, but with a sickening *slurp*, a sound that spoke of souls being ingested, of realities being breached. The spectral manifestation of the Master, cloaked in an aura of decay and ancient power, had opened a fissure, a tear in the world, and with a final, heart-wrenching cry from Lily that echoed with a terror far beyond her years, she was gone, swallowed by the hungry maw of the "Rooms Between."

The room snapped back into a semblance of normalcy, the violent energies receding as quickly as they had appeared, leaving behind only a profound stillness, a vacuum where a child's laughter had once filled the air. But the normalcy was a cruel illusion. The lingering scent of ozone and something akin to decay, a scent Harmony would forever associate with utter devastation, clung to the air. The indentation in Lily's bed was a stark, physical testament to the impossible violation, a gaping wound in the fabric of their lives.

Harmony stood frozen, the scream dying in her throat, replaced by a ragged gasp. Her hands, reaching for a daughter who was no longer there, trembled uncontrollably. The mundane objects of the room – the stuffed animals scattered on the floor, the colorful drawings taped to the wall, the faint scent of lavender from Lily's pillow – all seemed to mock her with their ordinary existence. They were anchors to a reality that had just been irrevocably shattered.

She stumbled forward, her movements jerky, her mind struggling to process the impossible. She fell to her knees beside Lily's empty bed; her gaze fixed on the spot where her daughter had last been. The silence that followed was deafening, broken only by the frantic thumping of her own heart, a drumbeat of pure agony. The Master's act was not merely an abduction; it was a declaration of war, a brutal assertion of his power, a desperate attempt to break the one being who had dared to resist him. He had taken what was most precious, most vulnerable, a calculated strike aimed at the core of Harmony's being, at the very essence of her strength.

The world outside the bedroom window continued its oblivious cycle of night and dawn. The crickets chirped their nightly chorus, the distant hum of traffic a familiar sound. But for Harmony, the world had ceased to spin. It had fractured, its familiar contours replaced by the terrifying, unknown geography of the "Rooms Between." The mundane had been violated by the monstrous, leaving behind not just a missing child, but a mother irrevocably changed, standing at the precipice of a terrifying new reality.

Her grief was a tangible entity, a suffocating weight that threatened to crush her. It was a grief born not just of loss, but of witnessing the unconscionable. The image of Lily, her small form ensnared by those spectral chains, her terrified cries echoing in the sudden void, was seared into Harmony's consciousness. It was a vision that would haunt her waking hours and invade her dreams, a constant reminder of the Master's cruelty and the profound helplessness she had felt in that moment.

The Master's intent was brutally clear. He had sought to inflict maximum damage, to dismantle Harmony's spirit by tearing away the very reason for her defiance. Lily was not just a pawn; she was the fulcrum upon which Harmony's resistance had been built. By taking her, the Master aimed to sever that connection; to plunge Harmony into a despair so profound it would render her incapable of further opposition. He was attempting to break her will, to obliterate the very spark that had ignited her fight against him.

Harmony's mind, still reeling from the shock, grappled with the enormity of what had happened. This was not a crime that could be solved with police reports or missing person posters. This was a transgression of cosmic proportions, a violation of the fundamental laws of existence. The Master had stepped from the shadows of legend and into the stark reality of her life, leaving behind a trail of shattered normalcy and a gaping wound that seemed to bleed into the very soul of her world.

She remembered Lily's soft hand in hers, the warmth of her embrace, the innocent trust in her wide, curious eyes. These memories, once a source of joy and comfort, now served as agonizing reminders of what had been so brutally stolen. The Master had not just taken a child; he had stolen a future, a lifetime of laughter and love, a tapestry of shared moments that would now remain forever unfinished.

The violation felt deeply personal. It was a calculated act of psychological warfare, designed to dismantle her resolve through the most agonizing means possible. The Master, in his ancient, alien understanding, knew that a mother's love was a powerful force, perhaps the most powerful force in existence. And by targeting Lily, he was attempting to extinguish that force, to extinguish the light that Harmony represented in his dark, corrupt world.

As Harmony knelt there, the silence of the room pressing in on her, a single, chilling realization began to dawn. The Master had not just taken Lily to inflict pain; he had taken her to *use* her. To what end, she could not fathom, but the implication sent a fresh wave of terror through her already ravaged spirit. He had demonstrated his power, his ability to breach the veil between worlds, and now he had a piece of Harmony's world, a piece of her very being, in his grasp.

The residual energy of the abduction still seemed to hum in the air, a low thrumming that vibrated in Harmony's bones. It was the echo of a door opening and closing, a passage between realities that had been brutally forced. The sheer audacity of the act, the raw, untamed power displayed, left her feeling impossibly small and fragile. She, who had found a nascent strength in her defiance, was now confronted with a power so overwhelming that it threatened to swallow her whole.

The spectral chains, the impossible speed, the very being of the Master – these were not figments of a nightmare. They were the chillingly real tools of a predator who operated beyond the confines of human understanding. And Harmony was left with the agonizing aftermath, the stark, undeniable proof of an otherworldly violation that had ripped her daughter from her arms and plunged her into an unknown abyss. The gaping wound in her heart was mirrored by the tear in the fabric of reality itself, a wound that would require more than just time to heal, a wound that demanded a desperate fight for what had been so cruelly taken. The night had truly fallen, not just over the world, but over Harmony's soul, ushering in a darkness she had never imagined possible.

The silence that descended after the terrifying spectacle was not a void, but a deafening roar in Harmony's ears. It was the sound of her own world imploding, of every cherished sound – Lily's laughter, her sleepy murmurs, the cheerful hum of her favorite songs – being abruptly extinguished. The air, once familiar and comforting, now felt thin and alien, as if the very molecules had been rearranged by an unholy force. The vibrant, almost tangible energy of Redwater Crossing, the subtle thrum that had always resonated beneath the surface of the town, seemed to recede, a collective gasp from the very land itself, as if it too had witnessed the impossible violation.

Harmony remained on her knees, her body a rigid monument to shock. Her hands, still outstretched as if to ward off the spectral chains, now trembled with a violence that threatened to dislocate her bones. The intricate floral pattern on Lily's rug, a detail she had once admired for its delicate artistry, now seemed to twist and writhe before her eyes, morphing into grotesque, mocking shapes. Every object in the room, from the worn teddy bear perched precariously on the bookshelf to the crayon drawing of a lopsided sun taped to the wall, screamed of a life that had been irrevocably stolen. They were relics of a stolen past, fragments of a shattered present, and the horrifying prologue to an unimaginable future.

The grief that seized her was not a gentle sorrow, but a physical assault. It was a tearing, a ripping sensation that began in the pit of her stomach and clawed its way up her throat, threatening to choke her. Her lungs burned with a desperate need for air, but each inhale was a sharp agony, a reminder of the emptiness that now resided within her. The Master, in his ancient, twisted wisdom, had aimed directly for her heart, for the very core of her being. He had believed that by taking Lily, he would shatter her will, that the crushing weight of maternal despair would render her utterly broken, incapable of further resistance. And for a fleeting, terrifying moment, as the initial shock gave way to the raw, unadulterated pain, it seemed he might be right. The world, once a kaleidoscope of vibrant colors and shared joys, had narrowed to a single, agonizing point of darkness.

A guttural sob tore from her, raw and ragged, a sound that seemed to echo the very dismantling of her soul. She pressed a hand to her chest, as if to physically contain the rupture, to hold together the fractured pieces of herself. The image of Lily, her daughter's small face contorted in terror, her eyes wide with an incomprehension that was far too profound for her tender years, was seared behind Harmony's eyelids. The spectral tendrils, the unnatural shimmer of the Master's form, the sickening finality of Lily's disappearance – these were not memories she could bury or forget. They were now permanent fixtures in the landscape of her mind, a constant, gnawing reminder of the monstrous reality that had intruded upon her peaceful existence.

The Master's objective was undeniably clear: to inflict a wound so deep, so devastating, that it would cauterize any remaining spark of defiance within her. He had witnessed her strength, her resilience, her unwavering protection of Lily, and he had recognized it as a threat. He understood, in his own alien way, the profound power of a mother's love, and he had sought to corrupt it, to twist it into a weapon of self-destruction. He had believed that by severing the object of that love, he would extinguish the source of her power. He had aimed to drown her in an ocean of despair, to leave her gasping for air in the suffocating darkness of her loss.

As Harmony knelt amidst the wreckage of her former life, the vibrant pulse of Redwater Crossing seemed to dim perceptibly. The familiar hum of the town, the subtle ebb and flow of its energy, felt muted, subdued. It was as if the very earth mourned the violation, as if the unseen forces that governed the town had recoiled from the sheer malevolence of the Master's act. The colors of the world seemed to leach away, leaving behind a sterile, desaturated panorama. The chirping of the crickets outside, once a soothing lullaby of the night, now sounded hollow and distant, a soundtrack to her desolation.

Her mind, still reeling from the impossible violence of the abduction, struggled to grasp the enormity of what had occurred. This was no ordinary crime, no earthly transgression that could be addressed by law enforcement or community support. This was a breach of cosmic proportions, a tear in the very fabric of reality, orchestrated by a being who operated outside the known laws of physics and existence. The Master had stepped from the realm of myth and legend, not as a shadowy figure in a distant tale, but as a tangible, terrifying force that had ripped her daughter from her very arms. The violation was not just an act of separation; it was a profound desecration.

The indentation on Lily's bed, a subtle but undeniable mark of absence, was a constant, tormenting focal point. It was a gaping wound, not just in the mattress, but in the very soul of Harmony's world. She traced its outline with a trembling finger, the coarse fibers of the fabric a stark contrast to the phantom softness of Lily's skin. Memories flooded her, each one a fresh wave of exquisite agony: Lily's tiny hand tucked securely in hers as they walked through the park, the warmth of her small body curled against Harmony's side during story time, the infectious gurgle of her laughter as they played games. These were the moments that had woven the tapestry of her life, and now, with brutal swiftness, the Master had slashed through those threads, leaving behind a jagged, unfinished canvas.

The Master had anticipated this. He had foreseen that the profound, primal instinct of a mother to protect her child would be the most potent weapon against her. He believed that by removing Lily, he was removing Harmony's reason for being, her anchor to the world, her wellspring of courage. He had imagined her collapsing under the sheer, unbearable weight of her grief, her spirit crumbling into dust. He envisioned her succumbing to a despair so profound that it would render her a hollow shell, incapable of ever again posing a threat. He had sought to annihilate her will by destroying what she held most dear.

But even as the pain threatened to consume her, a flicker of something else began to stir within the darkness. It was a tiny ember, buried deep beneath the ashes of her shock and sorrow, a nascent defiance that refused to be extinguished. The Master might have taken her daughter, he might have inflicted a wound that bled into the very essence of her being, but he had not yet broken her. The image of Lily, not just in terror, but in her inherent strength, her curiosity, her unwavering belief in her mother, began to surface through the haze of despair.

Harmony's mind, still struggling to reconcile the impossible with reality, began to piece together the fragments of the encounter. The spectral chains, the speed that defied comprehension, the palpable aura of ancient power – these were not elements of a shared hallucination. They were the undeniable proof of an otherworldly entity, a being who operated on a plane far removed from human understanding. And this entity had breached the sanctity of her home, had stolen her most precious possession, and had left behind a wound that pulsed with an unimaginable darkness. The Master's act was not merely an abduction; it was a declaration, a chilling testament to his power and his intent. He had declared war, not just on Harmony, but on the very fabric of light and life that she represented.

The scent of ozone, now mingling with a faint, metallic tang that Harmony couldn't quite place – a scent she would forever associate with terror and loss – still lingered in the air. It was a phantom perfume, a cruel reminder of the unnatural forces that had invaded her sanctuary. She breathed it in, forcing herself to confront the reality of it, to anchor herself to the present moment, however horrific. The silence of the room pressed in on her, no longer an absence of sound, but a heavy, suffocating blanket of dread. The Master had stolen Lily, but in doing so, he had also inadvertently ignited a fire within Harmony, a fire fueled by a mother's unyielding love and a primal, unshakeable will to reclaim what had been so cruelly taken. The gaping wound in her heart was a testament to the depth of her love, and in that love, lay the seed of her retribution. The Master had made a terrible mistake.

He had underestimated the ferocity of a mother's protection, the unyielding strength that could be forged in the crucible of unimaginable loss. He had shattered her world, yes, but in doing so, he had also revealed a strength within her that even she had not known existed, a strength that would now be honed into a weapon as sharp and unforgiving as his own. The night had indeed fallen, but for Harmony, it was not the end of everything. It was the grim, terrifying beginning of a battle for survival, for redemption, and for the return of her daughter.

The Master, a figure cloaked in an aura of ancient malevolence, felt a tremor of something akin to satisfaction ripple through his ethereal form. It was a sensation so alien to his usual state of detached observation and calculated cruelty that it momentarily surprised even him. He had orchestrated countless acts of terror, sowed seeds of despair across epochs, but this felt... different. This was a precision strike, a surgical incision into the very heartwood of his adversary's existence. He had studied Harmony, observed her fierce protectiveness, the radiant, almost incandescent love she harbored for the child, Lily. He had seen it as a weakness, a vulnerability ripe for exploitation. And now, witnessing the raw, animalistic grief that contorted her features, the ragged gasps that tore from her throat, he allowed himself a moment of profound, albeit chilling, triumph.

He had always understood the primal bonds that tethered mortals, the fragile threads of connection they clung to with desperate ferocity. Love, he had discovered, was a particularly potent fuel for despair when severed. It was the anchor that kept them grounded, the light that guided them through the darkness. To snatch away the object of that love, to extinguish that light, was to plunge them into an abyss from which escape seemed impossible. He had seen it happen before, countless times, in myriad forms. But with Harmony, there had been a certain... resilience. A spark that even the most calculated cruelties had failed to fully extinguish. Until now.

The 'tall man,' the spectral manifestation that served as his earthly vessel, seemed to swell, his shadowy form pulsating with a dark, exultant energy. The air around them, already thick with the palpable dread Harmony had been feeling, thickened further, growing heavy and suffocating. It was as if the very atmosphere of Redwater Crossing had become a tangible extension of the Master's malevolent glee. The ambient terror, the subtle hum of unease that always permeated the town when he was near, seemed to amplify, reaching a crescendo as he savored this perceived victory. He could almost taste the despair on the wind, a sweet, intoxicating nectar that promised to finally break her.

He had anticipated this outcome with a chilling certainty. He had foreseen the shattering impact of Lily's absence, the implosion of Harmony's world. He had meticulously calculated the precise angle of attack, targeting not her physical strength, which he knew to be formidable, nor her intellect, which he recognized as sharp, but the very core of her emotional being. This was not merely an abduction; it was a masterstroke of psychological warfare. He had believed that by removing Lily, he was not just taking her daughter, but her purpose, her joy, her very will to fight. He had imagined her collapsing, her spirit succumbing to a grief so profound it would leave her utterly incapacitated.

The Master reveled in the image he conjured: Harmony, a broken husk, her eyes hollowed by unshed tears, her body wracked by sobs that would never truly alleviate the pain. He pictured her stumbling through the days, a phantom haunted by the ghost of a vibrant life, her every breath a testament to her loss. This was the intended aftermath, the carefully curated consequence of his intervention. He had aimed for the deepest, most sensitive nerve, and he believed, with a fervent certainty, that he had struck true. The silence that followed Lily's disappearance was not an emptiness to Harmony; it was a deafening roar of what was no longer there, a void that the Master intended to fill with unending torment.

He watched, a silent, invisible observer, as Harmony's hands, once capable of such gentle reassurance, now clenched into fists, her knuckles white. The trembling that wracked her body was a testament to the seismic shock that had ripped through her. He felt a dark kinship with that destructive force, a mirror reflecting his own capacity for annihilation. He had sought to inflict a wound that would fester, a gaping chasm in her soul that would swallow any flicker of hope. And in this moment, as he felt the raw power of her devastation radiating outwards, he believed he had succeeded. The Master's brief triumph was the potent, intoxicating sensation of seeing his design come to fruition, of witnessing the expected outcome unfold with devastating precision. He had found her Achilles' heel, the one vulnerability that could bring her to her knees.

He could feel the energy of Redwater Crossing responding to his presence, the subtle shifts in its unseen currents. The town, usually a tapestry of mundane anxieties and quiet joys, now pulsed with a shared apprehension. The Master had always been a discordant note in the town's symphony, a dissonant chord that disrupted its fragile harmony. But this time, his presence felt more profound, more invasive. He was not merely an external threat; he was an internal poison, seeping into the very foundations of its existence. The fear he sowed was not just a reaction to his power, but a recognition of the profound violation that had just occurred within its borders.

The Master, in his ageless existence, had learned to dissect the intricate mechanisms of mortal despair. He understood that the most profound pain often stemmed not from physical suffering, but from the loss of what gave life meaning. For Harmony, that meaning was unequivocally Lily. He had observed their interactions, the easy affection, the unspoken understanding, the shared laughter that echoed through their home. He had cataloged every gesture of love, every protective instinct, every whispered endearment. And he had meticulously planned their obliteration.

He allowed himself to linger in the aftermath, to absorb the potent cocktail of shock and nascent grief. He was a connoisseur of suffering, and this was a vintage he had been cultivating for some time. The sheer, unadulterated agony radiating from Harmony was a testament to the depth of her love, a love he now sought to corrupt and weaponize against her. He envisioned her future, a desolate landscape devoid of the warmth and light Lily had brought into her life. He saw her isolation, her despair, her eventual surrender. This was not a fleeting victory; it was the prelude to a sustained campaign of psychological destruction.

The Master, reveling in the raw agony that emanated from Harmony, felt a flicker of something akin to understanding ignite within his ancient, unfeeling core. He had always perceived love as a weakness, a tether that bound mortals to their fragile existences, making them susceptible to his manipulations. He had honed this understanding over millennia, wielding despair as a sculptor's chisel, chipping away at the spirits of those who dared to stand against him. He saw Harmony's love for Lily as the most exquisite vulnerability, a glowing beacon in the darkness of her being, perfect for extinguishing. He had anticipated the crushing weight of grief, the debilitating paralysis that would follow the child's vanishing. He had envisioned her world collapsing, her formidable will dissolving into a puddle of inconsolable sorrow. This was the intended outcome: a broken woman, stripped of her purpose, her joy, her very essence.

But as he observed her, a subtle, almost imperceptible shift occurred within the ethereal plane. The sheer intensity of Harmony's anguish, instead of dissipating her, seemed to coalesce, to condense into something potent, something *other*. He had seen grief manifest in countless ways – in shattered minds, in withered souls, in the slow erosion of hope. Yet, this was different. This was not the passive surrender he had come to expect. This was a crucible, and the heat within it was not consuming Harmony, but forging her anew.

The Master, cloaked in the ephemeral form of the "tall man," felt a searing, unexpected jolt ripple through his being. It was a sensation he had not experienced in centuries, a prickling, burning agony that radiated from his spectral core. He recoiled, a phantom gasp tearing through his ethereal lungs, a sound unheard by mortal ears. What was this? He had expected despair, a corrosive agent that would eat away at her resolve from the inside. Instead, he was feeling... pain. A sharp, debilitating pain, as if a thousand needles of pure, incandescent energy were piercing his very essence.

He narrowed his focus, his ancient gaze, usually detached and clinical, now filled with a sudden, unwelcome bewilderment. He had meticulously dissected Harmony's emotional landscape, cataloging every facet of her protectiveness, every nuanced expression of her maternal devotion. He had believed he was striking at the very heart of her being, severing the most vital connection. And in a way, he had. But he had miscalculated the nature of that connection. He had seen it as a chain, easily broken. He had failed to recognize it as a conduit, a channel for something far more powerful than he had ever accounted for.

Harmony's love for Lily was not a passive emotion, a gentle ebb and flow of affection. It was a force. A primal, untamed power that surged through her, fueled by an instinct as old as creation itself. It was the unwavering roar of a mother lioness defending her cub, amplified and transmuted into something ethereal. When Lily was ripped away, it was not her heart that shattered, but a dam that burst. The pure, unadulterated essence of her love, unleashed by the violent act, had found its only available target – the source of its violation.

The Master's ethereal form shimmered, his shadowy contours rippling like disturbed water. The pain intensified, a relentless, burning sensation that spread through him like wildfire. It was a wound, a deep, gouging wound that defied his incorporeal nature. He could not bleed, could not scar, in the mortal sense, but the agony was undeniably real, a feedback loop of pure, cosmic torment. He had expected to inflict a gaping wound in Harmony's soul, a chasm of despair that would swallow her whole. Instead, he had inadvertently created a wound in himself, a self-inflicted injury born from the very emotion he sought to exploit.

He had always understood the concept of energy, of its manipulation, its redirection. He had manipulated fear, sowed discord, and reveled in the resulting chaos. But Harmony's love was an energy of a different order. It was a pure, unyielding light, a beacon of fierce devotion that, when weaponized, became a searing blade. It was the antithesis of his own being, a force of creation and protection colliding with his own inherent darkness and destruction. And in that collision, he was the one suffering the damage.

He saw Harmony then, not as the broken figure he had envisioned, but as a tempest. Her grief was still present, a roiling sea beneath the surface, but it was no longer the dominant force. It was now tempered by a burning, righteous rage. Her eyes, moments before clouded with shock and disbelief, were now blazing with an inferno of protective fury. The tremors that wracked her body were not of weakness, but of contained power, a coiled spring ready to unleash its full force.

The Master's triumph evaporated, replaced by a dawning, unsettling realization. He had underestimated the fundamental nature of her love. He had viewed it through the lens of mortal frailty, mistaking its tenderness for weakness. He had failed to comprehend that the very strength he had sought to break was the source of its unparalleled power. He had attacked the vessel, but the essence, the pure, undiluted love, had found a way to retaliate.

He felt the wound within him pulse, a constant throb of agony that distracted him, a stark contrast to his usual state of serene detachment. It was as if a part of his spectral being had been cauterized, seared by an unimaginable heat. This was not the fleeting discomfort of a minor setback; this was a fundamental violation of his own incorporeal existence. The raw, untamed power of Harmony's love, channeled through the lens of her maternal rage, had struck him with the force of a supernova, leaving an indelible mark.

He had built his power on the ruins of mortal spirits, on the ashes of broken dreams and extinguished hopes. He had been the ultimate predator, always in control, always inflicting the damage. But now, he was the victim, the recipient of a pain he had not inflicted, but had, in a perverse twist of fate, brought upon himself. The irony was not lost on him, a bitter, acrid taste that mingled with the burning sensation. He had sought to create a gaping wound in her, a wound that would fester and consume her. Instead, he had created a wound in *himself*, a wound that he suspected would not heal, a wound that would serve as a constant, agonizing reminder of his miscalculation.

The ambient dread that usually permeated Redwater Crossing when he was near felt different this time. It was no longer solely a reflection of his power, his ability to instill terror. It was now mingled with a sense of something ancient and elemental stirring. Harmony's love, amplified and weaponized, was a force that resonated beyond her immediate being, touching the very fabric of the town's unseen energies. He could feel the subtle currents of fear and unease, but beneath them, a new vibration was emerging, a defiant hum of protective energy that seemed to push back against his malevolent presence.

He had intended to shatter Harmony's world, to reduce her to a state of utter desolation. He had meticulously planned to exploit her deepest love, to turn it into her greatest undoing. But he had failed to account for the inherent resilience of that love, its capacity to transform and to fight back. He had underestimated the sheer, unadulterated power of a mother's fierce protectiveness. He had thought he was dimming a light, but instead, he had ignited a wildfire. And the Master, for the first time in an eternity, found himself on the defensive, reeling from an unexpected, agonizing blow dealt by the very weapon he thought he had so expertly wielded. The gaping wound was not in Harmony's soul, but in his own spectral form, a searing testament to the power of a love he had so catastrophically misjudged. He could feel the wound festering, a constant, gnawing pain that echoed the agony he had intended to inflict. This was not victory; this was a brutal, humbling defeat, and the Master, for the first time, was experiencing the raw, unadulterated sting of his own creation.

The spectral edifice of Earl's Honest Rides, once a beacon of calculated normalcy, began to fracture. It wasn't a sudden, dramatic implosion, but a sickening, insidious decay, like a photograph left too long in the sun, its colors bleeding into a muddy, unrecognizable mess. The psychic residue that had meticulously maintained its illusion of a thriving, albeit slightly seedy, used car dealership was fraying, threads of malevolence unravelling under the relentless, incandescent pressure of Harmony's unleashed love. The Master, so accustomed to his dominion over the subtle energies of fear and despair, found himself reeling, his carefully constructed dominion cracking around him. He had intended to forge a wound in Harmony, a gaping chasm of grief that would consume her very being. Instead, his own spectral form had become the site of a searing, agonizing tear, a wound born not of his own design, but of the raw, untamed power he had so spectacularly underestimated.

The psychic backlash, a tsunami of pure, maternal fury and protective agony, had slammed into the Master with the force of a celestial body. It was a pain so profound, so utterly alien to his eons of detached existence, that it threatened to tear his ethereal essence asunder. He had wielded terror like a surgeon's scalpel, precise and devastating, but Harmony's love, now weaponized by her anguish, was a crude, overwhelming force, a sledgehammer against his carefully constructed reality. The very foundations of his influence in Redwater Crossing began to tremble. The spectral energy that had held the town in a pervasive, suffocating grip, whispering doubts and fanning the flames of discord, now stuttered and warped. The oppressive atmosphere, a constant, low hum of dread he had meticulously cultivated, began to flicker. It was as if the very air was struggling to breathe, choked by the sudden, violent surge of a power antithetical to his own.

Earl's Honest Rides, in particular, was a nexus of this destabilization. The spectral constructs that gave it its semblance of solidity, the phantom sales pitches echoing in empty showrooms, the spectral hum of unreliable engines, all began to glitch. The polished chrome of the cars seemed to ripple, reflecting distorted images of a reality struggling to maintain its disguise. The "Honest" in Earl's Honest Rides became a cruel mockery as the spectral veneer peeled back, revealing the avaricious greed and desperate lies that lay beneath. Shadows writhed and stretched unnaturally, detaching themselves from their corporeal anchors, dancing with a frantic, dislocated energy. The cheerful, if slightly worn, signage flickered erratically, the neon tubes sputtering and dying one moment, flaring with an unnatural intensity the next. It was as if the very building was suffering from a profound, agonizing fever, its systems breaking down under the overwhelming strain.

The Master, his incorporeal form writhing in silent agony, felt the structural integrity of his influence in Redwater Crossing disintegrating. He had woven a complex tapestry of fear and despair, a subtle yet pervasive control that seeped into the very soul of the town. But Harmony's pain, amplified by the primal force of her love, was an acid eating away at the threads. He could feel the connections weakening, the tendrils of his influence snapping one by one. The subtle whispers that preyed on insecurities, the insidious nudges towards self-destruction, the carefully manufactured paranoia – all of it was faltering. The energy that sustained these manifestations was being actively repelled, absorbed, and transmuted by the sheer, unadulterated power of Harmony's retaliatory love.

He had always viewed emotions as tools, levers to pry open the vulnerabilities of mortals. He had dissected grief, analyzed fear, and cataloged desperation, understanding their mechanics as instruments of his will. But Harmony's love was not a tool; it was a fundamental force, an elemental power that operated on a plane he had never truly comprehended until now. It was the antithesis of his own essence – he, a creature of entropy and decay, and her love, a force of creation and fierce protection. The collision of these two opposing powers had not merely repelled; it had caused a catastrophic implosion within his own spectral being. The wound he had intended to inflict upon Harmony had instead opened within him, a bleeding tear in his incorporeal existence that pulsed with agony, a constant, agonizing reminder of his monumental miscalculation.

The spectral energy holding Earl's Honest Rides together began to unravel with alarming speed. The illusion of prosperity, the carefully crafted image of a reputable business, dissolved like mist in the morning sun. Cars that had appeared pristine now seemed to rot from within, their spectral paint blistering, their metallic shells warping as if succumbing to an unseen decay. The sales staff, who had once slithered with insincere smiles, now flickered in and out of existence, their forms becoming indistinct, their voices reduced to guttural whispers that dissolved into static. The very ground beneath the dealership seemed to groan, the asphalt cracking and crumbling, revealing not earth, but a void, a gaping maw that echoed the wound within the Master himself.

The intensity of the psychic backlash was immense. It was not just Harmony's pain that was being reflected; it was the collective, buried unease of Redwater Crossing, the suppressed anxieties and unspoken fears that the Master had so expertly stoked, now being amplified and turned back upon their source. The town, once a canvas for his malevolent artistry, was now fighting back. The subtle currents of dread that had permeated its existence were being overwhelmed by a surging tide of protective energy, a wave of defiance that originated from Harmony's shattered heart but resonated through every soul that had ever suffered under his unseen dominion.

The Master, his ethereal form flickering like a dying candle flame, felt his grip on Redwater Crossing weakening with every passing second. He could no longer impose his will with the same effortless precision. The psychic landscape was in turmoil, a maelstrom of unleashed emotion. Earl's Honest Rides, a symbol of his mundane manipulation, was the first casualty of this psychic storm. Its collapse was not merely the destruction of a physical structure, but the shattering of a carefully constructed illusion. It was a visible manifestation of the Master's internal unraveling, a testament to the power of a love he had so grievously misjudged.

The spectral energy that had held the dealership together was not merely dissipating; it was actively being consumed, transmuted by the raw, potent energy of Harmony's anguish. It was like a dark, tar-like substance being devoured by an inferno of white-hot light. The sales office, where countless desperate deals had been forged in shadow, now flickered with a malevolent intensity, the paperwork on the desks swirling in phantom eddies, the air thick with the scent of decay and ozone. The showroom floor, usually a polished expanse reflecting the deceitful gleam of the vehicles, now seemed to warp and buckle, its polish cracking, revealing fissures of darkness beneath.

The Master felt the instability in Redwater Crossing as if it were a physical tremor running through his own being. He had always thrived on the subtle control, the quiet manipulation that allowed him to sow discord and harvest despair without overt confrontation. But Harmony's response had been anything but subtle. It had been a violent, earth-shattering eruption, a force of nature unleashed. The psychic wound he now carried was a constant, throbbing reminder of his hubris, a searing pain that made coherent thought a struggle. He had sought to break Harmony, to extinguish her light by plunging her into the deepest abyss of grief. Instead, he had inadvertently forged a weapon of unimaginable power from the very emotion he sought to destroy.

The manifestations of Earl's Honest Rides began to collapse inward. The cars didn't just decay; they imploded, their metal folding in on itself, their glass shattering into shards that rained down upon the asphalt. The building itself seemed to sigh, a long, drawn-out sound of despair, as its walls buckled and dissolved, the roof caving in with a silent crash. It was a cataclysm of proportions, a violent unravelling of the Master's influence, a tangible manifestation of his internal turmoil.

The Master's reign of subtle terror over Redwater Crossing was beginning to crumble, not under the weight of overt defiance, but under the overwhelming force of a love he had mistakenly perceived as weakness. The psychic backlash, a wound that festered within his very essence, had destabilized the foundations of his control. Earl's Honest Rides, once a proud monument to his ability to twist the mundane into something sinister, was now a testament to his downfall, a gaping wound in the fabric of Redwater Crossing, mirroring the agonizing tear in his own being. The wind, which had always seemed to carry a whisper of his insidious influence, now howled with a mournful, yet defiant, cry, signaling the inevitable end of his suffocating reign. The town, long held in his psychic thrall, was beginning to stir, its unseen energies resonating with Harmony's unleashed power, pushing back against the darkness he had so carefully cultivated. The collapse of Earl's Honest Rides was not an isolated incident; it was the first tremor of a seismic shift, the overture to the Master's unraveling.

CHAPTER 13

The Master's Demise

Harmony's counter-attack was not a battle waged with fists or weapons, but a detonation of pure, unadulterated truth, a primal scream against the cosmic injustice that had ripped her world asunder. The spectral wound she had inadvertently inflicted upon the Master, a consequence of his own audacious attempt to fracture her maternal spirit, was now the very conduit through which her defiance flowed. It was a tear in his incorporeal being, a bleeding fissure from which his carefully constructed dominion over fear and despair was hemorrhaging, replaced by the searing, incandescent light of her love and rage.

She didn't manifest in a grand, ethereal form, nor did she summon legions of spectral warriors. Her power was more elemental, more profound. It was the raw, unvarnished force of a mother's grief, transmuted into a weapon of pure spirit. Every tear shed for her lost child, every sob that had wracked her body, every desperate prayer whispered into the indifferent void – all of it coalesced, not into a passive lament, but into an active, aggressive force. This wasn't the mournful wail of the bereaved; it was the battle cry of the protector, the furious roar of the wounded beast defending its young.

The Master, still reeling from the initial shock of Harmony's potent counter-wave, felt the onslaught not as a physical blow, but as an invasive contamination. His existence was predicated on the subtle manipulation of negativity, on feeding upon the insecurities, the doubts, and the despair of mortals. He thrived in the shadows, a parasite of the soul, his essence woven from the threads of broken promises and shattered dreams. Harmony's love, however, was anathema to his very being. It was light where he was shadow, creation where he was decay, an unyielding rock against which his spectral entropy shattered.

The wound he carried was a raw, gaping wound, not of spectral flesh, but of corrupted spirit. It was a place where his own power had been turned against him, a festering testament to his miscalculation. Through this breach, Harmony's essence poured, not as a gentle balm, but as a corrosive agent. She was flooding his being with the unadulterated truth of his actions, the stark, undeniable reality of the pain he had inflicted. This wasn't a philosophical debate; it was a spiritual exorcism. She was stripping away the layers of his deceit, exposing the hollow core of his parasitic existence.

He had always perceived emotions as tools, instruments to be wielded with calculated precision. Fear was a lever to pry open minds, despair a wellspring to be tapped, greed a siren song to lure the foolish. But Harmony's love, particularly when amplified by her anguish, was something beyond his comprehension, beyond his control. It was a force of nature, a tidal wave of primal energy that cared nothing for his intricate machinations. It was the antithesis of his carefully cultivated atmosphere of dread. Where he sought to smother, she sought to ignite. Where he sought to isolate, she sought to connect.

Her spirit, forged in the crucible of her loss, was now an unassailable fortress. She pushed back against the spiritual corruption that had permeated Redwater Crossing, a corruption that was the Master's lifeblood. It wasn't about casting spells or wielding mystical artifacts; it was about the sheer, indomitable power of her will, amplified by the righteous fury of a mother scorned. She projected her truth into the very fabric of his being, a truth that resonated with the stolen innocence, the extinguished hopes, and the silenced voices of all those he had preyed upon.

The Master felt his hold on the subtle currents of Redwater Crossing faltering, not just weakening, but actively being dismantled. The spectral threads he had so meticulously woven, the invisible strings that had dictated the town's atmosphere of unease, were snapping under the pressure of Harmony's pure, focused energy. He had relied on the quiet erosion of spirits, the slow, insidious decay of hope. Harmony's retaliation was a lightning strike, a sudden, overwhelming force that bypassed all his defenses.

He could feel the edifice of Earl's Honest Rides, once a nexus of his influence, now actively rejecting him. The decay he had orchestrated within its walls was being accelerated, twisted into a form of self-immolation by the sheer power of Harmony's unleashed spirit. The phantom chrome gleamed with an unnatural, almost sickly luminescence, reflecting not the deceitful promise of a good deal, but the stark, ugly reality of avarice and exploitation. The sales pitches that echoed in its empty halls were no longer seductive whispers, but the desperate cries of trapped souls, their voices amplified by Harmony's amplified grief.

The Master, accustomed to operating from the shadows, found himself exposed. Harmony's truth was a blinding light, searing away the comforting darkness he had always inhabited. He felt his very essence being scrutinized, his parasitic nature laid bare. He had built his existence on the foundation of human frailty, on the ease with which mortals could be manipulated. But Harmony was not frail. She was broken, yes, but in her brokenness, she had found an unyielding strength. Her love, no longer a gentle warmth, had become a consuming inferno, incinerating the spectral constructs of his power.

He tried to push back, to reassert his control, but it was like trying to reassemble a shattered mirror. The pieces were too numerous, too sharp, and too utterly inimical to his purpose. The psychic backlash, originating from the wound he carried, was no longer just a pain; it was a constant influx of Harmony's unwavering spirit. He felt the echoes of her love for her child, a love so pure, so fierce, that it was anathema to his own decaying existence. It was a love that sought to protect, to nurture, to preserve – all things that were antithetical to his own drive towards entropy and destruction.

The Master's spectral form began to flicker more violently. The carefully maintained illusion of his power was crumbling, revealing the insubstantial, leech-like entity beneath. He was not a god, not a cosmic entity of unfathomable power, but a scavenger, a creature that fed on the detritus of human misery. Harmony's unleashed love was not merely an attack; it was a revelation, a stripping away of his carefully constructed mystique. She was showing him, and by extension, showing the very fabric of Redwater Crossing, what he truly was.

The wound he carried was a focal point for this spiritual assault. It was not just a source of pain; it was a gateway. Through it, Harmony's grief and fury poured, not as a destructive force aimed at annihilating him, but as a force of purification. She was not seeking revenge in the traditional sense; she was seeking to cleanse, to excise the malignancy that had taken root in their lives. Her motive was not destruction, but restoration, a fierce, unyielding desire to reclaim what had been stolen.

He felt the whispers of doubt and despair that he had so expertly sown in Redwater Crossing turning against him. The very emotions he had cultivated were now fueling Harmony's counter-attack. The collective unease of the town, the suppressed anxieties, the unspoken fears – all of it, now amplified by Harmony's potent grief, was battering against his spectral defenses. It was as if the town itself, long a passive victim of his influence, was now actively resisting, its collective consciousness resonating with Harmony's defiant cry.

Earl's Honest Rides began to collapse not just physically, but spectrally, in a more profound way. The illusion of its prosperity, the sheen of success, dissolved. The cars no longer represented opportunities for a fresh start, but mausoleums, monuments to broken dreams and failed hopes. The showroom floor, once a stage for his subtle manipulations, became a mirror reflecting the emptiness of his own being. The office, where deals were struck in the shadows, now echoed with the wails of the tormented, their anguish amplified by Harmony's righteous indignation.

The Master found himself drowning in an ocean of pure emotion, an experience utterly alien to his detached, calculating existence. He had always viewed emotions as predictable, quantifiable forces. But Harmony's love, magnified by her pain, was a chaotic, overwhelming surge, an elemental power that defied analysis. It was the force of creation itself, a stark contrast to his own inherent nature of decay. The collision was catastrophic, not just for him, but for the very foundations of his influence.

He could feel his spectral tether to Redwater Crossing fraying. The psychic connections he had painstakingly forged over centuries were weakening, snapping one by one, not under the weight of direct assault, but under the relentless pressure of Harmony's unyielding spirit. He had planned to inflict a wound, to create a lasting scar. Instead, he had opened a portal, a wound through which the very essence of what he feared most – pure, untainted love and protective maternal rage – was flooding his being.

His incorporeal form writhed, not in pain alone, but in a profound sense of existential dread. He was being consumed, not by an external force, but by the reflection of his own actions, amplified by the unshakeable spirit of a mother's love. The wound within him was a constant reminder of his failure, a bleeding testament to the fact that he had underestimated the power of a heart driven by love and fueled by righteous fury. Harmony's counter-attack was not a fleeting moment of defiance; it was a fundamental unraveling of his being, a spiritual reckoning that was far more devastating than any physical destruction.

The cars themselves, the supposed prizes of mortal ambition, became the most potent symbols of this collapse. They shimmered erratically, their forms losing cohesion as if viewed through rippling heatwaves on a sunbaked highway. A sedan, a model that had always represented a step up, a hint of the good life, now flickered violently, its tires seeming to spin without purchase, its windows darkening as if sucked into an unseen abyss. A hulking SUV, the kind that promised security and capability, began to buckle in the middle, its frame groaning with a soundless agony, its headlights dimming to impotent embers. The illusion of solidity, the very foundation upon which the Master had built his empire of desire, was evaporating with a terrifying, audible hiss, a sound like a thousand tiny souls sighing their last. The once gleaming asphalt of the lot, a seemingly stable foundation for so many dreams, cracked and fractured, not into fissures of earth, but into gaping voids that seemed to swallow the ambient light, revealing glimpses of the raw, churning psychic energy that lay beneath. It was the unvarnished truth of the Master's domain, a truth he had meticulously concealed behind layers of spectral artifice.

He had always viewed emotions as tools, instruments to be played with calculated precision. Fear was a key to unlock minds, avarice a current to steer desires, and despair a fertile ground for his insidious influence. He understood their mechanics, their predictable ebb and flow. But Harmony's love, amplified by the searing anguish of her loss, was a force of nature, a primal tide that dwarfed his sophisticated machinations. It was not something to be manipulated; it was something that *demanded* to be felt, to be acknowledged, and in its overwhelming purity, it was poison. The wound, he now understood with dawning horror, was not a static injury, but a living conduit, actively channeling Harmony's unleashed spirit into the core of his being. It burned with an unnatural intensity, a spiritual cauterization that stripped away the spectral illusions he had woven over centuries.

His control over Redwater Crossing, once an intricate web spun with invisible threads of suggestion and fear, began to unravel with alarming speed. The spectral hum of unease that had been his constant companion for generations was being drowned out by a discordant symphony of raw emotion emanating from Harmony's relentless spiritual assault. He felt the delicate tendrils of influence he had extended into the town's collective consciousness snapping like brittle string. The sales pitches echoing through the dealership, once laced with subtle promises of prosperity and escape, now twisted into frantic, desperate pronouncements, their tones cracking with an alien cacophony. The illusion of order, the carefully curated atmosphere of plausible deniability, was dissolving into a chaotic maelstrom.

He writhed, an incorporeal being experiencing a sensation akin to drowning. He had always been the predator, the unseen force orchestrating the downfall of mortals. The concept of being prey, of being fundamentally *threatened* by something so pure and potent, was a paradigm shift that sent tremors through his spectral foundation. The wound was not just a point of agony; it was a festering nexus where his own power was being turned against him, amplified by Harmony's unwavering spirit. He felt the echoes of her maternal love, a fierce, protective force that was the very antithesis of his own existence, seeping into his being, corrupting his spectral essence. This was not the calculated pain of a rival entity or the destructive force of a natural disaster; this was a visceral, spiritual purging.

The Master's spectral form flickered, its edges blurring and reforming as it struggled to contain the onslaught. He had maintained his dominion through an intricate dance of manipulation and misdirection, always operating from the periphery, a ghost in the machine of human desire. Harmony, however, had bypassed all his defenses, striking directly at his core. The 'wound' was more than a breach; it was a revelation. It exposed the hollow core of his existence, the parasitic nature of his being that fed on the detritus of mortal lives. He saw, through the searing lens of Harmony's grief, the true extent of his cruelty, the sheer waste of potential he had fostered, the countless stolen joys and extinguished hopes that were the foundation of his power.

He tried to shore up the spectral integrity of Earl's Honest Rides, to reassert his control over the illusion of prosperity that clung to its chrome and glass. But the very fabric of the place was rebelling. The spectral mechanisms designed to subtly reinforce the illusion of legitimacy were now glitching violently, their phantom gears grinding against each other, their wires sparking with uncontrolled energy. The cars, once gleaming symbols of aspiration, began to warp and twist, their engines emitting screams, their chassis buckling inwards as if under immense, unseen pressure. The asphalt of the lot cracked and splintered, revealing not earth, but a swirling vortex of raw, untamed psychic energy – a direct consequence of the Master's internal unraveling.

The Master's attempts to quell the agonizing influx were futile. He had always been the puppeteer, the one pulling the strings. Now, he was a marionette whose strings had been cut, whose very being was being deconstructed from the inside out. The psychic backlash from the wound was not merely a sharp, piercing pain; it was a continuous, overwhelming surge of pure, unadulterated emotion. He felt the raw force of Harmony's love for her child, a love so potent, so fiercely protective, that it was anathema to his own decaying existence. It was a love that sought to nurture, to preserve, to create – all concepts that were diametrically opposed to his own inherent drive towards entropy and destruction.

He had expected resistance, perhaps a desperate struggle, but not this. Not an all-consuming, spirit-purging onslaught. His existence had been predicated on the subtle erosion of hope, the slow decay of spirit. Harmony's counter-attack was a lightning strike, a sudden, overwhelming force that bypassed all his carefully constructed defenses. He had never conceived of an opponent capable of wielding such potent, primal energy, let alone one driven by the unyielding force of maternal love. His spectral form, accustomed to the quiet hum of despair, was now buffeted by the tempest of Harmony's grief and fury. It was a symphony of righteous indignation, an anthem of maternal defense that resonated through the very bones of his spectral existence, a sound he had never encountered, and now, a sound that was tearing him apart.

This was not the subtle erosion of influence, the gradual dimming of hope that he typically orchestrated. This was a spectacular, public disintegration, a testament to his profound miscalculation. Harmony's intervention, fueled by a mother's unyielding love and a righteous fury, was not a surgical strike; it was an earthquake, a demolition that brought the entire edifice of his deceptions crashing down. The Master, whose power was intrinsically tied to the maintenance of these elaborate charades, found himself powerless to halt the spectacular implosion. He had always been the conductor of a carefully orchestrated symphony of deception; each note meticulously placed to create a desired effect. Now, the orchestra was in disarray, instruments shattering, melodies devolving into discordant shrieks, and the conductor himself was being swept away by the tidal wave of his own unraveling.

The sales pitches that had once echoed with such persuasive sincerity began to twist into a cacophony of nonsensical pronouncements. The carefully crafted phrases designed to appeal to avarice and vanity now sputtered and died, their tones cracking like brittle glass. "Unbeatable deals!" became a strangled gasp. "Drive away today!" devolved into a desperate wail. The very language of commerce, the hypnotic balm of consumerism, was being undone, stripped of its meaning by the overwhelming surge of raw emotion that Harmony had unleashed. The salespeople, once embodiments of slick, insincere charm, now writhed with agony, their fixed smiles contorting into grimaces of terror as their own forms began to fray at the edges. They were no longer extensions of the Master's will, but victims of his hubris, their phantom existence dissolving along with the illusions they had helped to perpetuate.

The Master's own spectral form, intrinsically linked to this physical manifestation of his power, was experiencing the collapse firsthand. He felt the tearing sensation not just in the architecture of the dealership, but within his very essence. Each flaking piece of paint, each dissolving car, was a fragment of his presence being ripped away. He had always prided himself on his detachment, his ability to observe and manipulate mortal desires from a safe, incorporeal distance. But Harmony's intervention had bypassed his defenses, striking at the heart of his connection to this plane, forcing him to experience the disintegration of his influence as if it were his own physical demise. The wound he carried was no longer a localized point of pain; it was a gaping maw through which his very existence was hemorrhaging.

He desperately tried to reassert control, to weave new illusions, to shore up the crumbling foundations of Earl's Honest Rides. He channeled what remained of his spectral energy, attempting to imbue the fading chrome with a renewed sheen, to solidify the glass of the showroom windows, to coax a semblance of order from the escalating chaos. But his efforts were like trying to cup water in a sieve. The energies he now wielded were corrupted, tainted by the overwhelming purity of Harmony's emotions, which acted like a spiritual acid, corroding his every attempt at manipulation. The spectral constructs he attempted to create flickered and died before they could even take form, dissolving into the swirling vortex of psychic debris.

The collapse was not merely visual; it was sensory. The spectral hum of unease that had always permeated the dealership, a subtle undertone of desperation and longing, was replaced by a deafening silence, punctuated only by the tearing sounds of illusions being unmade. The phantom scent of exhaust fumes and cheap air freshener was gone, replaced by the sterile emptiness of pure void. He felt a profound sense of violation, as if his very soul were being scoured clean. He, who had feasted on the despair of others, was now being purged by the potent elixir of a mother's love. The irony was not lost on him, even in his torment. He had sought to break Harmony, to grind her spirit into the dust of despair, and in doing so, he had inadvertently created the very weapon that was now dismantling him.

The illusion of prosperity that had clung to Earl's Honest Rides like a shroud began to tear away in earnest. The signage, boasting of "Finest Selection" and "Lowest Prices," warped and melted, the letters slurring into illegible streaks of light. The flags that had snapped smartly in the breeze now drooped, their fabric fraying into wisps of nothingness. The very concept of "honesty," a word mockingly emblazoned on the dealership's name, was being systematically eradicated. Earl's Honest Rides was not just an illusion of a car lot; it was a monument to the Master's deepest lies, and now, that monument was being reduced to rubble by the sheer force of an undeniable truth – the truth of a mother's unwavering love.

He felt the tendrils of his influence over the town itself beginning to snap. The spectral whispers that had nudged Redwater Crossing towards his desires, the subtle currents of greed and discontent he had fostered, were being severed. The collective consciousness of the town, so long susceptible to his machinations, was now recoiling, as if sensing the fundamental rot at the core of the Master's power. The cars, the tangible symbols of his influence, were dissolving into the ether, taking with them the hopes and dreams he had so carefully cultivated. Each fading vehicle was a broken promise, a stolen ambition returning to the void from which it had been conjured.

The Master recoiled, an incorporeal entity experiencing a sensation akin to being physically torn apart. The spectral wound he bore was no longer just a source of pain; it was the epicenter of his undoing. Through it, he was witnessing the spectacular implosion of his life's work, the meticulous tapestry of deceit he had woven over centuries being unraveled with a terrifying speed. He had always operated from the shadows, a master of subtlety and misdirection. But Harmony, in her raw, unfiltered power, had dragged him into the harsh, unforgiving light of truth, and in that light, his illusions were turning to dust. The charade had not merely failed; it had self-destructed, leaving him exposed and vulnerable, the architect of his own spectacular, agonizing demise.

The collapse of Earl's Honest Rides was not just the fall of a dealership; it was the shattering of an entire reality, a testament to the ultimate failure of manufactured hope in the face of an unyielding, indomitable spirit. The chrome and glass were dissolving, but the truth they had so desperately tried to conceal was now burning brighter than ever, an incandescent testament to Harmony's triumph and the Master's ultimate, irredeemable failure. He was no longer a puppeteer pulling strings; he was a broken doll, his strings severed, his stuffing spilling out into the void. The illusion had not just been broken; it had been annihilated, leaving behind nothing but the raw, painful truth of his parasitic existence.

The scream, a sound that had resonated with the insidious promise of corrupted desire for so long, finally fractured, dissolving into a series of staccato shrieks that seemed to tear at the fabric of reality itself. It was not a prolonged, agonizing wail of defeat, but a sudden, violent implosion of energy, a final, futile struggle against the inevitable. The imposing silhouette of the 'tall man,' a figure that had loomed over Redwater Crossing like a perpetual storm cloud, began to warp, its edges blurring not into smoke or mist, but into an absence, a void that consumed its own substance. The spectral light that had emanated from him, a sickly, avaricious glow, flickered and died like a snuffed candle, leaving behind only the chilling darkness of absolute oblivion.

There was no grand, theatrical collapse, no dramatic explosion of spectral energy. Instead, it was a reverse unfolding, a terrifying regression. The Master's form, a carefully constructed facade of power and authority, began to contract inward. The illusion of his physical presence, the source of so much dread and manipulation, imploded upon itself. It was as if every strand of his parasitic being, every corrupted essence that had latched onto the town's dreams and desperations, was being violently retracted, pulled back into the infinitesimal point from which it had emerged. The air, which had always thrummed with a subtle, malevolent energy whenever he was near, grew unnaturally still. The oppressive weight that had settled upon Redwater Crossing for generations, a suffocating blanket of manufactured discontent and unfulfilled longing, began to lift, not gradually, but with a sudden, almost startling lightness.

Harmony watched, her breath catching in her throat, a strange mixture of terror and vindication warring within her. She had expected a struggle, a final, desperate battle of wills. But this was different. This was the unraveling of something that was never truly whole, a deception so profound that its demise was almost anticlimactic in its completeness. The Master, the architect of so much misery, the weaver of despair, was simply... ceasing to be. His power, so meticulously accumulated through the exploitation of mortal frailty, had no substance of its own to sustain it when confronted with the pure, unadulterated force of a mother's love and a child's stolen innocence. It was a poison that could only thrive in darkness, and Harmony, in her unwavering resolve, had flooded his domain with an unyielding light.

The remnants of Earl's Honest Rides, which had been dissolving into nothingness just moments before, now seemed to accelerate their demise. The chrome of the cars winked out of existence, the paint jobs vanished, and the illusion of solid ground beneath them crumbled into the nascent void. The very concept of the dealership, a monument to the Master's insidious influence, was being scrubbed from existence, leaving behind only the stark reality of the empty lot under the pale, indifferent moon. It was as if the universe itself was exhaling, expelling a foreign contaminant that had lingered for far too long.

The echoes of his final, desperate cry faded not into silence, but into a profound, resonant emptiness. It was the sound of absence, the void where a malevolent presence had once resided. There was no lingering specter, no residual haunt, no shadowy echo to torment the townsfolk further. The Master, the parasitic entity that had fed on Redwater Crossing's collective anxieties, had finally been starved. Harmony's act of defiance, fueled by the raw, primal instinct to protect her child, had severed his connection to the psychic energies he had so expertly manipulated. He had been a parasite, and she had, in essence, surgically removed him, leaving behind only the clean, unscarred flesh of the town.

A collective sigh seemed to ripple through Redwater Crossing, though no one had uttered a sound. It was an involuntary release of tension, a shared recognition of a burden lifted. The oppressive atmosphere that had clung to the town like a damp shroud for generations, the subtle undercurrent of despair that had whispered in the back of their minds, had vanished. The dreams that had been deferred, the ambitions that had been subtly crushed, the very essence of their collective will that had been sapped by his unseen influence – all of it began to stir, a slow, tentative reawakening.

Harmony felt a tremor run through the ground, not an earthquake, but a subtle thrum of returning life. The spectral energy that had been bound to the Master's will was not destroyed but dispersed. It was like a dam breaking, the pent-up waters rushing out and dissipating into the wider landscape, rejoining the natural flow of existence. The raw, untamed power that had been funneled into his manipulative schemes was now free, and as it dispersed, it carried with it the lingering traces of his influence, cleansing the psychic residue he had left behind.

She looked down at her hands, still tingling with the residual energy of her defiance. Her gaze swept across the empty lot, the spectral remnants of Earl's Honest Rides now fully extinguished. The Master was gone. Truly gone. Not vanquished in a glorious battle, but simply unmade, his existence negated by the power of a truth he could not comprehend. He had thrived on illusion, on the manufactured desire that blinded people to their own inner strength. Harmony, in her desperate love, had offered something far more powerful: an undeniable reality, a force of will that could not be deceived or corrupted.

The 'tall man' figure, the spectral embodiment of his power, had imploded like a collapsing star, all its borrowed light and stolen energy sucked back into an eternal darkness. There was no physical evidence of his passing, no ash, no residue, only the profound absence of a presence that had been a constant, unwelcome fixture for too long.

Redwater Crossing was, at last, breathing freely. The insidious grip had been broken, the parasitic entity's life force extinguished. Its energy, no longer tethered to its manipulative will, dispersed into the ether, a final, silent surrender to the natural order of things.

The town was no longer under a dark enchantment; it was simply a town, ready to reclaim its own destiny, free from the spectral chains that had bound it for generations. The oppressive silence that had fallen was not a void, but a pregnant pause, a breath taken before the first tentative sounds of renewal. The air, once thick with unspoken anxieties and manipulated desires, now felt crisp and clean, carrying the faint scent of damp earth and the promise of a new dawn.

Harmony stood on the edge of the dealership's former grounds, a solitary figure bathed in the fading moonlight, a testament to the fact that even the most ancient and insidious darkness could be banished by the unwavering light of courage and love. The Master's final moments were not a spectacle of power, but a silent testament to his ultimate weakness: his inability to understand the enduring strength of the human spirit when pushed to its absolute limit. He had sought to break Harmony, to extinguish her spirit and claim her child, but in doing so, he had inadvertently forged the very weapon that would bring about his own annihilation. His reign of terror, built on a foundation of fear and deceit, had crumbled not under a mighty blow, but under the gentle, yet unstoppable, pressure of unconditional love. The void left by his dissipation was not an empty space of despair, but a fertile ground for hope to once again take root and flourish in Redwater Crossing. The master was dead, and in his absence, life was finally able to begin.

The silence that descended upon Redwater Crossing was not a gentle quietude, but the stark, echoing stillness that follows an earth-shattering tremor. The spectral scream, once a piercing shard of malevolent energy, had imploded, taking with it the oppressive aura that had suffocated the town for generations. Harmony stood on the grounds of Earl's Honest Rides, the remnants of the Master's influence dissolving around her like frost in the morning sun. The chrome, the paint, the very illusion of commerce and corrupted dreams – all were being scrubbed from existence by an unseen hand. It was a cleansing, a profound exhale from a town that had been holding its breath for far too long. The Master was gone. Truly gone. Not vanquished in a glorious, drawn-out battle, but simply unmade, his essence erased by a force he had fundamentally misunderstood: the unyielding, potent truth of a mother's love. He had thrived on illusion, on the manufactured desires that blinded people to their own inner strength, and Harmony, in her desperation, had offered something far more real.

Yet, as the oppressive weight lifted from Redwater Crossing, a new, far more intimate burden settled upon Harmony's shoulders. The Master's demise was a victory, undeniably so. The spectral chains that had bound the town were broken, and a collective sigh of relief, unspoken yet palpable, rippled through the land. The air, once thick with unspoken anxieties and manipulated desires, now felt crisp and clean, carrying the faint scent of damp earth and the undeniable promise of a new dawn. The oppressive silence was not a void of despair, but a pregnant pause, a breath taken before the first tentative sounds of renewal. The Master's reign of terror, built on a foundation of fear and deceit, had crumbled not under a mighty blow, but under the gentle, yet unstoppable, pressure of unconditional love.

But Harmony's gaze wasn't on the nascent hope blooming in Redwater Crossing. Her eyes, sharp and unwavering, scanned the emptiness where the Master's spectral form had imploded. The void left by his dissipation was fertile ground, yes, but it was a ground that now contained a chilling, agonizing absence. The victory, so hard-won, was irrevocably tainted. The immediate, existential threat to her community had been neutralized, but her personal war, the one that gnawed at the very marrow of her bones, had only just begun. The death of the Master was not the end of her suffering; it was merely the closing of one harrowing chapter, a prelude to a far more perilous, deeply personal odyssey.

The spectral energy that had once been bound to the Master's will was not annihilated but dispersed. But this dispersal, this cleansing of the town's collective consciousness, did little to soothe the raw wound in Harmony's own soul. For while Redwater Crossing began to awaken from its long nightmare, Harmony was now faced with the stark reality of her daughter's continued captivity.

The Master, in his final moments, had not simply ceased to be. He had been a collector, a connoisseur of stolen innocence, and he had taken the most precious thing Harmony possessed. His death, therefore, was not a release, but a grim ultimatum. The battle against his influence might have been won, but the war for her child was now a solitary, desperate struggle against an enemy whose power, though diminished, was still immense, and whose motives were inextricably linked to the very essence of her child. The spectral scream that had finally fractured was a sound that had promised a perverse form of oblivion for the Master, but for Harmony, it was the sound of a future stolen, a future she now had to reclaim, piece by agonizing piece.

But the remnants of Earl's Honest Rides, while dissolving into nothingness, did not erase the searing image etched into Harmony's mind: the spectral glow of her daughter's eyes, held captive in a gilded cage of the Master's making. The victory was hollow. The relief that swept through Redwater Crossing was a cruel mockery of the gnawing dread that had taken root in Harmony's heart. The Master had been a parasite, and she had, in essence, surgically removed him, leaving behind only the clean, unscarred flesh of the town. But the wound he had inflicted upon her own life, the wound that bled a constant, searing pain, remained.

The whispers of the wind through the spectral lot seemed to carry a new lament, a mournful echo of the joy that had been so cruelly snatched away. Harmony had expected a struggle, a final, desperate battle of wills, and she had found one. She had unearthed the strength within herself to face down an ancient evil and emerge victorious. But the victory was incomplete. It was a foundation built on sand, a triumph that felt like a profound, soul-crushing loss.

The Master's power, so meticulously accumulated through the exploitation of mortal frailty, had no substance of its own to sustain it when confronted with the pure, unadulterated force of a mother's love and a child's stolen innocence. Yet, in his final act of malice, he had ensured that the very force that destroyed him would also become the instrument of his ultimate revenge – a revenge that targeted Harmony's heart.

The void left by his dissipation was not an empty space of despair for the town, but for Harmony, it was a vast, cavernous abyss where her daughter's laughter should have been. The remnants of Earl's Honest Rides were now fully extinguished, leaving behind only the stark reality of the empty lot under the pale, indifferent moon. Harmony stood on the edge of it, a solitary figure bathed in the fading moonlight, a testament to the fact that even the most ancient and insidious darkness could be banished by the unwavering light of courage and love. But the light that had banished the Master now served only to illuminate the depth of her own personal darkness. His reign of terror, built on a foundation of fear and deceit, had crumbled, but the deepest scar he had inflicted, the one etched onto Harmony's very soul, remained.

He had sought to break Harmony, to extinguish her spirit and claim her child, but in doing so, he had inadvertently forged the very weapon that would bring about his own annihilation. His final moments were not a spectacle of power, but a silent testament to his ultimate weakness: his inability to understand the enduring strength of the human spirit when pushed to its absolute limit. He had thought to win by corrupting, by destroying, by stealing. He had failed to grasp that the greatest power lay not in destruction, but in creation, in love, and in the fierce, unwavering determination to protect what is most precious.

The power that had surged through Harmony, the raw, unadulterated force that had unmade the Master, was a testament to her love, a love so profound it could shatter spectral entities. But that same love now acted as a siren's call, a beacon that drew her towards the lingering tendrils of the Master's influence, towards the whispered promises of a rescue that might never come. The energy that had been bound to his will was now dispersed, a wild, untamed force scattered across the land. And Harmony knew, with a chilling certainty, that some of that dispersed energy, some of that residual power, would inevitably be drawn to the potent psychic tether that bound her to her daughter. It was a terrifying prospect, a dark irony that twisted the knife of her victory.

She had flooded his domain with an unyielding light, and he had imploded. But the light, while it had extinguished him, had not illuminated the path to her child. The spectral scream of his demise had dissolved not into silence, but into a profound, resonant emptiness. It was the sound of absence, the void where a malevolent presence had once resided. There was no lingering specter, no residual haunt, no shadowy echo to torment the townsfolk further. The Master, the parasitic entity that had fed on Redwater Crossing's collective anxieties, had finally been starved. Harmony's act of defiance, fueled by the raw, primal instinct to protect her child, had severed his connection to the psychic energies he had so expertly manipulated. He had been a parasite, and she had, in essence, surgically removed him. But the extraction had not been clean. It had left behind a gaping wound, a chasm of loss that threatened to swallow her whole.

The immediate threat to Redwater Crossing was gone, a ghost of a nightmare banished by the dawn. But Harmony's personal quest, the one that clawed at her sanity and threatened to consume her, had just begun. The Master's death, though a profound relief to a town finally free, represented only the end of one battle, a brutal, earth-shattering clash that had cost her dearly. It was the beginning of a far more perilous war, a clandestine struggle fought in the shadows, a desperate fight for her child's very soul. The heavy burden of this new reality settled upon her, a crushing weight that made the victory feel like the heaviest defeat. She had saved the town, but she had lost her daughter, and the spectral remnants of the Master's empire, though gone, had left behind a chilling legacy of stolen innocence and a mother's unending pain.

CHAPTER 14

The Lingering Threat

The spectral scream had fractured, and in its shattering, the Master had been unmade. Redwater Crossing exhaled, a collective sigh of relief that rippled through the now-clean air. The oppressive weight that had pressed down on the town for generations had lifted, leaving behind a quietude that was not an absence of sound, but the pregnant pause before a new beginning. Harmony, however, felt no relief. The victory, so hard-won, was a bitter pill, a triumph that tasted like ash in her mouth. Her daughter, Lily, remained lost, stolen by the very entity she had just destroyed. And in the aftermath of the Master's implosion, a terrifying clarity had descended upon Harmony, a chilling understanding of where Lily was being held.

She now understood the 'Rooms Between.' The knowledge settled upon her not like a revelation, but like a creeping frost, numbing her with its grim truth. These were not mere prisons in a conventional sense, not cells of stone and iron. They were spaces of consumption, existential traps woven from despair and malice, places where entities like the Master ensnared their victims, feeding on their hope, their innocence, their very essence. The Master had been a gatekeeper, a curator of these desolate dimensions, drawing power from the fractured psyches of those he imprisoned. And Lily, his most prized possession, was now adrift in this horrifying interdimensional labyrinth.

Harmony's mind, still reeling from the raw energy of her defiance, began to piece together the fractured echoes of the Master's dying moments, the desperate whispers he had uttered not in pain, but in a twisted sort of revelation. He had spoken of "harvesting," of "dimensional anchors," of "psychic resonance." Terms that had once been an incomprehensible jumble of arcane pronouncements now clicked into place with a horrifying precision. The Rooms Between were not static locations, but fluid, shifting constructs, their architecture dictated by the desires and weaknesses of the entities that presided over them. They were parasitic spaces, designed to bleed their occupants dry, to transform them into sustenance for the beings that dwelled in the void.

She saw it now, not as a physical place, but as a manifestation of absolute despair. Imagine a dream, a beautiful, vibrant dream, slowly decaying, its colors leaching away, its joyful sounds warping into discordant wails, its comforting embrace turning into a suffocating grip. This was the essence of the Rooms Between. They were prisons for the soul, forged from the shattered fragments of stolen lives. The Master, in his infinite cruelty, had perfected the art of creating these spaces, not just for himself, but for his patrons, for the ancient, nameless things that lurked in the deeper darkness, things that craved the raw, potent energy of lost hope.

Harmony recalled the fleeting images that had flashed through her mind during the confrontation, glimpses of a place that defied earthly logic. It wasn't a room with four walls and a ceiling; it was a space where gravity seemed to be a suggestion, where light was a scarce commodity, and where the air itself tasted of decay and regret. She had seen Lily's form, a small, flickering ember of light against an overwhelming darkness, her face etched with a terror that went beyond the physical. Now, she understood that this was not a hallucination, but a window into the hell her daughter was enduring. The Master had used Lily's psychic tether to Harmony, her love and her desperation, as a beacon, a way to solidify his hold, and more importantly, to draw her into his game.

The knowledge was a heavy, suffocating shroud. It was a roadmap, yes, but one that led through a landscape of unimaginable horrors. She understood that the Rooms Between were not merely passive holding cells. They were active environments, designed to break down their inhabitants, to strip them of their will, their identity, their very humanity. The Master had been able to create these spaces by tapping into a primal energy, a force that existed beyond the veil of their reality. He had learned to bend the fabric of existence, to weave pockets of despair where he could feed and hoard his stolen treasures.

Harmony's own raw power, the force that had unmade the Master, was now her only weapon, but it was also a double-edged sword. It was the key that could potentially unlock the doors to these dimensional prisons, but it was also the very energy that had drawn the Master's attention in the first place. He had recognized her potential, her fierce maternal love, and had seen it as a potent source of energy, a rich vein to be exploited. Her defeat of him had not banished him from existence entirely, not in the way one would banish a ghost from a haunted house. Instead, it had dispersed his essence, scattering it like dust on the wind. And that dispersed energy, she feared, was still tethered to the Rooms Between, still a beacon, albeit a weaker one, drawing attention to the prison where Lily was held.

She closed her eyes, trying to focus the swirling chaos in her mind. The Master's final moments, the implosion of his spectral form, had been like a dam breaking. The immense power he had accumulated, the psychic energy he had hoarded from countless stolen lives, had been unleashed. But it hadn't simply dissipated into nothingness. It had reformed, coalesced, and in doing so, had illuminated the path. The dispersed energy, the residual fragments of his malevolence, were like breadcrumbs leading directly to the heart of his prison network.

Harmony understood now that the Rooms Between were not uniformly constructed. Each entity, each powerful being that existed beyond their realm, had its own dominion, its own twisted creation within this interdimensional space. The Master's rooms were designed for the slow, agonizing consumption of innocence, for the systematic erosion of hope. She pictured them as vast, desolate plains under a bruised, perpetual twilight, where the ground itself seemed to weep sorrow, and the air whispered doubts into the ears of its captive souls. There were no exits, no doors, only illusions of escape that led deeper into the despair. The very act of trying to leave, of yearning for freedom, only strengthened the walls, tethering the victim more firmly to the consuming void.

She remembered the feeling, the sickening lurch in her gut when the Master had first hinted at Lily's location, a casual cruelty that had been far more devastating than any physical threat. He had spoken of "hollow spaces," of "echoes of stolen joy," of "the hunger of the in-between." At the time, it had sounded like the ramblings of a madman. Now, it was a blueprint for hell. These were not just dimensions; they were psychological battlegrounds, where the very fabric of reality was warped to exploit a victim's deepest fears and vulnerabilities.

The Master had been a predator, a hunter of souls, and his network of Rooms Between was his hunting ground, his pantry. He would lure them in with promises, with manufactured desires, with the illusion of fulfillment, and once they were ensnared, he would begin the process of breaking them down. He fed on their despair, their regret, their fading memories of happiness. Lily, pure and innocent, would have been a particularly potent source of energy, her uncorrupted spirit a blinding light in the Master's desolate dominion. And in his dying moments, he had ensured that Harmony would not only know where her daughter was but would be drawn to it, compelled to follow.

The knowledge was a terrifying burden, but it was also a stark directive. She could no longer afford to be passive. The dissolution of Earl's Honest Rides, the cleansing of Redwater Crossing, was a victory that now felt hollow. The immediate threat was neutralized, but the true war had just begun. She had confronted an ancient evil and emerged victorious, but the cost was the knowledge of her daughter's suffering. The Rooms Between were no longer a theoretical concept, a dark rumor whispered in the shadows. They were Lily's reality, and Harmony was now armed with the terrible understanding of what that meant.

She knew that these spaces were not built for rescue. They were designed for eternal imprisonment, for the slow, agonizing decay of the soul. To enter them would be to step into a realm where the rules of existence were rewritten by despair. The Master had been the premier architect of such places, and his demise had not dismantled his creations, but had rather, in a cruel twist of fate, made them more accessible. The dispersed energy of his being, the lingering echoes of his power, were now like spectral guides, pointing the way into the labyrinth.

Harmony understood that the Master had not simply been a collector of souls; he had been a conduit, a bridge between their world and the darker realms. The Rooms Between were the spaces he had carved out, utilizing the raw, unformed energy of the void, shaping it with his malevolence. They were pockets of corrupted reality, where the fundamental laws of physics and consciousness were twisted to serve his purpose. He had fed on the fear and desperation of Redwater Crossing, but his ultimate goal was to extract the purest essence of life, the untainted spirit of a child, and to use it to empower himself and his unseen masters.

The clarity that came with the Master's demise was a terrifying thing. It stripped away the illusion, the comforting ignorance that had shielded her from the true depth of Lily's peril. She could now see the architecture of Lily's prison, not with her eyes, but with her soul. She understood that the Rooms Between were a reflection of the Master's own fractured psyche, a manifestation of his insatiable hunger and his profound emptiness. They were spaces of consumption, designed to drain the life force from their inhabitants, to leave them as hollow shells, mere echoes of their former selves.

Harmony braced herself, the weight of this newfound knowledge pressing down on her. It was not a comforting revelation, but a terrifying imperative. She had been given the map to her daughter's suffering, and now, she had to navigate it. The Master's power was gone, but the space he had created, the horrifying interdimensional prison, remained. And Lily was still trapped within its consuming maw. The victory was not an end, but a brutal, soul-shattering beginning. The spectral scream had silenced the Master, but it had amplified Harmony's own resolve. She would find Lily, even if it meant venturing into the very heart of the darkness the Master had so meticulously crafted. The Rooms Between were no longer a mystery; they were her next battlefield.

The implosion of the Master, a cataclysmic event that had shattered the oppressive silence of Redwater Crossing, was not the final curtain call for the insidious forces that preyed upon the liminal spaces of existence. Instead, it was a thunderous opening salvo, a seismic tremor that rippled far beyond the immediate vicinity of the now-liberated town. The raw, untamed energy unleashed by the Master's unmaking, a cosmic scream of defiance and destruction, had not merely dissipated into the ether. It had acted as a beacon, a violent signal flare in the darkness, announcing the existence of a vulnerability, a tear in the veil that allowed passage between worlds.

For generations, entities like the Master had operated with a calculated discretion, their operations often masked by the mundane horrors of human existence. They were parasites, feeding on the despair, the fear, and the stolen innocence of sentient beings, weaving their prisons, the 'Rooms Between,' from the psychic detritus of their victims. They thrived in the shadows, their existence a carefully guarded secret, lest humanity discover the true nature of the predators that stalked the edges of their perception. But the Master's end, so spectacular and so profoundly *other*, had changed everything. It had been a public, violent, and utterly inexplicable demise, a spectacle that had ripped through the established order of their predatory ecosystem.

Harmony understood this with a chilling certainty that settled deep in her bones. The 'Rooms Between' were not individual fortresses belonging solely to their architects. They were interconnected, a sprawling network of predatory domains, each overseen by a different entity, each with its own unique horrors tailored to its master's predilections. The Master had been one of many, a gatekeeper, perhaps, or simply a particularly ambitious collector. His destruction had not closed the doors of this interdimensional menagerie; it had, in a terrifyingly ironic twist, swung them wide open.

The residual energy of the Master's implosion had been like a thunderclap in a silent forest, alerting every lurking predator. Other entities, sensing the sudden shift in the cosmic balance, the inexplicable absence of a known presence, began to stir from their own dark slumber. They felt the void, the space where the Master's influence had once been a steady, albeit malevolent, hum. And in that void, they saw opportunity. The shockwave of his destruction was a declaration of war, not against humanity, but amongst themselves. It was a signal that the established territories were no longer secure, that the old rules of engagement might be broken.

Harmony could feel it, a prickling sensation at the back of her neck, a subconscious awareness that the silence that had fallen over Redwater Crossing was deceptive. The absence of the Master's oppressive aura was a vacuum, and into that vacuum, others, perhaps even more ancient and ravenous, appetites were beginning to turn their attention. They were drawn by the very force that had unmade him, a force they could not comprehend but recognized as potent. Her defiance, her maternal fury unleashed, had not only saved her town but had inadvertently painted a target on it, and by extension, on the path that led to Lily's prison.

These other entities were not necessarily allied with the Master. Their motivations were likely as diverse as their forms, but their methods of sustenance were disturbingly similar. They were cosmic opportunists, drawn to places where the veil between worlds was thin, where despair was fertile ground for their insidious creations.

Redwater Crossing, having already been the site of such a powerful manifestation of darkness, now bore a faint, but detectable, psychic signature. It was a place that had demonstrated its capacity to host, and to be preyed upon by, otherworldly forces.

She visualized it not as a single, unified threat, but as a multitude of hungry eyes turning towards their shared prey. Imagine a flock of vultures, sensing the death throes of a great beast. They may not be coordinated, they may even be rivals, but their collective focus was on the inevitable feast. The Master's death had been the announcement of that feast, and Harmony, in her desperate rescue of Lily, had stumbled onto the dining table.

The implications were staggering. If the Master's Rooms Between were designed for the slow erosion of innocence, what were the designs of others? Were there entities that fed on raw terror, on the primal scream of agony? Were there those that reveled in the meticulous dismantling of sanity, leaving their victims as gibbering husks? The Master had dealt in despair, but perhaps others dealt in madness, in sheer, unadulterated horror that went beyond the existential.

Harmony thought of the faint, almost subliminal whispers she had sometimes heard on the fringes of her awareness, before the Master had fully manifested. They had felt like the distant murmur of a vast, uncaring ocean, a constant undertow of unease. Now, she realized, those whispers might have been the stirrings of these other entities, sensing the ebb and flow of power, the rise and fall of their kind. The Master's fall had created a ripple, and that ripple was now attracting predators from deeper, darker currents.

The fear was a cold, sharp thing, but it was also strangely invigorating. It fueled the nascent resolve that had begun to bloom in the ashes of her grief. She understood that this was not a battle she could win by simply eradicating one threat. It was a war against a pervasive darkness, a war that would require constant vigilance, constant adaptation. The Master's demise had been a necessary step, a surgical removal of a cancerous growth, but the underlying disease, the susceptibility of her world to such entities, remained.

She had glimpsed the architecture of the Master's prison, a testament to his particular brand of torment. But now, she had to consider that Lily was not just in *a* Room Between, but in *the* Room Between, or rather, *one of* the Rooms Between. The Master had been a curator, and his collection was now vulnerable to the predatory gaze of his peers. If Lily was a prize, a source of potent energy, then other entities, sensing her value and the Master's absence, would undoubtedly seek to claim her for themselves. The interdimensional prison was not a fixed location, but a fluid, shifting landscape, and Lily could be moved, transferred, or worse, exposed to new horrors.

Harmony's mind raced, piecing together the fragments of knowledge gained during her desperate struggle. The dispersed energy of the Master, the echoes of his power, were still a faint tether, a spectral breadcrumb trail. But if other entities were now drawn to this resonance, they would also be able to follow that trail, perhaps even more effectively than she could. They understood the language of such energies, the subtle shifts and currents that spoke of opportunity and sustenance.

She imagined them as beings of pure instinct, driven by an insatiable hunger. They didn't operate with human notions of territory or ownership, but rather with a predatory immediacy. If something of value was left unguarded, if a weakness was revealed, they would descend. The Master's demise had been a loud, unmistakable signal of such a weakness. The psychic resonance of Lily's captivity, coupled with the violent unraveling of her jailer, was an irresistible lure.

This awakening of other entities was not a distant, abstract threat. It was immediate, a direct consequence of her actions. The victory over the Master, so hard-won, had inadvertently escalated the danger. It was the classic 'kill the dragon, only to find out the dragon was guarding an even greater evil' scenario, but on a cosmic scale. She had confronted a single monstrous entity, but in doing so, she had alerted the entire horde.

Harmony's gaze swept over the quiet streets of Redwater Crossing. The houses seemed to hold their breath, the trees stood sentinel, their leaves rustling with an unspoken unease. The people were oblivious, reveling in a peace they could not comprehend the fragility of. They saw the Master's end as a definitive resolution, a vanquishing. They did not see the widening ripples, the hungry shadows that were now gathering on the horizon, drawn by the very act of their liberation.

She knew, with a certainty that chilled her to the core, that she could not allow herself to be complacent. The Master was gone, but his legacy was a more dangerous, more widespread threat. Lily was still lost, and now, the very fabric of her captivity was potentially shifting, becoming a crossroads for multiple predatory powers. The 'Rooms Between' were not just the Master's domain; they were a vast, interconnected ecosystem of suffering, and the Master's fall had merely opened the door for other inhabitants to explore new hunting grounds.

The lingering threat was no longer a singular entity. It was a multiplicity, a constellation of darkness now aware of its prey and its new, unexpected vulnerability. Harmony felt the weight of this realization settle upon her shoulders, a crushing burden. She had faced one demon and emerged, somehow, victorious. But now, she had to face the possibility of an entire legion, each with its own unique horrors, its own insatiable hunger, and all potentially drawn to the faint, spectral echo of her daughter's stolen light. The fight for Lily had just become immeasurably more perilous.

The silence that had descended upon Redwater Crossing was a fragile thing, a thin veneer stretched taut over a chasm of unspoken horrors. The Master was gone, a phantom of malice unmade, but Harmony knew, with a visceral certainty that chilled her to the bone, that this was not an end, but a terrifying beginning. The echoes of her desperate struggle, the raw, explosive energy that had ripped through the veil between worlds, had not simply faded. They had announced her presence, her capability, to a far vaster, far more ancient audience. The Master had been but one thread in a tapestry of predation, and his unraveling had only revealed the intricate, monstrous pattern of the whole. The thought of other entities, drawn by the scent of vulnerability, by the psychic resonance of her daughter's captivity and the sudden, violent disruption of its hold, was a cold, sharp jab to her already frayed nerves. Yet, amidst the encroaching dread, a different kind of power began to coalesce within her.

It was the power of a mother's love, a primal force that had already defied the impossible. Grief was a heavy cloak, woven from the strands of loss and the gnawing fear for Lily's unseen fate. But it was not a shroud that would smother her. Instead, it became the fuel for an unyielding resolve. The chilling realization that Lily was not merely imprisoned by a single entity, but potentially caught in a larger, more complex web of interdimensional predators, should have shattered her. It should have sent her retreating into despair, overwhelmed by the sheer scale of the darkness. But Harmony was no longer the woman who had been blindsided by the Master's insidious influence. She had faced the abyss and had not flinched. She had confronted a creature of nightmares and had, against all odds, prevailed.

This newfound understanding of the interconnectedness of these malevolent realms did not paralyze her; it galvanized her. The Master's Rooms Between were not isolated dungeons. They were nodes in a vast, predatory network, and his destruction had merely illuminated the pathways for others. Imagine a vast, unseen city, humming with unseen activity, where each building represented a prison, a trap, a feeding ground. The Master's building had collapsed, but the city remained, its other inhabitants now keenly aware of the disruption, and the potential for new acquisitions. Harmony had seen the inner workings of one such building, its cruel architecture designed to break the spirit, to drain the essence. Now, she had to prepare for the possibility that Lily might be moved, her torment amplified, her very existence subjected to the unique cruelties of entities whose motives and methods were as yet unknown, but undoubtedly horrific.

The fear, the bone-deep terror of what Lily might be enduring, was a constant thrum beneath her skin. But layered over it was a hardening, a sharpening of her purpose. She accepted the mantle that had been thrust upon her, not as a victim of fate, but as a warrior of necessity. The truth of these entities, their existence no longer a whispered rumor or a fragmented nightmare, but a terrifyingly concrete reality, was both a weapon and a burden. It meant she could no longer afford to be naive, to be caught off guard. Her eyes were now open, truly open, to the shadows that lay just beyond the edge of human perception.

Her resolve was forged in the crucible of her recent battle. She had felt the Master's power, had seen its manifestation, and had found a way to strike at its heart. This experience, however harrowing, had demystified the ethereal. These were not omnipotent gods or abstract forces. They were beings, however alien, with weaknesses, with vulnerabilities. The Master had been undone by a raw, untamed love, a maternal fury that bypassed his intricate defenses. Harmony clung to that knowledge, to the memory of that surge of power, as a life raft in a sea of uncertainty.

She pictured Lily not as a lost child, but as a captive, a valuable commodity in an interdimensional black market. The Master had been a collector, and his collection was now ripe for the taking by his peers. This was not simply about rescuing Lily from one prison; it was about intercepting her, about fighting for her across a landscape that defied the familiar laws of physics and sanity. It was about understanding that the trail she had followed to the Master's lair was not a dead end, but a potentially dangerous thoroughfare, now thronged with new, unseen travelers.

The instinct to protect, amplified by the agony of Lily's absence, became her guiding star. She would not wait for these new threats to manifest fully, to claim her daughter. She would become the hunter, not the hunted. The path ahead was fraught with unimaginable peril, a labyrinth of unknown horrors. But Harmony's will, tempered by loss and sharpened by knowledge, was now an unbreakable force. She was a mother, and her daughter was her world. The entities that preyed on the liminal spaces had made a grave mistake. They had awakened a mother's fury, and that fury, in its purest, most unadulterated form, was a power they could not possibly comprehend.

Her gaze, once filled with confusion and dawning horror, now held a steely determination. The silence of Redwater Crossing was no longer a lull between storms, but a strategic pause. Harmony knew that the forces that had orchestrated the Master's existence, and by extension, Lily's abduction, would not simply vanish. Their influence was a persistent stain, a psychic residue that lingered long after the source was gone. The Master's unmaking had been a spectacular event, a blinding flash that had drawn attention, but it had also revealed a crack in the foundation of their hidden world. This crack, she now understood, was not a weakness to be exploited by Harmony alone. It was an invitation to others, a beacon for entities that operated on principles far more ancient and terrifying than human comprehension.

The weight of this realization pressed down on her, a physical burden that settled into her shoulders and her chest. It would have been easy, so agonizingly easy, to succumb to the sheer terror of it all. To imagine Lily in the clutches of beings whose very essence was defined by suffering, by the consumption of light and life. But Harmony found that the sheer magnitude of the threat, the chilling certainty that her daughter's predicament was now even more precarious, paradoxically, stripped away her fear. It was replaced by a cold, hard clarity, a singular focus that burned brighter than any apprehension.

She saw herself not as a victim fighting against insurmountable odds, but as a force of nature, an unstoppable tide against a monstrous sea. The Master had been a significant obstacle, a formidable guardian of the pathway to Lily. His destruction had been a monumental victory, a testament to Harmony's resilience and her unwavering love. But it had also been a turning point, a shift in the cosmic balance that had not gone unnoticed. She imagined a vast, interdimensional game board, where the Master had been a powerful piece, strategically placed. His removal had disrupted the game, and now, other players, unseen and unknown, were taking notice. They saw the open space, the unclaimed territory, and the tantalizing prize that lay within it: her daughter.

This was not a battle she could win with brute force, not in the conventional sense. The entities that inhabited the spaces between were not bound by the same rules of reality. Their power was derived from more abstract sources – fear, despair, the erosion of sanity. To combat them, Harmony understood required a different kind of strength. It required an unyielding core of resilience, an ability to face unimaginable horrors without succumbing to them. It required a will as strong and as sharp as any blade, a will that refused to break, no matter how profound the despair, no matter how terrifying the revelation.

Her resolve was not a sudden surge of adrenaline; it was a slow, steady burn, a deep-seated conviction that had taken root in the fertile ground of her maternal instinct. She had seen the architecture of the Master's domain, the carefully constructed environments designed to break a soul piece by piece. She had navigated its horrors, had resisted its temptations, and had emerged, not unscathed, but unbroken. This experience had been a brutal education, a harsh but invaluable lesson in the nature of these otherworldly threats. She now knew what they were capable of, and, more importantly, she knew that they could be fought.

The knowledge that other entities were now aware of Lily, of her potential, of the vulnerability created by the Master's absence was a heavy burden. It meant that Lily was no longer simply a prisoner of one entity, but a potential prize for many. Harmony envisioned these other beings as apex predators, drawn to the scent of weakness and the promise of sustenance. They did not operate on logic or reason, but on instinct and an insatiable hunger. Her daughter, a source of immense psychic energy, was a beacon in their dark world, and the Master's demise had simply made that beacon more accessible.

Yet, this understanding did not breed despair. Instead, it forged a new kind of determination within Harmony. She accepted the role of hunter, not out of a desire for vengeance, but out of an absolute necessity to protect. Her purpose was no longer solely to rescue Lily from a specific prison, but to confront the very nature of the darkness that held her captive, and now, threatened to ensnare her further. She was armed with the brutal truth of their existence, with the memory of her own courage, and with the unwavering certainty of her love for Lily.

The lingering threat was no longer a singular monster lurking in the shadows. It was a vast, interconnected network of predatory forces, and Harmony had inadvertently shone a spotlight on their operations. But she would not be a victim of their attention. She would turn it to her advantage. She would use the very awareness she had sparked as a weapon, drawing them out, identifying them, and ultimately, confronting them. Her will, unbreakable and unyielding, was the only weapon she truly needed. Lily was waiting, and Harmony would move heaven and earth, and the very fabric of reality, to bring her home. The fight for her daughter had just entered a new, terrifying, and ultimately, resolutely determined phase.

Sheriff Brody stood at the edge of Harmony's porch, the late afternoon sun casting long, distorted shadows across the familiar, yet now profoundly altered, landscape of Redwater Crossing. His uniform, usually a symbol of order and authority, felt strangely inadequate, a flimsy defense against the unseen currents that had reshaped this small town and the lives within it. He watched Harmony, her gaze fixed on some distant, internal horizon, her posture radiating a new, fierce resolve that both awed and troubled him. The Master was gone, a chilling testament to Harmony's strength, but the silence left in his wake was not one of peace. It was the charged quiet before a storm, a silence pregnant with the whispers of new dangers.

Brody knew his place in this unfolding drama. He had witnessed horrors that defied logic, that shredded the fabric of his understanding of the world. He had seen the raw, elemental power unleashed by Harmony, the maternal fury that had burned through the unnatural constructs of the Master's domain. He understood, with a gut-wrenching certainty, that the battle Harmony had waged, the victory she had achieved, was not the end of her struggle. If anything, it was the opening salvo. The 'Rooms Between,' as Harmony had come to call them, were not just the Master's private hell; they were portals, conduits, and his unmaking had undoubtedly sent ripples through those unseen networks.

He could not follow her. The sheer psychic and ontological demands of those spaces were beyond him, a realm where the laws of physics bent and broke, where sanity was a currency easily spent and rarely recouped. He had seen the lingering traces, the residual energy that had clung to Harmony even after her return, a faint aura of the otherworld that marked her as irrevocably changed. He was a man of the tangible, of the here and now, of bullet casings and crime scene tape. His strength lay in the grounded realities of his profession, not in the spectral battlegrounds Harmony was now destined to navigate.

But that did not mean he was powerless. It meant his role had to adapt, to pivot. He was no longer just the sheriff of a small town; he was now, by virtue of circumstance and a profound, shared trauma, an ally to a woman fighting a war on planes he could barely comprehend. His commitment to Harmony, already solidified by the desperate events that had transpired, now took on a new, more focused dimension. He would be her anchor, her point of contact with the world she was fighting to protect, and, more importantly, the world that was fighting for her.

"Harmony," he said, his voice a low rumble, careful not to shatter the fragile calm she seemed to be cultivating. He approached slowly, his hands held open, a gesture of peace and solidarity. "You know I can't go with you, not into... that." He gestured vaguely towards the air, towards the unseen spaces that separated their reality from the Master's. "But that doesn't mean I'm not with you. Not even for a second."

Harmony turned, her eyes, a deep, unsettling shade of blue that seemed to hold the echoes of unseen stars, met his. There was a weariness there, profound and bone-deep, but also a fire that had not been there before. It was a terrifying, beautiful thing to witness. "I know, Sheriff," she replied, her voice raspy but firm. "And I appreciate it more than you can ever know."

He nodded, a sense of purpose settling over him. "My job, now, is to make sure you have a world to come back to. And to make sure no one else has to go through what Redwater Crossing, and now

Redwater Crossing, has endured." He paused, the weight of his words settling. "I'll be watching. Keeping my eyes open for anything... unusual. Any whispers, any odd occurrences in neighboring towns. Anything that smacks of the kind of thing the Master was, or worse."

The thought of "worse" sent a shiver down his spine, a primal fear that he had to actively suppress. He had seen enough to know that the Master, in all his terrifying complexity, was likely just one player in a much larger, much darker game. Harmony's victory had been a beacon, and not necessarily a positive one for her. It had announced a vulnerability, an opening, to beings whose motivations and methods were beyond human reckoning.

"I'll be the eyes and ears on the ground," Brody continued, his voice regaining its official tone, a subtle anchoring in the familiar. "If I see anything that even hints at a new presence, a new pattern emerging... I'll document it. I'll try to find parallels, try to anticipate. I'll be looking for the signs, Harmony. The subtle shifts, the whispers that might precede a larger manifestation." He knew the limitations of his search. He couldn't scan for psychic energy or interdimensional incursions. But he could look for the ripple effects, the societal tremors that might precede such events. He could observe the anxieties of a community, the unexplained disappearances, the unsettling changes in behavior that often preceded larger, more terrifying events in the folklore of the uncanny. He would become a student of the shadows, an observer of the precipice.

"I'll be talking to other sheriffs, subtly, of course," he mused, already strategizing. "Asking about unusual cases, strange phenomena. Trying to build a network, a silent alarm system, if you will. Because what happened here... it can't be allowed to spread. Oaklawn and King George was one thing, a tragedy. Redwater Crossing was something else, a descent into madness. We have to prevent a fourth." His gaze swept over the quiet street, the few residents who were tentatively emerging from their homes, their faces etched with a mixture of relief and lingering fear. They were survivors, but they were also marked.

"I'll also be your link," he stated, his gaze returning to Harmony, unwavering. "When you're... in there, fighting, you'll need to know what's happening out here. If there are any developments, any changes in the local situation, anything that might be relevant to your fight, I'll be the one to get it to you. How we'll do that, I don't know yet. But we'll figure it out. You'll have your methods, your... connections, I imagine. And I'll have mine. We'll bridge the gap."

He understood the immense pressure Harmony was under. The knowledge that Lily was not merely lost, but potentially a prize being contended for by multiple, unknown entities, was a terrifying prospect. He had seen the toll the Master had taken on Harmony, the physical and emotional exhaustion that had accompanied her ordeal. Now, that ordeal was likely to intensify, to expand. She would need more than just her own courage. She would need the support of the world she was fighting for.

"And if... if anyone else starts sniffing around, looking for whatever the Master had, or whatever he was protecting," Brody added, his jaw tightening, "they'll have to go through me first. I can't fight them in the 'Rooms Between,' but I can make it damned difficult for them to operate in this world, in this reality. I can contain the fallout. I can be the bulwark." He wasn't deluding himself. He knew he was outmatched on a fundamental level. But he was stubborn, and he was fiercely protective of the people he was sworn to serve, and Harmony was now, unequivocally, one of those people.

He considered the implications of Harmony's fight. It wasn't just about Lily anymore. It was about understanding and combating a whole new stratum of threat, one that operated outside the established frameworks of human law and order. He felt a profound sense of inadequacy, a stark realization of the limitations of his own skills and knowledge in the face of such an existential challenge. Yet, within that inadequacy, a resolve hardened within him. He had a duty, a responsibility that extended beyond the conventional boundaries of his badge.

"I'll be researching," he said, his voice gaining a determined edge. "Anything and everything related to the kind of phenomena that occurred here. Local legends and historical accounts of unexplained events. I'll be looking for patterns, for common threads that might point to the nature of these... entities. If the Master was one, what were the others like? What were their appetites? Their weaknesses? The more information we have, the better your chances." He knew it was a long shot, digging through dusty archives and folklore, but he was willing to try anything. Desperation bred unconventional approaches.

"And I'll be coordinating with any authorities who might be able to help on a larger scale, without revealing... too much, of course," he continued, navigating the delicate balance of secrecy and necessary communication. "There are agencies that deal with the... unusual. If I can find the right people, the right channels, without endangering you or compromising what you're doing, I'll try. It's a long shot, I know, but we can't afford to leave any stone unturned." The idea of conventional authorities being able to grasp the reality of the situation was almost laughable, but the possibility of finding individuals within those structures who were already aware, already prepared, was a flicker of hope.

He stepped closer, his gaze meeting Harmony's directly. "You go and fight your fight, Harmony. You do what you have to do to bring Lily back. And I'll stand here, in this world, and hold the line. I'll be your watchtower. I'll be your shield, as best as I can. I'll make sure that while you're battling in the shadows, the light here doesn't get extinguished. And I'll be waiting, ready to help you rebuild, ready to help you heal, when you're done."

He placed a hand on her shoulder, a gesture of firm support. "You're not alone in this. Even when you're in places no one else can reach, you're not alone. I'll be here. Always." The words felt inadequate, the promise almost impossibly vast, but they were sincere. He would do everything in his power to ensure Harmony had the support she needed, the space to fight, and a stable world to return to. His continued support was a silent vow, a promise etched in the stark reality of their shared experience, a commitment to holding the line against the encroaching darkness. He would be the sentinel, the steadfast guardian of the world Harmony fought to preserve.

The quiet aftermath of the Master's defeat was a deceptive peace. Harmony Jakes, standing on the porch of her now-scarred home, felt the hum of the world beneath her feet, a low thrumming that was no longer just the mundane heartbeat of Redwater Crossing. It was a resonance, a subtle vibration that spoke of unseen currents, of a vast, terrifying ocean of existence where monsters swam, and where her daughter, Lily, had been swept away. The victory over the Master, a man who had woven nightmares into reality, had been a brutal, primal act of maternal defense. But it had also been a revelation. It had peeled back the veneer of normalcy, exposing the raw, visceral truth: that the world was far more dangerous, and far more ancient, than anyone in Redwater Crossing had ever imagined. And she, Harmony, was no longer merely a victim caught in its gears. She was something else entirely.

The transformation had been involuntary, brutal, and absolute. The fear that had once paralyzed her had been transmuted, through the crucible of unimaginable loss and the desperate fight for Lily, into a cold, hard resolve. It wasn't the fear of what *could* happen that drove her now, but the potent, all-consuming certainty of what *must* be done. Her personal tragedy had become her genesis. She had been a mother, a survivor, and now, she was a hunter. The Master's defeat had not been an ending, but a violent, necessary beginning, a shedding of her old skin to reveal the predator beneath.

The very act of confronting the Master, of delving into the twisted architecture of his 'Rooms Between,' had been a baptism by fire. She had navigated labyrinths of corrupted memory, faced down apparitions born of his twisted desires and his victims' deepest fears, and in doing so, she had discovered a resilience she never knew she possessed. The psychic backlash, the sheer ontological weight of those spaces, had nearly crushed her, had threatened to unravel her very being. Yet, she had held on. Love, a fierce, unwavering love for Lily, had been her compass, her anchor, and her most potent weapon. It was a force that transcended fear, that burned brighter than any darkness.

Sheriff Brody's words, spoken with a quiet sincerity that belied the immense weight of his promise, had been a balm. He would be her bulwark in the tangible world, her eyes and ears on the ground, a grounding presence in the maelstrom that was to come. But she knew, with a certainty that chilled her to the bone, that his world, the world of laws and evidence and tangible threats, was no longer enough. The Master, in his malevolence, had been but a single, albeit powerful, manifestation of something far larger, far more ancient, and infinitely more dangerous. His defeat had not eradicated the threat; it had merely alerted the other predators to the scent of vulnerability, to the potential for a prize.

Harmony looked at her hands. They were no longer the hands of a woman who worried about baking cookies or tending a garden. They were the hands that had gripped, that had fought, that had clawed their way through the impossible. They had felt the cold, dead flesh of the Master's constructs, the searing heat of his corrupted energy. They were capable now. Not just of defending, but of pursuing.

The knowledge she had absorbed, piecemeal and terrifying, during her ordeal, was a heavy burden, but also her greatest asset. She understood, in a way that Brody could only glimpse, the intricate tapestry of unseen forces that influenced and preyed upon the human world. The Master had been a weaver of illusions, a puppeteer of fear, but he had also been a gatekeeper. And by unmaking him, she had, inadvertently, opened the gates wider.

She had seen the subtle signs that led to the Master's rise, the quiet desperation of those who sought solace in his twisted promises, the gradual erosion of their will. She had seen how fear and greed could twist people into instruments of darkness, how easily they could be led astray by whispers in the dark. These were the same vulnerabilities that other entities, perhaps even more ancient and cunning than the Master, would exploit. And she, Harmony, now recognized the subtle shifts, the nascent tremors that preceded their arrival.

The battle for Lily was far from over. It had merely shifted from a desperate rescue within the confines of one man's madness to a relentless pursuit across planes of existence she was only beginning to comprehend. She was no longer just a mother seeking her child. She was a hunter, driven by a love that had been tempered into a blade, armed with the knowledge of the enemy's methods, and propelled by an unyielding spirit.

The 'Rooms Between' were not just a place; they were a state of being, a fractured dimension where the rules of reality were fluid and subjective. The Master had built his domain within them, but he had also drawn power from their inherent instability. Now, Harmony knew, other forces would seek to exploit that same instability, to draw sustenance from the psychic residue of human suffering, to manipulate the very fabric of perception.

She felt a new kind of instinct awakening within her, a heightened awareness that stretched beyond the five senses. It was a primal recognition of danger, a subtle perception of disturbances in the unseen. She could feel the echoes of the Master's defeat, a ripple effect that had not only unsettled his followers but had also broadcast her own emergence, her own capability, to a much wider, much more dangerous audience. She had announced herself, and now, she had to be prepared for the inevitable attention.

Her resolve was a quiet, unwavering force. It was not the boisterous roar of a warrior charging into battle, but the silent, inexorable advance of a glacier. She would move with purpose, with precision, and with a relentless determination. Every step she took, every decision she made, would be guided by the singular objective of bringing Lily back, and in doing so, of safeguarding humanity from the predatory forces that lurked just beyond the veil of their understanding.

The world had changed, and so had she. The woman who had wept in despair just days ago was gone, replaced by a figure of steely determination, a mother who had looked into the abyss and had not flinched. She would venture into the unknown, into the 'Rooms Between' and wherever else these entities might lurk, not as a victim, but as a hunter. And she would not rest until Lily was safe, and until the shadows that threatened to consume their world were pushed back, one by one, by the unyielding light of her love and her newfound strength. The genesis of the hunter was complete. The hunt had begun.

CHAPTER 15

The Hunt Begins

The silence in Harmony's home was no longer the peaceful quiet of respite, but the charged stillness of a predator coiled. Each tick of the grandfather clock in the hall, a relic from a more settled time, felt like a countdown. The Master's defeat had been a shattering victory, a brutal unburdening, but it had also ripped open a chasm. The 'Rooms Between,' the interstitial spaces where the Master had woven his nightmares, were not merely his domain; they were the veins of a hidden reality, pulsating with a dark life of their own. And Lily, her Lily, had been pulled into those currents.

Harmony moved with a newfound economy of motion, each action deliberate, imbued with the weight of her purpose. Her focus was a laser, honed by the sharp edge of maternal desperation. The world outside, the familiar streets of Redwater Crossing, the comforting routine of Sheriff Brody's patrols, felt increasingly distant, like a fading dream. The real work, the soul-grinding, reality-bending work, lay ahead, within the fractured landscapes of the 'Rooms Between.'

She had begun by systematically dismantling the remnants of the Master's influence in her own home. Not physically, but psychically. It was like sweeping out dust after a hurricane, but the dust was made of lingering fear, of corrupted thought-forms. She burned every scrap of paper that had once held his insidious scribblings, not with matches, but with the focused intensity of her will, channeling the residual energy that still clung to them. The air in the house, once thick with the Master's oppressive presence, now felt thin, almost brittle, as if holding its breath.

The real preparation, however, was an internal one. The Master's defeat had been a violent upheaval of her own psyche, a forced evolution. She had glimpsed the raw mechanics of the 'Rooms Between,' the way they twisted and warped perception, feeding on emotion. She had learned, through agonizing trial and error, that brute force was insufficient. It was understanding, a deep, intuitive comprehension of the rules, or rather the *lack* of rules, that would be her true armor.

She spent hours in the hushed sanctuary of her study, a room that had once been a haven of domesticity, now transformed into an arsenal of knowledge. Books, once stacked haphazardly, were now arranged with a strategic purpose. Not just fiction, though she had devoured tales of the uncanny since childhood, but obscure tomes on folklore, forgotten histories, and even esoteric philosophical texts. She wasn't looking for practical guides; there were none. She was searching for patterns, for recurring themes, for the whispered warnings of those who had brushed against the edges of these realities before.

She reread passages about liminal spaces, about the thin places where the veil between worlds grew permeable. She cross-referenced tales of fae realms, of the underworld, of ghost stories that hinted at more than mere spectral echoes. The Master had been a crude architect, a builder of traps, but his constructs were built upon the very foundations of these 'Rooms Between.' Understanding his methods was like deciphering a single dialect of a vast, ancient language.

One particular book, bound in cracked leather and smelling faintly of dust and decay, became her constant companion. It was a collection of fragmented accounts, purportedly gathered by a reclusive scholar who had vanished without a trace decades ago. The scholar's notes were rambling, often bordering on madness, but they contained chillingly accurate descriptions of spatial anomalies, of sensory distortions, and of entities that thrived in the spaces *between* conscious thought. He spoke of 'echoes' – not just sounds, but impressions, emotions, entire realities that could be trapped and replayed within these interstitial zones. He even posited the existence of a 'psychic sediment,' a residue of intense experiences that could form the very substance of these 'Rooms.'

Harmony traced the brittle pages with a fingertip, her brow furrowed in concentration. The scholar's descriptions of 'anchors' resonated deeply. He theorized that these liminal spaces, while inherently chaotic, could be stabilized, even navigated, by individuals who possessed strong emotional anchors, points of intense, unyielding connection to the tangible world. For the Master, his anchors had been his victims, their fear and despair his perverse scaffolding. For Harmony, there was only one anchor strong enough to hold her steady: Lily.

Her daughter. The thought was a constant hum beneath the surface of her consciousness, a vibrant, burning point of light in the encroaching darkness. She visualized Lily's face, the curve of her smile, the earnestness in her eyes. She remembered the feel of Lily's hand in hers; the warmth of her small body pressed against her side during a thunderstorm. These were not just memories; they were talismans, imbued with the power of her love, now sharpened into tools.

She practiced a form of mental discipline, a rigorous honing of her inner landscape. The fear was still there, a cold knot in her stomach, but it no longer dictated her actions. It was a signal, a warning, nothing more. She learned to observe it, to acknowledge its presence without succumbing to its paralyzing grip. She focused on her breath, on the simple, undeniable reality of air filling her lungs, of her heart beating a steady rhythm against her ribs. These were the small, concrete victories that built the foundation for larger ones.

Sheriff Brody had been a solid, reassuring presence, but his world, the world of tangible evidence and procedural justice, could offer little solace here. He had promised to keep an eye on Redwater Crossing, to be her earthly anchor, but he could not follow her into the 'Rooms Between.' Their last conversation had been brief, tinged with a quiet understanding of the gulf that now separated their realities.

"Be careful, Harmony," he had said, his gaze steady but his voice laced with a concern that transcended his official capacity. "You're walking into places... places we don't have maps for."

Harmony had met his gaze, her own reflecting a resolve that even he, a man who had seen his share of the strange and unsettling, could recognize. "I'll find her, Sheriff. I have to."

She had accepted his offer of any available resources. He had provided her with a sturdy, all-terrain vehicle, packed with basic survival gear – water purification tablets, high-energy rations, a powerful flashlight, a first-aid kit that felt woefully inadequate for the dangers she anticipated. He had also, with a hesitant air, procured a heavy-duty rope, the kind used for mountain climbing, and a sturdy hunting knife. These were tools for the physical world, meager defenses against the metaphysical.

But Harmony knew the most important tools were not in the trunk of the vehicle. They were within her. She had begun a regimen of physical conditioning, pushing her body to its limits. The Master's defeat had left her physically and emotionally drained, but her reserves of strength, ignited by the primal need to protect her child, were far from depleted. She ran until her lungs burned, performed calisthenics until her muscles screamed, pushed herself through a gauntlet of exertion that left her bone-weary but clear-headed. She needed her body to be as resilient as her spirit.

She also began to explore the subtler abilities that had begun to manifest since her encounter with the Master. It was a terrifying, exhilarating process. She found she could sense disturbances, subtle shifts in the air that weren't just weather-related. It was like a faint static electricity on her skin, a prickling awareness that something was *wrong*, or about to be. She practiced focusing on this awareness, trying to distinguish between ambient psychic noise and genuine danger.

One evening, while sitting on her porch, watching the fireflies begin their nightly dance, she concentrated on a patch of woods at the edge of her property. She closed her eyes, picturing the trees, the undergrowth, the fallen leaves. She reached out with her mind, not to see, but to *feel*. At first, there was nothing but the familiar hum of the natural world. Then, a faint, almost imperceptible tremor. It was like a ripple in a still pond, a disturbance that didn't belong. It wasn't a creature, not in the conventional sense, but a fleeting impression, a residue of unease. She held onto the feeling, trying to trace its source, but it dissipated as quickly as it had appeared, leaving behind only a faint, lingering chill.

It was enough. It was a confirmation. The 'Rooms Between' were not some distant, inaccessible dimension. They bled into their reality, their influence seeping through the cracks in the mundane. And if they could bleed in, she could bleed out.

She meticulously packed her bag, each item chosen with agonizing deliberation. The scholar's book, nestled carefully amongst spare clothing. A small, smooth stone she had picked up on the beach during a rare family vacation years ago, Lily had called it her "lucky stone." Harmony clutched it now, feeling its comforting weight. She included a locket containing a miniature photograph of Lily, its metal cool against her skin. These were her talismans, her anchors in the storm.

She also packed a small, worn leather-bound journal, similar to the scholar's but blank. She intended to document her journey, to record what she found, what she learned. If she didn't return, perhaps someone else would find it, someone who might be better equipped, or at least forewarned. The thought was a stark reminder of the stakes, but it didn't waver her resolve.

The knowledge she had gained, however incomplete, was her most potent weapon. She understood that the 'Rooms Between' were not static environments. They were fluid, responsive, and deeply personal. The Master had exploited the universal human fears, but other entities might have more specialized tastes, more insidious methods of manipulation. Some might prey on greed, others on loneliness, still others on forgotten guilt. She had to be prepared for anything and for everything.

She found herself replaying the moments after Lily's abduction, searching for any subtle signs she might have missed, any flicker of strangeness that had been dismissed as imagination or stress. The unsettling stillness in the air before Lily vanished, the way the shadows had seemed to deepen unnaturally, the almost imperceptible shift in the light. They were the early warning signs, the subtle tremors that preceded an earthquake. She vowed to be more vigilant, to trust her instincts above all else.

Her preparation was not just about gathering supplies and knowledge; it was about forging an unshakeable mental and emotional resilience. She imagined the 'Rooms Between' as a vast, disorienting labyrinth, where logic dissolved and perception became a weapon against her. She visualized herself moving through it with a clear mind, her resolve a beacon that cut through the illusions and the despair. She practiced disassociating herself from the fear, treating it as an external force to be observed, not an internal state to be succumbed to.

She revisited the concept of 'thresholds.' The Master had created artificial thresholds, elaborate gates and doorways. But the 'Rooms Between' themselves were thresholds, places that existed in the gaps, in the moments of transition. She understood that entering them would require a conscious act of crossing, a deliberate step into the unknown. She visualized that step, that commitment, over and over again, until it felt less like a terrifying plunge and more like a necessary, if daunting, progression.

The final act of preparation was a silent communion with her own strength. She stood in the center of her living room, the space still echoing with the psychic residue of the Master's defeat and reached deep within herself. She acknowledged the fear, the grief, the overwhelming burden of her task. But she also acknowledged the love, the fierce, unwavering love for Lily, and the potent, transformative power it had unleashed within her. This was not a mother driven by blind panic, but by a deep, unyielding purpose. She was a hunter now, and the hunt had begun. The 'Rooms Between' awaited, and she was ready.

The Master, for all his depravity and twisted ingenuity, had been a singular focus, a tangible evil that Harmony had been able to confront and, ultimately, overcome. His defeat had been akin to eradicating a particularly virulent strain of a disease. But the sickness, she now understood with a chilling certainty, was far more pervasive. The 'Rooms Between' were not a dominion built by one man's malevolence; they were a natural, albeit horrifying, habitat, teeming with life that had evolved over eons, sustained by the very fabric of human frailty. The Master had been a predator, yes, but he had been a known quantity, his motives, however abhorrent, discernible. The beings that now awaited her were something else entirely.

She envisioned them not as individuals, but as a complex, interwoven ecosystem of dread. The Master had been a wolf, perhaps a particularly savage one, but a wolf nonetheless, with familiar hunting patterns. What lay ahead were the unseen predators that haunted the deeper woods, the things that moved in the peripheral vision, the whispers that coiled in the dark. These entities were likely older, their existence predating human comprehension, their forms and methods shaped by an alien logic, or perhaps, by the absence of logic altogether. They were not necessarily driven by the same base desires for control or suffering that had motivated the Master. Their hunger might be more abstract, their torment more existential. Some might feed on emotions, not just fear, but also despair, regret, or even misplaced hope. Others might subsist on the very essence of reality, subtly twisting and warping it for their own inscrutable purposes.

Harmony recognized that her approach had to evolve. The tools and strategies that had served her against the Master would need to be augmented and refined. Her understanding of the 'Rooms Between' as a place responsive to emotional anchors was still valid, but she suspected that the nature of those anchors might need to be more diverse. The Master had fed on the pain of his victims, using their fractured psyches as building blocks. What if other entities were drawn to different emanations of the human spirit? Could greed be a lure? Could ambition, twisted and corrupted, become a beacon for something predatory? The possibilities were a dizzying, terrifying landscape, and she knew that her ability to adapt, to read the subtle cues of these new threats, would be paramount.

She found herself poring over the fragmented writings of the reclusive scholar with a renewed intensity. His ramblings about 'psychic sediment' and 'echoes' now felt less like abstract theories and more like descriptions of the raw materials these ancient beings manipulated. He spoke of entities that could "wear the echoes of joy like a shroud," or "weave despair into tapestries of false memory." This suggested a level of cunning far beyond the Master's crude methods. The Master had forced his victims to confront their fears; these beings might compel them to relive their deepest regrets, to drown in oceans of what-ifs and should-haves.

Harmony practiced a heightened state of awareness. She began to notice the subtle shifts in the ambient atmosphere, the almost imperceptible hum of psychic energy that existed even in the mundane world. It was like learning to hear a new frequency, a constant undercurrent of the supernatural. She would sit in quiet contemplation, her focus extending outward, trying to differentiate between the natural psychic 'noise' of a living place and the discordant signatures of something alien and hungry. She imagined these signatures as tendrils, reaching out, probing, seeking vulnerabilities.

The Master's presence had been a loud, obvious roar; these new enemies might be the silent, creeping vine, suffocating life from the shadows.

She understood that the 'Rooms Between' were not a single, unified dimension, but rather a vast, interconnected network of pocket realities, each with its own subtle distortions and unique dangers. The Master had carved out a territory within this network, a gruesome playground. But what existed beyond his influence? Were there realms where the very laws of physics were inverted, where time flowed backward, or where gravity was a mere suggestion? The scholar's notes hinted at such places, describing "zones of temporal anomaly" and "gravity wells of pure dread." Harmony braced herself for the disorientation, the fundamental challenge to her perception of reality.

Her physical preparation continued, a desperate attempt to create a vessel that could withstand the onslaught of psychological and perhaps even physical assault. She pushed her body to its limits, not just for strength, but for resilience. She imagined her nerves as wires, capable of carrying immense loads without fraying, her mind as a fortress, its walls reinforced against insidious infiltration. She practiced grounding techniques, not just to maintain her connection to the tangible world, but to center herself against the disorienting effects of these alien environments. The feel of solid ground beneath her feet, the scent of rain-washed earth, the warmth of sunlight on her skin – these were her anchors, and she clung to them with a fierce, almost desperate, grip.

She also began to consciously cultivate a broader range of emotional responses. The Master had been susceptible to the raw power of her maternal rage and her unwavering love. But if these new entities fed on more nuanced emotions, she would need to be a more complex target, or perhaps, a more complex weapon. She meditated on her capacity for empathy, for understanding, even for a detached form of curiosity. Could she, in some strange way, learn to understand the motivations, however alien, of these beings? Or would that simply make her a more palatable meal? The thought sent a shiver down her spine.

The idea of a 'hidden ecosystem of predators' was a recurring motif in her thoughts. She pictured it as a vast, dark ocean, with the Master as a shark, easily spotted and formidable. But beneath the surface, in the crushing depths, were creatures of unimaginable strangeness, adapted to an environment that would crush a human mind. These were the leviathans, the bioluminescent horrors, the things that had no eyes but saw everything. Her hunt was no longer just a rescue mission; it was an expedition into the unknown, a reconnaissance into a hostile territory populated by beings whose very existence challenged the definition of life.

She revisited the concept of the 'Rooms Between' as fluid, not static. The Master had imposed his will, shaping his domain to his perverse specifications. But the underlying fabric of these spaces was likely far more malleable, far more chaotic. What if these new entities were not builders, but weavers, intricately threading together disparate elements of reality to create their hunting grounds? What if they could manifest entire landscapes out of a victim's deepest anxieties, or conjure illusions so perfect they were indistinguishable from truth? Harmony knew that she couldn't rely on recognizing a 'place' in the conventional sense. Every corner, every shadow, could be a deliberate construction, designed to deceive and ensnare.

She thought about the different ways these entities might manifest. The Master had projected his physical presence, albeit in a corrupted form. But what if others existed purely as forces, as psychic energies that could influence and manipulate without ever taking a discernible shape? What if they were more akin to atmospheric phenomena, a psychic storm that could descend without warning, its effects devastating and irreversible? The scholar's notes mentioned 'ephemeral intelligences,' beings that existed only as patterns of thought or emotion, and whose interaction with the physical world was subtle, insidious.

Harmony began to practice what she termed 'active observation.' Instead of just passively sensing disturbances, she would actively probe them, sending out tentative threads of her own consciousness, trying to gauge the nature of the anomaly. It was like sending a reconnaissance drone into enemy territory, hoping for telemetry data without triggering an alarm. She learned to interpret the subtlest of responses: a fleeting resistance, a ripple of unnatural stillness, a flicker of discordant energy. These were the silent communications of a world teeming with unseen life, and she was determined to learn its language.

The awareness of this ecosystem of dread was a constant hum beneath the surface of her thoughts, a dissonant chord that never quite resolved. It made her hyper-vigilant, her senses attuned to the slightest ripple in the psychic fabric. Walking down a busy street, she could almost *feel* the ambient emotional energies, the faint trails of desperation from a man facing eviction, the sharp sting of envy from someone observing a more successful peer, the dull ache of loneliness radiating from an elderly woman sitting alone on a park bench. These were not just random human emotions; they were potential bait, subtle signals that could attract the attention of the unseen. Harmony understood, with a chilling certainty, that these entities could use these very emotions to lure their prey, weaving narratives of hope or solace that ultimately led to deeper entanglement.

This knowledge, this terrible foresight, was both a curse and a weapon. It was a curse because it alienated her, painting the world in shades of gray and dread that others couldn't perceive. She saw the potential victims everywhere, the unwitting souls walking blindly towards the precipice, their vulnerabilities broadcasting like distress signals. It was a constant battle to maintain her own emotional equilibrium, to avoid succumbing to the pervasive despair that this knowledge threatened to inflict. The temptation to retreat, to seal herself off from the world and its inherent dangers, was a siren song, promising a fragile peace. But she knew, with a ferocity born of experience, that such a retreat would be a form of surrender.

And yet, it was also a weapon. This intimate understanding of the 'Rooms Between' and its inhabitants, this hard-won knowledge of the subtle forces at play, gave her an edge. While others were blind, she could see. While others were deaf, she could hear the whispers of danger. This was the power that fueled her resolve, the grim determination that propelled her forward. It was the knowledge that had saved her that had allowed her to break free from the Master's grasp, and it was this same knowledge that would allow her to protect Lily, and perhaps others, from falling into the same abyss. She was a sentinel, standing guard against a threat that no one else acknowledged, armed with an understanding that was both a heavy burden and her greatest strength.

The implications for her strategy were profound. The Master had been a singular point of failure, a dark star around which his twisted world revolved. His defeat had been a surgical strike, removing a malignancy. But these new adversaries were like a pervasive mold, an insidious rot that had infiltrated the very structure of reality. They were not confined to a single 'room,' but were woven into the fabric of existence, their influence subtle and far-reaching. Harmony understood that her approach had to shift from confrontation to something more akin to an ongoing vigil, a constant effort to identify and disrupt their subtle manipulations. She couldn't simply defeat them; she had to learn to live with their presence, to navigate their unseen currents, and to protect the innocent from their predatory reach.

She began to see the mundane world through a new lens. A particularly intense argument between strangers on the street was no longer just a display of human friction; it was a potential psychic flare, a beacon for entities that fed on discord. The pervasive sadness that clung to certain places, the residual grief of a tragedy long past, was not just a historical echo; it was a potential feeding ground, a reservoir of energy that could be tapped and amplified. The scholar's writings, once arcane ramblings, now felt like an instruction manual for a world she was increasingly inhabiting. He spoke of 'psychic residue,' of 'emotional imprints,' concepts that now resonated with the chilling accuracy of lived experience.

The burden of this knowledge manifested in a constant state of low-level anxiety, a persistent feeling that the ground beneath her feet was not as solid as it appeared. She found herself scrutinizing her own thoughts and emotions with a newfound intensity, aware that her own internal landscape could be a vulnerability. Had she ever harbored a flicker of true malice? A moment of overwhelming greed? A selfish ambition that had twisted into something darker? She knew that these entities could exploit even the most fleeting of negative impulses, weaving them into a tapestry of illusion that would draw her deeper into their influence. It was a constant process of self-examination, a mental purification that was both exhausting and essential.

This self-awareness, however, was also a source of strength. The Master had preyed on her maternal love, twisting it into a weapon against her. But she had learned to compartmentalize, to channel that raw power into focused action. Now, she needed to expand that capacity. She needed to understand not just her own emotional triggers, but the broader spectrum of human feelings that these entities might exploit. It was a daunting task, a journey into the labyrinth of the human psyche, but she knew it was a necessary one. To protect others, she had to understand the very nature of the temptations and vulnerabilities that these ancient predators leveraged.

The scholar's fragmented accounts of 'temporal anomalies' and 'zones of warped perception' haunted her waking thoughts. These were not merely places of physical danger, but realms where the very fabric of reality was frayed, where cause and effect could become entangled, and where the perception of time itself could be a fluid, unreliable thing. This meant that her understanding of her environment, honed by her experiences with the Master, might be insufficient. She couldn't rely on the stability of space or time, couldn't assume that a location remained constant, or that the sequence of events would unfold in a predictable manner. This added another layer of complexity to the burden of her knowledge, demanding a level of adaptability that stretched her mental faculties to their breaking point.

She began to practice a form of cognitive camouflage, a deliberate effort to project an aura of emotional neutrality, to dampen her psychic emissions. It was like learning to whisper in a world of shouts. She envisioned herself as a quiet presence, a shadow that moved without disturbing the ambient energies, making herself less of a target, less of a tempting morsel. This was a difficult discipline, requiring a constant suppression of her own powerful emotions, a stoic facade that masked the churning depths of her fear and determination. The burden of this internal performance was immense; a silent scream trapped behind a mask of calm.

Yet, amidst the isolating dread and the overwhelming weight of her awareness, there was a nascent sense of purpose. This knowledge, however terrifying, was not merely a passive observation of impending doom. It was an active understanding, a blueprint for survival, and potentially, for resistance. It gave her the foresight to anticipate threats that would blind others, the resilience to withstand the subtle erosions of psychic attack, and the resolve to continue her hunt, not just for Lily, but for the very idea of safety that these entities sought to extinguish. The burden was heavy, the path fraught with unseen dangers, but it was her path to walk, illuminated by the chilling, empowering light of what she knew. The fight was not merely against external foes, but an internal struggle against despair, a testament to the indomitable human spirit, even when burdened by the knowledge of horrors beyond comprehension.

The oppressive silence of the sheriff's office was a familiar blanket to Sheriff Brody, a stark contrast to the chaotic symphony of sirens and shouted commands that usually punctuated his days. Yet, tonight, the silence was a conscious choice, a deliberate act of stillness. He sat at his worn oak desk, the glow of the desk lamp casting long shadows that danced with the rhythmic sweep of the clock on the wall. Each tick was a small hammer blow against the silence, a reminder of the hours he was dedicating to his vigil. His gaze, though weary, was sharp, scanning the flickering television screen that cast a pale, anemic light across the room. He wasn't watching the evening news for entertainment; he was dissecting it, sifting through the mundane reports of local traffic accidents and political squabbles for any hint, any tremor, of the unnatural.

He'd developed a keen eye for the discordant note in the symphony of everyday life. A news report of unusual animal behavior in a neighboring county, dismissed by the anchor as a seasonal anomaly, might, to Brody, be a faint echo of something far more sinister. A local farmer's story of livestock vanishing without a trace, officially attributed to coyotes, might prickle the hairs on the back of his neck, reminding him of the Master's insatiable hunger, his uncanny ability to prey on the vulnerable and the unseen. He kept a meticulously organized file, a patchwork quilt of newspaper clippings, hastily scribbled notes, and transcribed whispered rumors. Each entry was a potential thread, a single, seemingly innocuous detail that, when woven with others, might reveal the shadowy tapestry of the 'Rooms Between' and the horrors that dwelled within.

His role had shifted, evolved. Once, he was the unwavering hand of law and order, the bulwark against tangible threats. Now, his battles were fought in the realm of the intangible, his arsenal comprised of skepticism, vigilance, and an unwavering belief in Harmony. He understood, perhaps better than most, that some threats didn't leave fingerprints or DNA. They left behind a psychic residue, a lingering miasma of fear and despair that could fester and grow. He was Harmony's anchor, her connection to the world she was fighting to protect, a constant reminder of what she was risking everything for.

He was her eyes and ears in the tangible world, the one who kept watch while she navigated the treacherous, unseen currents.

He poured himself another cup of lukewarm coffee, the bitter taste a familiar companion. It was past midnight, and the small town of Redwater Crossing slept, blissfully unaware of the unseen war being waged beyond their dreams. Brody, however, was wide awake, his mind a finely tuned instrument, perpetually scanning the horizon for signs of trouble. He would revisit Harmony's detailed account of the Master, the chilling descriptions of his abilities, the subtle ways he manipulated his victims. He would pore over the cryptic notes she'd managed to salvage, searching for patterns, for anything that might offer a clue to the nature of the entities Harmony now faced. He knew they were not the same as the Master; the Master, for all his depravity, had been a tangible evil, a focal point of malevolence. These new adversaries, as Harmony had explained, were more diffuse, more insidious, feeding on subtler forms of human weakness.

He remembered the day Harmony had left, the quiet strength in her eyes, the grim determination that had settled upon her features like a second skin. She had promised to return, and he had no doubt she would. But the waiting was the hardest part. It was a hollow ache in his gut, a constant hum of anxiety beneath the surface of his stoic demeanor. He imagined her out there, alone, facing horrors that he could only dimly comprehend, armed with knowledge that had cost her dearly. He pictured her sifting through ancient texts, deciphering cryptic warnings, her every instinct honed to a razor's edge. He saw her navigating the 'Rooms Between,' the disorienting, terrifying spaces that existed just beyond the veil of normal perception.

His commitment to her was an unspoken vow, a silent promise he'd made to himself, and to her. He would hold the fort, keep the home fires burning, and ensure that when she returned, she would find Redwater Crossing unchanged, a sanctuary waiting for her. He would continue to monitor the news, to listen to the whispers, to be the steady hand on the tiller while she weathered the storm. He would reassure the townsfolk if any strange occurrences were reported, offering logical explanations, his voice calm and steady, while his mind raced with the unspoken possibilities. He was the gatekeeper, the one who stood between the fragile reality of their town and the encroaching darkness.

He picked up the worn photograph on his desk – a smiling Harmony, her eyes bright with life, her arm slung around a younger, less burdened version of himself. It was a reminder of what he was fighting for, of the innocence that was at stake. He traced the outline of her smile with a calloused finger. She was more than just a resident of his town; she was a survivor, a warrior, and a friend. He owed her a debt that could never be repaid, a debt born of the horrors she had faced and the strength she had shown. His vigil was a small offering, a way of acknowledging that debt, of doing his part in the grand, terrifying scheme of things.

He leaned back in his chair, the springs creaking in protest. The news anchor droned on about a minor political scandal, a distraction from the real battles being fought in the shadows. Brody closed his eyes for a moment, picturing Harmony. He imagined her moving through the unseen world, her senses sharpened, her will a shield against the encroaching dread. He sent her a silent message, a flicker of reassurance, a bolster of his unwavering support.

I'm here, Harmony. I'm watching. Come home safe.

The hours bled into one another, each one a testament to his quiet dedication. He checked the security cameras around the perimeter of the town, not for petty criminals, but for anything that didn't belong, anything that moved with an unnatural stillness or a disconcerting fluidity. He reviewed the dispatch logs, looking for any calls that seemed out of place, any reports of unexplained phenomena that might have been dismissed as pranks or local folklore. He was the last line of defense, the mundane world's unwavering sentinel.

He thought about the fear that must grip Harmony, the immense pressure she must be under. She was not a soldier trained for this war, but a civilian thrust into its heart. Yet, she faced it with a courage that humbled him. He knew that the knowledge she carried was a heavy burden, a constant weight that could crush the spirit. But he also knew her strength, her resilience. She had faced the Master and survived. She had emerged from the 'Rooms Between' with scars, yes, but also with a resolve that was unbreakable.

He ran a hand through his thinning hair, the fatigue a dull ache behind his eyes. The coffee had long since lost its warmth, but the resolve within him remained as potent as ever. He would continue his watch, through the long, silent hours of the night, until Harmony returned. He would be the constant, the unwavering presence, a reminder that there was still a world of normalcy and safety, a world worth fighting for. His vigil was not just about watching for danger; it was about maintaining hope, about keeping the beacon of Redwater Crossing lit, a silent promise that home was waiting, a sanctuary from the encroaching shadows. He was Sheriff Brody, and he would stand his post, a silent guardian against the night, until his warrior returned.

The clock on the wall chimed softly, marking the approach of another hour. Brody shifted in his chair, the stiffness in his limbs a testament to the long hours of his vigil. The television screen, once a source of flickering light, now seemed to cast a more somber glow, the early morning news offering a fresh slate of mundane worries – a forecasted drizzle, a minor pothole discovered on Main Street, the upcoming bake sale at the community center. To Brody, however, even these seemingly insignificant details were part of the intricate tapestry of normalcy he was determined to preserve. They were the threads that held their world together, the quiet affirmations that life, in its ordinary, predictable rhythm, continued.

He traced the outline of a faded stain on his desk, a ghost of a spilled coffee from a forgotten night. It was these small, tactile reminders of the passage of time, of the routine of his days, that grounded him. While Harmony delved into the abstract horrors of the 'Rooms Between,' he remained firmly rooted in the tangible, the familiar landscape of Redwater Crossing. He was the guardian of the mundane, the protector of the everyday, and in that role, he found a profound sense of purpose. He was the calm eye of the storm, the steady presence that ensured that even when Harmony was facing unimaginable terrors, there was still a place for her to return to, a place that remained, by his quiet vigilance, intact.

He thought about the whispers he sometimes heard, the hushed conversations at the diner, the worried glances exchanged over garden fences. There were those in Redwater Crossing who remembered the strange events surrounding Harmony's initial encounter with the Master. They remembered the fear, the inexplicable occurrences, the lingering unease. And while they might not grasp the true nature of the threat, their anxieties were a subtle resonance, a faint echo of the larger struggle. Brody, with his quiet assurances and his steadfast demeanor, served to soothe those anxieties, to gently guide them back towards the comforting certainty of the ordinary. He was the voice of reason, the steady hand that held them steady when the ground beneath their feet felt a little less solid than usual.

He adjusted the tie of his uniform, a small, almost unconscious gesture of maintaining order. His commitment was not a dramatic show of force, but a persistent, quiet dedication. He was the unwavering anchor, the silent promise that Harmony was not alone in this fight. He would continue to sift through the detritus of daily news, to listen to the subtle shifts in the town's atmosphere, to remain ever-watchful. He was the repository of Harmony's trust, the one she knew would keep the home fires burning, the one who would be waiting, ready to offer support and a quiet haven upon her return.

The first rays of dawn began to paint the sky in hues of soft pink and orange, a gentle awakening of the world. Brody felt a pang of longing for Harmony, a silent wish for her safety. He knew the hunt had begun, and that it would be a grueling, perilous journey. But he also knew Harmony's strength, her determination. She would not falter. And he would be here, waiting, a steadfast beacon in the ordinary world, his vigil a silent testament to his unwavering faith. He would continue to be her eyes and ears, the quiet guardian of Redwater Crossing, ensuring that the home she fought to protect remained a sanctuary, a place of refuge, a testament to the enduring power of normalcy against the encroaching darkness. His watch would continue, unwavering, until the moment she walked through the door, safe and sound, her mission accomplished.

The threshold of the mundane world shimmered, a veil so thin it was almost invisible, yet it marked the precipice of an abyss. Harmony stood before it, a warrior clad in the ordinary guise of a worried mother, her heart a battlefield where love warred with a primal, chilling fear. Each breath she drew was a conscious act, a deliberate intake of air that tasted of the familiar, of late-night coffee and the scent of pine from the surrounding woods – the scent of home. But soon, that air would be replaced by something else, something alien and suffocating. This was the beginning of the hunt, not just for her daughter, but for the sliver of hope that existed in the heart of Redwater Crossing, a hope that was under siege from an enemy that understood the vulnerabilities of the soul.

Her gaze swept over the quiet streets of Redwater Crossing, a familiar tableau bathed in the soft, pre-dawn light. Sheriff Brody's vigil was a silent promise, a bulwark against the visible world, but Harmony's journey led her beyond the reach of tangible defenses. She saw the silhouettes of houses, the gentle curve of the river, the steadfast presence of the old oak tree in the town square. These were the markers of normalcy, the things she was fighting to protect, the tangible reality that the encroaching darkness sought to unravel. The image of her daughter, laughing, her eyes bright with life, flashed through her mind, a potent fuel for the fire that burned within her. That image was the compass guiding her steps into the uncharted territories that lay beyond the familiar.

Her first step was not a grand stride, but a hesitant placement of her foot onto what felt like solid ground, yet pulsed with an unnerving, almost imperceptible vibration. It was as if the very fabric of existence had been stretched thin, and beneath it lay a churning, unformed potential. The air grew heavy, thick with an unidentifiable scent – a metallic tang mixed with the cloying sweetness of decay, a fragrance that whispered of forgotten places and stolen moments. The familiar sounds of Redwater Crossing began to recede, muffled as if by a great distance, replaced by a low, persistent hum that seemed to resonate not in her ears, but in the very marrow of her bones. This was the symphony of the 'Rooms Between,' a disquieting overture to the trials that awaited her.

She remembered the desperate words of her daughter, the fragmented pleas for help that had been snatched away by the suffocating silence of the void. Those words were not just a cry for rescue; they were a testament to the resilience of a child's spirit, a spirit that refused to be extinguished. And it was that same spirit that now propelled Harmony forward. She was not merely a mother searching for her child; she was a warrior answering a desperate call, venturing into the heart of the unknown to reclaim what had been stolen. The 'Rooms Between' were a maze of psychological torment, a landscape designed to break the spirit, but Harmony carried a weapon far more potent than any physical blade: an unbreakable will forged in the fires of love and loss.

The visual distortion began subtly, a slight warping of the edges of her perception. The trees, once distinct and familiar, began to blur, their branches twisting into grotesque shapes, their leaves shimmering with an unnatural, phosphorescent light. The ground beneath her feet shifted from the familiar soil to a surface that felt unnervingly like tightly packed dust, yet yielded slightly with each step, as if treading on the dried husks of countless forgotten dreams. The silence, once a heavy blanket, now felt like a suffocating shroud, broken only by the rhythmic thumping of her own heart, a desperate drumbeat against the encroaching stillness.

She clutched the worn locket around her neck, its cool metal a small anchor in the swirling disorientation. Inside, a tiny photograph of her daughter smiled up at her, a beacon of innocence in this encroaching darkness. This was her purpose, her undeniable reason for embarking on this perilous journey. The world beyond the veil was a hungry place, a realm where the vulnerable were preyed upon, where the seeds of despair were sown and nurtured by entities that thrived on misery. Her daughter had been taken because she was pure, because her light was a stark contrast to the pervasive gloom, a light that these creatures sought to extinguish.

As she ventured deeper, the environment began to morph and shift with a disquieting fluidity. Walls that seemed solid moments before would dissolve into shimmering curtains of light, only to reform into distorted reflections of places she knew – her own kitchen, the sheriff's office, the bustling main street of Redwater Crossing – all warped and twisted, like a carnival mirror reflecting a nightmare. These were not mere illusions; they were manifestations of the subconscious, the psychic detritus of lives lived and lost, a landscape sculpted by fear and regret. Each distorted image was a test, a temptation to succumb to the familiar, to the comfort of what was known, even if that known was now a grotesque mockery of itself.

Harmony's training, the cryptic knowledge she had painstakingly gathered, became her shield and her guide. She understood that these were not physical traps, but psychological ones. To resist the allure of the distorted reflections, she had to anchor herself to the reality of her mission, to the concrete purpose that had driven her into this alien realm. She focused on the image of her daughter, on the warmth of her hand, the sound of her laughter, the scent of her hair. These were not mere memories; they were tangible points of reference, anchors in the sea of illusion.

She encountered pockets of profound silence, areas where sound ceased to exist, where the very concept of auditory perception seemed to vanish. In these zones, a gnawing unease would creep in, a primal fear of isolation, of being utterly alone. It was in these silences that the creatures of the 'Rooms Between' often made their presence known, not through overt attack, but through subtle manipulation of the mind. Whispers, too faint to be distinct words, would brush against the edges of her consciousness, planting seeds of doubt, of hopelessness.

She's gone. You'll never find her. You're all alone.

Harmony countered these insidious whispers with her own internal monologue, a steady stream of affirmation. She spoke her daughter's name aloud, her voice a small, brave sound that seemed to push back against the suffocating silence. She recited the names of the people she was fighting for, the community of Redwater Crossing, the fragile peace they had managed to preserve. She reminded herself of Sheriff Brody's unwavering support, his quiet strength, a testament to the enduring bonds of friendship and loyalty. These affirmations were not just words; they were spells, incantations against despair, woven from the very fabric of love and connection.

The journey was not linear. The 'Rooms Between' defied logic, folding in on themselves, presenting impossible geometries and shifting pathways. What might appear as a direct route could lead her in circles, or deposit her back where she started, the landscape subtly altered, the psychological pressure intensified. It was a test of her resolve, a deliberate effort to break her spirit through exhaustion and frustration. But Harmony had learned patience. She understood that in this realm, brute force and haste were liabilities. It was a hunt that required observation, intuition, and an unwavering commitment to the objective.

She began to notice patterns, subtle shifts in the spectral light, the faintest of currents in the heavy air that indicated a direction, a pathway not immediately apparent. The entities that inhabited this space were masters of deception, their camouflage near perfect, their presence often felt rather than seen. She learned to trust these subtle cues, the almost imperceptible disturbances in the spectral fabric, the faint echoes of emotions that did not belong to her. A sudden chill that had no earthly origin, a fleeting scent of ozone, a sense of being watched by unseen eyes – these were the breadcrumbs leading her deeper into the labyrinth.

One particular section of this liminal space was a vast, echoing expanse, a plain of shimmering, opalescent mist. Here, the emotional residue of countless lost souls seemed to coalesce, manifesting as faint, spectral figures drifting aimlessly, their forms indistinct, their faces etched with an eternal sorrow. They were the forgotten, the abandoned, the ones who had succumbed to the despair of the 'Rooms Between.' They offered no resistance, no threat, but their silent lament was a powerful testament to the dangers of this realm, a stark warning of what could happen if one allowed the darkness to consume them. Harmony offered them a silent prayer, a moment of empathy, before continuing her solitary path.

She felt the presence of the entity that had taken her daughter, not as a distinct form, but as a pervasive influence, a malevolent awareness that seemed to permeate the very air. It was a vast, ancient hunger, a force that sought to consume innocence and twist it into something dark and despairing. It was a predator that moved not by physical pursuit, but by subtle manipulation of the environment, by exploiting the deepest fears and insecurities of its quarry. Her daughter was not being held captive in a physical cage but was likely ensnared by the psychological tendrils of this entity, her spirit slowly being eroded.

The knowledge was both a burden and a source of strength. It fueled her urgency, her determination to reach her daughter before the corruption became irreversible. But it also brought a profound sense of responsibility. She was not just fighting for her daughter's life, but for her daughter's very soul. The 'Rooms Between' were a spiritual battleground, and the stakes were eternal.

She stumbled upon a clearing, a place where the mist thinned, revealing a landscape that was a chilling mockery of Redwater Crossing. The old general store stood, its sign warped and illegible, the windows dark and vacant. The town square was there, but the familiar oak tree was a skeletal, withered thing, its branches grasping at the oppressive, starless sky. A profound sense of desolation permeated this twisted replica, a palpable aura of despair that threatened to overwhelm her senses. This was a place where the entity was actively shaping the environment, drawing power from the fear it generated.

In the center of the warped town square, a single, flickering light emanated from what would have been the sheriff's office. It pulsed with a sickly yellow hue, a beacon of false hope designed to lure the unwary. Harmony knew instinctively that this was a trap, a projection designed to exploit her longing for the familiar, for the sanctuary of her home. It was a manifestation of the entity's cunning, its ability to understand and manipulate the desires of its victims. She averted her gaze, focusing on the faint, almost imperceptible trail of energy that led away from this deceptive spectacle, a faint shimmer that suggested a true path, hidden from view.

The journey was a constant negotiation with her own mind. Every twisted tree, every distorted reflection, every chilling whisper was a potential snare. The entity sought to unravel her resolve, to make her question her own sanity, to break her down until she was as lost and despairing as the spectral figures in the mist. But Harmony's love for her daughter was a shield against these psychological assaults. It was a constant, unwavering flame that illuminated the darkness, a reminder of the precious life she was fighting to save.

She pushed onward, her steps deliberate, her focus unwavering. The 'Rooms Between' were a testament to the hidden fears and anxieties that festered just beneath the surface of ordinary life, a mirror reflecting the darkness that lurked in the human heart. And Harmony, the ordinary mother turned warrior, was stepping into that darkness, not to conquer it, but to reclaim what was hers, to bring her daughter back from the brink, and to ensure that the light of Redwater Crossing would not be extinguished by the encroaching shadows. The hunt had truly begun, and with each step, she moved closer to the heart of the unseen world, a world where the future was unwritten, and where courage was the only currency that truly mattered.

Epilogue

[Anchor: Kelly Burns | WCLN Channel 7 Coastal News]

"Tonight, a bit of good news for residents across Knox County looking for affordable transportation. A new car dealership—Robert's Reliable Rides, which opened 5 weeks ago—held its grand opening this afternoon just off Route 11 near the old lumber mill site. The owner, known locally simply as Robert, says the goal is to provide, and I quote, 'honest prices for honest people.' The lot features a rotating stock of used sedans, trucks, and family SUVs, with financing options said to be available regardless of credit history."

"The dealership has already seen strong community turnout, with nearly four dozen vehicles sold in pre-opening appointments alone. Robert says he hopes to 'give folks of Knox County a fair deal in a tough economy.' Residents we spoke with praised the business, calling it a welcome alternative to high dealer fees and big-city pricing."

"And in other economic news..."

"The Mississippi State Department of Labor released new numbers this morning showing a 24% increase in personal bankruptcy filings across Knox County compared to the same quarter last year. Financial advisors attribute the trend to inflation, fluctuating fuel prices, and the increasing difficulty for residents living paycheck to paycheck."

"Local banks declined to comment on whether lending policies have recently changed."

"In other news, the Knox County Sheriff's Office has issued a statement addressing what they call a 'worrying upward pattern' in reported suicides since late summer. While officials have not released full statistics, Sheriff Dale Mercer confirmed that the department has responded to 'a notable rise' in calls over the past four weeks."

"Mental health advocates urge residents struggling financially or emotionally to reach out to available community resources. The Sheriff's Office declined to comment on whether any of the cases are connected."

"Coming up after the break—Camden's Clam & Chowder Festival returns this weekend, promising live music, local vendors, and what organizers say will be 'the best chowder on the coast.' More when we come back."

The lot of Robert's Reliable Rides sits in silence after dusk; cars lined like sleeping cattle beneath the streetlights.

No one noticed how quickly they sell, or how quickly families unravel afterward.

No one asks where Robert came from.

And no one ever asked where he goes next.

Honest prices for honest people.

That's all anyone remembers——until they can't remember anything at all.